THE WIDOW

"There should be clouds," Kathleen thought as she stared out of the porthole. "It should be raining and storming to match my feelings!" She closed her eyes to the beauty of the night. "Yes, there should be bolts of jagged lightning rending the sky, as Reed's loss is tearing my heart to pieces! And loud, angry thunder to match the rage in my soul! Oh, God! How can you do this to me—to Reed—to our innocent little babies?" The words were ripped from her throat in a shriek of despair.

Hot tears stung beneath her swollen eyelids. "No! No!" she cried, shaking her head violently. "If Reed had died, wouldn't I have felt his loss? Could Reed die, be it a thousand miles away, and I not feel anything at all? I cannot believe that I would not know. My heart would have told me. Surely, as much as Reed and I love one another, there would have been some indication, some reaction. My heart should have stopped at the same moment as his. This awful pain would have begun then, I know it!"

A tiny glimmer of hope rose in her, even as the sun was beginning to rise in the eastern sky. Alone in the dawn, she vowed, "Reed, I know you are still alive somewhere! I feel it at the very core of my being. I'll find you, my darling, I promise. Wait for me, my love! As quickly as the *Starbright* can carry me, I'll come to you!"

ASHES AND ECSTASY

CATHERINE HART

LEISURE BOOKS   ∞   NEW YORK CITY

*For my adorable husband and my three children,
who have learned to cook in self-defense and
desperation. Also, for Patty and Karen,
who have tried to make up for Leslie's absence
as stand-in sounding boards.*

A LEISURE BOOK

Published by

Dorchester Publishing Co., Inc.
6 East 39th Street
New York, NY 10016

Printed in the United States of America

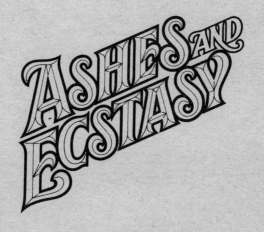

Chapter 1

The carriage drew to a jarring halt at the front of the dock where the *Kat-Ann* was moored. A tall, broad-shouldered man stepped out and made his way toward the frigate. His hair was as midnight black as that of any of the inhabitants of this inland riverport of Córdoba, Spain, his skin nearly as bronzed by the hot sun. Only his brilliant blue eyes gave the lie to the impression that he was a native of the region.

Halfway up the boarding plank, he was met by an excited bundle of silk skirts, long legs, and flying red-gold hair who promptly launched herself into his embrace. Her slim arms twined intimately about his neck and she kissed him soundly on the lips. Then, still clinging to him, she leaned back with a gamine grin.

"Hello, Captain! Haven't we met like this before?" Her emerald eyes twinkled with unsuppressed merriment.

He carried her to the ship's deck, where he promptly set her on her feet and planted a firm whack on her backside. His answering grin belied his admonishment. "Behave yourself, Kat! Is this any way for a wife and mother of two young babes to act?"

Kathleen smiled up into his face, twitching her hips and retorting saucily, "That depends on whose wife she is, I suppose, Captain Taylor."

He gathered a huge handful of her flowing hair, a decidedly possessive look on his handsome face as he drew her up to him once more. "You are *my* wife, Kathleen O'Reilly Haley Taylor, and don't you ever forget it!"

"Yes, Reed," she murmured in a rare moment of docility as his lips descended on hers with forceful mastery.

For long moments, they were oblivious to anything around them as they lost themselves in the kiss and one another. Their lips met and clung, hers softening and molding beneath the firm warmth of his. At his unspoken command, her lips parted to permit entrance to his invading tongue. Tongues touched and tangled in a mating dance that sent hot spears of desire darting through them both. Reed's hands tightened in her hair; his other at the small of her back brought her body into smoldering contact with his, leaving her in no doubt of his ardent arousal.

In retaliation for the waves of heat he was sending through her, Kathleen's tongue snaked out to trace and tease the soft inner edge of his lip. She felt him shiver in response, and then his strong white teeth were nipping sharply at her full lower lip, mingling little shafts of pain with fiery pleasure.

With a low groan of unfulfilled need, Reed tore his lips from hers and raised his head, obvious regret reflected in the sea-blue depths of his eyes. Kathleen's thickly lashed eyes fluttered open slowly, revealing emerald eyes still clouded with unbanked fires of desire.

"Shall we depart to the captain's quarters and conclude what we've begun in more privacy?" Kathleen suggested huskily, only now aware of the smothered chuckles of several members of the *Kat-Ann's* crew.

"You tempt me, wench," Reed admitted with a heavy sigh, "but I haven't spent the morning tracking down your schoolmate's address and hiring a carriage for nothing.''

Kathleen's face lit up with delight. ''Oh, Reed! You've located Isabel?''

''I've got an address for her parents, Kat,'' he corrected. ''Don't forget, it's been five years since you were together at that English boarding school. She's probably married with a family of her own by now, so don't raise your hopes too high. Isabel may live in Madrid or Granada or heaven knows where.''

''But we will go see if we can find her,'' Kathleen insisted excitedly.

''Yes, kitten. Now, go get yourself ready and see that Della has the children in hand. I need to give a few instructions to the crew before we leave.''

Reed shook his head and smiled as she dashed off. Kat never did anything by half measures. Her volatile Irish nature left no room for complacency. When she was happy, the entire world knew her delightful smile, her joy, and her infectious laughter; and when she was angry, everyone near her felt the lash of her tongue, the flash of her expressive green eyes, the heat of her wrath. In turn, when she was sad, Reed almost expected clouds to shut out the sun in response to her tears; and when she turned to him with the full measure of her passion, he swore he felt the earth tilt and catch fire as he held her in his arms. In every area of her life, she gave all of herself or nothing at all.

The past three years had been comparatively peaceful. He and Kathleen were secure in the love they shared and with their two lovely children. For Reed, contentment was waking up next to her each morning, basking in the glow of her smile each day, and hearing her glorious cries of ecstasy when he made love to her. All Reed wanted in this world was to spend the rest of his life with Kathleen.

Below deck, Kathleen was saying goodbye to her son and daughter. "Now you be a good little boy, Katlin, and don't give Della any trouble," she told her twelve-month-old son, fluffing his soft jet-black baby curls.

He looked up at her and gave her the same crooked grin his father often displayed, his new baby teeth gleaming, his clear blue eyes alight with glee. "Dell," he repeated.

Kathleen kissed his chubby cheek. "Yes, my smart boy. Dell."

"I'm smart, too, Mommy," piped up the little girl standing next to Kathleen. Her auburn hair caught the glow of light streaming through the porthole and held it.

Kathleen laughed and stooped down to hug her daughter. "You are a very bright little penny, my adorable Alexandrea. Give Mommy a kiss before I go."

"I want to go, too!" Alexandrea Jean Taylor, more commonly called Andrea, thrust out her lower lip in rebellion. Her unusual aqua eyes, a perfect blending of her mother's vivid green and her father's sky-blue, clouded in anticipation of Kathleen's refusal. At two and a half, she was by turns angelic and precocious.

Kathleen kissed the protruding lips. "Not this time, Andrea." She stood and straightened the folds of her gown. "Mind Della and I'll be back soon."

"An' pull in dat lip afore yo' steps on it," Della advised. Tall, black, and an absolute jewel with the children, Della was a godsend to Kathleen. And, wonder of wonders, she hadn't even gotten seasick the entire six weeks, though they'd hit a couple of nasty storms between Georgia and Spain.

10

"Don't hurry on our account, Miz Kafleen. Deze two gwine eat some lunch an' take a nice long nap."

Kathleen nodded and hurriedly took her leave. Behind her, she heard Andrea arguing, "I don't want to take a nap! I'm a big girl now. *Babies* take naps!"

Kathleen was still grinning as she climbed into the carriage with Reed.

"What's so funny?" he wanted to know.

"Your daughter. She's giving Della trouble about taking a nap. Andrea is a real minx sometimes."

Reed laughed. "What did you expect? She takes after her mother!"

Kathleen could not honestly argue that point, especially to Reed; not after what she had put him through.

It was true that Kathleen's father, Lord Edward Haley, had spoiled his only child. When she had returned from boarding school in England, he had taken her sailing with him on business trips for his shipping firm, teaching her to sail the eight frigates he owned. She learned everything she could from the crewmen, and soon she was acting as captain on most of their jaunts.

The crew didn't mind, for she was an excellent captain. In addition to a quick mind and good reflexes, Kathleen had a special feel for the sea; something rare and inborn, as if the sea were divulging her closely hoarded secrets to the girl. At times, the link was so strong that it was eerie, as if Kathleen could communicate with the gods of the deep; as if she had been born on the waves, a part of the mysterious depths and its creatures.

When Kathleen had begged and pleaded persistently enough, her father had also allowed her to take fencing lessons, and soon she was besting her teachers. The heavy rapier soon became almost an extension of her arm, and with her natural agility, she became an expert duelist. Rarely could anyone best her, even Reed, as good as he was . . .

As the carriage slowed to enter a private drive leading to a palatial estate, Kathleen jolted out of her reverie. A sidelong glance in Reed's direction told her he was eyeing her quizzically.

"What were you thinking, kitten?" he asked.

Kathleen smiled softly, her hand reaching automatically to brush back the errant lock of black hair that fell across his forehead. "About the past, and about how much I love you," she said.

Reed's smile answered hers. "And I love you, my darling, more than life itself." His lips reached down to touch hers softly as the carriage pulled to a stop.

The building before them was an imposing structure; three and a half stories of solid stone with balconies and high, narrow windows behind iron grillwork. A shiver ran over Kathleen's skin as she thought it more resembled a fortress than a residence—or perhaps a prison.

Reed let out a low whistle. "Awesome, isn't it, even if it is slightly depressing?"

"Shouldn't it have gargoyles guarding the entrance?" Kathleen suggested wryly. She almost wished she hadn't made the comment, as she watched Reed reach for the doorknocker. It was large, heavy, and in the shape of a fierce, fire-breathing dragon. "Oh, Lord!" she whispered, choking back a giggle.

The gentleman who opened the door was dressed severely in black, enhancing the somber effect of the exterior. His face held no sign of emotion as he asked in Spanish, "May I help you?"

"We'd like to speak with Isabel Fernandez," Reed replied, also in Spanish.

A frown barely registered on the servant's face. "She's not here." Immediately he began to shut the door.

Reed put out a hand to hold it open. "Then may we speak with Señor or Señora Fernandez?"

"Do you have an appointment?" came the haughty reply.

"No, but we have traveled a long distance, and my wife was looking forward to a visit with her friend."

Indecision flitted across the man's features. Finally he opened the door wider. He motioned them into a lofty dark hallway. "Wait here. I will get the master."

When he had left them, Kathleen let out the breath she'd been holding. "Good grief! You'd think we were asking for an audience with the queen!" Then another thought struck her. "Heavens! I can only wonder what Isabel thought when she came to visit me in Ireland the summer after school was out! She probably thought us a tribe of uncouth barbarians!"

Reed shook his head and smiled. "Somehow I doubt that."

"Oh, but Reed!" Kathleen moaned in mortification. "I even talked my fencing instructor into letting Isabel share my lessons!"

Reed rolled his eyes. "Why is it I am not surprised?"

Further comment was cut short as the manservant returned to usher them into a small parlor off the hallway. This room, too, was deeply shadowed and decorated in dark tones. "Please be seated. The señor will be with you in a moment," he said.

No sooner had he left them than a man and woman entered the parlor. The man was tall and thin, with a prominent nose that gave him a distinctly hawklike appearance. The woman was petite, with dark hair and eyes. In spite of her pale, ashen complexion, Kathleen noted her resemblance to Isabel, and was sure this must be her mother.

At first no one spoke, and the tension in the room was nearly palpable. The man seemed tense, even wary; and the woman was visibly nervous, perhaps frightened, as she repeatedly twisted her handkerchief.

At last he spoke. "I am Rafael Fernandez, and this is my wife, Carmen. We are told you are looking for Isabel. I would like to know who you are and why you seek her."

Frowning slightly at Rafael Fernandez's imperious attitude, Reed stated, "I am Captain Reed Taylor, and this," he gestured toward Kathleen, "is my wife, the former Lady Kathleen Haley. My wife and your daughter were classmates in England a few years ago. We are in Spain on business for a few days, and Kathleen wished a short visit with Isabel, if it could be arranged."

"Yes," Kathleen inserted. "Surely you recall that you let Isabel visit me in Ireland one summer. Is she still living here with you? Will she be home soon?"

A cold look of disdain further hardened Sr. Fernandez's stern features. "Isabel has not lived here for three years, and if she is wise, she will not attempt to darken my doorstep with her presence. She is no longer welcome in my home!"

A dismayed gasp escaped Señora Fernandez's lips as Reed and Kathleen stared at each other in surprise. "She is our daughter, Rafael," the woman whispered faintly.

Sr. Fernandez shot her a quelling look. "I no longer have a daughter!" To Reed and Kathleen he said, "I am sorry you have wasted your time and mine."

14

As he turned to leave the room, Kathleen jumped up. "Wait! Can you at least tell me where I might find her? I am sorry you are at odds with one another, but I should still like to see her."

The look Sr. Fernandez leveled at her would have frozen water. "I have no idea where she is, and I care less. To me she is dead." He stalked from the room, leaving them alone with the distraught señora.

"I am so sorry," the woman murmured, unshed tears glistening in her huge dark eyes. "My husband is a hard, unforgiving man, but he has his reasons."

"Why?" Kathleen asked softly, still stunned by Fernandez's outburst.

"I cannot tell you. He has forbidden me to speak of it, or of her. I am surprised he consented to see you at all." She sighed deeply, as if it was an effort to breathe. "This much I can tell you. You would be wasting your time to try to find Isabel. Others have been looking for her for weeks without success, and if my prayers are answered, she is not to be found in Córdoba or all of Spain."

Sorrow contorted her features into a grimace of pain. "I must ask you to leave now. Manuel will see you out."

As they climbed into the carriage, Kathleen and Reed were still stunned. "What was that all about?" Reed wondered aloud.

Kathleen shook her head in dismay. "Poor Isabel! What could she have done that is so dreadful?"

"I suppose we'll never know," Reed answered.

The carriage pulled out onto the street, and as it slowed at the nearest corner, an old woman waved at them frantically. She resembled a scrawny black crow, dressed as she was all in black. They were about to ignore her and go on, when she approached the carriage, looked furtively back at the house they'd just left, and asked in hushed tones, "You are looking for Isabel?"

Kathleen exchanged a quick look with her husband and nodded hurriedly. "Yes. Do you know where we can find her?"

"Perhaps," the woman answered hesitantly, "but I would need to know what you want with her." Again she glanced worriedly toward the house.

Impulsively, Kathleen threw open the carriage door. "Get in. We can talk in privacy as we ride."

Once settled, the woman still did not drop her guard. "Why do you seek Isabel?" she asked abruptly.

"I am a friend of hers," Kathleen offered.

"Why have I never seen you before?" the woman returned suspiciously, her small, beady eyes narrowed.

"This is my first trip to Spain," Kathleen explained. "Isabel and I were friends at school in England. She visited me once in Ireland."

"What is your name?"

"I am Kathleen Taylor, and this is my husband, Reed." When she got no response, she added, "Before my marriage, I was Kathleen O'Reilly Haley."

This brought a nod from the old crone. "I have heard the name. What are you doing in Spain?"

The mystery and interrogation of the past hour were starting to bother both Kathleen and Reed. They exchanged an exasperated look, and Reed took over. "I am a ship's captain, and I own a shipping firm and several vessels in America. We are here on business to trade goods. While here, my wife wished to arrange a visit with Isabel, but I am beginning to wish I'd never heard of her."

Kathleen laid a restraining hand on his arm. Leaning

toward the old woman, she asked intently, "Is she in some sort of trouble? What is going on? Where is she? Why is everyone acting so strangely?"

The old woman shook her head. "I cannot tell you that yet. I must know that you can be trusted before I say more." Her eyes grew piercing as she studied Reed and Kathleen. "Did you come by ship?"

At their answering nod, she asked, "Where are you staying?"

"We are staying aboard our ship, the *Kat-Ann,* at the docks." Reed wondered if he were making a mistake in telling her this.

"How long will you be there?"

"We plan to leave late tomorrow evening."

"Are you leaving Spain? Where are you headed?" the woman persisted.

"We are making a short stop at Seville for additional goods, since the port of Cádiz is under French blockade and we cannot trade there. Then we proceed to Ireland to attend to Kathleen's estate there," Reed told her.

"And then we will return to Savannah," Kathleen added.

"That is in America?" the woman asked, as if it were of great importance.

"Yes."

Again she nodded. "That is good."

"Why?" Kathleen prodded.

The woman disregarded her question, posing instead another of her own. "Will you be aboard your ship tonight and tomorrow?"

They assured her that one of them would be there if it was necessary.

"*Bueno.* Someone will contact you. I only hope that I

17

am not placing Isabel in danger by talking to you." Her concern and suspicion were evident.

"I swear to you that I am Isabel's friend," Kathleen vowed. "If she is in trouble, I want to help her if I can."

"Bah!" The woman spat the word in contempt. "Her own father has turned his back on her. You must place your trust carefully when your own flesh and blood turn you out."

Reed pinned the woman to her seat with his own determined glare. "If my wife says we will help Isabel, then help her we will."

The woman motioned for the carriage to stop. "You will hear from Isabel or from me soon. Be alert, and beware of strangers lurking about or asking questions. Isabel's life may depend on your discretion. Tell no one that you have spoken to me, or what we have discussed." With that, she descended from the carriage and disappeared into a nearby alley.

Kathleen and Reed stared after her in bewilderment. "This is getting stranger by the minute," Reed said with a frown.

"Oh, Reed!" Kathleen raised worried eyes to his in a long look. "Isabel is in trouble of some sort! I'm wondering if we should alert the authorities?"

He smiled wryly. "I have an odd feeling that it may be authorities who are searching for her so diligently, Kat."

Kathleen slumped in her seat. "But why?"

"If we knew that, I wouldn't be so worried," he answered thoughtfully. "On second thought, knowing might make it worse. We'll just have to wait and see."

"I hope she is all right."

"So do I, kitten, and I hope her troubles don't become ours. I hear Spanish jails are not the most hospitable places in which to find oneself.''

"Strange talk for someone so deeply involved in piracy,'' she commented dryly, a sparkle lighting her green eyes.

"Privateering,'' he corrected with a mocking look. "*You*, my dear, are the only one in this family who has ever practiced actual piracy.''

Three years of relative tranquility in his marriage had dulled Reed's mortification at finding out that his own wife had pirated him very successfully. Now Reed could almost laugh about it; or at least he could accept and understand why Kathleen had done it. In all honesty, he had to admit he admired her courage and skill in handling both her ship and her rapier.

Kathleen had been stunning as the piratess Emerald of the *Emerald Enchantress*, he recalled. Disguising herself so that Reed would not recognize her, she had dyed her hair raven black and wore a mask and an extremely bold, revealing outfit consisting of long black boots, a green vest, and matching green trousers cut off short to just cover her buttocks . . .

Later that evening aboard the *Kat-Ann*, Kathleen snuggled deeper into Reed's enfolding embrace. "Alone at last,'' he mumbled gruffly into her hair. "Is Della still in charge?''

"Yes,'' Kathleen laughed. "The children are all hers until morning, and I am all yours.''

"That is the best news I've heard all day.'' Reed's lips found the smooth skin of her neck, trailing tiny, nipping kisses to her creamy shoulder and sending shivers of delight dancing across her skin.

Her seeking fingers feathered sensuously through the

dark mat of hair on his chest. Kathleen always marveled that the tufts were both coarse and soft at the same time. She loved the feel of it against her palms, and brushing the tips of her breasts when Reed made love to her.

She nuzzled her nose into his neck and worked her way upward to nip at his earlobe. Her tongue traced the shape of his ear, and she blew softly into it, laughing when she felt him shudder in response.

"Witch!" he muttered huskily, turning his head to meet her eager mouth with his own. Their breath mingled, and her lips melted beneath his like warm wax. Tongues met and teased and tangled. Beneath her open hand, Kathleen felt Reed's heartbeat accelerate to match her own.

With his hands, he spread her coppery hair across the pillow. Then his fingers traced her slightly slanted eyes, her high, delicate cheekbones, her up-tilted nose; and on to her stubborn chin, her luscious, kiss-reddened lips.

"You are so lovely," he whispered. "So very beautiful. I'll never get enough of you, sweetheart; not if I live to be a hundred."

"I'm sure I won't be beautiful then," she teased, gazing into his passion-darkened eyes.

"You will always be beautiful to me, my love," he assured her.

His lips traced the path his fingers had taken, and while he tenderly teased the rosy nipple of one breast between a finger and thumb, his lips pulled insistently at the other. His teeth gently grazed the pert nub, and her back arched as she drew in a sharp breath. Her fingers laced through his dark locks as she held his head tightly to her.

"Reed! Oh, Reed! Yes!" Her mind was whirling as she felt his hand wending its way across her hip; her thigh. His fingers feathered lightly up the inside of her leg and on across her stomach, before delving down to stroke the tiny, throbbing essence of her femininity.

Kathleen was on fire for him. Without thought, her hands caressed the width of his shoulders in broad, sweeping gestures, as his mouth came up to ravage hers and silence her moans of ecstasy. She clutched him to her, unconsciously reveling in the feel of his muscled strength under her hands. She writhed beneath his touch, and as his fingers delved deeply into her silken warmth, he found her moist and ready.

With her body she urged him to take her. Her hand reached down to find his velvet shaft, the hard proof of his desire, and her fingers stroked out their urgent plea.

As he positioned himself above her, her body rose to meet his. "Tell me, Kat. Let me hear the words," he whispered hoarsely.

"Take me," she gasped. "Make me yours. I need you so badly!"

The first spasms shot through her body as he plunged deeply into her. Her long nails dug into the bunched muscles of his back, and he let out a low hiss. His kitten had turned into a tigress, and her passion fired his. The rhythm of their lovemaking gradually increased, taking them both higher and higher on an ever-building wave of desire. Their damp, slick bodies strained toward the peak, the pleasure almost unbearable. Then the wave crested, and they rode the sparkling wake together until it lowered them into gentler waters.

Weak with the force of their loving, Kathleen lay limply in his embrace, her head now cushioned on his broad shoulder. A long sigh of contentment shuddered from deep within. "I love you, Reed, more and more each day.''

He smiled, and his arm tightened about her small waist. Reed never failed to treasure her words of love, for there was a time when each of them had feared to let the other know of their deep feelings. Now he tenderly kissed the damp tendrils of hair on her forehead. ''I love you, too, kitten. Forever.''

Kathleen fought the intruding sounds that repeatedly forced their way into her deep slumber. She mumbled groggily, feeling the mattress give as Reed shifted position, and then the light of the lantern pierced her closed eyelids. Just as the fog of sleep was lifting from her brain, she heard the creak of the cabin door, and Reed talking to whoever was on the other side.

''All right, I'll take care of it. Give me a minute,'' she heard him say.

''What is it?'' she croaked sleepily, as she watched him tug on his pants.

''Just some little wharf rat caught sneaking on board. He probably intended to stow away, but he got caught instead.''

''Why can't Kenigan take care of it?'' she frowned.

''Because the cheeky little waif keeps spouting something to him in Spanish, and the only thing he can make out is that he wants to see the *capitán*. So, the captain he shall see, and no doubt be sorry he disturbed my rest.''

Reed looked so put out that Kathleen almost felt sorry for the lad. Just as she was about to plead with him to be gentle with the boy, the sound of shouts and running footsteps reached their ears. The noise came closer, and just as Kathleen concluded that the pursuit would lead past their cabin, the door flew open, and in tumbled a dirty,

22

skinny little urchin. Clutching the bedcovers to her chest, Kathleen watched in open-mouthed amazement as four burly seamen crowded in after the ragamuffin.

At Reed's enraged bellow, the boy scrambled to his feet, gesturing wildly and chattering excitedly in rapid Spanish. Beneath the shouts of the men, the lad's voice was barely heard.

Suddenly the young scamp spied Kathleen in the bed, and he lurched unsteadily toward her, his black eyes seeming to plead with her for help.

Reed grabbed his arm, pulling him back. "What the hell are you trying to prove here?" he shouted.

The boy's eyes never left Kathleen's, and Kathleen's own gaze was swiftly transmitting signals to her sleep-dazed brain. Those eyes! Those huge black eyes, heavily fringed with long, dark lashes. Those lips, perfectly shaped into a cupid's bow! Those eyebrows; delicate arches as fine as a bird's wing!

"Oh, my God!" Kathleen gasped in disbelief.

Before she could say more, Reed was shepherding the men from the cabin, dragging the lad after him.

"Wait!" Kathleen shrieked, gathering the covers about her as she leaped from the bed.

"For heaven's sake, Kat! Get back in bed!" Reed exploded.

"No! You don't understand!" she interrupted. "Let the boy speak! Let him go!"

"Have you gone daft?" Reed demanded.

Kathleen took a deep breath and said more calmly, "Reed, please. Send the men away and let me explain. I know what I am doing, believe me."

Something about her absolute certainty made him relent. "All right, but I'm staying, and we are going to get to the bottom of this."

When the men had gone, Kathleen said, "You can let him go now, Reed."

He looked at her doubtfully, but reluctantly complied. The lad stood mutely as Kathleen approached. With a mischievous smile, Kathleen reached out and pulled off the boy's cap, releasing a mass of waist-length black hair.

Through Reed's amazement, he heard Kathleen say softly, "I'd like you to meet Isabel Fernandez."

One huge sob tore loose from the very depths of the bedraggled Isabel as she flung herself into Kathleen's open arms. Her hot tears wet them both as Kathleen clutched her friend and the covers tightly, rocking Isabel gently as she often did in comforting her own children.

As she stroked the tangled hair, Kathleen's own eyes shimmered with tears. "What on earth has brought you to this end, my dearest Isabel?" The girl weighed less than nothing, and Kathleen could feel her bones through the thin shirt she wore.

Full of pity, Kathleen pulled herself slightly away, looking down at her diminutive friend. Pleading jet-black eyes looked up into hers. When Isabel spoke, her voice quavered with fatigue, and she sagged weakly against Kathleen's supporting arm. With obvious effort, she begged faintly, "*Ayudeme*, Katrina. Help me! For the love of God, hide me! Save me!" With the last of her strength, she added, "*Por favor*—please." Then, as if aware she had reached safety at last and could finally relax, she wilted in a dead faint.

Reed caught her before her head hit the floor. Scooping the frail girl into his arms, he looked questioningly at Kathleen. "Well, Kat? Do we find her a bed and let her rest, or do we give her a bath first?"

Kathleen smiled her thanks. "I think she needs the sleep more, or she wouldn't have fainted."

Reed frowned. "That, or she passed out from sheer hunger. Good grief, but she is a skinny little thing! Was she always so thin?"

"No." Kathleen shook her head in dismay. "She was always very tiny and petite, but never anything like this! The poor girl is practically dying of starvation, Reed! I wonder when she last had decent food?"

"Well, I can tell you she will have plenty of it as soon as she wakens, my love," he promised solemnly. "But we may have another problem first."

At her quizzical look, he explained. "Kat, she's burning up with fever. We have a very sick lady on our hands."

Kathleen let out a cry of dismay.

"Don't worry," Reed soothed. "We'll tend to her. It is a good thing we have our own doctor aboard, since we obviously do not dare risk calling in a physician from town, not knowing what kind of trouble Isabel is running from. But, until the doctor confirms that whatever ails her is not contagious, I want you and the children to stay well away from her."

"But, Reed . . ." Kathleen started to protest.

He cut her off, his words sharp and brooking no more argument. "No, Kathleen. She is your friend, and we will help her, but I'll not risk your life or the children's for anyone. You mean too much to me."

By the following morning, Isabel's fever was raging, and she was shaking with chills so badly that her teeth chattered. Completely delirious and incoherent as she was, there was no way Reed could find out what sort of trouble she was in. The ship's doctor assured them that her fever was a result of her run-down condition. It appeared she had survived for some time on barely enough food to keep body and soul together. With proper food and care, he told them, Isabel would survive, as long as they managed to get her fever down soon.

In view of the doctor's diagnosis, Reed relented and allowed Kathleen to help care for Isabel. With Della's help, she stripped the dirty, vermin-ridden rags from her friend's thin frame. Together they bathed the filth from her body, and even managed to shampoo her hair. The tepid water helped to cool her and keep the fever from rising further.

By mid-morning Reed had noticed three men hanging about the docks who didn't look like the usual sailor or dock worker. Something about them nagged at him, but he could not put his finger on what was different about them. They were dressed no differently from any of the other workers and they seemed busy enough . . .

Reed watched them for a while. As he watched one of them lift a heavy crate, something suddenly clicked in his brain. The man had bent from the waist, instead of stooping and letting his legs take the weight, something every sailor or laborer learned early on. It could be the men were merely new on the job, but Reed doubted it. Several times in a few minutes, he saw them dart quick, surreptitious looks about them, often directing their attention toward the *Kat-Ann*.

Reed searched out his quartermaster and quietly pointed out the men in question. Finley confirmed his suspicions. He, too, had noticed the trio, adding that they'd first appeared yesterday afternoon, to his knowledge. Also, while on watch last evening, he'd seen a couple of men, either these or others, skulking about in the shadows of the nearest buildings.

Reed could only hazard a guess, but he bet that Isabel was the reason. The men could be looking for someone to rob, or planning to stow away, but he doubted it. He and Kathleen had openly visited Isabel's parents the previous morning, and after the old woman's warnings in the carriage, the coincidence was too obvious.

"Did anyone see our young stowaway come aboard last night?" Reed asked.

"I can't say for positive, but if you mean those three spies, I think not," Finley replied. "None of us saw him come aboard. If I hadn't gone to the galley for a cup of coffee before starting my watch, we may not have discovered the scamp until we'd sailed. I caught him stealing food."

Reed nodded. "Then whatever occurred happened belowdeck, with our observers none the wiser," he concluded.

Finley concurred.

"Those three bear watching," Reed commented, his eyes squinting in thought. "Go about the ship's business, but keep an eye on them, and alert me to anything out of order. Tell the crew not to discuss anything at all, no matter how trivial, with anyone they don't know, and I particularly want them to keep quiet about our starving stowaway."

Finley quirked a questioning brow at Reed.

In answer, Reed said, "I can't explain now, but you are to consider that a direct order from your captain. The consequences will be dire, indeed, to the man who disobeys it."

Finley did not attempt to question Reed further. "Aye,

27

Captain. I'll pass the word along. Anything else?''

"No. Let's just get loaded. The sooner we're gone from here, the happier I will be.''

Later that day, Reed sent two of his most trusted men into the town. Several hours and taverns later, they returned with the information he sought. He waited to approach Kathleen until he was certain she was alone in their cabin. He told her about the men lurking about on the dock, and then related what the two crewmen had heard.

"Kat, they found out why Isabel has been in hiding.'' His face betrayed his reluctance to hurt her with his news.

Kathleen's teeth worried her bottom lip. The news was obviously bad, or Reed would be faster to reveal it. Steeling herself mentally, she said, ''Tell me.''

Reed heaved a deep sigh and seated himself on the edge of his desk. "Isabel has been married for the last three years to Count Carlos Santiago, a very rich and important nobleman. That is, she *was* married to him until two months ago. Apparently he was an extremely dominating man, well known for his cruelty to his servants and disliked by many of his fellow noblemen. All that aside, he was found one morning in his private drawing room, slain. A sword was found in his hand, and another near the door to the courtyard.

"At first it was thought that an unknown adversary had entered the room, sparred with him, killed him and left. However, both rapiers belonged to Don Carlos. Also, Isabel was nowhere to be found. A maid identified a shredded piece of fabric found near the body as part of one of Isabel's favorite nightrobes.

"Isabel has not been seen since early on the evening of the murder. The authorities have been searching for her for two months now. Needless to say, she is their prime suspect.

"I'm sorry, Kat."

Kathleen was stunned. She shook her head vigorously in denial. "No! A nobleman has been killed, and they need a scapegoat. There has to be another explanation."

"Then why hasn't Isabel come forward to clear herself?" Reed insisted.

"Really, Reed!" she huffed. "She might just as well buy the rope they'd hang her with! Do you think they'd listen? They most likely want someone to blame so they can conclude their case all nice and tidy, and justice be damned!"

"Alright, I'll give you that much. The fact remains that we are now knowledgably harboring a wanted woman. The question is—what do we do about it?"

Kathleen looked at him squarely, her emerald eyes glittering with determination, her chin jutting out stubbornly. "Nothing," she answered firmly. "We go on as if we knew nothing of what you have just relayed to me; as if Isabel never burst through that door last night; as if we've not seen her at all."

"And if the authorities question us?" Reed persisted. "They surely know we visited the Fernandez home yesterday. I believe that is why those three men are observing the *Kat-Ann* so closely. Since they have not approached the ship, I assume they did not see Isabel sneak aboard last night."

"If they question us, we know nothing," Kathleen insisted. "If they come to search the ship, we'll hide her somehow."

"And what if she truly *is* guilty of killing her husband?"

Kathleen shrugged. "Then I can only assume he deserved it," she stated confidently. "I know Isabel. She is a fine, gentle person. If she was driven to murder, she had good reason."

Reed sighed. "Alright, Kat. As you say, you know Isabel. We'll keep her aboard, hide her if necessary. Then, when she is able, we'll hear her side of it."

Kathleen's tense body relaxed, and she offered him a grateful smile. "Thank you, Reed. I owe you a debt of gratitude for this."

He grinned lecherously at her, his blue eyes blazing. "And I'll collect with interest, my love."

Chapter 2

That evening they traveled down to Seville, where they stayed for two days. Then, under cover of darkness, they slipped out of the river and were soon heading north toward the British Isles. It wasn't until they were well out into the Atlantic that Isabel's fever finally broke and she regained consciousness at last. Weak as a newborn kitten, she could barely swallow the nourishing broths Kathleen and Della spooned into her. Through cracked lips, she managed to whisper her gratitude to Kathleen and Reed, but explanations were postponed until she was stronger.

Isabel slept for long periods of time, waking only when the women forced her to eat. Gradually, some of her strength returned, and she could sit up in her bed, propped by pillows. Broths slowly gave way to soft foods, and Isabel's color improved.

They were a day's sailing from Ireland when Reed decided the time had come for their talk. "Isabel," he began, "after you arrived aboard ship, we heard tales that you were wanted by the Spanish government in connection with the death of your husband. You sought our help, and we gave it. Now we would like an explanation, please."

Reed had not spoken harshly, or with condemnation. Nevertheless, Isabel's face took on a hunted look, and she turned frightened black eyes toward Kathleen, seeking assurance.

"It will be all right, Isabel," Kathleen soothed. "My husband is a fair and decent man. My goodness! You look as if we might dump you straight into the Atlantic! My dear friend, you are safe with us. Besides, I've told Reed there must be some mistake. I do not believe you could have killed your husband."

Isabel's eyes filled with tears, and her lips quivered as she spoke softly. "But I did, Kathleen. I stabbed him and watched him die; and that much, at least, I do not regret, may God forgive me!"

Amazement held Kathleen speechless. It was Reed who asked quietly, "Why?"

Tears were sliding unnoticed one after another down Isabel's cheeks. With a helpless, pained look, Isabel recounted sadly, "How do I make you understand what it was like to live with such a man day after day, year after year? Even my own father could not see what a beast he was, but perhaps that was because Papa had arranged the marriage in the first place. Carlos seemed such an aloof, polite person when we were out in public. It was only in the privacy of our own home that he showed his true nature. The servants could tell you how hateful he was."

Her voice began to shake with emotion, but Isabel struggled on. "It started on our wedding night. The charming man who had courted me suddenly became very impatient with my shyness. I was very frightened and unsure of what to expect, and Carlos was—less than gentle with me that night. From then on, I hated those nights he would visit my bed. I lived in fear of the pain and of him.

"Looking back, that first year was bad enough, but it became worse—much worse. Carlos was anxious for a son, and he was furious when, after more than a year, I had failed to conceive. He blamed me. At any time, he would suddenly fly into a rage and drag me off to my bedchamber, day or night. Then he started coming home with all sorts of strange powders and concoctions he'd gotten from some witch-woman, and he would force me to drink the evil mixtures. So eager was he that I honestly feared that he would risk poisoning me in the process.''

Isabel brought her hands to her face, as if to hide her shame. ''I cannot begin to tell you the unspeakable things he did to my body, all for the sake of begetting a child! He beat me so regularly that I was always covered with bruises, often so obvious that I could not leave the house. I became his prisoner, the focus of all his anger.''

''Oh, Isabel! Why didn't someone stop him?'' Kathleen asked.

Reed agreed. ''Surely your father did not condone such treatment of his daughter.''

An eerie, mirthless laugh escaped Isabel's throat. ''When my father noticed the bruises, he told me if I were a proper wife to Carlos, he would not treat me so badly. He advised me to learn to please my husband.'' The laughter ended on a strangled note. ''Only my mother and my *dueña* Josepha seemed to understand my plight, and they could do nothing. As Carlos's wife, I was his property, to do with as he wished. In Spain, men have killed their wives, and the authorities do nothing; but for a wife to murder her husband is a crime of great magnitude.''

''What happened that night you finally killed him?'' Kathleen asked. ''Surely you had been tempted many times before.''

''Ooh! I cannot tell you!'' Isabel wailed. ''You will

33

never want me near you again! You will be too disgusted, and I shall lose my only true friend!''

Kathleen could see that Isabel was on the brink of hysteria. Gently she gathered the sobbing girl into her arms, stroking her hair. ''Isabel, listen to me,'' she urged. ''Perhaps what you have to say is shocking and very terrible, but I will always be your friend. You came to me in trust. Trust me now.''

''But Caterina! Kathleen! How can I make you see? It is obvious that you love your husband, and he loves you. You must have led such a serene, pleasant life together with your children.''

For one crazy moment, Kathleen wanted to laugh. As she caught Reed's eye, she was afraid Reed might as well. ''No, Isabel. It wasn't all that quiet at first,'' she said solemnly.

The corners of Reed's mouth twitched. ''*Emerald* could tell you differently,'' he stated mockingly.

A frown of confusion wrinkled Isabel's brow. ''Who is this Emerald?''

Kathleen shook her head. ''Another time, my friend. Tell us about the night you killed Carlos.''

With a weary sigh of resignation, Isabel hung her head. Her hair shielding her face, she began to speak in a voice so low and trembling it was a mere whisper. ''That night Carlos entertained two friends. They were men I'd never met before. He'd invited them for dinner, telling me they were business associates, and ordering me to dress and come down to dinner on time.

''As soon as I could politely do so after the meal, I returned upstairs to my rooms. I assumed the men would take brandy and discuss business with Carlos. No sooner had I prepared for bed, than the door to my bedroom

34

opened, and in came Carlos, bringing his two friends with him! You cannot imagine how shocked I was! But that was just the beginning of a nightmare that will always haunt me. If just one day would go by that I could forget what happened that night . . . ! It was like being thrown into hell, with Carlos as the Devil, his demons at his side!''

A long moan of pure agony escaped her, and Isabel paused to collect herself. Kathleen continued to hold her, seeking to calm the terrible trembling that had overtaken the girl. ''What happened?'' she urged, although by now she had a fairly good idea.

''Carlos told me he had instructed his friends to bed me. I couldn't believe what I was hearing! He'd gone mad! He said that I was a hopeless excuse for a wife; that I deliberately expelled his seed. He claimed I was of no use to him as a wife, so now I would whore for him. He even went so far as to suggest that I might conceive from one of these men, and thus redeem myself to some extent. He was even crazy enough to say that he would claim the child as his heir!''

Isabel choked on her tears, and Kathleen tightened her hold. Fury and misery made her long to strike out at Isabel's attackers. ''They raped you,'' she sighed, closing her eyes against hot tears. ''How dreadful!''

Isabel nodded. ''Yes, each of them; *all* of them. I tried to fight, but I was not strong enough. The pain and humiliation were unbearable. At some point I must have fainted, but I remember hearing Carlos's demonic laughter all the while. I remember that most of all, for it seemed a sound straight from Hell! I still hear it in my dreams!

''When I finally awoke, they were gone, and the house was quiet. I crawled from my bed to wash as best I could.

35

My reflection in the mirror was almost unrecognizable. My lips and eyes were swollen, and my cheek was already turning purple. I remember thinking I should get some raw meat from the kitchen to put on my face, so I slipped on a robe and crept down the stairs.

"The hallway to the kitchen led past Carlos's private drawing room, and the door was open. He was sitting in a chair by the fireplace, smoking a cigar. I probably would have gone on by, had Carlos not looked up just then and seen me. He couldn't resist taunting me. 'Did you enjoy the party, Isabel?' he asked me. 'I hope so. My friends and I did. In fact, we are going to repeat it quite often, until you are with child.' Then he laughed that evil, crazed laugh I remember so well."

Closing her eyes, Isabel drew in a painful breath. "I don't know quite how it happened, but the next I knew, I'd gone into the room. I had taken down both rapiers from the wall, and was handing one to Carlos. Suddenly, I was strangely calm, and I recall enjoying the look of astonishment on Carlos's face as I told him I was going to kill him.

"Carlos was a fair swordsman, and I remember wondering if it might be I who would die that night. At that point, it didn't matter. Dying would be a welcome relief from living with that madman.

"Carlos seemed amused at this new 'game.' Warning me that if I failed to kill him, things would go worse for me, he promised not to kill me. He swore he'd find more refined ways to torture me in the future.

"As we faced one another with no more than four feet between us, I felt no fear. I was beyond fear, I think. Perhaps he had pushed me over the edge of sanity at that point. His sword came up and slashed at my gown, grazing my thigh. It was much later I realized he'd cut me. Somewhere in my brain, I must have been recalling some of what your fencing instructor taught me, Kathleen, though I was too dazed to realize it then. Carlos threw back his head and laughed at me, never dreaming I'd have the strength to raise the sword against him with any results.

"That laugh was the final straw. Something snapped in me, and from somewhere within I found the courage and strength to attack. Taking advantage of his confident inattention, I raised my rapier and drove it straight through his heart.

"He was dead before he hit the floor, I believe, but not before he realized what I had done. Always, I shall savor the look of absolute amazement on his face as I pulled the sword from his chest!

"How long I stood in dazed triumph over his body, I do not know. I do not recall leaving the house. Instinct must have led me to my parents' home, for I awoke on the seat of a coach in their carriage house, still dressed in my nightrobe. Recalling what I had done, I was debating whether or not to go into the house, when I saw the civil authorities arrive.

"After they'd gone, I crept up the backstaircase into Josepha's room and waited for her. When she arrived and found me there, she warned me not to go to my father. He was horrified that I had been accused of killing Carlos, and was determined to turn me over to the officials and see me pay for my crimes if I came to him for help. The entire household was instructed to inform him the minute they saw me.

"Josepha, my nurse and companion from childhood, decided to help me. As I had no money or clothes of my own, she gave me one of her old dresses. She hid me until nightfall, then took me to the poorest section of town, to the house of friends of her family. With her own money, she paid for my keep.

"The people I hid with did not know who I was, or they would have been tempted to turn me in for the reward. They were extremely poor, and had many mouths to feed. Josepha returned every week to see how I was doing, but even the small weekly basket of food she brought was insufficient for our needs, and I soon learned to beg on the streets with the others. We would raid the garbage pails of inns and taverns for scraps. Almost immediately, I traded my dress for boy's clothing and cap. It was much safer to be a boy on those filthy streets than a young girl."

"Was Josepha the old woman who talked with us in the carriage?" Reed questioned.

Isabel nodded, but did not look up. "It seemed a miracle when she told me you were here. I had nearly given up hope of finding a way out of Spain. I feared I was doomed to live in squalor and hunger until I either starved to death or was eventually caught. The taste of fear was more common than that of food on my tongue."

"Considering the condition you arrived in, that is easy to believe," Reed mumbled, shaking his head at her incredible story.

A look passed between Reed and Kathleen of instant communication and understanding. Kathleen voiced their mutual thoughts. "Isabel, you are welcome to stay with us as long as you wish. If you want, you can come with us when we return to Savannah. There will be an entire ocean between you and Spain. You can feel safe there, and build your life anew, forgetting all the abuse and laying to rest all the awful memories."

Sobs shook Isabel's frail frame as she huddled in Kath-

38

leen's embrace. "There are no words to express my gratitude! I know you must be shocked and disgusted, yet you still offer your help. I will repay you somehow; this I promise. I will work for you. I will scrub and clean for you, and help with the children," she babbled.

"No," Kathleen answered firmly.

A stricken look made Isabel's features dissolve anew. "I do not blame you. Who would want a murderess caring for their children?" she choked.

"It is not that, Isabel," Reed corrected gently, taking her thin hand in his own and kissing it gallantly. "Kathleen is saying that you will not be a servant in our home. You will live with us because we are your friends and we want you there. We will be your family."

"You would do this for a friend of Kathleen's? A confessed murderess? Someone you barely know?" Isabel was incredulous.

"I would do this for Kathleen's friend, yes," Reed concurred, "and also for a young woman who has been severely mistreated; who brought none of her problems upon herself, but took the only course open to her. You did what you had to, Isabel, and now you are free; free to forget the past and build a better life in a new land; free to seek the happiness you deserve."

Kathleen hugged the frail girl to her. "Welcome to the family, Isabel."

Because of the increasing unrest between England and the United States, Reed did not think it wise to advertise the arrival of an American vessel in Ireland. Thus, Kathleen suggested they sail the *Kat-Ann* around to a little-used cove near the rear of her estate. It was close, convenient, and private.

Reed was astounded when they finally arrived. The house was immense, of solid, rough-hewn grey stone, and the dimensions of it dwarfed Chimera, their plantation home. The surrounding land which was not wooded, was tilled and planted, with small, neat crofter's cottages dotted here and there.

"My God, Kathleen! Is all this land yours?" he gasped.

She nodded, her brilliant green eyes matching the Irish landscape.

"Aye, 'tis indeed." How easily that familiar Irish brogue came back to her tongue!

"And the house!" Reed exclaimed. "The blasted thing is a castle!"

"Nay, actually it is thirteen rooms shy of being classified as an authentic castle."

Reed laughed. "So what is it then, a castlette?"

"No, it's merely a mansion," Kathleen chuckled in return.

"Well, whatever it is called, I must admit I am impressed. And I thought you would be so awed by Chimera!" He laughed again. "You could put Chimera inside this mansion and have room enough left over for your Aunt Barbara's house, too!"

"Now, Reed, you know how much I love Chimera. There isn't a plantation to compare with it anywhere near Savannah. The house is large and airy, the architecture is absolutely beautiful, and the rooms are lavish, yet tastefully designed."

"Still," he argued, "it is nothing like this."

"Thank your lucky stars, you befuddled sea captain!" she teased, rolling her eyes to the heavens. "Do you realize how cold and drafty this old place is in the winter? The fireplaces barely lessen the chill; mostly they throw smoke back into the rooms. The stone floors are like ice. There is no way to keep a home this size as clean as you'd like, so most of the rooms are closed off, and only aired when company comes. Nanna used to let me lead the spider brigade each year during spring cleaning!

"Everything smells musty. And you'll notice the lack of windows compared to the newer houses you are used to. Many of these big old places were used as fortresses at one time or another. What windows there are were small and placed high in the walls. They let very little light into the rooms, even on a bright, sunny day, so the entire house is in perpetual gloom. It is very depressing at times."

Reed gazed down at her tenderly. "Yet you still love it."

Kathleen swallowed the lump in her throat as she let her eyes roam over her ancestral home for the first time in four years. "Yes, I still love it. I wish Grandmother Kate had come back with us! I know she still misses Ireland even after all these years."

Reed's arm stole about her waist. "Perhaps it holds some painful memories, Kat. When I asked her to come with us, she was very staunch in her refusal, saying she preferred to remember it as she last saw it. Also, she told me that one cannot hold onto the past if one intends to take a firm grasp on the future."

Kathleen thought about her grandmother's words. "Kate is a very wise lady," she concluded, with a faint smile.

The last few days of June slipped into July, but no one noticed. They were all too busy. In addition to purchasing Irish whiskey, lace, and linen to take home, Reed was overseeing the estate. The crops were doing very well this year,

41

from barley to potatoes. He and Kathleen were well pleased when they went over the books with her solicitor, Mr. Kirby. The livestock were thriving, and it seemed that more than the usual number of kids and lambs had been born this spring as well as new foals and several calves.

The biggest problem was the mansion itself. The house had been run by a minimal staff during Kathleen's protracted absence, so most of the rooms had been closed off for the past four years and were smothered in dust and mildew. Many of the draperies and carpets were irreparably ruined by moisture and mold, as were a few tapestries, most of the mattresses, and upholstered chairs.

When Kathleen had departed four years previously, she had taken very little with her on her journey. Now she had the chore of sorting through and packing those items she wished to take back to Chimera. There was the family silver, of course, and the china and crystal, and Mr. Kirby had held most of her mother and father's jewelry for her. Now he brought them from his bank vault and returned them to her.

There were also portraits, family heirlooms, and long-forgotten mementos of Kathleen's youth. What clothing she'd left in chests and wardrobes were now either outgrown or outdated. These, along with those of her father's which she had not had time to sort through before, she donated to her tenant farmers and their families.

Reed and Kathleen visited the crofters and were pleased to find that Mr. Kirby had seen that the cottages were kept in good repair. Most were freshly whitewashed, with thrifty garden plots on small, well-kept lots. Many had small sheds in which to house a cow or goats and a few chickens. Compared to most, Kathleen's tenants were very well looked after, and she was both glad and proud, for she loved her homeland and its people.

In addition to the tenant families, many of Kathleen's former neighbors and friends came to call. Word had spread of her marriage to an American and many of their visitors were surprised that Reed was not the uncouth backwoodsman they'd envisioned. They were fascinated by his deep Southern drawl, and Reed in turn was amused by their thick Irish brogue.

They'd been there nearly a month, when one late afternoon found Reed and Kathleen on the vast front lawn, staring thoughtfully up at the slate roof. Most of their work had been tended to, and they were now preparing for their return journey to Savannah.

"What do you think, Reed?" Kathleen queried, shading her eyes with her hand. "Can we just patch the leaky spots and get by with that?"

Reed looked doubtful. "I don't know, Kat. I should get a couple of men and go up and take a good look at it. My guess is, it is in worse repair than we know. A few leaks can be patched until next year, but the entire roof should be inspected closely just to be sure. This may be a major project, and it should be done right if it's done at all."

"Drat! I was looking forward to going home, Reed. Even if we leave by the end of the week, it will still be mid-September at the soonest before we reach Georgia."

Reed's grin was triumphant, his teeth flashing white in his deeply tanned face. "You're homesick!" he gloated. "My little Irish rose has thrust her roots deeply into that rich Georgian soil, and now she misses it!"

Wrinkling her nose at him, Kathleen pushed a slim finger at his chest. "Listen to me, you Yankee upstart.

43

First of all, I am anything but little! Just because you cast a shadow longer than most trees hereabouts, is no reason to jeer at me. Furthermore . . ."

"Hereabouts? Hereabouts?" Reed drawled with a hooting laugh. "Honey, you sound more Georgian every time you open your mouth!"

She ignored his interruption. "*Furthermore,*" she repeated, "I would not compare myself to a rose, Irish or otherwise. A rose is weak and fragile and . . ."

"And beautiful and soft," he interjected, "which you are, even when you are scratching me with your thorns. A rose is also intricate, and delicate, and extremely fragrant," he added, nuzzling his nose in her neck.

Kathleen gave a shiver of delight as his warm breath raised goose bumps on her skin. "Fine. I'll concede to the rose concept, if you will admit I'm not little."

His warm hand curved to cradle her breast. "Agreed," he chuckled.

Kathleen swatted at him and hid her smile. "Crazy man!"

"Crazy about you, my sweet Irish rose," he teased.

Kathleen leveled a warning look at him. "Speaking of flowers, Kate wanted me to bring back an arbutus shrub for her, and a start of that mint growing by the springhouse, and a few strawberry plants if I can. I'd nearly forgotten. Remind me to dig them up just before we leave."

"I'll try to remember," Reed promised.

Kathleen looked back at the roof with a grimace. "How long will that job delay us?"

"I think, if I can find a few reliable men, that we can still leave soon. If Kirby will keep an eye on the repairs, there is no reason we have to stay. I'll talk to him about it.''

Kathleen squinted her eyes in the direction of a rapidly approaching coach. "You can speak to him sooner than you think. If I'm not mistaken, that is his carriage barreling down the drive."

"I wonder why he is in such a hurry?" Reed mused.

Kirby met them halfway across the lawn. The first indication that something was wrong came as Kathleen noted that his usually impeccable appearance was quite ruffled. "Mr. Kirby, is something wrong? First you come tearing up the drive hell bent on destruction, and now you look as if your best hunter broke a leg," she said.

Kirby's thin lips compressed even further, and he looked from Kathleen to Reed in obvious discomfort. He cleared his throat nervously. "There is no easy way to say this. We have just received word from London that on June eighteenth, President Madison of the United States formally declared war on Great Britain."

It took a moment for the words to sink in. "That was over a month ago!" Kathleen exclaimed.

At the same time, Reed cursed, "Damn! I wanted to be home before it happened."

"You know how slowly news travels from overseas. We just got the word today, and I rushed right out to tell you. They say President Madison is also issuing privateering commissions against England," said Kirby.

Reed ground his teeth in impatient frustration. "And I have eight ships that cannot be used until I get home!"

"*We* have eight ships," Kathleen corrected, "and we must get them back to port and authorized as privateers as soon as possible."

Reed grabbed Kathleen by the shoulders, his blue eyes ablaze. "We must head for Savannah immediately, Kat!"

"Yes, of course," she agreed. "Ask Mr. Kirby about the roof while I inform the others." She started toward the house.

"Wait!" Mr. Kirby exclaimed excitedly. His face reflected despair as he said more quietly, "There is more."

"More bad news?" Reed guessed.

Kirby nodded. "Two days after King George received the declaration of war, he, in a fit of rage, declared that all British properties now held by Americans are now revoked. The same courier brought both announcements today."

Kathleen stood rooted to the spot at this information. Slowly the blood drained from her face, leaving her deathly pale. Her eyes sought Kirby's for confirmation. "And my estate has legally belonged to Reed for the past four years," she rasped.

"And I am an American," Reed added.

"Yes," Kirby confirmed.

"But this is not an estate awarded by favor of the King," Kathleen reminded him hopefully. "It has belonged to my mother's family for years, and I am her heir also."

Kirby shook his head sadly. "It doesn't apply here, Kathleen. Your mother, being Catholic, would have forfeited the land if your father had not happened along just then. When they married, the property became his through marriage, yes, but only because he was Protestant. Had he been Catholic, the property would have been lost."

"My father was also a lord," Kathleen argued, "and I inherited the title."

Kirby sighed. "It has now been rescinded by order of the King. All British subjects married to Americans and living in the United States have been divested of their titles and lands."

"Is there no way to reverse the decision?" Kathleen asked.

"Only if you and Reed swear allegiance to the British crown, give up your holdings in America, and live here."

"Never!" Reed shouted. "Not in a million years!"

Kathleen rejected Kirby's words as well. "No. There is no way we would do that. I'd never ask it of my husband, not even to save my lands. I'd hold little respect for him if he had agreed."

Reed's arms enfolded her, his thoughts now entirely on her loss. "Kat, I'm so sorry."

Twin emerald pools shimmering with tears gazed up at him. "I guess I've always been more Irish than English, and I'll be damned if I'll let that pompous idiot dictate to me from his throne! My children are American, and so am I now. Let him have the estate, but it will be a hollow victory if I have my way."

Squaring her small shoulders, she directed a question to the barrister. "Mr. Kirby, do you have any indication who the new owner of this property might be?"

The poor man flinched openly as he told her. "Sir Lawrence Ellerby."

Kathleen teetered as if hit by a blow. "Larry Ellerby!" she shrieked. "That imbecile couldn't run a one-horse farm, let alone an estate of this size! He'll ruin it within weeks!"

"I know," Kirby agreed readily. "He's done just that in the last six years with both the inheritance his grandfather left him and the lands willed to him on his father's death.

He's a notorious Jonah when it comes to property. The man can take an estate worth a fortune and within months, he's bankrupt again."

"He's not a Jonah," Kathleen corrected indignantly. "He's an out-and-out fool! Ellerby bleeds the land for its immediate profits. The money goes to support his gambling, his drinking, and his whoring. Never does he think to reinvest some of the money back into the property. Anyone with an ounce of sense knows crops don't seed themselves and come up year after year just begging to be harvested, but Ellerby seems to expect just that! Then he is supremely surprised when the profits stop rolling in and his coffers are empty! The man is a moron; a hazard to society! No wonder the King is banishing him to Ireland! Left to his own devices, he could single-handedly defeat England from within, and the Americans would never need fire a shot!"

At the end of her discourse, Kirby was staring at her open-mouthed, and the corners of Reed's lips were twitching suspiciously. Kathleen glared at them both.

"I'm sorry, Kat," Reed explained, "but you've shocked poor Kirby, I'm afraid. I haven't seen you on such a tirade since—since Emerald." He smiled wryly at the thought of her Irish temper.

"I'll tell you one thing, Reed Taylor. You haven't seen anything yet!" she promised. Her eyes spouted green flames. "All I ask is a few more days before we sail."

"Till the end of the week?" he suggested.

"Fine. Mr. Kirby, when can we expect Ellerby's arrival?"

"I'd say a week at most. The man is desperately in debt."

"Then we'd best get started right away. Mr. Kirby, I do

hope you can stay to supper. There is a lot I must discuss with you.'' Kathleen started for the house at a fast pace.

''I take it you have a plan!'' Reed called after her.

The look she flashed him was delightfully wicked; her tinkling, brazen laughter promised trouble. ''Do fish swim?'' she retorted saucily.

As Reed watched her prance away, he was bursting with pride. He'd almost forgotten how fabulous his Kat could be in a true temper. She had taken a severe blow, but to watch her, you'd never guess it. For mere seconds, he'd watched her flounder. Then she'd found her feet again and was off and running. She bounced back so quickly, spinning plans and plotting revenge.

It was marvelous to watch her in action, her eyes flashing; and it was a unique treat to see her temper directed at someone else for a change! If he didn't know how deeply Kat had been hurt, Reed could almost pity Ellerby. As it was, Reed suspected if she broke down at all, it would be tonight in the privacy of their bedchamber, and he intended to be ready and able to comfort her. He wanted to lend her his strength; to hold her, cradle her in his arms and kiss away all the pain and tears; to make her world shine again.

Chapter 3

Reed awoke in the middle of the night, wondering sleepily what small noise had awakened him. Automatically, his arm reached out for Kat and found her gone. Just as his searching gaze saw her shadowed outline at the window, he heard a stifled sob.

Silently he slid from the bed and went to stand behind her. His arms curled protectively about her waist, and he pulled her back to rest against his solid form. Though the night was warm, she was trembling violently. Reed rubbed his chin soothingly across the top of her head, ruffling her hair. Hot salty tears fell from her lowered face like raindrops onto his forearms.

"Oh, Kat," he groaned, hating the pain he knew she was feeling. He kissed her head and the side of her neck. "I'm here, kitten."

"It . . . hurts like the devil!" she stammered between sobs.

"I know," he murmured, tightening his grip as he felt another tremor seize her. It dismayed him to realize how useless he was to her just now. Kathleen was given more to flashes of rage than to tears. Rarely did anyone see her cry. She was always so strong, so vibrant. Now, when she was feeling defeated and weak, all he could offer was his strength and understanding.

Instinctively, Reed knew she would reject anyone's pity, his included. Kathleen detested weak, weeping, self-pitying women. Relying as she did on her own strength, she rarely displayed a need for his, though he knew how deeply she loved him. At times, it irritated him that she was not more dependent on him, but her stubborness was one of the first things about her that had caught his attention, and he admired her self-reliance.

"It always hurts to lose something you love, sugar," he said softly, his breath ruffling her soft hair. "I know how deeply you care about this place. All your roots are here. A lot of memories were born here."

"*I* was born here. So were Mama and Kate," she added mournfully. "I wanted Katlin to inherit the estate, to carry on the heritage that has been passed down for generations."

"Katlin will still have Chimera as his birthright," Reed pointed out gently. "I'm not saying he would not appreciate an added inheritance, but I doubt he would make it his home, Kat. And it is not easy to manage property so distant from your home."

"I've managed so far," she argued.

Reed shook his head. "With the aid of Mr. Kirby. Even so, you see how some things have been sadly neglected; the roof for instance."

Kathleen nodded reluctantly. "That doesn't ease the pain of losing it, though. Especially when it is going to be in the hands of someone like Ellerby. I feel as if I am placing one of my children into the care of a rapist! He'll strip the land of its prosperity and beauty, and leave it bereft and lifeless! It isn't fair!"

"Few things in this life are, kitten. You must concentrate on your blessings. You are hurting now, but you still have Chimera to return to, and people who care about you there; Kate, Barbara, Mother, Susan and Ted." He turned her slowly in his arms to face him. "And you have the children—and me, love."

His hand lifted her trembling chin until tender blue eyes met those of shimmering green. "Kat, my darling, you'll always have me," he reminded her gently. "Doesn't that help at all?"

He watched as her eyes overflowed with tears that coursed down her flushed cheeks. "Oh, Reed!" she choked. "Of course it helps, my love. I could lose everything else, and if I had you, I'd still be rich! I'm just being a silly, sentimental female, and I *hate* it when I act this way!"

Reed smiled tenderly. "You are not being silly, Kat," he corrected. "You are merely human. When cut, you bleed; when hurt, you cry."

He brushed a lingering tear from her cheek, and bent to taste her trembling lips with his. "Mmm, salty," he commented in low tones.

With a quivering sigh, Kathleen leaned against him. Her hands slid up his warm, furry chest to lock at the back of his neck. "Hold me, Reed. Love me," she implored softly, her shaky voice conveying her need of his comfort and strength.

Wordlessly, he complied. Gathering her close to him, he kissed her deeply. There was no urgent demand as his lips covered hers; only tenderness. The moment was timeless as his mouth warmed hers, his tongue gently tracing the salty contours of her lips.

As he held her, Reed ran his hands over the muscles of her back, gently kneading the tension away. From shoulders to waist, the soothing circles repeated until he felt her relax with a shuddering sigh of contentment.

It was like stroking a kitten. Her hair, her skin were as warm and sleek as satin. And like a cat, she stretched and snuggled at his touch, wriggling her body provocatively against his. A sound very much like a purr escaped her lips, and a primitive flush of desire surged through him, sorely testing his waning control.

With swift strides, he carried her to the bed. As he laid her upon it, Kathleen reached out for him, but he captured her wrists gently and put them aside. "No, kitten. Tonight let me love you." His blue eyes blazed even in the darkness of the room. "I want to touch every inch of you, caress every curve, kiss every crevice, excite every nerve. I want to love you as never before; as no one ever will again."

Time held no meaning; the darkened room became their only existing world as Reed's hands and lips slowly traversed her body from head to toe. His knowing fingers found every sensitive area, every erotic spot on her skin. Not one inch was neglected as his hot, moist kisses covered her body.

He took her small feet, cool now from standing on the stone floor, and warmed them in his palms. His strong fingers massaged her arches, and she sighed in blissful contentment. Feeling almost drugged by his ministerings, Kathleen jerked back to full awareness as Reed's teeth nipped at her toes.

"Reed! For heaven's sake, the floor was *dusty*!" she objected, trying to pull her foot away.

Anticipating her move, his hand held her ankle firmly. "Hush! Relax!" he ordered, laughing huskily.

"Relax!" she nearly shrieked as his tongue slid across her ticklish sole. "This borders on torture!"

His chuckle was decidedly devilish as he administered the same treatment to her other foot. His fingers blazed a path for his silken tongue to follow; curling about her ankles and tracing intricate patterns up her legs, pausing momentarily at the sensitive hollows of her knees, and alternating slowly up the insides of each thigh.

While Kathleen felt her bones melting at his leisurely traversal, she felt her muscles tightening in delightful anticipation of his next move. Her skin had come alive in his sensual touch, every nerve awakened and more sensitive than she could ever recall. The blood seemed to boil in her veins, rushing through her body at a startling rate, and her heart was racing. Her breath came in irregular gasps, and her mind seemed to focus only on the pleasures he was evoking.

Before she knew what he intended, Reed had flipped her onto her stomach, and began tracing lazy circles on her back with his wet tongue. He lingered at the nape of her neck and along the delicate cords of her shoulders, biting gently and laughing softly at her predictably spasmodic responses. How deftly he teased the hollows along her shoulder blades, and the pleasure points all down her spine. He deliberately disregarded her instinctive tensing as his attentions wandered lower, his hands cupping and fondling her round buttocks, his mouth delivering nipping kisses here and there on its way to the tender flesh of her inner thighs.

When he finally turned her onto her back once more, Kathleen was trembling with the force of her arousal. Once more she reached out for him, but Reed was far from finished. Gently he captured her hands, nipping and licking at the delicate pads of her fingertips, running his tongue tantalizingly across each palm in turn, and up the inner curve of each outstretched arm. His lips caressed the curve of her neck, teasing the sensitive flesh and nibbling their way up to each ear.

Kathleen was nearly mindless, her senses awash with sensual delight. She drifted in a fog, where only the glorious sensations Reed was creating made any impression. She shivered in wondrous bliss as his tongue playfully traced the inner shell of her ears, his strong white teeth nipping at her lobes as he whispered endearments. She felt treasured and tormented at the same time.

His warm lips feathered lazily across her face, as if memorizing each feature they encountered. The attack on her senses was doubled as his hands trailed seductively along the contours of her body.

Kathleen was aflame with the most basic, primeval need she'd ever felt. Deep, agonized moans seemed to be wrenched from the depth of her being, and her body arched toward his as she writhed beneath his wizard's touch. His hot mouth at last enclosed a swollen, pouting nipple. Cradled in his warm palm, she could almost feel her breast swell to fill his hand. As he sucked and teased first at one breast, then the other, she felt fires race through her body. His hand found the throbbing center of her femininity, and he teased her mercilessly until she was delirious with desire.

By now she was calling out his name repeatedly, clutching at him, pleading with him to take her. With practiced ease, he eluded her grasping hands, his lips trailing tiny kisses across her stomach, until they at last replaced his hand between her thighs.

Kathleen writhed against the sheets, her fingers clenching at his shoulders, her nails digging crescents into his flesh. Her cries seemed to echo from the stone walls, resembling those of some demented creature. A swirling mist seemed to surround her; she was mindless with desire and need of him.

Trembling on the edge of ecstasy, she at last felt Reed's body cover hers. As he came into her, she cried out, receiving him eagerly as if long denied this ultimate fulfillment. Rapture coursed through her in swell after endless swell, until the leaping flames engulfed them both with devastating force, burning into their very souls, hurtling them toward the heavens like glowing embers in a gale; and they floated slowly back to earth as if on lazy puffs of cloud, the last remnants of their blazing flight still warming their sated spirits.

Reed continued to hold her as Kathleen drifted off to sleep, her head pillowed on his shoulder. Profoundly glad he had succeeded in taking her mind off her loss, he realized that the respite was only temporary. As if his thoughts had touched some semi-conscious corner of her mind, he heard her mutter, "Damn, bloody English!" Her terse cursing creased an amused smile across his handsome face, and he stifled a chuckle. One thing, at least, was evident. The worst of her grieving was past. If Reed was correct, the morning light would revitalize her anger and need for revenge; and he'd rather see her angry any day, her green eyes flashing defiantly, than weeping. Content that his goal had been achieved, he joined his wife in deep, reviving slumber . . .

As Reed had predicted, Kathleen awoke in a rare rage the next day. After a few sweet moments of reflection over the previous night's loving, a few lingering kisses and caresses beneath the bedcovers, she was ready to do battle. Time was of the essence now, and Kathleen's mind was spinning off ideas faster than anyone could follow. Orders were flying right and left. Everyone but Reed seemed stunned by her energy and outrageous plans.

"Mr. Kirby, have you sent in the bi-annual income report to London yet?" she asked the attorney that morning.

"No," he answered hesitantly. "What do you have in mind?"

Instead of answering, she posed another question. "What sort of winter did you have here last year?"

"Colder than normal," came the reply. "Much more harsh than usual."

"Good!" she said, making them all wonder if she'd lost her mind. "I want every bit of livestock cleared off the property. The books can be altered to the effect that several disasters struck the estate. I'll be blistered if I leave that moronic fop so much as a chicken to roast!"

"What will you do with the animals?" Isabel asked, wide-eyed.

Kathleen waved a hand in the air. "Give them to the cottagers," she suggested magnanimously. "While I wish to leave nothing for Ellerby, I do not wish to cause hunger or oppression to the tenants."

"And how should I word the report, lass?" Kirby wanted to know.

Kathleen chewed a fingernail thoughtfully, then smiled wickedly. "I'm afraid, Mr. Kirby, that the harsh winter caused a great loss of cattle, sheep, and goats. The remainder had to be used for food, in addition to all the chickens, ducks, and geese."

"And the hogs?"

"A mysterious swine disease killed them all."

Kirby's eyebrows shot upward at this. He could hardly

bring himself to ask the next question. "What of the horses?"

Kathleen shook her head in mock dismay, as Reed silently applauded her cunning. " 'Tis a pity we'll have to burn the stables to cover my tales, but I fear all the horses were lost when the stables caught fire earlier this spring," she invented.

This caused even Reed to roll his eyes. "Kat, are you sure about burning the stables?"

She frowned, but then nodded. "I'm sure. I'd burn the barns and the fields, too, but it would only cause hardship to the tenants. Some crops are already in, and others are near harvest. I would not cause hunger for the families so loyal to us all these years just to vent anger on Ellerby.

"However, I will not leave so much as a crumb in the pantry! The larders will be cleaned out, and what food there is distributed among the crofters. And the devil take Sir Lawrence!" Kathleen nearly spat the last words.

"Too bad you cannot burn the house," Isabel added.

"Oh, no! No!" Kirby exclaimed. "Kathleen wouldn't want to do that, even were it possible!" As Kathleen narrowed her eyes, he went on, "Perhaps someday, after this war between England and America is over, the King will return the property and the title to you."

Kathleen gave him a doubtful look. "Is that likely?"

Kirby shrugged. "It is not probable, but it has happened. If Sir Lawrence becomes a bankrupt, the King may return it to you after a time, should you petition him."

Kathleen considered this possibility briefly. "Well, short of tearing the place down to stone, I cannot destroy it. However, I intend to strip it bare! What I cannot take with me, or do not want, the crofters may have. I'll set what is left aflame with the stables. Let Ellerby supply his own furnishings. When I've finished, he'll even have to buy his own candles and candlesticks!''

True to her word, Kathleen set the servants to the task of stripping the house of its contents. In addition to the items she'd already selected and had loaded aboard the *Kat-Ann*, she now added everything else of value, whether sentimental or monetary. Besides the portraits she'd already selected, she now added those remaining ancestors she'd originally decided to leave behind. Tapestries and paintings were carefully packed, as were stacks of books and Irish linens. Silverware, china, and crystal found their way aboard ship. Room was made for vases, knicknacks, figurines, mirrors, and clocks.

A few choice pieces of furniture were carried aboard, but most of it, by necessity, had to be left behind, and Kathleen stoically set about distributing it to her tenants. The crofters were delighted to have her cast-offs, down to the crockery, pots and pans and even the fireplace screens.

Like a whirlwind, Kathleen went through the house from attic to cellar, clearing out treasures. One afternoon, Reed found her standing in the center of the empty dining room, staring toward the ceiling with great concentration. He knew it was a mistake before he even opened his mouth, but he asked anyway. ''What is the problem, Kat?''

She threw him a sheepish look from the corner of her eye. ''I was trying to decide what to do with the chandelier. I'd nearly overlooked it,'' she admitted.

''God forbid!'' he chided, tongue-in-cheek.

''Well, I certainly don't intend to leave it for Ellerby!'' she huffed. ''Nor the one in the main hall.''

"Your crofters will love them," he teased. "Just what every cottage needs!"

In the end, he found himself directing the workers as they dismantled and packed the great crystal and silver monstrosities. After this, Reed thought surely there was little else Kathleen could do to stun him. The empty rooms threw back echoes as he strolled through them. Not a matchstick was left that he could see. Kathleen had given away everything, including the kitchen broom, stating that Ellerby could provide his own to clear away the cobwebs and spiders, which she benevolently bequeathed to him.

But, Reed thought she was going a bit far when she ordered the wallmounted sconces taken down and the door knocker removed. "Are you sure you don't want to dismantle the entire mansion and rebuild it stone by stone in Savannah, Kat?" he inquired mockingly.

"If it were at all possible, I would, indeed," she retorted, her emerald eyes snapping.

As a parting shot, she watched as dozens of workers scaled the steep roofs, dragging huge rocks up with them. These they wedged into the chimney openings, where they could not easily be seen or removed.

"There!" she chuckled slyly. "Let Ellerby try to get a decent draught now! I hope he chokes on the first fire he lights! May all his toes turn blue and drop off!"

Reed laughed helplessly. "Oh, Kat! What a devious, conniving female mind lies behind that delicate form and angelic face of yours! Remind me never to underestimate you!"

The look she gave him was at once calculating, tantalizing, and totally feline. Her emerald eyes shimmered with deviltry and her merry laughter rang out like a hundred tiny bells. "Just stay on my good side, darling, and you have nothing to worry about!"

The mist lay heavily across the bay, matching Kathleen's sorrowful mood as she watched Ireland fade from sight. A heavy sigh caught in her throat, threatening to become a sob. Turning from the rail, she saw Reed watching her intently. She mustered a wan smile. "I think I'll go below-deck for a while," she told him.

Kathleen worked her way carefully across the crowded deck and passageway to the captain's quarters. The *Kat-Ann* was carrying three times her usual crew, as well as numerous other passengers on her return voyage to Savannah. Before leaving Ireland, Reed had offered passage to those servants and crofters' families who wished to emigrate to America. He issued the same invitation to those sailors and personnel who had worked for years for Edward Haley's shipping firm. A goodly number of loyal crewmen, many of whom had sailed under Kathleen's command years earlier, accepted Reed's offer of employment in Savannah. A couple of the firm's bookkeepers followed suit. Several crofters and a few of the servants, whose hatred of the English had grown steadily over the years, decided to try their luck in America rather than work for the infamous Ellerby. Those with trades could find work as carpenters, masons, blacksmiths, cooks, and seamstresses. Kathleen was certain that her grandmother, who had never approved of the concept of slavery, would hire many of the farmers and their families at her own estate, Emerald Hill.

The *Kat-Ann*, designed to carry cargo, and outfitted as a

privateer, was never meant to house so many passengers. The few cabins were crammed to overflowing, as were the crew's quarters, and there were even bedrolls and hammocks strung on deck. Every nook and cranny from bow to stern was filled with cargo, supplies, or people, and the *Kat-Ann* rode low in the water.

Kathleen fought her gloomy mood as best she could. She spent extra time with her children and talked for hours with Isabel, who was by now physically recovered from her ordeal and beginning to put on a few much-needed pounds. Additional energy was spent making sure the crofters' wives and children had everything they needed. Sewing circles were organized to provide useful outlets for energy and the opportunity for companionship among the women. Katlin and Alexandrea's large cabin was converted into a makeshift nursery during the day, with mothers taking turns watching the youngsters. This gave the women a few hours' respite from the constant demands of their children, and at the same time provided the children with playmates and organized activities to compensate for the restriction of their normal freedom aboard ship.

Once a day, all the children were shepherded on deck for fresh air and sunshine, carefully watched by anxious mothers to be sure that their natural exuberance would not take them near the ship's rail. The roll and pitch of the frigate on the ocean swells made many of the women lurch along at an unnatural gait, and Reed laughingly commented that they resembled a flock of waddling mother ducks with their brood stumbling along in their wake.

Still unable to shake her depression by the fifth day, Kathleen fell back on her old remedy. Rising early, she donned a pair of trousers she kept in her sea chest, and a boy's full-sleeved shirt. Inwardly, Kathleen winced at what Reed's reaction might be, but she squared her shoulders and marched out on deck. By now Reed was used to the idea that his adorable wife had some very unfeminine talents, but Kathleen usually took great care to conceal them in public. Alone with Reed and their usual crew, she often took the helm and sailed the *Kat-Ann* herself, as she had done several times on the trip over. At home, she donned trousers when she helped Kate train the horses they raised at Emerald Hill, or for a wild early morning ride on her palomino stallion with Reed. Together they would race across fields and pastures, Kathleen on Zeus and Reed astride his own black stallion, Titan.

Reed had learned long ago to accept Kathleen's unorthodox behavior and dress as a natural part of her charm and unusual allure. It did no good to rail at her; the more he ranted, the more outrageous she became, as if to spite him. He really didn't mind as long as she was discreet about it. Most of the time he enjoyed sharing the excitement of his world with her. Kathleen was so much more vibrant than any other woman he'd ever met, that others paled in comparison. She had a daring and zest for life, adding a sparkle and spice to their marriage that he'd never imagined possible. Not even in his angriest moments would he trade his mercurial mate for a more conventional spouse, but there were times when she tried his patience sorely, and this was one of them.

Kathleen strode boldly onto the deck, bound for the mainmast. Reed took one look at her trim figure, accentuated by the men's clothing, and was instantly vexed. A deep frown creased his brow and his eyes narrowed in annoyance. Handing the wheel over to the nearest man, he stalked over to where she was already climbing the mast.

Hands on hips, he glared up at her. "What in hell's half acre are you up to now?" he bellowed.

With a graceful dexterity that always amazed him, she swung about, clinging to the mast with one hand, one foot balanced precariously on a spar. Looking down at him, she measured the distance separating them and announced pertly, "I'd say about twenty feet and climbing."

His face clouded at her answer. "Get your sweet self down here," he ordered, "before I climb up and carry you down over my shoulder."

Her own eyes narrowed into green slits. "Your caveman tactics don't impress me, Reed," she smirked.

"My hand on your backside will make quite an impression," he warned sternly. "Are you coming down?"

Kathleen shook her head, her flaming hair flying in the breeze. "No!"

"Kathleen," he said slowly, striving for some remnant of patience, "be reasonable. The ship is overflowing with passengers, and you are making a spectacle of yourself."

"At this point, I couldn't care if the king and his court were watching!" she spat out irritably. Her eyes closed on a deep sigh, and when she opened them, she gazed at him imploringly. "Reed, please. You are quite right when you say the ship is crowded. I can't go three feet without tripping over someone, and frankly, it's driving me insane! I've taken all I can in my present mood, and I'm sorry if I am embarrassing you, but I need some space. I desperately need some time to myself; to think, to release the pressures building up inside me; to deal with my anger over losing the estate; to settle my mind." Green eyes glittering with unshed tears, she begged him for understanding.

The moment he glimpsed her tears, Reed was defeated. When faced with her ire or tart tongue, he could spar with her on even ground; but under the force of her tears, his anger rapidly disintegrated. He smiled wryly, gave a frustrated sigh, and waved her on with a flip of his hand. "Up with you then, sprite," he said gruffly. "Off to your clouds and your private musings. Just make sure you come down in a brighter mood than you've been in lately."

Smiling her thanks, she blew him a kiss and scurried up the mast before he could re-think his decision.

Perched high above the deck, at the very top of the mast, Kathleen found the solitude she craved. The wind whistled in her ears, blowing her hair wildly about her face, creating a unique music she loved. Up here the noise from the deck was muted by the wind, the flapping of the huge sails and the creak of wood. At this height, the sway of the mast as the ship sliced through the sea was magnified, but Kathleen was used to it. It soothed her as a babe is comforted by the rhythmic movements of a rocking chair.

Far below, she saw the deep blue waves, stretching endlessly toward the horizon. With no land in sight, it was easy to imagine the swells rolling off the edge of the world in a gigantic waterfall. For a long time, Kathleen sat on her lofty throne, letting her thoughts and agitation drift away on the wings of the winds; letting the motions and sounds of her beloved sea sift into her being and fill her with peace.

Tranquil as she was, it took several moments for her mind to register what her eye had already unconsciously realized. Instantly alert, she peered intently at the small dark speck in the otherwise undisturbed azure sea.

"Ship to the starboard stern!" she shouted.

Reed's head snapped up, his eyes searching for her in the shrouds above him. "Can you see her colors?" he barked back.

"Not without the glass," came her answer. "She's too far off. But by the shape and size of her, I'll lay odds she's British."

Immediately Reed sent a man up the mizzen mast with the glass. Kathleen kept her post, awaiting the identity of the craft. A chill up her backbone told her what the sailor confirmed seconds later.

"She's a limey brig; all sails unfurled, and closing fast!"

"A British warship!" Reed cursed under his breath.

Kathleen lost no time shinnying down the mast. Her face was tense, her supple mouth drawn into a thin line. "Damn and double damn!" Normally the sleek, fast *Kat-Ann* could outrun and outmaneuver any ship on the sea, but now she was burdened by her extraordinarily heavy load.

Kathleen raced to Reed's side. "We can't outrun them, Kat," he told her unnecessarily.

She nodded briskly. "Then we'll have to stand and fight."

Pride shone in his eyes, making them a brilliant blue as he gazed at her. No simpering Miss here, but a tigress, ready and willing to defend her young.

"I'd rather it not come to that. There are too many passengers aboard. Perhaps we can outwit them instead." The *Kat-Ann* was flying no colors, in case of a situation such as this.

"I have an idea," Kathleen said. "Run up the Irish

flag! Let them come alongside, thinking they approach an ally. We cannot hope to avoid their guns otherwise, but once they are upon us, their cannon will be of little use, as will ours.''

Reed nodded thoughtfully. ''They'd risk a broadside from us, and the odds would be even then. Either could sink the other readily.''

''Precisely.''

''They'll be looking to impress sailors into service,'' Reed surmised, his thoughts flying furiously. ''If we let them board in their usual imperious manner, we could surprise them.''

''Like unsuspecting trout to a lure,'' Kathleen agreed with a sly smile. ''And with so many seasoned seamen, we should have no problems. We've three times our normal crew, and all good fighters.''

''Reformed pirates, mostly.'' Reed suppressed a rueful grin, but his eyes gleamed momentarily. Quickly they outlined their plan, and set out to inform the men.

It took Kathleen all of five minutes to gather her rapier, knife, and pistol, and order the women to stay belowdeck with the children. Now she stood behind Reed, watching as the English brig pulled alongside. Their plan was simple, but Reed's acting abilities and timing would be crucial to the outcome.

''Heave to and prepare to be boarded!'' The shouted order sang across the short space separating the two ships.

Over his shoulder, Reed said, ''Kat, if anything should go wrong . . .''

With a jab of her elbow in his unsuspecting ribs, she cut his words short. ''Nothin'll be goin' wrong, me laddie,'' she answered in an exaggerated Irish brogue. ''Newgate prison is not on me list o' places t' visit this season.'' The anticipation of the encounter kindled an added gleam in her sparkling eyes as she threw Reed a wicked wink.

"You're a sassy wench, Kathleen Taylor," he retorted with a grin.

Their attention was brought to the business at hand as grappling hooks found their marks, linking the two vessels like multiple umbilical cords. A plank served as a bridge, and in short order a score of British seamen boarded the *Kat-Ann* behind their commanding officer. From what Kathleen could see from beneath Reed's arm, he was short, chubby, and pink-cheeked. Only his impeccable naval uniform and dour expression prevented him from resembling an elf.

"Who commands this vessel?" he demanded imperiously.

"I captain the *Kat-Ann*," Reed replied, aping Kathleen's Irish accent.

The British officer eyed Reed with obvious disdain. Drawing himself up to his full height, which still left him several inches shorter than Kathleen, he stated, "In the name of the King of England, I command you to release all British seamen and subjects into my command immediately."

Doing his best to assume a humble pose, Reed said, "I do not believe we carry any, sir, but you are welcome to check."

"Oh, we shall—we shall indeed!" The officer sniffed haughtily. "We shall also appropriate any arms, ammunition or supplies we deem useful to His Majesty's Navy." He motioned for his men to search the ship.

When the British seamen spread out to investigate, the *Kat-Ann*'s crew went into action. While a number of

Reed's men stood quietly on deck, meekly watching and making no move to stop them, the British seamen selected several for impressment into England's service. These men were relieved of their weapons and herded together into one group to be guarded by three of the British, while others went belowdeck to search out more men and confiscate goods.

Kathleen stood quietly behind Reed and watched the enemy disappear one by one into the passageways. Several minutes went by with no apparent disturbance occurring. Except for an occasional dull thud, no sounds reached the upper deck.

Meanwhile, several innocuous-looking sailors slipped quietly into position on deck, awaiting the signal from Reed. Laughing to herself at the British officer's superior expression, Kathleen stepped quickly from behind Reed, rapier in hand. "My, my! Rats aboard my ship!" she exclaimed loudly. "What shall I do about them?" She looked down her tip-tilted nose at the short man before her. At the sound of her decidedly female voice, all heads turned her way, all eyes drawn to her. The sight of Kathleen in form-fitting trousers and low-buttoned blouse, her fiery tresses blown wild by the breeze, was startling, to say the least.

Reed's slight nod went unnoticed by all but those who had been waiting for it. Within seconds, Reed's rapier blade was at the small officer's throat. The three seamen guarding their prisoners suddenly found themselves at gunpoint. Before any of the British were aware of what was happening, the grappling lines were cut, and the two vessels lurched apart. With amazing speed, the *Kat-Ann*'s crew flew into action releasing lines and unfurling sails, as

Kathleen took the wheel. Finley signaled from below that the remaining English sailors were subdued.

As the space between the *Kat-Ann* and the British warship widened, so did Reed's grin. With their commanding officer and several of their crew held prisoner, it was safe to assume the English would not fire on the *Kat-Ann*.

A few hours later, Kathleen stood at the stern rail with a much less assured British commander. She wore a broad smile, while he wore a very red face and a ragged towel about his otherwise naked body.

"I do hope you can swim, Commander," she taunted, her voice rich with laughter. She flicked at his towel with the tip of her rapier.

One by one she and Reed had forced their captives overboard to flounder in the briny Atlantic until they could be rescued by their ship. With each man released, the distance between the two vessels widened, until the British brig could no longer be seen. The commander was the last to be set adrift, and by the time his ship retrieved his water-wrinkled, pruny person, the *Kat-Ann* would be long gone.

With a final nudge of her sword, Kathleen prodded him over the edge, at the same time hooking his towel. Kathleen hid her eyes with her hand in mock embarrassment as the chubby officer flailed the air and finally hit the water as bare as the day he was born. Her rippling laughter floated down to him as he surfaced, as did her parting comment:

"Damn fool Englishman!"

Chapter 4

The next few weeks were trying on everyone's nerves. Being confined in such crowded quarters made tempers short, but the voyage was surprisingly smooth for the most part. They encountered no more British vessels, and they gave a wide berth to Bermuda, an English controlled island. The sea was calm for most of the crossing, and the trade winds favorable. Not until they entered the warmer southern waters a few days from Savannah did the weather give them problems. This region was now in the midst of the hurricane season, and tropical storms were known to appear out of nowhere, swooping down with surprising speed and force, only to disappear just as suddenly, leaving behind destruction beneath blue skies and sunshine.

Having encountered a couple of smaller squalls, it was no surprise to Reed when another threatened this day. Still, he had an uncomfortable feeling about the coming storm.

"What do you think, Kat?" he asked, trusting her mysterious intuition about the sea more than his own experienced opinion. "I'm uneasy about this one for some reason."

Kathleen nodded. "So am I. I think we may be on the

fringes of a hurricane. See how murky the water has become?''

Reed agreed. With the rising wind, the waves had become larger, and the *Kat-Ann* now bounced roughly on the choppy seas. "The winds keep changing instead of blowing steadily from one direction. You must have noticed how many times we've had to trim sails already.''

Kathleen was staring into the hazy waters below. ''The fish have gone deep,'' she commented. Reed did not question how she knew this. Some things about Kathleen would always be a mystery to him, especially her strange affinity with the sea and its creatures. He simply accepted her statement as truth.

''I wish I knew whether we were heading into it or merely catching the edge,'' he mused.

''I can't help you there,'' Kathleen answered. ''You've told me often enough that hurricanes are notoriously unpredictable. All I know is that I've not seen a dolphin all morning, and that is a warning in itself.''

Reed's frown deepened, lines creasing his forehead. ''We'd better prepare for the worst, just in case. The way the winds are changing, I'd say we are on the outer edge, but whether it is the leading edge or the tail of the storm is anyone's guess. If it is a hurricane, it won't matter anyway. They've been known to stay in one location for a week or more, then take any direction you'd care to name. They'll gather strength or lose it without any particular rhyme or reason.''

''Let's just hope we stay on the edge of it,'' Kathleen said. ''The *Kat-Ann* is carrying too much weight to withstand a major storm.''

''We may have to jettison some of the cargo,'' Reed told her.

Kathleen considered this a moment and nodded her assent. A smile found its way to her curved lips. "I suppose we could start with Uncle Haviland's portrait. He always seemed such a stern, forbidding character. Besides, he was some distant relation on the Haley English side of the family, and therefore not in my favor at the moment."

Reed laughed and shook his head. "I doubt that throwing old Haviland overboard will lighten the load much."

"No, but we could start there and work up. If nothing else, it gives me a good excuse to get rid of the oppressive thing!"

Luck was with them after all. Though the *Kat-Ann* was tossed about like a matchstick on a pond, they stayed on the edge of the storm. The rain came down in torrents, creating a thick curtain that made visibility impossible beyond a few feet. Throughout the hours it took to weather the storm, Kathleen and Reed stayed on the bridge. Rain and waves drenched them as they stood together at the helm. They'd taken the precaution of lashing themselves to the wheel, and Kathleen stood in the shelter of Reed's arms as together they rode out the storm. Rather than being frightened, Kathleen was exhilarated. As the wind and waves rose, so did her spirit, until she felt at one with the sea and the elements. Her face shone as if she'd just been handed the most precious of gifts. She glowed with a sort of peaceful tranquility and joy, like a captive bird suddenly set free. As the *Kat-Ann* fought her way through deep troughs and over mighty crests, Kathleen rode her own high wave of exultation, transported for a time into a world consisting only of herself, Reed, and her beloved sea.

As Reed stood behind her, his arms straining with hers

to keep the wheel steady, he was reminded of another time he and Kathleen had ridden out a hurricane together. Then she had been disguised as the piratess Emerald, bold as brass, with hair dyed black as midnight. Then, as now, she had been energized and enthralled by the storm; vibrantly alive, yet at the same time somehow peacefully mesmerized.

"We're crazy to be enjoying this!" he shouted over the noise of the storm.

Tilting her head back to look at him, she laughed.

The breath caught in his throat as Reed gazed down at her rapt face. Here she stood, drenched to the skin, her hair straggling in her face, and he'd never seen her more enchanting. He kissed a drop of rain off her nose, and she snuggled more closely against his broad chest. At this moment Reed knew he loved Kathleen with all his heart, and would for the rest of his life. Surely he could never feel this way about any other woman; no other woman could ever compare to Kathleen. She had completely bewitched him, and he loved it.

The remainder of the voyage was calm and sunny. The final hurdle before reaching Savannah was to successfully run the English blockade along the Georgia coast. Fortune blessed them with a black, moonless night, and their arrival coincided with a high tide in their favor. Reed guided the *Kat-Ann* unfalteringly up the Savannah River, past islands and around sandbars as familiar to him in the dark as by daylight. It was in the wee hours of the morning of September eighteenth that the *Kat-Ann* slid silently into her berth at the base of Savannah's white-bluffed port. They were home at last.

As much as he wished, Reed could not go directly home

with Kathleen, Isabel and the children the next day. He stayed in town to see to the unloading of the *Kat-Ann*'s cargo and the housing of the passengers. Kathleen's Aunt Barbara and Uncle William Baker insisted that he stay with them while in town. Reed readily agreed, since it gave him the opportunity to discuss business with their son Ted, his sister Susan's husband. Ted and Susan had a two year old son, and were expecting another child in December.

When Reed had relocated the shipping firm from Ireland to Savannah, Ted had expressed interest in helping to run the operation. The brothers-in-law worked well together. Ted, with a good head for figures, managed the offices and warehouses. While he knew next to nothing about sailing a ship, he had a sharp mind for business. Most people wondered why he had not followed in William's footsteps and become a lawyer, but while Ted admired his father immensely, law had never interested him.

On the other hand, Reed had sailed for years, captaining vessels first for other owners, and finally his own fleet. There was little he did not know about ships and ports, cargos and the sea. He devoted his time to seeing that all eight frigates were kept in good repair, hired the captains and crews, charted their courses and determined what merchandise was to be bought and sold in which ports, and saw to the loading and unloading of goods. At any given time Reed knew where each of his ships was, who was captaining which run, and which frigate would dock in Savannah at what time.

With both the plantation and the shipping firm to run, Reed was more than happy to let Ted handle the management of the office and warehouses. Paperwork bored him, and he appreciated having Ted to rely upon, knowing his young brother-in-law was not only capable, but honest.

Unable to stay away from the sea for long, Reed would occasionally take one of the voyages himself. Sometimes Kathleen would accompany him as she had this time. Their mutual love of sailing was one of the many things they shared. Reed's responsibilities to his family and home kept him tied to shore more now than he'd been used to before his marriage. Not that he regretted his commitment to Kathleen and his children, but he could not spend as much time aboard ship as when he was younger and more carefree. But Reed knew Kathleen understood his love affair with the sea, for she, too, was under its hypnotic spell. Neither of them could resist its call for long.

While Reed saw to business in Savannah and caught up on news of the war with Britain, Kathleen took Isabel and the children on to Chimera. The Taylor plantation was but a few hours' ride outside the city, along the southern bank of the Savannah River.

The house itself was large, bright, and airy, and Kathleen had loved it on sight. To her, Chimera was beautiful to behold; warm and welcoming. This was home, all the more precious now since she'd lost her estate in Ireland. After greeting her mother-in-law, Mary Taylor, and introducing Isabel, Kathleen set about getting her friend settled in one of the spacious guests suites. Once Della put the children to bed for their naps, Kathleen sat down with a soothing cup of tea to hear all the news from Mary.

"I can't tell you how relieved I am that you are home again, Kathleen," Mary told her. "I've worried that you might not make it back safely now that war has begun."

"We started home as soon as word reached us, Mary.

You should know wild horses couldn't have kept Reed away once he'd heard.''

Mary nodded. ''I've missed you all terribly! Lands, I swear those children have grown a foot since you left!''

''So has Susan's little Teddy,'' Kathleen pointed out. ''I was so surprised to find Susan so far along with child. It made me realize how long we've been away. She wasn't even expecting when we sailed.''

''Now that you are home, I'll stay a few weeks and spend time with Andrea and Katlin. Then I shall be going to Savannah to stay with Susan until after her baby is born,'' Mary added.

Kathleen smiled. ''She'll like that, I know. It was sweet of you to take such good care of me when Andrea and Katlin were born. I don't know if I've ever properly thanked you for that, but I appreciate it more than I can say.''

''You are like my own daughter, Kathleen,'' Mary said, gently waving aside Kathleen's words of gratitude. ''That is what mothers are for.''

After being brought up to date on everything that had happened at Chimera during their absence, and all the local gossip about friends and neighbors, the talk turned once more to the war.

''They've started rebuilding old Fort Wayne, and there is talk of building another where Fort Greene stood before the hurricane of 1804 destroyed it,'' Mary mentioned with a frown.

''It was too dark to notice anything last night when we arrived, but on the way out here today, I saw quite a few slaves digging ditches of some sort. What is that all about?'' Kathleen asked.

Mary explained, "The town fathers decided we should have earthworks built around the city; hence the trenches."

A worried look passed between the two women. "Perhaps you should think about moving into town, too, Kathleen," Mary suggested. "It might be safer for you and the children."

"We'll see," Kathleen replied slowly. "I want to see what Grandmother Kate is going to do, and what Reed suggests."

That afternoon, Kathleen rode over to Emerald Hill, her grandmother's plantation adjoining the Taylor holdings. Kathleen had been named after her grandmother, and the resemblance between the two was striking. Though Kate, who had just celebrated her seventieth birthday, now displayed more grey hair than red, her green eyes still sparkled just as brightly. Her Irish brogue still lingered on her tongue after nearly two decades in America, and her active mind and quick sense of humor had not dimmed with the passing years. Kate O'Reilly was very active in Savannah society, and had taught Kathleen the art of horse breeding at Emerald Hill when Kathleen had first arrived in Savannah.

It nearly broke Kathleen's heart to tell her grandmother that the estate which had been in their family for centuries was no longer theirs. There was no way to soften the blow.

"Gran, I'm so sorry, but there was nothing we could do. Mr. Kirby did say that after the war is over, perhaps we could petition the King for its return."

Her green eyes misting with sentimental tears, Kate shook her head sadly. "Don't be blamin' yerself, lass. 'Twould have been lost years ago if yer father hadn't come along and married yer mother when he did. Maybe

80

'tis best the last ties have been broken. We're Americans now, and have our land and lives here. O'course, I'm saddened by the news. There's a wealth o' memories wrapped up in thet place, both good and bad. 'Tis glad I am thet I didn't go back with ye t' visit. Now I'll always be rememberin' it jest the way we left it, Sean and I.''

''I did bring back the plants you wanted, and a few other things, like the silver and the portraits and such,'' Kathleen offered, hoping to ease the older woman's grief.

A glow lit Kate's face. ''Did ye now? And what of the O'Reilly banner?''

Kathleen nodded. ''It's in one of the trunks Reed will be sending from Savannah. I tell you, Gran, I was so furious that I left not so much as a broomstraw for Ellerby. What I couldn't bring back with me, I gave to the crofters. I even brought the door knocker!''

Kate laughed. ''Kathleen, me own, ye're Irish through and through! I'll not be believin' a drop o' English blood runs in yer veins, not matter what yer Aunt Barbara says.''

''And proud of it, Gran,'' Kathleen proclaimed. She then proceeded to tell Kate everything that had transpired. In the end, as Kathleen had predicted, Kate agreed to hire many of the Irish crofters who had come to Savannah with them.

''Aye, 'tis time t' even out the odds a bit. All o' Scotland seems t' be wantin' t' settle here, and we need some good Irish stock t' balance the scales. There's no one better with horses than an Irishman, and I'd be willin' t' bet Reed would agree thet there's none t' compare with Irish whiskey and Irish women either,'' she boasted with a broad wink.

Reed arrived home full of news of the war and his plans

to aid the American cause. "Do you realize that what the United States calls its naval protection consists of sixteen frigates and sloops of war; this pitted against nearly six hundred British naval vessels?" He was incredulous and incensed at the same time.

Kathleen felt chills dance up her backbone. She and Mary shared a dismayed look across the dining table. Kathleen knew what Reed would say next, and she barely choked back a groan.

Reed did not notice her reaction. "President Madison is calling on all owners of seaworthy vessels to help balance the odds. We have three frigates in port now, and two more expected this week, one of them the *Starbright*. Since the *Kat-Ann* and the *Starbright* are already heavily armed, we've only the others to worry about."

"Meaning you intend to add more guns to the other frigates before they sail again," Kathleen stated.

"Yes."

"Does that also mean that you intend to use them as warships instead of cargo vessels?"

The tense tone of her voice finally registered, but Reed met her intent gaze steadily. "For the most part, yes. We may use one as a blockade runner, if needed. I'm not sure yet."

Her appetite completely gone, Kathleen pushed her plate away from her. "Which frigate will you be captaining, Reed?" she asked softly.

Blue eyes locked with green, registering the multitude of emotions each was feeling in that moment. Like most men, Reed's first reaction had been an immediate thrill of patriotism and anticipation at engaging in battle with the enemy. Now, as he saw the worry on Kathleen's face, he realized all that this war could cost. In that moment, he faced his own mortality, and his fragile hold on life and happiness.

Kathleen was facing her own fears for his safety, and at the same time she felt a distinct twinge of jealousy. She envied Reed the freedom and excitement of fighting the British from the deck of a ship. For just a second she hated him for daring to risk his life and their future together, and also for the very fact that he was a man and had the freedom of choice denied her as a woman.

Above all, she felt torn by her love for him. A part of her was bursting with pride that he would brave the dangers of war to defend his country and his family, and she yearned desperately to be able to stand at his side while he did so. The other side of her despaired his absence, already missing him; even now she was gnawed by fear that he might be seriously wounded or killed.

Reed's reply was equally soft, but determined. "I'll be taking the *Kat-Ann*."

Unconsciously, Kathleen fingered the necklace at her throat, as if it was making it difficult for her to breathe. "When will you be leaving?"

Regret and male pride mixed, making Reed's reply brusque. "I expect to sail early next week. There are a few things I need to catch up on in order to leave the business in Ted's hands and the plantation running smoothly under your supervision and Mother's."

"I see." Blinking rapidly, Kathleen barely held back her tears. "In other words, your mother and I are to keep the home fires burning until your return." She could not keep the sharp edge from her voice. The slight hesitation gave weight to her next words, as she added, "*If* you return."

Mary Taylor paled visibly, and her choked gasp was

clearly heard in the silence following Kathleen's words. She gazed helplessly from Kathleen to Reed as they sat locked in silent combat. Seconds ticked by, endlessly long, before Reed spoke.

"I have to go."

Kathleen swallowed hard. Pushing her own pride aside, she begged, "Take me with you!"

"I can't." His eyes pleaded with her to understand.

"You *won't*," she countered angrily, two plump tears wetting her cheeks. Her chin jutted out stubbornly.

"All right, I won't," Reed conceded with a slight nod of his head. He waited, and when she failed to comment or soften in her manner, he pushed his chair from the table. "Would you have me be a coward, Kat?" he asked.

"No, but I want to be with you."

"And I want you here." With that, he strode from the room.

Kathleen alternately cursed the war, the British, Reed, and the world in general in the following days. Reed took up where she left off. Kathleen's attitude angered him, but he often had occasion to regret his sharp words to her.

Mary and Isabel constantly found themselves trying to smooth ruffled feathers and calm edgy tempers. Also cast in the role of peacemaker, Kate O'Reilly could have banged Reed and Kathleen's heads together.

"Two stubborn fools, that's what they are," she complained to Mary. "They should be treasurin' these precious days together instead o' hissin' and clawin' at one another."

Mary folded her hands together in her lap and sighed heavily. "They'll work it out," she predicted hopefully. "One thing that helps is that Reed hopes to stay within a few days of Savannah much of the time. He wants to concentrate on harassing the British blockade along the coastline from Charleston to the Floridas. He'll be able to come home often, and if the British try to attack Savannah, he may be able to warn us in time for Kathleen to leave Chimera and get the children to safety. That, at least, relieves my mind somewhat. It bothered me that you and Kathleen would be alone out here, knowing that the British would reach Emerald Hill and Chimera before Savannah.''

Kate chuckled, her emerald eyes alight with life. ''Kathleen told me she refused t' go t' Savannah t' stay, and I have t' agree with her. I'll not be leavin' Emerald Hill, either, unless I absolutely must.''

Mary eyed the older woman in exasperation. ''I know where Kathleen gets her stubborn streak, Kate. She inherited more than her looks from you! To quote your granddaughter, she'll be hanged if she'll let those bloody British run her out of a second home.''

''Aye,'' Kate agreed. ''She's still hurtin' over losin' her Irish lands.''

''That, and the fact that she has to remain behind while Reed is gone,'' Mary added. ''She's having a harder time accepting that than anything else for some reason.''

Kate could have told Mary why, but she kept still. Kate alone, of all their friends and relatives in Savannah, knew of Kathleen's escapades as Emerald. No one else was aware of her dual identity except Kathleen's friend Eleonore and the Lafitte brothers, and they were all in New Orleans now. If Kathleen had confided in Isabel, the young woman had not mentioned it to anyone.

Chapter 5

That first night, Kathleen was so upset and angry at Reed that she locked him out of their bedroom, the first time in three years that she had denied him his husbandly rights.

"Blast it, Kat! Open this door!" Reed's fist connected with the solid door with a resounding thump.

Inside the bedroom, Kathleen sat cross-legged in the center of their huge bed. She glared at the door, clearly envisioning Reed on the other side. She'd put pillow and sheets on the settee in their private sitting room. As Reed was now standing less than three feet from the settee, she was positive he'd noticed. The locked door and the bedding spoke for themselves. Kathleen saw no need to respond to Reed's rantings. Stubbornly mute, she cursed him silently, if thoroughly.

At length, Reed stopped beating on the door, though Kathleen could still hear him mumbling to himself in the next room. Finally all was silent, and Kathleen hoped Reed had given up and gone to sleep. In a way, she was surprised, for a locked door had never kept him at bay before. She could only assume that Reed had not wanted their argument heard throughout the house.

Kathleen deliberately waited until Reed had left the house before coming down to breakfast the next morning. When he failed to appear at luncheon, she knew he, too, was avoiding a confrontation. All day, Kathleen vacillated between wanting to make up and feeding her anger. She knew she was being irrational and taking her frustrations out on him, but she couldn't help herself. Reed was not responsible for the war, nor could he change the fact that she was a woman and therefore relegated to the role of waiting at home for her husband's return. Still, she balked at the injustice of it all. She was young and strong and willing to fight. No one was more competent with a rapier than she. Nobody could hold a candle to her at the helm of a ship, except Reed himself. If he needed to throw himself headlong into danger, she wanted to be there with him; side by side, hand in hand, not waiting at home for news of his death or worrying herself sick.

He, of all people, should know how she felt! It was she who had outsailed, outfought, and outmaneuvered him for the better part of their first year of marriage. And not only him, but many others, including the infamous Jean Lafitte. She keenly resented being unable to take part in this war against the British when she possessed the necessary skills. But society would not stand for it, and perhaps would never allow women the freedom they deserved. Meanwhile, Kathleen strained at the tethers that bound her to home and children.

Reed was not blind to Kathleen's needs and feelings, but there was no way he would allow Kathleen to accompany him. If she should be wounded, even killed, he would never forgive himself for exposing her to such dangers. Then, too, if something should happen to him, the children would still have Kathleen to care for them. Reed would stand firm on this, and Kathleen would just have to come to her senses. He hoped that it would be soon, and that she could restrain her volatile temper and reason things out. Hating the idea of being separated from her, he did not want their parting marred by harsh words and anger.

Reed took matters into his own hands the next evening. Kathleen, intending to escape to the seclusion of her room, excused herself shortly after dinner. She discovered Reed's sabotage as soon as she attempted to lock the bedroom door, only to find he had removed the locks from all the doors of their private suite.

Nearly speechless with anger, she nevertheless managed to sputter several choice epithets. In a royal rage, she stomped to her dresser, extracting the first nightgown her hands encountered. Still seething, she marched to the bed, tore the sheets off it, grabbed her pillow, and strode toward the door.

With the bedclothes piled high in her arms, and her mind in a fury, she failed to see Reed until she almost barreled into him. Pulled up short, her eyes shot emerald arrows through him as he stood smugly in the doorway, his arms crossed across his chest, a self-satisfied smile on his face.

"And just where do you think you are going?" he taunted.

Gritting her teeth, she snarled, "I should think that would be obvious, even to someone as dense as you. I am going to find other quarters in which to sleep—*alone.*" She attempted to shoulder her way past him, but he blocked her path.

One dark eyebrow raised mockingly as he slowly shook his head. "No, my lovely little spitfire. You are going to stay right here, and we are going to settle things once and for all." The stern tone of his voice and the forbidding look in his ice-blue eyes negated the smile still curving his mobile mouth.

Anyone who knew Reed well would have been warned to caution by his attitude, but Kathleen was too angry to heed the signs. "Get out of my way, you big buffoon! I have nothing to say to you." She pushed at the arm blocking her way.

He moved, not to let her pass, but to clamp an iron hand about her wrist. Effortlessly, he tossed her back into the room, to tumble awkwardly onto the bed. Linens flew everywhere. Before Kathleen could untangle herself from their hindering folds, Reed was towering over her.

"If you do not wish to speak, so much the better. You may sit quietly and listen to what I have to say for a change," he instructed firmly, yet quietly.

Kathleen opened her mouth, a quick retort on her tongue, but the dark look on his face made her think better of it. Her jaws clamped shut with a snap.

Reed gave a short, humorless laugh. "That's wise of you, Kathleen." The use of her full name was an indication of just how angry he was. His eyes dared her to budge from the bed.

When he spoke, his words were clipped and precise. "In the last couple of days, you have worked yourself into a lather over a situation which neither you nor I can change. The facts are these. I am leaving in two days' time aboard the *Kat-Ann* to do my level best to help defeat the British naval forces in this war. You, my shrewish wife, are staying *here* to fulfill your duties toward me, our children, and Chimera. There will be no further discussion of this agreement!"

Kathleen glared up at him, silently fuming, as he continued. "In the interim, you will resign yourself to the situation and resume your usual activities as mistress of my home. You will carry out your wifely duties with a cheerful, obedient attitude, or I will be quite within my rights in beating you black and blue.''

At this, Kathleen sprang from the bed, only to be shoved back down again. ''You wouldn't dare!'' she hissed, narrowing her eyes at him.

''Try me.'' Reed was implacable, his blue eyes as hard and brilliant as diamonds.

Kathleen's chin rose at least three notches as she matched him glare for glare. Crouched on the bed, her red-gold hair in a tumble about her shoulders, her tip-tilted emerald eyes shooting daggers at him, she resembled a spitting orange cat. Unconsciously, her fingers curled into claws, digging viciously into the sheets in her anger.

Reed stepped back from the bed long enough to close the bedroom door. He threw her a calculating look as he started to remove his shirt. ''Make up the bed, and get yourself undressed,'' he ordered.

Leaping from the bed as if it were on fire, Kathleen railed at him, ''Your barbarous demeanor doesn't impress me, Reed! I'll not be bedded if I have no wish to be.''

''We covered this same ground years ago, Kathleen,'' Reed pointed out tersely. ''I don't recall that you ever won a battle in our bed.'' His smile mocked her. ''All I have to do is touch you, and you melt like butter. Your own sensual nature defeats you long before I do.''

His remark, correct as it was, struck a nerve. A flicker of hurt flashed unbidden across her face, quickly hidden as Kathleen thrust out her lower lip mutinously. In that moment, she wondered exactly how far she could push him; how angry he really was. Suddenly unsure of herself, she wished she could erase the last two days and go back to the easy, loving relationship she and Reed usually shared.

Finished undressing, Reed closed the distance between them. Knowing her as he did, he'd seen the hurt in her eyes, and silently chastised himself for causing it. By sheer will, he hardened his heart toward her. "Don't fret, Kat," he laughed, his lips curving into a devilish smile. "I intend to see that you thoroughly enjoy every moment. In fact, it wouldn't surprise me if, in the end, you are begging me to satisfy your aching body with mine." He reached out a hand to cup her breast.

Kathleen slapped his hand away. "Your ego is monumental!" she retorted hotly. Not for the world would she admit that he was probably right. Long ago she had admitted to herself that Reed had a devastating effect on her.

His fingers found the row of buttons on her bodice, deftly loosening the first three before Kathleen could react. She jerked away from him, the fabric ripping in the process. "Drat it, Reed! Will you stop this? I don't want it to be like this between us." Her voice cracked, and her eyes were shimmering with unshed tears.

"How *do* you want it to be, Kat?" he asked bluntly. "Last night, you locked me out of our bedroom. For two days you've locked me out of your life, your thoughts, showing me nothing but anger. How did you expect me to react?"

She gazed up at him in despair. Wetting her lips, she mustered her courage and whispered, "I love you, Reed. I want to be with you. I want to know that you are safe."

His hands gripped her shoulders as Reed looked down at her earnest face. "I love you, too, Kat," he said gruffly, "and I, too, need to know that you are safe. That is why I will not permit you to risk your life in combat."

Once more, Kathleen's face became set in mutinous lines, and she shook off his hands. "Just what would you term my activities as Emerald, if not combat? A Sunday picnic? A civilized tea?" she shouted. "I'm not a hothouse flower, Reed! Time after time I faced you over crossed swords. What more must I do to prove that I can defend myself? You've seen me fight my foes and win. We've fought against one another and on the same side."

"Yes," he interrupted sharply, "but I've never seen your blood stain the deck, and I never want to. You can't hold off a bullet or a cannon shot, Kat. I can not even promise you *I'll* come home whole, if at all, but I at least want to know that our children will have their mother to raise them if the worst should happen."

A tense silence followed his words, as he awaited her reaction. Neither moved, and then suddenly she flung her arms about his neck, burying her face in the hollow of his throat. "I'm sorry. Oh, Reed, I'm so sorry!" she choked, her tears wetting his chest. "I just love you so much! I *hate* the thought of you leaving."

His hands framed her face as he kissed the tears from her cheeks. "Send me off happy, kitten. Let me go with the memory of you in my arms. Let me remember the glorious look on your face when I'm loving you. Let your smile and the warmth of your love linger in my mind and beckon me home again."

His tender words destroyed the last of her defenses. Her body melted into his, her soft feminine curves the perfect complement to his muscular contours. His lips claimed hers, molding them to his will, as his hands quickly divested her of her clothing. With her gown a silken puddle at her feet, her hair a fiery mantle falling in riotous waves across her shoulders, she stood within the circle of his warm embrace; proud, passionate, and his.

As she leaned into him, her breasts brushed lightly against the curly mat of dark fur on his chest, their rosy tips instantly roused to marble-hard attention. Like a contented cat, she rubbed her body provocatively against his; thigh to thigh, breast to chest, skin against skin. Wild and wanton, as only he and nature had taught her to be, she was his fallen angel; an exotic flower begging to be plucked.

With fluid motions, he picked her up and lay her atop the unmade bed. Neither noticed the tangled sheets as he lay down beside her, his leg thrown over hers as if to further reinforce his claim on her. The thick fans of her long lashes fluttered down to lie dark against her flushed cheeks as he bent to kiss her forehead, her temple. His warm lips feathered a path ever nearer her waiting mouth. As his lips lightly touched hers, their breath mingled. Her lips trembled invitingly beneath his, urging the full weight of his mouth on hers. Still he teased her, his tongue tracing and tickling the outline of her lips, his teeth nipping gently to part her lips and admit the hot probing of his tongue into the moist recesses of her mouth.

A satisfied sigh escaped her as Kathleen gave herself fully to the deepening kiss. Her fingers slid from his shoulders to delve into his thick dark hair, holding his mouth firmly to hers.

His hands were making a langourous journey over her skin, from shoulder to knee, lingering lovingly at the curve of her hip and the indentation of her waist. That such work-roughened hands could bring her such pleasure never failed to amaze her. His long, strong fingers sought and found all the most sensitive spots on her body, creating havoc with her nerves. The calloused palms alternately soothed and aroused her in the most sensual manner. Like a great artist, Reed's hands painted her body with passion in a kaleidoscope of glorious colors and emotions.

With her head still spinning and her lips warm and swollen from his fervent kisses, Kathleen felt his mouth slip from hers to slide in a velvet caress along the curve of her jaw to the tender skin of her neck. His warm breath tickled her ear, making her shiver in delight. Slowly, as if to savor the taste of her flesh, he worked his way from neck to shoulder, and back to the pounding pulse at the base of her throat.

Caught up in the tingling enchantment of their lovemaking, Kathleen's hands stroked his muscled shoulders, patterning sensuous circles with her long nails, urging his head downward toward her aching breasts.

As his warm, moist mouth closed over a pouting nipple, pleasure blazed through her like an exotic fire dance. His ebony hair created a startling contrast against her pale, blue-veined breasts as he suckled and nipped and teased at first one, then the other.

Her muscles tensed and then melted under his touch as his fingers found and fondled the nub of sensuality at the junction of her thighs. Liquid fire raced through her veins, and she curved her body into his in an unspoken plea for fulfillment. The bold proof of his virility lay hot and hard against her thigh.

His lips wandered to the quivering muscles of her stomach, and then, as if hungry for the taste of her, came back to claim her mouth. Unwilling to prolong the pleasurable agony any longer, Kathleen's trembling hands found him and guided him to the molten cave that was the center of her yearning.

Her body welcomed his intrusion, clutching and clinging as their bodies merged in the ancient ritual of love. She gloried in his powerful thrust, rising to greet his penetration, feeling as if he were searing her very soul, marking her for life as his alone.

As their rhythm became more frantic, her nails scored his back and buttocks. Whispered words of love mingled with gasps of desire and moans of pleasure.

Then it was as if the earth had opened up beneath them, and they were hurled into the white-hot molten center of a volcano. Waves of heated rapture washed over them, surrounded them, caressed them. The receding aftershocks left them limp as melted candlewax, warm and content in each other's arms.

"I don't have the energy to move," Reed groaned into her ear when he was able to speak.

Kathleen sighed. "Neither do I, but the bed isn't made. The sheets are half on the floor."

"We'll fix them later," he suggested lazily.

"Mmm-hmm," she agreed, already more asleep than awake.

"I love you," he murmured huskily, his head nestled comfortably on her breast.

A smile curved her love-swollen lips. "I love you, too." Her arms cradled him close to her, as if loath to let him go, even in sleep.

Kathleen did not go into Savannah to see Reed off the day he left. Instead, she said her final goodbye to him in the privacy of their bedroom, where they made love one last time. His promise to be home soon echoed in her mind, and his farewell kiss lingered on her lips as she slowly climbed the stairs to the third floor, where she stood alone and strained to see the *Kat-Ann* as it sailed silently past Chimera on its way down the Savannah River to the ocean. As she watched the frigate slide out of sight around the bend, she knew that solitude would become very familiar to her in the lonely months ahead.

Kathleen filled her days to the brim with constant activity, for only if she was dead-tired could she stave off the spectre of loneliness that invaded her bedchamber each night. Only if she could collapse on their huge bed and fall instantly into an exhausted sleep, could she keep the tears and yearning at bay. Even then, too often did she awaken in the still of the night, listening for the sound of his deep breathing, reaching for him with aching arms that remained empty.

Fall was a busy time at Chimera, with crops being harvested and the pantries filling with preserved vegetables and fruits from the gardens. The smokehouse was brimming with hams and chops, roasts and sides of beef, turkey and chickens being cured for winter. Fruits were drying on huge racks or stocked in the fruit cellar alongside plump potatoes and onions.

When she was not managing affairs at Chimera, Kathleen often went to Emerald Hill, where she continued to be tutored in the art of horse-breeding by Kate. Kathleen was an apt pupil, her natural love of horses making it a joy to learn from her grandmother. She also aided Kate in helping the newly arrived Irish immigrants accustom themselves to their surroundings and the workings of the plantation. It became a familiar sight to find Kathleen working side by side with them in the fields, her long legs more often than not encased in snug breeches, her copper hair tied securely at her nape or tucked up beneath a floppy straw hat. Never a stranger to hard work, Kathleen now drove herself relentlessly.

Many a late evening found her at Reed's desk, diligently applying herself to the never-ending chore of keeping the plantation books. Often she was late for supper, once in a while missing it altogether, though she tried to dine often with Isabel and spend some time with Katlin and Alexandrea before bedtime, trying to make up for Reed's absence. Often she would take them with her to Kate's, or into Savannah to visit their cousin Teddy. They also found time for short jaunts into the woods to gather berries and to wander along the streams and fields of Chimera, and for trips to the barns and stables to visit the horses, pups, and kittens.

As much as possible of Kathleen's spare time was devoted to Isabel, and to helping the gentle girl adjust to her new home at Chimera. Two weeks after Reed's departure, Mary had left for Savannah to stay with Susan. This gave Kathleen and Isabel ample opportunity for private talks together, of which the two friends took full advantage.

By now, Isasbel was fully recovered physically from her ordeal. She had gained back most of her weight and once more resembled the young girl Kathleen had known. But Kathleen knew Isabel's emotional scars ran deep. Her beautiful face was often shadowed by sadness, her brow furrowed by a frown. She smiled rarely, and almost never without sorrow dimming its radiance. Many times Kathleen would come upon Isabel unexpectedly, to find her lost in a private world of dark memories, her eyes vague and filled with pain. Too often a flicker of fear would flash across her delicate features, and her small frame would react in spasms of uncontrollable shudders.

Isabel avoided speaking of her husband, and Kathleen

did not press her on the subject. Instead, the young women talked of their days together at Mrs. Bosley's Academy for Young Ladies. They laughed over some of the pranks they'd played on poor Mrs. Bosley and their classmates, and enjoyed reliving their happy times there.

"Do you remember when Fran Carrington thought she was pregnant because her beau had kissed her during the Christmas holiday?" Kathleen laughed. "How worried she was!"

Isabel smiled. "Yes, and then when she came down with that beastly cold soon after, she nearly died when old Bosley was going to call Dr. Frobisher."

Kathleen shook her head in mock dismay. "How young and naive we all were then!"

"Stupid, but blessedly innocent," Isabel agreed with a sigh of regret.

An impish grin made Kathleen's eyes sparkle like cut glass. "What about the time we stole a pair of Bosley's bloomers and hung them from the tower window!" she chortled.

Isabel laughed delightedly. "I'd forgotten about that, though heaven knows how! I've never seen anyone turn as many shades of purple as the poor old thing did then. I thought she was going to have heart failure!"

"When she found out who was responsible, I wished she had," Kathleen pouted. "I swear my knees still have indentations from those three weeks of scrubbing floors she gave us as punishment."

Isabel frowned, and then smiled again in remembrance. "Ah, but you got back at Cynthia Oberly for telling on us. Do you remember?"

Kathleen roared with laughter. "Oh, Lord, yes! I just wish I could have seen her face when she woke up and

99

found her long blonde braids whacked off at her scalp!'' Tears of mirth rolled down her cheeks.

Isabel rocked back and forth, trying to control her own laughter. ''We didn't *need* to see her. The entire school heard her shrieking! I was just glad Bosley couldn't pin the blame for *that* one on us!''

Kathleen nodded. ''Everyone knew we'd done it. Bosley just couldn't prove it.''

''Just as she couldn't prove who put the blue dye in her face cream!'' Isabel giggled.

Spasms of laughter had Kathleen holding her sides in acute pain. ''She had blue wrinkles for a solid week!'' she sputtered. ''That was even better than the time we sneaked into the laundry and put itching powder in the starch!''

Peals of laughter had Isabel crying helplessly by now. ''I nearly died laughing at everyone trying to scratch delicately.''

''And in a lady-like manner,'' Kathleen added, aping Mrs. Bosley's stiff way of speaking.

''You were incorrigible!'' Isabel assured Kathleen.

''*Me!*'' she shrieked. ''*You* were the one who decided we should butter all the doorknobs, Isabel, and glue Bosley's book pages together on exam day, and empty all the inkwells and refill them with lemon juice.''

''You inspired me,'' Isabel declared vehemently, ''when you hid the limburger cheese in Audrey Humphrey's bedsheets.''

''Is that why you exchanged ground-up bird droppings for Dotty Saunders' dusting powder?'' Kathleen challenged.

Long minutes later, their laughter hiccuped to a stop.

"It is a miracle we survived those years," Isabel smiled in wonderment.

"No, but it is a wonder the others did," Kathleen corrected. "It was all that mischief that kept me sane until I could go home."

"Do you suppose after all these years we should write to Mrs. Bosley, confess all, and apologize?" Isabel suggested.

"Bite your tongue!" Kathleen exclaimed on an exaggerated gasp. "She'd probably arrange for British spies to abduct us and deliver us up before her for past due punishment! My grandchildren would be grown before she let me loose again, and we'd be permanently stooped and missing our kneecaps from years of scrubbing floors!"

Isabel's dark eyes twinkled. "Bad idea?"

Kathleen nodded vigorously. "Very bad idea, Isabel. *Extremely* bad idea!"

And so, bit by bit, Isabel recovered. Her sparkling laughter came more readily, as did her charming smile. Slowly she emerged from her protective shell, responding to the honest and unselfish love of her friend. Kathleen was delighted to see the improvement in Isabel, but wondered if Isabel would ever completely get over the dreadful things that had happened to her. It hurt to see Isabel close up around other people, to glance fearfully about as if expecting to be arrested and hauled off to Spain at any moment.

Especially in the presence of men, Isabel had a tendency to flinch if touched unexpectedly. She hated meeting strangers, and particularly detested riding about Savannah in an open carriage. Kathleen could literally feel the fear tearing at Isabel at those times, and she despaired that her friend would ever feel truly comfortable and unafraid again. Trying to convince Isabel that she was safe was a monumental task. Only love and time itself could work that miracle, and perhaps even that would not prove enough. She could only pray that someday Isabel would be wholly free of her dreadful memories and debilitating fear. In the meantime, she had to content herself with smaller victories; a smile here, a laugh there, Isabel's obvious affection for Andrea and Katlin, her willingness to help Kathleen in any way she could. Isabel had taken an immediate liking to Kate, and Kathleen was sure her grandmother was guiding Isabel on the road to recovery in her own unobtrusive way. While Isabel had cautiously accepted the friendship proffered by Mary Taylor, Ted and Susan Baker, and Kathleen's Aunt Barbara and Uncle William, she readily trusted Kate at once, recognizing the same sterling qualities in the older woman as in Kathleen.

Chapter 6

Savannah continued with most of its usual fall activities, as well as some new ones instigated by the war. Work went on steadily toward the restoration of old Ford Wayne and building the new fort. Slowly but surely, the breastwork around the city was taking shape. Otherwise, no one visiting Savannah would have guessed a war was going on. No enemy troops threatened, though rumors flew constantly that the British were near, or had landed on this island or that along the Georgia coast. The only guns fired were those of the local militia training to defend the city in the event of enemy attack. A soon as uniforms could be sewn for all of them, a parade was being planned.

News of the war was slow to filter into Savannah, due to the British blockade which cut severely into shipping trade and port traffic. The residents had already learned of Isaac Hull's victory in August, when his ship, the *Constitution,* had defeated the *Guerrière.* Just recently, word had come from the North of General William Hull's surrender of Detroit to British Commander Isaac Brock in mid-August, and the surrender of Fort Dearborn and the subsequent Indian massacre at nearly the same time. It seemed the entire Northwest was now in British hands, which made the *Constitution*'s victory all the more dear. But there was also welcome news of smaller sea victories by various privateers such as Reed's in single-ship encounters of their own. The Americans appeared to be holding their own against the powerful British Navy and doing remarkably well compared to their counterparts on land, though they could do little to alleviate the British stranglehold on all the ports.

The church bazaar was held the first weekend of October, and Kathleen donated her time to work in one of the stalls. In deference to Reed's absence, she prudently refused to serve in the kissing booth, choosing instead to work with Isabel in the fortune teller's tent, a new attraction this year. Their booth did surprisingly well, collecting a good deal of money for the war effort, and Kathleen had a marvelous time making up ridiculous predictions for everyone. She foretold that Kate would meet a tall, dark stranger who would sweep her off her feet. For Susan she predicted triplets, all with an abundance of freckles. To Uncle William she prophesied another son to follow in his footsteps. When Aunt Barbara heard this, she told Kathleen she'd better dream up a second wife to present him with the child, for *she* certainly wouldn't at this late date!

Another of the annual fall events was St. Teresa's Ball in mid-October. Held each fall at this time, it was an elaborate affair where all eligible young ladies made their official debut into society.

That evening, as Kathleen stood watching the white-gowned girls be led down the magnificent staircase on the arms of their escorts and presented to Savannah's elite, she recalled her own debut a few short years past. She'd worn a specially designed gown of glimmering white satin, with long sheer sleeves of pleated silk that opened up like butterfly's wings when she lifted her arms. Scores of jeweled butterflies were sewn painstakingly into the fabric, creating a unique and dazzling effect, catching and reflecting the light in a sparkling rainbow of colors.

Reed, devastatingly handsome, had escorted her down the long staircase. Together they had become Savannah's darlings that evening. No one could recall a time in the history of the ball, and certainly not since that night, when any couple had made such a dramatic entrance or had had such a stunning impact on Savannah society. Since that time, Kathleen and Reed had enjoyed being considered one of the city's most attractive couples—though they'd shocked and delighted its leading citizens with their outrageous behavior many times over. Savannah, it seemed, was willing to forgive Kathleen and Reed Taylor almost anything. . . .

In spite of Reed's absence, Kathleen found herself invited to many other fall festivities, harvest balls, parties, barbecues and feasts. She attended most of them, finding it an excellent way to introduce Isabel to their friends and neighbors in a relaxed, casual manner. While Isabel balked a bit at first, she realized that Kathleen was sparing her the intimate prying that often resulted at more intimate gatherings. Grateful for this small reprieve, Isabel allowed herself to be pulled along in Kathleen's wake, frequently with Kate on her other side to fend off curious inquiries and would-be suitors.

The twenty-second of October brought Alexandrea's third birthday. This year Kathleen deemed her old enough to have a party, to which several of her little friends were invited. In this way, Kathleen helped to ease the disappointment of Reed's absence.

Susan, adhering to her mother's advice not to travel any

more than necessary at this late stage of her pregnancy, sent Teddy in Mary's care. Altogether, there were fifteen children aged two to four, enjoying refreshments and games at Chimera that afternoon. The weather was fine, and the party was held outdoors. Andrea received many lovely gifts on her special day—as well as a full set of teeth prints from Randall Wicker, who had bitten her within five minutes of his arrival. But by the time Della brought out the birthday cake, all animosity was forgotten, and Alexandrea Jean blew out her three candles with a proud smile.

At the end of the day, Kathleen gratefully kissed her two tired children goodnight earlier than usual and retired to her own bed more weary than if she'd worked in the fields all day.

Reed arrived home without warning at the end of October. He had been gone for four weeks, and Kathleen thought he looked thinner and in dire need of rest. The furrows in his broad forehead and the tiny lines fanning out from the outer corners of his eyes seemed deeper than before, though he assured her he was getting adequate sleep. And most important of all, he was alive and in one piece!

Kathleen was thrilled to have him home, though the visit was short. As she listened to Reed recounting various encounters with the British, she was sure he was glossing over the rough spots for the benefit of his mother and sister. He knew Kathleen was fully aware of the perils of sea battles, as well as the exhilaration of facing a worthy opponent over crossed swords.

What he did have to say that surprised her, was that he had been to Washington to register his fleet with the authorities. As a result, he was now involved in various secret missions on behalf of the government, in addition to his privateering ventures and general harassment of English vessels.

"I don't like the sound of that," Kathleen told him when they were finally alone.

Reed stopped in the act of unbuttoning his shirt, looking at her in surprise. "Why?"

She shrugged, her frown deepening. "I don't really know, Reed. It's just a feeling."

"Kitten, your imagination is working overtime. Nothing is going to happen to me. There is no more danger in carrying out government missions than in forays of my own."

Kathleen disagreed. "Yes there is, darling. When you attack a ship, no one knows your plans ahead of time, but when you are employed on a so-called 'secret' mission for Washington, others must know about it, too. What if someone tells the wrong person? What happens if a British sympathizer finds out and warns them? What if there is a British spy right there in Washington, working side by side with American officials, privy to all the same information?"

Reed drew her into his arms, smiling down into her worried face. "You are getting all upset over something that has little chance of happening, honey. I'm not a careless man—not when I have you to come home to." His soft words, spoken close to her ear, made her shiver, and his lips gliding down her neck almost made her forget what they were discussing.

"Just be especially careful. Promise me, Reed," she whispered as her eyes closed in delight at what his hands and lips were doing to her.

"I will be, love. Now, can we stop talking for a while? I

won't be home for very long, and I certainly don't want to spend all our precious time together discussing war strategy." His hands, splayed across her back, arched her lower body into closer contact with his, as his lips nudged her loosened gown off her shoulders.

"What did you have in mind?" she teased, as her own hands slipped inside his shirt, her fingers weaving into his chest hair, palms gently teasing his hard nipples.

He laughed easily. "Working out some lovely strategy, instead."

Kathleen wriggled enticingly against him. "Sounds fine to me, Captain Taylor," she purred, pulling his lips down to meet hers.

Much time was spent over the next few days showing Reed just how much she had missed him. What remained of his time was divided between playing with his children and readying the *Kat-Ann* for her next voyage.

Regretting having missed Andrea's birthday, Reed had nonetheless not forgotten it. He presented his daughter with a beautiful doll, and listened intently to her detailed description of her birthday party. Andrea's version differed a bit from Kathleen's recollections, which Reed solicited later. He wished he'd been here to celebrate with them, and he privately conceded with a grin that Kathleen's re-telling was probably closer to the truth than Andrea's wide-eyed tale.

Amidst all else that was going on, Kathleen organized an early birthday celebration for Reed; just a small dinner party of their closest friends, since Reed would not be home on the actual date some two weeks hence. The dinner was relaxed and enjoyable, and the gifts well chosen for being such a spur-of-the-moment idea.

Everyone seemed to come up with something Reed needed or could use on his jaunts. From his children he received miniature portraits that he could carry with him wherever he went. Kathleen had found a local artist who was quite good, and she had also had him paint a miniature of herself, which she gave to Reed along with an oilskin slicker which she knew he desperately needed.

In addition, he received a thick wool jacket to ward off the November chill. Mary and Susan had worked hard together to finish it. There were new gloves from the Bakers, a knit scarf from Isabel, and an intricately detailed copy of the most recent map Ted could lay his hands on. The entire Atlantic coastline, with all the islands as far south as the Leeward Islands, was included, as well as Louisiana and most of the Gulf of Mexico. Reed was deeply touched by their thoughtfulness.

Reed spend as much time as he could alone with Kathleen and the children. His young daughter delighted him with the recitation of a poem she had learned especially for him. Her auburn curls bounced as she nodded her head in rhythm to the words, and her small nose wrinkled as she concentrated. Reed choked back a chuckle when she finished and she eyed him expectantly with enormous long-lashed turquoise eyes.

"Very good, Andrea," he complimented. He laughed outright when she bobbed a proud curtsy and scrambled immediately into his lap, unconcerned that her ruffled skirts were askew and being crushed in the process. She grinned up at him, patting his cheeks with her tiny hands.

Returning her grin, he kissed her pert nose. "Are you Daddy's little darlin'?"

Andrea nodded, cuddling close. Over her head, Reed caught Kathleen's eye. "I wonder where she learned all

109

her feminine wiles," he commented wryly. "Could it be she's been taking lessons from Mama?" His blue eyes sparkled with merriment.

Responding to his mood, Kathleen gave him a wide-eyed look, fluttering her thick lashes. "Why ever would you think that, Reed? She's probably seen Daddy pawing Mama when he thought no one was watching. I warned you to be more circumspect," she teased.

Reed's eyebrow rose in an arch as he smiled wickedly. "Meaning I can 'paw' Mama all I want as long as I do it privately?"

Kathleen's green eyes glowed as she ran her tongue provocatively across her lips before she answered. "Precisely."

Reed mentally undressed her as his eyes roved over her curved body. "And what will Mama be doing while Daddy is busy with all this 'pawing'?" he drawled suggestively.

Struggling to keep a sober face, she answered simply, "Tickling."

"Tickling?" he echoed, his tone definitely devilish, his eyes burning into her.

Kathleen nodded, a smile tugging at her lips. "Tickling."

Adrea giggled delightedly, recalling their attention to her presence. "I *like* tickling," she announced decisively.

"I think I do too," Reed laughed softly. Over his small daughter's head he grinned at Kathleen, who somehow managed to retain her composure and return his look with a serene and confident smile.

Katlin, too, came in for his share of attention from his father. At nineteen months, he was a lively, chubby-cheeked imp; half angel, half elf, with a wide, dazzling

110

smile exactly like Reed's. The cuddly toddler had everyone wrapped securely about his pudgy fingers, most especially Reed. It still stunned Reed every time he looked into the small face so much like his own; the dancing blue eyes were a perfect match for his; the same midnight black hair, with that unruly lock falling across his forehead. It made Reed feel almost immortal and so proud he could burst. He could hardly wait until Katlin was old enough to come with him on his rounds of the plantation. Already Reed was anxious to teach him to ride his first pony, to fish, to hunt, to sail.

"But first he has to get out of diapers and into perpetually dry breeches," Reed thought wryly, handing Katlin over to Della and wiping ineffectually at the unsightly wet spot left on his own trousers. Katlin was undoubtedly adorable and charming, but definitely a hazard at this stage.

It seemed Reed had only gotten home when he was off again. He'd stayed for four days. Regardless of how busy Kathleen kept, the November days dragged by.

Barbara invited Kathleen and Isabel to her home for Thanksgiving dinner. Mary Taylor was going to be there, as well as Susan and Ted. The previous year everyone had gone to Susan's, and the year before to Chimera. This year, with Reed gone and Susan so near her due date, Barbara had decided to host the holiday feast. At first Kathleen declined, and Barbara was hurt, thinking her niece had refused the invitation because Amy was coming from Augusta with her husband, Martin Harper.

Barbara's only daughter, Amy, had years ago set her cap for Reed, and when Kathleen had first arrived in Savannah, Amy had bristled immediately. Amy was livid with jealousy, and right from their first meeting, Kathleen and she had resented one another.

But then Martin Harper had come to Savannah. The young Augustan gentleman was much taken with Amy's blond, blue-eyed beauty, but he refused to worship at her feet as so many had before him. Gently, but firmly, Martin took her in hand, and before anyone could quite believe the change in her, they were married and had gone to live on his plantation in Augusta.

Amy and Martin had only been back to Savannah a half dozen times since their wedding three and a half years before. Now they were coming to stay until after Christmas if the war allowed, and Barbara was delighted. It wasn't until Mary Taylor shed some light on the situation that she understood Kathleen's reluctance to accept her invitation.

"Oh, Barbara! Surely you don't think Kathleen still resents Amy!" Mary exclaimed in surprise.

"Why else would she refuse?" Barbara asked.

"I would imagine she feels she should spend the holiday with her grandmother," Mary suggested quietly, her gentle brown eyes silently rebuking her friend. "I don't suppose it crossed your mind to think of inviting Kate."

Barbara's hands flew to her face in dismay. "Of course! Oh, how stupid of me!" Her light blue eyes, so like Amy's, were full of embarrassed regret. Though the Bakers and Kate O'Reilly were both related to Kathleen on opposite sides of her family, their English and Irish backgrounds were at odds. For years they had resided in the same town, attended most of the same functions, and never admitted any family ties until after Kathleen had moved to Savannah. Now Barbara realized that she had unwittingly slighted Kathleen by her thoughtlessness, and she vowed to set things right. She addressed an invitation to Kate O'Reilly and sent it immediately by messenger, then repeated her invitation to Kathleen. Upon learning that Kate had also been asked to attend, Kathleen accepted. Barbara was relieved, hopeful that Mary was right in believing there would be no hard feelings between Kathleen and Amy when they met once again.

Amy surprised everyone by arriving unexpectedly and quite undeniably pregnant. Her bulging body made her petite height seem even shorter. Martin was touchingly protective of her; understandably so, since Amy had miscarried the year before. She seemed healthy enough now, however, and happily expecting the arrival of their first child sometime toward the end of January. Consequently, their visit would be extended until after Amy had recovered from childbirth.

Martin was eager to hear any and all news of the war from his brother and father-in-law. If it had not been for Amy's condition, he admitted he would have left the plantation in his father's care and gone off to Tennessee to join Andrew Jackson's troops, now busily fighting the Creek Indians whom the English had incited to war. As it was, he had to content himself with joining the local militia.

Kathleen shook her head in a mixture of amazement and amusement. It seemed every remaining man in Georgia wore the same frustrated expression as Martin. They all resembled small boys who had just been told that Christmas had been cancelled. While she understood only too well their yearning to participate, the more realistic side of her knew exactly what they were missing—which none of them did.

Kathleen knew both the taste of victory, and that of fear. She'd experienced both during her pirating days.

Fighting was not the glory they imagined it to be. It was dirt, smoke and fire; the clash of metal against metal, will against wit. It was the feel of flesh giving way to steel, the stench of sweat and blood, the cries of wounded and dying men about you. No, battle was not all glorious banners waving proudly in the breeze and victorious songs and parades of smartly dressed soldiers. Kathleen's heart cried out silently in a prayer for Reed's safe return.

December brought with it the usual onslaught of festivities. By now the effect of the blockade was being felt more severely. Unable to obtain current fashion guides from Europe, ladies made new gowns from old patterns, if they were fortunate enough to find material to work with. With a sigh of regret, old bonnets were brought forth to be worn yet another year.

Food supplies were grown locally, and most families had prudently put up enough to see them through for some time. Many holiday recipes underwent revisions, however, when certain ingredients were unavailable, spices in particular. Holiday gifts were mostly homemade this year for the same reason. From time to time, a ship slipped through the blockade and found its way to Savannah port, but with less and less frequency.

The militia continued to drill regularly and ammunition was hoarded, awaiting a British attack. The ladies' auxiliaries had been rolling bandages and collecting medical supplies in church basements for months.

With most of the holiday festivities held in Savannah itself, Kathleen now spent most of her time in the city. Time lay heavy on her hands, and she was beginning to loathe attending functions without Reed beside her. But for the sake of Isabel, Kate and the children, she smothered her anxieties and lack of enthusiasm, putting on a smiling face for the benefit of friends and family.

One function she thoroughly enjoyed was the Christmas pageant which both Andrea and Katlin participated in. All the children were so adorable in their costumes, and if they sometimes forgot their lines, they were immediately forgiven amidst smiles and smothered chuckles from the audience.

Alexandrea portrayed an angel which Kathleen thought was in direct contrast to her oft-times stubborn attitude. As she sat listening to the sweet, pure tones of their little voices raised in song, Kathleen forgot her worries for the moment and lost herself in the joy of the season. Teddy Baker had won the coveted part of one of the three wise men. As he lisped his way through his solitary line, his turban fell down across one eye, and he pushed it up again with an exaggerated sigh. The audience winced in unison as the little girl playing Mary dropped the Christ child doll on its porcelain head, but she plucked the baby up and went on as if nothing untoward had happened. Katlin, because of his limited vocabulary, was given the role of a lamb. Soon bored, he fell asleep and had to be awakened at the conclusion of the program and carried home in his fleecy costume to be put to bed.

Waddling valiantly through the pre-Christmas festivities in her advanced pregnancy, Susan drew Kathleen's full sympathy. Her soft grey eyes looked out from her puffy face in serene resignation, and she hardly ever complained, though her feet and ankles were swollen and painful. Her stomach preceded her like an advance guard; even Amy, due a mere month later, was not nearly as uncomfortable as Susan.

In an effort to help her sister-in-law, Kathleen took

Teddy back with her to Barbara's. Andrea and Katlin were overjoyed with his company, and for once the children decided to behave and play well together. Mary stayed with Susan and took over running the household, trying her best to keep Ted calm at the same time. One would think he had never gone through all this before, so nervous was he. He worried and fussed constantly over his bulging wife, driving everyone around him nearly crazy in the process.

Ted reminded Kathleen of Reed when she had been carrying Alexandrea. Reed had pampered her and hovered over her until she thought she would pull her hair out— or perhaps his. When Andrea had finally decided to be born, Reed had almost missed her birth in his mad dash to fetch the doctor. He'd barely returned in time, so quickly did his daughter make her entrance into the world. The fact that Kathleen had presented him with a daughter instead of a son mattered not at all; he lavished praise and love on both his precious ladies. . . .

Chapter 7

Exactly a week before Christmas, Susan went into labor—and labor it was! For twenty hours she struggled in immense pain. Ted was in nearly as bad shape as she. He prowled and paced in the downstairs parlor, pale and shaken, as William consoled him with sage fatherly advice which Ted barely heard. At long last, his baby daughter was born. Despite her ordeal, Susan met him with a tired smile as he took his first peek at Marlana Noelle Baker, just minutes old in her mother's arms.

Not knowing whether Reed would be home in time for Christmas, Kathleen went hopefully about the business of preparing gifts for everyone. There were toys and clothes and candy for the children. She'd found material in the attic at Chimera for a new dress for Isabel and a shawl for Kate. With much concentration and sore, pricked fingers, she'd remodeled and redecorated two exquisite bonnets for Mary and Susan. Her artistic talents amazed even herself as she made a door wreath for Barbara and Uncle William and a dried flower arrangement in a cut-glass vase for Amy and Martin. For Ted she managed to find a bottle of vintage wine in Chimera's well-stocked cellars.

One of their ships came in unexpectedly, bringing needed goods and a few more luxurious items, but no news of Reed. Kathleen managed to acquire, at great expense, a new bolt of wine-colored velvet, from which she made Reed a warm robe, trimmed in matching satin from one of her old dresses. Just enough materal was left to fashion slippers to go with it. Also from the ship's cache she obtained a gold watch chain and a magnificent ruby stickpin.

These she wrapped lovingly in hopes that Reed would be home to receive them soon. Again she was spending the holiday at Barbara's, though she'd made sure each of the servants at Chimera would receive baskets of fruit and food and the gold coins she and Reed always gave each of them at Christmas.

Late Christmas Eve found Kathleen staring solemnly into the flames of the slowly dying Yule log. Hours before, the entire family had attended Christmas Eve services at church, returning to drink punch and sing carols. Now they'd all retired, leaving the house silent and dark as Kathleen sat alone, snuggled against the fluffy pillows in the corner of the divan. The clock on the mantel chimed three times, and Kathleen sighed softly, two fat tears spilling from her shimmering emerald eyes. A shudder ran through her, and she hugged her arms tightly about her, as if to contain the pain of loneliness for Reed lancing through her. She closed her eyes and more tears forced their way past her lashes, wetting her cheeks in a growing stream. As if her tears had opened a floodgate, Kathleen found herself unable to control the sobs that shook her frame, and she turned her face into the pillows to stifle the sound of her crying.

How long she had wallowed in her private misery, she could not tell, but suddenly she felt strong arms enfolding her. Her mind must be playing tricks on her, for the deep male voice crooning softly over the noise of her sobbing sounded like Reed's. As she was pressed against a broad, protective chest, she blinked hard to clear the tears from her eyes. When she finally dared to raise her gaze, she thought she must indeed be dreaming, for the face she beheld above hers was Reed's. Warm blue eyes scanned her features as if starved for the sight of her. She blinked once more, but when she raised her wet lashes, the vision remained, and it was Reed's voice softly saying her name over and over again as he gathered her close to him.

"Oh, Reed," she whispered on a shuddering sigh. "Please tell me I'm not dreaming! Please tell me you are really here, holding me in your arms!"

"I'm really here, sweetheart, and so glad to be holding you again. I can't begin to tell you the trouble I've had trying to get home for Christmas, and I'm so sorry if I'm the cause of all those tears making green seas of your eyes."

"I don't care—it's all right," she stammered. "You are here at last, safe and sound, and I'm so happy to see you I could cry all over again!" She sniffed loudly and scrubbed at her cheeks with her hands, a joyous smile lighting her face. With a rueful look, she brushed her hair back. "Would you happen to have a handkerchief in your pocket?"

Reed laughed heartily, hugging her to him again briefly before producing the needed handkerchief. "Here, imp. Blow your nose and mop your tears. I don't want you getting us both wet and sloppy when I kiss you, which I am dying to do as soon and as thoroughly as possible."

Their reunion on the divan lasted only long enough for the heat of their passion to rage hotter than the embers in the fireplace. Sanity restored itself momentarily, and they realized that they could not make love in the middle of

Barbara's parlor, where anyone could walk in on them.

They retired to Kathleen's bedroom, and as Reed shut the door, he looked around and his eyes lit with deviltry. "I see Barbara put you in your old room. If memory serves me correctly, one of the last times I made love to you in this room, your Uncle William burst in on us under very embarrassing circumstances, indeed!"

Kathleen's eyes narrowed warningly. "You just can't help but gloat, can you, Reed? Nothing thrilled you more than seeing me forced to admit our marriage after I'd kept it a secret for so long."

"I wouldn't go so far as to say nothing has thrilled me more," Reed corrected with a grin, "but it definitely ranks high on my list." He crossed to her and pulled her tightly to him. "I want the world to know you belong to me."

His eyes dared her to object, and when she silently melted against him, his lips claimed hers in a hard, possessive kiss that stole her breath.

"I'll always belong to you, my love," she whispered. "You've captured my heart, and I cannot ransom it back."

The late hour and their weariness was forgotten as together they rediscovered the pathway of passion. His hands and lips mapped the route, and her body followed his lead gladly. Long awaited pleasures were theirs at last, and the months of loneliness fell away under a more urgent longing. Their bodies strained toward a new closeness, as if to become one in body as well as in heart and spirit. When they finally rode high upon rapture's brilliant rainbow, their joy was complete, their love a bright and shining star in the heavens.

Wrapped once more in the arms she'd longed for, Kathleen was peaceful and ready for sleep, but there was so much to tell him and so much she wanted to know. In quiet whispers, Reed highlighted his trip briefly. She told him news of the family, of Susan's new baby, and the gifts she'd arranged for the children's Christmas. It was nearly time to get up before they finally closed their eyes and slept.

Alexandrea and Katlin were overjoyed to discover their father home when they came bounding into Kathleen's bedroom early that morning. Eager to begin unwrapping their gifts, they bounced up and down on the bed, prying open sleepy lids and squealing into their parents' ears to arouse them.

With a pitiful groan, Kathleen drew the covers over her head. "What time is it?" she croaked sleepily.

With an unsympathetic grin, Reed grabbed the covers back down. "Time to spread Christmas joy, Mama dear. Rise and shine!"

Della arrived to usher the children out of the room, and Reed, now dressed, tugged the covers down to Kat's toes. Shivering, she reached for her robe in bleary-eyed defeat. "Alright, you monster! I'm getting up." She eyed him with rueful disgust. "How can you be so cheerful and wide awake?" she complained.

He planted a quick kiss on her pouting lips. "Because it's Christmas, I'm with my family, and Andrea and Katlin wouldn't let us sleep if our lives depended on it right now. So, my dear, you'd better get dressed and face the day. I'll see you downstairs." He left smiling contentedly, and Kathleen could hear him whistling merrily as he went down the stairs.

Thrilled to have him home, Kathleen was surprised to find that Reed had somehow managed to obtain gifts for all of them. When she unwrapped a small, oblong box, she discovered a magnificent opal choker necklace. The perfect arrangement of sparkling gems was set in bands of fine filigreed white gold. "You've been to New Orleans!" she gasped delightedly, recognizing the distinctive work of Reed's favorite jeweler there.

He nodded his dark head in agreement. "I also stopped by Grande Terre to see Jean. He and Dominique send holiday greetings."

"Did you see Eleonore also?"

"Not this time," he answered evasively, then decided to tell her what he knew. "She's still in New Orleans with her brother, but the romance between her and Jean has cooled lately."

"Oh, no!" Kathleen's face was immediately downcast at the news.

Reed shrugged. "I think you are taking it more to heart than either of them. They are still friends, Kat. It's just that they are no longer lovers. Neither of them regrets the time they spent together, but as Jean explained, their relationship was not going forward, and it was time to give it up before their friendship was destroyed, too."

"I wonder how Eleonore feels?" Kathleen mused.

"Dominique said she has been homesick for France for some time now. She looks forward to the end of the war so she can return home." Then he chuckled lightly. "From what I heard, she is now conquering as many hearts as she can before leaving New Orleans. She'll leave many a broken one in her wake when she sails."

"I hope she's not hiding a broken heart of her own, Reed."

"I hope not, too, but I'm sure you'll hear from her as soon as she can get a letter through. Perhaps then she can set your mind at ease."

Reed stayed to see the new year of 1813 ushered in before he sailed once more. He and Kathleen attended several parties in that time, and everything seemed almost normal for a short while. Susan proudly introduced him to his new niece, whom he adored on sight; and he became reacquainted with his own children once more, Katlin and Andrea eagerly recounting their joys and woes.

Several days were spent at Chimera, where he reviewed the books with Kathleen and advised her as to what she should do next; which crops to plan for, which fields to ready, what changes and repairs to make. He made sure she had the seed and materials needed, and sufficient funds to tide her over during his absence.

At the wharf, he conferred with Ted about business, which was so slow as to be nearly nonexistant at this point. He discovered which of his vessels had reported in and when, whether repairs had been needed, what goods (if any) they had delivered. Instructions were left for those due in soon.

While Reed was still home, one of his frigates, the *Lady Fair,* limped into port, badly damaged. Several of the crew members required medical attention, but they jubilantly reported that they had sunk the English sloop they'd challenged. Thus far, in the first seven months of the war, American privateers had reportedly taken hundreds of English merchantmen and three warships out of commission. They, at least, were tasting success on the seas, though the blockade remained securely intact. The *Lady Fair* was not beyond repair, and Reed set men to the task immediately. Kathleen promised to oversee the work as it progressed, to insure that the repairs were properly done.

January and February dragged by interminably after

Reed's departure. Amy's baby was born—a healthy boy named after Martin. They stayed in Savannah until the end of February, when Martin decided they must return to Augusta and prepare for spring planting. The *Lady Fair* returned to the sea, replaced at the repair dock by her sister ship, the *Windfarer*. Some of Kathleen's time was taken up seeing to the renovations. One of her former crewmen, a burly Irishman by the name of Kenigan, had taken a shot in the shoulder, and Kathleen personally saw to his care.

The *Sea Cloud* slipped past the blockade the first of March, carrying a letter from Eleonore. In the missive, Eleonore explained further the reasons behind her decision to ease away from her close relationship with Jean. She assured Kathleen that she and Jean had parted on amicable terms, both of them agreeing to remain friends. Neither of them was suffering undue heartbreak, realizing that their affair had been gradually cooling for some time. Repeating what Reed had stated, Eleonore said she had become progressively homesick for France, and yearned to return as soon as the war allowed. Included in Eleonore's letter was a short note from Dominique, with greetings from Jean. Both men were faring well, and sent their loving affection to Kathleen and the children. They'd encountered Reed off the Florida coast in January and had spent a few hours exchanging news of the war and their individual exploits.

March drifted into April, and spring planting was underway. The birth of several new foals at Kate's kept Kathleen dizzy going from Chimera to Emerald Hill. Katlin's second birthday heralded the advent of spring, followed closely by Easter and Kathleen's birthday. Kathleen and Reed's fifth wedding anniversary was fast approaching, but Kathleen held little hope of Reed's arrival in time to celebrate the occasion. Since early January he'd been able to send only two messages to her by returning ships, and those with little more than assurances that he was well, missed her and the children, and loved them all. Kathleen understood he dared not say more for fear his communication would fall into hostile British hands.

One May morning, Kathleen was just coming up to the house from the stables when she heard a rider approaching. The bright morning sun was behind him, and she shaded her eyes with her hand, squinting to make out his identity. The man was tall, dark, and bearded, and riding his mount hell-bent on destruction straight toward her. As she stood in confused astonishment watching horse and rider bear down on her, not slowing their pace one whit, the man's face split in a wide grin, revealing startlingly white teeth in the midst of his heavy beard.

Before Kathleen could fling herself out of his path, he dashed past, leaning down to grab her about the waist and pull her into the saddle before him. As the horse skidded to a jarring halt, the stranger drew her tightly against his chest, his mouth descending on hers before she had time to react. The odd familiarity of his kiss was offset by the strange soft caress of his beard and mustache against her skin.

Gathering her senses, Kathleen wriggled in his arms, trying to free herself of his iron hold. With doubled fists, she pummeled his chest, twisting her mouth free of his. Her indignant screeching set him laughing heartily, his chest heaving against her hands.

"Kat! For God's sake, are you trying to dump both of us onto the ground?"

The sound of his voice froze her in mid-scream. Her

startled green gaze flew to his face, scanning the dark beard and mustache for distinguishable features beneath. Her eyes collided with those of brilliant blue, full of merriment and deviltry.

"*Reed!* You scoundrel! You scared me half witless!" She aimed a fist at his broad shoulder. "I thought you were some crazed lunatic attacking me!" No sooner had she hit him, than her arms went about his neck and she clung to him. Her cheek again came into contact with the soft bristles covering his face. Easing back in his arms, she reached up a tentative hand, lightly touching her fingers and palm to the unfamiliar growth. Her eyes grew wide with wonder at the springy feel of it. "What made you decide to grow a beard—and a mustache?"

He grinned broadly. "Do you like it?"

She shook her head undecidedly. "I'm not sure. Heavens! I didn't even recognize you!"

"So I discovered. How does it feel to have the shoe on the other foot for a change? I never recognized *you* as Emerald, either."

"It's definitely a strange feeling," she admitted softly. Once again she held him near. "To tell the truth, I've missed you so badly, you could have grown another head and I'd welcome you."

Reed chuckled. "I really don't think I'll resort to that. In fact, my theatrical arrival was rather unnecessary, but so is sitting out here forever on this horse, don't you agree?"

It was marvelous having him home again, and once she was accustomed to his new look, Kathleen rather liked it. Andrea wasn't sure she shared her mother's opinion at first. "It scratches!" she complained, frowning up at her father and rubbing her pink cheeks.

"No, no!" Katlin disagreed, shaking his head. At this

age, he gloried in picking an argument with his sister whenever possible. "*Tickles,*" he corrected with a lofty male superiority.

Kathleen rolled her eyes toward the ceiling in exasperation, as if seeking patience from heaven. "He's your son, Reed, head to toe. He not only looks like you, he *acts* like you!"

Reed smiled proudly, if arrogantly. "Yes—isn't it a blessing he inherited my good nature instead of your stubbornness?" he teased.

Kathleen sighed in defeat. "If your head gets any bigger, your hats won't fit," she predicted wryly.

When Kathleen mentioned Eleonore's letter and Jean saying he'd seen Reed, Reed told her he had been to New Orleans since then. On a government mission, he'd been sent to Louisiana with orders from Washington for General Jackson. Years before, Reed had occasion to meet Andrew Jackson and his wife, Rachel. He'd liked them both, and it had been a privilege to be of service to the stalwart soldier now. Reed admired the older man tremendously, and Jackson had high praise for Reed's contribution to the war effort. While in New Orleans, Reed had gone to Jean's warehouse to find a worthy gift for Kathleen in honor of their wedding anniversary. Among Jean's contraband goods, he'd found a selection of French-made lingerie and nightware to delight any woman, and make any man foam at the mouth just imagining a woman in it. He'd chosen several sets of risqué French undergarments, embarrassingly sheer and lacy. In addition, he'd selected a shimmery emerald satin peignoir set. The gown was simply styled in the Greek fashion and designed to cling seductively beneath the sleek matching robe. Delicate, open-heeled slippers went with the ensemble. Reed could not resist them, thinking how the color matched Kathleen's eyes, and how magnificent her curvaceous body would look draped in the shiny, clinging fabric. But his imagination had not done justice to the actual sight when Kathleen modeled the outfit for him. She stood before him like a queen, proud and tall, and he could not take his eyes from her. Her long copper tresses hung loosely across one shoulder, her eyes sparkling like jewels. Her creamy breasts stood sentinel, pushed high against the low-cut bodice of the gown, while the folds of the skirt clung suggestively, outlining the shapely length of her long legs.

"Kat, I've dreamed of you in that gown since I bought it, but the reality takes my breath away," he confessed huskily, his eyes caressing where his hands would soon follow. "You have to be the most sensuous woman in the world."

She laughed softly, embarrassed and excited by his praise. "If I am, it is you who make me that way. When you look at me with that devilish gleam in your eye, you bring out the wanton in me. All I can think of is how your hands will feel on my body; your lips, your tongue. Then I want to reach out and touch you, feel your hot skin beneath my fingertips, please you and excite you in any way I can."

Her seductive words were more than he could take, and his well-intentioned patience flew out the window as he stripped out of his clothing. He looked down at himself mockingly. "If you were any more exciting, I swear I'd burst!" He pulled her with him onto the bed. "Come, my sultry vixen, show me how well you can please me. You've sung your siren's song—now fulfill all of my wildest fantasies!"

Laughing, she batted her lashes at him flirtatiously.

"Ah, but sir, after a night of exotic ecstasy and forbidden pleasures, will you still respect me in the morning? After all, a wife is supposed to restrain herself and not be too bold before her husband, or so I've heard."

He eyed her wickedly, his sparkling eyes sapphire-dark with desire. "I promise not to be shocked, my pet, and I swear that, not only will I respect you come morning, I'll make passionate love to you all through the night and again in the morning light."

A delicate eyebrow raised tauntingly. "Are you sure you can make good on all those rash promises?" she teased.

Leaping playfully at her, he pinned her to the mattress with a low growl, causing her to giggle. "I'll prove it, you minx, as long as you contribute your share." His lips hovered temptingly over hers.

"It is a bargain," she whispered silkily, already falling under his seductive spell. Suddenly she felt as if her body was on fire; her skin was actually aching for the feel of his. All teasing was forgotten as she gazed ardently into his face, the face she had longed to see for long, lonely months. Her lips trembled for the touch of his. "Kiss me, Reed," she prompted softly, her eyes adoring him. "Please kiss me now."

If some nights are made especially for love, this was one of them. Every move, every look, each touch heightened their desires. It was like sipping salt water; the more they drank of one another, the thirstier they became. They came together leisurely, lingering over time-sweetened kisses, their lips and tongues tasting fully of love's nectar. Hands and fingertips caressed slowly, as if memorizing every pore; as if loathe to overlook any pleasure point to be discovered in this sensual foray. His body adored hers, and hers worshipped his in turn. Fire danced in their veins, igniting sparks of passion that traveled through every nerve like bolts of lightning. All their senses were heightened, responding instinctively to the elusive magic woven into the fabric of this exquisite night of splendor.

Low moans of pleasure echoed in the night as they enticed one another to higher levels of passion. Kathleen abandoned herself to Reed's will, shamelessly following his daring lead, mindlessly obeying his every directive, satisfying his every wish. Their desire raged out of control, like a wind-fed forest fire, consuming them in its hungry flames. Their love was erotic and adventurous, raising them to breathless peaks of rapture and tossing them into the wild winds of the fiercest gale before spinning them dizzily back to earth.

So intense and lovely was their lovemaking, that Kathleen could not hold back the tears of joy that dampened her cheeks afterward. Thinking perhaps he had inadvertantly hurt her in his ardor, Reed was immediately concerned. "Sugar, what is it? What's wrong?"

She shook her head, whispering, "Nothing could be wrong, my darling, now that you are here. You make me feel so adored, so cherished. My heart is so filled with love for you, it is spilling over, that is all. These are not really tears you see, but the overflow of my love that my heart cannot contain because you have made me so happy."

Tenderly he kissed the tears from her cheeks, his eyes drinking in the sight of her love-filled face. "My sweet, you have just given me one of the most spectacular nights of my life. How can I tell you what it does to me when you give yourself so completely? Not one moment of this night would I trade for all the world's gold."

"Are you absolutely sure?" she teased gently.

"Not for ten times that amount," he told her, pulling

her close against him. "I love you, kitten. I love your spirit and your fire; even your stubborn, willful ways. I adore you from the top of your sun-kissed head to the tips of your dimpled toes."

"I love you, too, Reed—so much that I must confess it scares me sometimes," she sighed, relaxing in his embrace. "I fear there must be a price to be paid for all this happiness. That is why I hate it so each time you sail without me. I am afraid something will happen to you, and then I would simply die!"

"Nothing this side of the grave will destroy our love, Kat," he said tenderly.

She reached out a hand to touch his cheek, and encountered the beard again. "I have something else to confess," she said, stifling a giggle.

"What's that?" he asked curiously.

"Katlin was right. The beard and mustache *do* tickle!"

His rumbling laughter mingled with her giggles in the early morning air.

Reed left a few days later, telling Kathleen he was on his way to Washington. There was soon to be an important prisoner exchange at sea, Reed confided, in which the *Kat Ann* and another privateer were to play a major role. Where and when the exchange would take place would be revealed to him in the capitol.

Kathleen kept busy through the rest of May. June brought sultry summer temperatures, and everyone sweltered under the blazing sun and clear azure sky. It looked as if this summer was to be unusually hot, and everyone hastened to leave the city and take refuge on the cooler country plantations. By now, the war was twelve months old, and Savannah had yet to see its first British ship or soldier. The residents let down their guard, leaving that chore to the militia stationed at the forts, and sought comfort outside the city.

Kathleen welcomed Mary home, as well as Susan, Ted, and their two children. Chimera was too large and empty without Reed, and they helped to divert her attention from her loneliness. Barbara and Uncle William did not join them, deciding instead to visit Amy and Martin on their estate outside of Augusta.

July was hotter still. No one did a thing they didn't absolutely have to, avoiding all work in the hottest part of the day. Cooking was done at night, and cold meals served during the day. Everyone lazed about in the shade, consuming tall, cool glasses of lemonade and iced drinks, doing what was required in the cooler hours of morning and evening.

The *Starbright* limped into Savannah the first day of the month, reporting violent storms in the Caribbean. Dan Shanahan and Hal Finley, two of her former crewmen, were aboard, Dan having suffered two cracked ribs during the gale that had maimed the *Starbright*. Regardless of the heat, Kathleen made several trips into Savannah with Ted to see to the repair of her favorite frigate, the same vessel she'd disguised and sailed as the *Emerald Enchantress* years before.

She was at the docks the day a strange ship anchored at Savannah port. Like the others, she took note of it, reassuring herself that it was an American vessel, and went back to her work. It was a short time later that Ted came looking for her, a uniform-clad stranger in tow. Kathleen eyed the smart young lieutenant curiously, wondering why he would want to speak to her. Her ready smile was frozen by the serious look on his face and the worry on Ted's.

"Mrs. Reed Taylor?" he asked. At her answering nod, he continued. "I've been sent from Washington. It is my sorrowful duty to inform you that your husband, his ship, and all aboard are missing following a storm at sea. All are assumed drowned. I reget to inform you, ma'am, that it has been concluded that Captain Taylor is dead."

Chapter 8

At first Kathleen stared at the lieutenant as if he were invisible, a disembodied spirit voicing her worst fears. Then, as the full impact of his words reached her stunned brain, she staggered backward, as if struck a physical blow. Never had she felt such severe pain, like a rapier driven straight through her heart. Her delicate features contorted into a wordless grimace of agony, and she doubled over from the waist, clutching her arms about her midriff. She did not feel Ted's arms go about her to steady her as she struggled to regain her breath and fought the waves of nausea and blackness that assailed her. Her heart seemed to have lodged in her throat and was choking her, and her brain screamed an anguished denial, mentally retreating from the words she could not bear to accept.

When at last she found her breath, it came in great sobs and long, pitiful wails torn from the depths of her shattered soul. Her cries echoed off the water, bouncing off the sandy cliffs in great anguished waves of sound like the cries of the banshees of her native land. No one on the waterfront that day would ever forget the sound of her heartrent grief.

As the sobs tore the very heart from her body, Kathleen was dazed with pain. Her ears were closed to her own cries, as her mind screamed, ''This is only a nightmare! It's got to be a nightmare! Oh, God! Please let me wake up and find this is not real!'' It was all Ted could do to prevent her from stumbling off the dock and into the river.

The young lieutenant stood watching helplessly, in the face of the grief he had so unwillingly caused. Upon hearing her cries, Hal Finley and old Dan Shanahan came rushing from the deck of the *Starbright,* unable to fathom what would cause their beloved Captain Kathleen to behave in such a manner. Putting himself directly in front of her, Dan called her name several times, getting no response save her continual screams. Not knowing what else to do, he raised one calloused hand and slapped her smartly across the face.

Kathleen's head snapped to one side, and she sucked in her breath sharply. Her wild shrieking stopped. Tears of pain and bewilderment swam in her eyes as she slowly focused on Dan.

''Kathleen, lass,'' he coaxed gently, his own blue eyes filled with torment, ''what is it?''

Kathleen blinked twice, her mouth working in spasms to form words. ''He said he is dead. He said Reed is dead.'' Her words choked off as she shook her head. In a child-like gesture of seeking comfort, she took both of Dan's gnarled old hands in hers. ''That can not be, can it old friend? They say he drowned. My beloved sea would not do that to me, would she, Dan? She wouldn't take Reed from me!''

Kathleen was rambling now, making little sense to anyone but Dan, who had known her from childhood. Her emerald eyes were huge and glazed with shock and pain.

Still supporting her, Ted urged gently, ''Come, Kathleen. Let's go home, where you can lie down for a while.''

"*No!*" Her reply was so sharp that he feared she would resume her wild thrashing.

Dan gave a warning shake of his head. "Teddie, lad, ken ye not thet she's in shock? Let's get her aboard the *Starbright*. She can rest in the captain's cabin 'til the brunt o' the blow is past. She'll be more at home on the *Starbright* than anywhere else right now."

This made little sense to Ted, and even less to the befuddled lieutenant, but Kathleen made no objection as they led her toward the ship. Not knowing what to do, the lieutenant turned and started away from the dock. A large, beefy hand clamped down on his shoulder, staying his flight, and he looked into the frowning face of Hal Finley.

"You'd best come with us, Lieutenant," Finley advised. "We'll need you to fill in the details surrounding Captain Taylor's death. When Mrs. Taylor comes to herself, she'll be askin' questions and wantin' answers. I wouldn't want to be the one tellin' her I didn't know anything."

Dan led them to the captain's quarters. There, instinct told him Kathleen would rebel at being forced to lie down. Instead, he seated her in the large captain's chair behind the desk. As the others watched silently, he poured a good portion of whiskey into a mug and pressed it to her lips. Her hands automatically came up to hold the mug.

"Drink this, lass," Dan instructed gruffly, "and don't ye be spittin' none o' it back at me. 'Tis good Irish whiskey ye have there, and I'll not have ye wastin' it."

A ghost of a smile touched her lips, and she obediently took a huge gulp. The fire of it nearly set her coughing, but she choked back the spasm and followed it with several more swallows.

As the powerful brew began warming her shattered

137

system, Kathleen drew in a long breath and let it out in a shuddering sigh. Her head fell back against the high back of the chair, as if too heavy for her slender neck to support. Her lids shut wearily, squeezing twin tears past her thick lashes. The others quietly started to leave the room, but Kathleen's eyes flew open, still revealing deep anguish, but also coherent thought. The first shock was passing. "Stay," she ordered.

Slowly she straightened in the chair, laying her forearms on the desk for support. She spread her hands flat upon the desk to stop their trembling, and her eyes found the young man in uniform. "I'm sorry, Lieutenant, for my earlier behavior." Her voice was a husky whisper. With effort, she pulled her dignity about her. Clearing her throat, she spoke more strongly. "I am ready to hear the details of what you have to tell me," she said.

"Ma'am, there is little else I can tell you. I'm deeply sorry for your loss," the lieutenant mumbled.

"You said there was a storm," she persisted.

"Yes, ma'am."

"When and where?"

"A month ago in the Gulf waters off Florida."

"Was Captain Taylor on a mission for the exchange of prisoners?"

A look of surprise came over the lieutenant's features. "You knew about that?"

Kathleen nodded somberly. "There is little my husband does not share with me." Unconsciously, she used the present tense. "Had the exchange been accomplished?"

The lieutenant nodded. "Captain Taylor and Captain Guthrie of the *Seahorse* had completed their mission and were heading for port when the storm hit. According to Captain Guthrie, the storm was violent, and he was so

138

occupied with saving his own vessel that he was not aware of the *Kat-Ann*'s disappearance for some time.''

Kathleen immediately grabbed at this first straw of hope held out to her. Her keen gaze leveled on the lieutenant's face. ''Then no one actually *saw* the *Kat-Ann* go under?''

The man frowned and shook his head. ''No, but we are sure it did. Following the storm, Captain Guthrie retraced his route. For two days he and his men searched the seas and the surrounding islands. They found no sign of life.''

Something in his voice told Kathleen there were things he'd left unsaid, but she did not press him on this yet. Instead, she said eagerly, ''Perhaps the *Kat-Ann* was sent off course by the storm. Perhaps the ship was damaged and will yet show up in port somewhere.''

The look he gave her was filled with pity. ''Ma'am, Captain Taylor was due back in Washington three weeks ago. We've had no word of the *Kat-Ann* or her crew being sighted in any other port, or anywhere on the seas.''

Again Kathleen got the distinct impression he was not telling her everything. ''Why is it you are so sure the *Kat-Ann* has sunk? What information are you withholding from me, sir?''

He sighed deeply, obviously reluctant to continue, but her steady gaze compelled him to go on. ''In the afternoon of his second day of searching, Captain Guthrie's ship came across debris from a recent shipwreck. To our knowledge, there were no other ships in that area at the time of the storm, and he concluded the wreckage must be that of the *Kat-Ann*.''

Kathleen took a deep breath and forced herself to ask, ''What manner of wreckage was found?''

The lieutenant turned his gaze from hers, his voice low but clear. ''They came across boards, barrels, spars, floating bits of wood . . . ''

"Bodies?" Kathleen suggested, swallowing hard.

"Yes, ma'am," he muttered.

Kathleen could barely ask, "Did they identify any of the bodies as those of men from the *Kat-Ann*?"

"Ma'am," the young man turned sympathetic eyes to hers once more, "there was no way positive identification could be made. Most of the bodies had been in the water so long . . ." His voice trailed off.

The two bright spots of color in Kathleen's cheeks brought on by the whiskey faded to paper-white. "God, yes!" she whispered, her eyes growing even more enormous. Her voice rose in sickened panic. "Sharks would have moved in immediately!"

The lieutenant nodded miserably.

Kathleen shook her head violently, deliberately pushing back the vision her words had called forth. "*No!*" she shouted forcefully. "No! I refuse to believe it was Reed's ship! It must have been another." Her pleading gaze begged him to agree. "Surely the navy intends to continue the search. You *will* be doing that, won't you? You can't just assume a man is dead from what little evidence you have and let it go at that!"

He swallowed hard, his own eyes pleading with her to understand and accept. "We *have* searched, Mrs. Taylor. We've searched and we've waited and we've prayed. Captain Guthrie found not one survivor, nor any evidence of any. We've done all we can. Our nation is at war, and we must get on with the business at hand. I'm sincerely sorry, ma'am, but under the circumstances, we must accept that Captain Guthrie's assumption is correct."

Anger made Kathleen's eyes flash a brilliant green. Her chin rose sharply, and she sat proudly upright. "*You* may accept that, sir—you and the rest of the navy—but *I* do not have to! If I can not depend on the government, for which my husband did so much, for help, I shall search for him myself!''

Drawing a map out of a drawer, she spread it across the desk top. ''Show me the location where the *Kat-Ann* was last seen,'' she commanded. ''I want to know where she was when the storm hit, and where Guthrie came across the bodies.'' As he hesitated, looking to Ted and Dan for aid, she slapped her hand sharply on the surface of the map. ''*Now!*'' she ordered.

''She'll give ye no peace until ye show her,'' Dan said slowly.

The lieutenant pointed out the areas on the map, designating spots off the western coast of Florida. When she was satisfied with the information he had given, he looked at Kathleen's determined face and those of the two seamen who seemed to be in favor of her decision. Only Ted seemed unsure.

''Surely you are not seriously considering taking Mrs. Taylor on this search for her husband?'' he asked Dan and Finley incredulously.

''Son,'' Dan assured him with a wry look, ''if Kathleen says she's goin', then goin' she is, and we'll be goin' with her. An' it won't be so much us takin' *her* as her takin' *us!*''

The lieutenant left, totally baffled by Dan's last statement, and too emotionally drained to wonder over it for long. He was filled with pity for the lovely young widow, praying that she would soon find the strength to accept her loss. The more he considered it, the more he was certain that the sailors had simply been humoring her in her grief. He hurried along to his own ship, hoping he would not be called upon to perform similar tasks elsewhere. Of all his duties, this was the one he hated most—telling young wives and mothers that their loved ones were gone forever.

Kathleen seemed to wilt once the lieutenant had gone. Pride and anger had bolstered her spirits momentarily, but now she sagged with the immensity of the shock.

Ted, himself grief-stricken by the loss of his friend and brother-in-law, could only guess at the depth of her grief. "Kathy, I think we should go home now. Susan and Mary must be told."

Kathleen shook off the fog of grief that threatened to engulf her. "You go ahead, Ted. I know Susan will need you when she hears, and Mary will need you both." As he started to protest, she held up a slim, trembling hand. "I'll come along later, dear cousin. I need to be alone just now, to think and plan and come to terms with everything that has occurred today. It has all happened so quickly."

Ted still protested, out of concern for her. "You should not be alone right now. You need the love and support of those who care for you. Besides, what are we all to tell Andrea and Katlin?"

At the thought of her two small children, Kathleen winced. "Have Isabel and Della keep them occupied, and delay telling them anything until I get there." Her voice broke and she swallowed hard before turning tear-blurred eyes toward his. "Give me until morning, Ted. Dan and Finley will look after me."

Almost as an afterthought, she murmured, "I'll have to stop off and tell Kate myself. She loves Reed very much. She is getting on in years, and I hope she takes the news well. I'd hate to lose Gram, too." Kathleen's chin trembled dangerously, and she clamped her jaws tightly shut, blinking hard.

"You will be home in the morning?" Ted asked anxiously.

Kathleen nodded. Briefly she allowed him to draw her close. "Go on now, Ted," she choked. "Tell Susan and Mary before they hear it from anyone else. Bad news spreads like wildfire."

Dan ushered Finley and Ted out of the cabin, then stationed himself outside Kathleen's door while the others went up on deck. He would stay nearby in case she summoned him, but he knew she needed time to herself now to vent her grief in private. Tears coursed down the old sailor's weather-roughened cheeks when, a few minutes later, he heard heartrending sobs from the other side of the door. He'd have given his life to spare her this pain, and he would do anything he could for her in the months to come. This he vowed silently to himself, to God, and to Kathleen.

Kathleen stood in the center of the cabin and stared dumbly at the door for long minutes after it had closed. Hot tears slid down her face, and a terrible trembling was shaking her entire body. An ever-tightening band seemed to be squeezing her chest, creating unbearable pain in the empty cavity where her heart had been before the lieutenant's words had ripped it from her body. An awful nausea invaded her stomach, and she wondered vaguely if she were going to be sick. The pain that was rending her chest and stomach was echoed by a tingling ache in both her palms, causing her fingers to curl slightly. Slowly, as if in a trance, she raised her trembling hands and stared mutely at them. A part of her mind, oddly detached, wondered at this. "What a strange place to hurt," she thought. Then she shook her head. No, perhaps not so strange. "These hands have held Reed long into many nights," she said aloud. "These are the hands that have stroked his face and body countless times, learning every contour, each muscle, the very texture of his skin. They have held his children and soothed the worry from his furrowed brow." The first wrenching sob echoed loudly in the empty room. "And now, perhaps these hands will be forever empty. Why should it be strange that they would ache at the possibility of never touching his beloved face again, never tracing the laugh lines around his firm mouth and twinkling blue eyes?"

It was more than Kathleen could bear. Suddenly her knees folded under her, and she sank to the floor beside the bunk. As deep, choking sobs racked her body, she cradled her face in her arms, leaning against the mattress to cushion the bone-jarring spasms that continued uncontrollably now, wracking her with a pain more intense than that of childbirth. Her sobs soon became wails, each heartaching breath carrying Reed's name over and over again, as if to call him back. Thoughts of him flooded her mind. She longed to hold him near, to see his dazzling smile and hear his hearty laughter. Her anguish intensified as she recalled his firm, warm lips on hers and how his eyes would darken with desire when he made love to her. To think that he was gone forever was unbearable.

Gradually the jarring sobs eased, and without thought she crawled onto the bunk, pulling the rough blanket over her trembling body. "So cold," she murmured incoherently, her teeth chattering. "I'm so cold!" In spite of the warm night air wafting through the open porthole, she huddled under the blanket. Finally she drifted into a weary, uneasy sleep, her knees drawn up to her chest. But

144

even as she slept, hot tears escaped her closed eyelids, slipping silently across her temple to wet her cold cheeks and tangled copper curls.

Kathleen woke to the full darkness of the night-filled cabin. She felt no disorientation, no wonder at the aching pain within her breast. Immediately she recalled the source of her anguish; every word, every gesture, each thought came clearly to mind. A sob-laden sigh shuddered through her aching body, and she lay staring into the night, letting her thoughts come as they would.

Memories assaulted her from every corner of her mind. She recalled the first time she's set eyes on the man who was to become her husband and the very center of her life. She relived her wedding; how outrageously handsome Reed had been that day! Her traitorous thoughts turned to the night Reed first possessed her, so gently teaching her the ways of love . . .

Tears ran in torrents and she sobbed softly into her pillow as her precious memories tortured her, piercing her very soul. Mental images of Reed rocking Andrea to sleep in his arms, and the proud look of his face when he'd first seen his son, now brought agony instead of joy. Even remembering their battles brought tears of longing. The times when they had fought, when Reed had hurt or angered her, were trivial compared to what she was feeling now.

"I'd trade my soul to have him with me now," she vowed fervently. "I would pay any price. I would spend a lifetime worshipping at his feet if that would bring him back to me!"

Just when her sobs seemed to subside, new thoughts would cause renewed pain, and her tears would freshen again. Crying, praying and reliving bittersweet memories was all she seemed capable of.

At length, her tears finally ceased, as if she had cried all it was humanly possible to do. She pushed herself wearily off the bed, crossing to stand at the open porthole. The air held the salty tang of the sea, and the sky was clear and dotted with stars.

"There should be clouds," Kathleen thought. "It should be raining and storming to match my feelings!" She closed her eyes on the beauty of the night. "Yes, there should be bolts of jagged lightning rending the sky, as Reed's loss is tearing my heart to pieces! And loud, angry thunder to match the rage in my soul! Oh, God! How can You do this to me—to Reed—to our innocent little babies?" The words were ripped from her throat in a shriek of despair.

Hot tears stung beneath her swollen eyelids. "No! No!" she cried, shaking her head violently. "I have got to stop thinking like this! According to the lieutenant, the *Kat-Ann* ran into that storm a month ago. If Reed had died then, wouldn't I have then felt his loss? Could Reed die, be it a thousand miles away, and I not feel anything at all?" She voiced her doubts aloud. "I cannot believe that I would not know—that I would feel nothing. My heart would have told me. Surely, as much as Reed and I love one another, there would have been some indication, some reaction. My heart should have stopped at the same moment as his. This awful pain would have begun then, I know it!"

A tiny glimmer of hope rose in her, even as the sun was beginning to rise in the eastern sky. Alone in the dawn, she vowed, "Reed, I know you are still alive somewhere! I feel it at the very core of my being. I'll find you, my darling, I promise. Wait for me, my love! As quickly as the

Starbright can carry me, I'll come to you!''

Holding tight to her fragile seed of hope, Kathleen went in search of Finley and Dan, whom she discovered just outside her cabin door, slouched asleep against the bulkhead. After she had roused him, they found Finley on deck.

"How soon can the *Starbright* be made seaworthy?" she demanded.

"A week—week and a half at most," Finley replied, attempting to ignore her puffy face and swollen eyes.

"No sooner?"

Finley shook his head. "Sorry, Captain, but we can't chance sailing until she's fit."

"Alright," Kathleen sighed. "Dan, I want you immediately to assemble a crew that will not object to taking orders from me. I will be captaining this voyage with Finley as quartermaster and you as bosun."

"Jest like old times," Dan murmured softly.

A shadow darkened Kathleen's face. "Almost, old friend. I will leave it to you two to see that stores are laid in and everything put in readiness."

"Aye, Cap'n. Anything else?"

Kathleen nodded. "Yes. Find me a horse, Dan. It is time I went home to Chimera."

On her way, she stopped at Emerald Hill to tell Kate all that had transpired. Tears drenched the older woman's wrinkled cheeks as she listened. Her eyes were nearly as bright as Kathleen's, reflecting tears and sorrow. The two women, so similar in many ways, shared their grief, clinging to one another in mingled anguish and hope.

Kathleen finished her tale by telling her grandmother that she was going in search of Reed as soon as possible. "I refuse to believe I would not have known if he were dead,

Gram. He is alive! I know it, and I'll find him and bring him home again.''

"I pray ye are right, Kathleen. 'Tis not an easy task ye've set yerself, scouring the seas and countless isles in the midst o' a war," sighed the old woman. But she knew better than to attempt to dissuade her headstrong granddaughter.

"I'll have help, Kate. Now that the first shock is wearing off a bit, I am thinking more clearly. My best bet may be to ask Jean and Dominique for help. Jean Lafitte knows that area better than any man alive.''

Kate nodded her approval. "Aye, thet may be the fastest way t' find Reed. I will feel better knowin' ye have Jean and Dominique t' look after ye, too. They would ne'er let anything happen t' ye.''

As Kathleen prepared to leave for Chimera, Kate hugged her tightly and kissed her on the cheek. "Kathleen, me love, are ye sure yer heart is not playin' tricks on ye? If Reed truly is drowned, 'twould be like losin' him twice t' put so much faith in such slim hopes.''

Kathleen shrugged helplessly. "What choice do I have, Gram? I simply cannot bear to believe he is dead. As long as there is a chance he is alive, I must search for him. I'm not whole without him, Kate.''

"And if ye find evidence thet Reed *is* dead?'' her grandmother asked gently.

"I'll deal with that when the time comes,'' Kathleen said softly, "*if* the time comes, God forbid!''

The atmosphere that greeted Kathleen at Chimera was hushed and sorrowladen. A pall hung over the entire plantation. The pervading gloom had even affected the children, who sensed that something was gravely wrong,

148

though not understanding any of it.

The main doors to the house had already been shrouded in black crepe, the symbol of mourning, and Kathleen shivered when she saw it. Susan was upstairs tending to her mother, for Mary had collapsed upon hearing the dreadful news. The servants were all tiptoeing about, red-eyed and reverent in the face of the family's grief. In the library, Ted sat gloomily nursing a whiskey and trying to discuss details of a memorial service with the minister. Isabel was graciously and quietly receiving neighbors and friends who had come immediately upon hearing about Reed to offer their condolences.

Unwilling to face Reverend Whiting just yet, Kathleen sent a servant into the library to tell Ted she had arrived home safely and would be upstairs with Mary and Susan. The same message was relayed to Isabel and to Della, who was with the children in the nursery. Gently acknowledging hushed expressions of sympathy from several of the servants, Kathleen made her way to Mary's room. The curtains were drawn against the bright July sunshine; the sounds of soft weeping led Kathleen to Mary's bedside. Susan sat in a chair near the head of the bed, mopping her swollen eyes with a handkerchief and holding her mother's hand. Mary lay limply on the bed, dark circles accenting her eyes and the pallor of her chalk-white face.

Kathleen embraced her sister-in-law silently. Then, taking Mary's hand, she spoke softly. "Mary, I'm home."

The dark head shifted on the pillow, solemn eyes resting gently on Kathleen's ravaged face. Mary's arms came up to gather Kathleen close. For long minutes the women shared a silent communication of deepest loss. At last Mary whispered hoarsely, "Did you see Kate?"

"Yes."

149

"I hope she is alright by herself. She has always been so fond of Reed. It is bound to be hard on her. You should have brought her here with you." Even in her sorrow, Mary was still thoughtful of others.

"She will be along later," Kathleen assured her mother-in-law. "She is tougher than she looks. It is you we are worried about."

"Oh, Kathleen!" Mary moaned. "Here I lie wallowing in misery when you have sustained a loss equal to mine, my dear. I should be ashamed of myself, but I can't seem to help it."

"Dearest Mother, don't worry yourself over me. I shall be fine as soon as the *Starbright* is ready to sail and I can go in search of my missing husband," said Kathleen firmly.

Both Mary and Susan stared at her as if Kathleen's grief had affected her mind. "Oh, dear!" Mary wailed.

Abruptly, Susan rose, offering Kathleen her chair. "Kathleen, honey, I don't believe you are thinking clearly. Sit here and rest awhile by Mother."

"No, Susan, keep your seat, and both of you listen to what I've come to say." Kathleen perched on the edge of the bed next to Mary. "And would you kindly stop looking at me as if I've come unhinged? I am perfectly sane, I assure you."

Taking a deep breath, she plunged ahead. "Ted has undoubtedly told you all that that lieutenant had to say yesterday." At their confirming nods, she continued. "I've thought about it all night, and I am not convinced that Reed is dead."

"But the *Kat-Ann* is missing," Susan interrupted, "and Reed has not been seen anywhere since then."

"And the bodies," Mary added on a sob. "What of the bodies Captain Guthrie discovered?"

"My dears," Kathleen went on gently, "those bodies were unidentifiable as anyone from the *Kat-Ann*. I know you must think that I am grasping at straws and clinging to false hope, but I cannot accept Reed's death on this evidence alone."

"But, Kathleen, where is he then?" Susan asked tearfully.

"We know the *Kat-Ann* was hit by that storm," Kathleen conceded. "Perhaps she was thrown off course. Maybe she sustained heavy damages and floundered near one of the islands awaiting help."

"And perhaps she actually did sink in the storm as Captain Guthrie believes," Mary suggested sadly. "Kathleen, dear, don't fight fate. If Reed is alive, he will find his way home to us, but don't go off chasing elusive shadows."

Kathleen's eyes filled with tears and she brushed them away impatiently. "Believe me, Mary, I am not considering this lightly. I know my feelings are running high right now, and I know the odds of finding Reed are slim indeed, but *I have to try!* I cannot sit idly by and wait while Reed may be in desperate need of help. There is no way I can bring myself to accept someone else's lame explanations and calm assertations that Reed is drowned. Not for a moment can I allow myself to believe that, or my life no longer has meaning. Something deep within me tells me he is alive, and I must search for him. Please try to understand. If I truly thought he was dead, I'd shroud myself in black from head to toe and mourn him forever, but my heart refuses to accept that!"

Kathleen stood, bravely squaring her shoulders against her heavy load of grief. "He is alive," she whispered. "He simply *has* to be alive. I cannot live without him!"

Mary caught at her hand. "I cannot tell you what to do, Kathleen. You must follow your heart and do what you feel is right. If you must go, we will care for the children in your absence, but please take care. It would be even more tragic to have both parents taken from them."

"We will pray for you, Kathleen," Susan added. Her soft grey eyes searched Kathleen's. "We will pray for your safety—and your success."

"When will you leave?" Mary asked.

"In about a week. There is much work to be done before the *Starbright* will be seaworthy."

"And how long do you think you will be gone?"

"As long as it takes, Mary, to find your son and bring him home. Perhaps a fortnight—perhaps a month or more." Kathleen gazed solemnly at the two women so dear to her. "Reverend Whiting is downstairs with Ted, wanting to arrange a memorial service, I suppose. You may do as you wish, of course, but I shall not be attending any services for Reed—not while I hold a shred of hope that he still lives!"

Mary stared at her silently for a moment. "All right, Kathleen," she sighed. "We will have the services postponed until we see what your search reveals."

"And the crepe on the doors?" Kathleen pressed.

"That, too, will be removed."

"Thank you, Mary, and you, too, Susan," Kathleen said sincerely. "I realize how deeply you both are hurting, and not for the world would I purposefully do anything to add to your pain. If I am wrong . . ." her voice faltered.

"If you are wrong, we cannot blame you for wanting to believe otherwise, Kathleen," Mary assured her. "It may prolong our grief, but I fear it will compound yours unbearably. We can only pray that you are right."

Susan stood to enfold Kathleen in her slim arms. "I shall not fault you either, Sister. Whether your hopes prove fruitful or groundless, you act out of love, and that is the strongest of all emotions."

As speedily as repairs were made on the *Starbright*, it was not fast enough for Kathleen. Her impatience grew daily, as did her temper. Too often she found herself retorting sharply to well-meaning comments. Try as she might, she could not curb her tongue, though she was infallibly tolerant with her children. As she waited to set sail, she spent much time with Andrea and Katlin, treasuring her moments with them. Knowing it would be some time before she saw them again, the hours they spent together were doubly precious. As simply as she could, she explained that their father was missing, and she must go in search of him. Just how much they actually understood, she knew not, but they realized that she must leave them for a while, and readily agreed to be good children for Della and Grandmama Mary.

Isabel surprised everyone by insisting that she accompany Kathleen on the voyage. Disregarding all attempts to persuade her otherwise, she stood firm on her decision. "We have been through much together, Caterina," she told Kathleen. "You stood by me when no one else would —you and Reed. Now I shall stand by you, whether you need or want me to, or not. I am coming, even if I have to stow away again!"

There were still times when dreadful doubts assailed Kathleen, and she wondered if she was about to sail on a fool's errand. At these times, she would slip off to be alone with her thoughts, often racing away on her golden palomino, Zeus, or on Reed's big black stallion, Titan.

Away they would ride, flying over the ground, the wind blowing all doubts and fears out of her head. Sometimes they would head for the coast, where she would sit for hours staring at the ocean, drawing some measure of peace and consolation from the churning waves. When she came away refreshed, she could not believe the same sea that lent her such comfort could be cruel enough to steal her husband.

Finally her anxious waiting came to an end. She made her rounds, saying goodbye to everyone, and she and Isabel boarded the *Starbright*. The order was given to weigh anchor, and they made their way slowly down the river to the sea. Outwardly calm and inwardly quaking, she prayed for the strength to face whatever she might find.

Chapter 9

They sailed south under fair skies. Bountiful breezes filled the sails and carried them swiftly toward the tip of Florida. Twice they sighed English men-of-war, but the *Starbright*, with Kathleen at the helm, quickly outdistanced them.

Kathleen was once again in her element, confident and completely in control of her destiny for the first time since the lieutenant's dreadful announcement. Once more she was sailing the seas, the salt spray in her face, the deck rolling beneath her firmly planted feet. She strode the deck in fitted trousers, full-sleeved tailored shirt, and high black boots. Her red-gold tresses blew wildly in the wind like a copper banner, and her rapier in its sheath slapped smartly against her thigh, a symbol of courage and defiance.

As comfortable as Kathleen felt in her own sailing attire, it came as a shock to her to see Isabel similarly garbed. Isabel's snug trousers and billowing blouse revealed voluptuous curves heretofore disguised by her demure dresses. With her long black hair held back by a ribbon and her black eyes snapping in her delicate face, she practiced daily with her rapier. Her blade was nearly half as long as she was tall, and she resembled a nimble pixie as she and Kathleen rehearsed the finer points of swordplay. There was nothing childish about either her figure or her attitude, however, for she took her lessons seriously, determined to regain her former competence with her weapon.

As they cruised the warm waters of the Gulf, Kathleen and her crew diligently searched every island they encountered, though they were far south of the area where the *Kat-Ann* had supposedly gone down. While it was impossible to cover all the hundreds of islands without months of searching, they did their best, at the same time heading steadily west and north. It was always possible, if not probable, that the storm had blown the *Kat-Ann* this far off course, and Kathleen was compelled to cover all possibilities.

In due course, they reached the area designated by Captain Guthrie. Kathleen was dismayed at the multitude of islands dotting the west Florida coastline as far as the eye could see. It was easy to understand why Jean Lafitte had called it "the land of ten thousand islands." Discouraged but still determined, the *Starbright* and her crew scoured the area as best they could, discovering nothing of note. After a cursory inspection, it was clear they needed help in their cause, and Kathleen headed her ship for Barataria Bay and Grande Terre.

Two and a half weeks after her departure from Savannah, the *Starbright* ran up the signal for entrance and sailed easily through the tricky straits into Barataria Bay. No sooner had they dropped anchor than a dinghy was sent out to greet them. Dominique You, busy at the fort at the time, had been the first to identify the frigate as the *Starbright*. He easily recognized the sleek lines of the vessel once disguised as the *Emerald Enchantress*, the fabled green ship of the Gulf. At once he notified his brother Jean that Reed's frigate was entering the bay, and they both went down to the dock to meet them.

Their surprise was boundless and their curiosity immediately piqued as they caught sight of Kathleen's flaming tresses, gleaming brightly in the setting sun. Their interest rose as they watched her petite dark-haired companion follow her into the dinghy. Search as they did among the many familiar faces of the crew, they could not make out Reed's among them. A tingling feeling of unease wafted across the bay, and Jean turned to Dominique with a frown.

"There is something wrong, *mon frère*, to bring Kathleen to Grande Terre at this time. I feel it in my bones."

"I would feel easier if I could spot Reed among the men," Dominique answered. "For Kathleen to leave her children in the midst of a war, the situation must indeed be serious."

They had no more time to contemplate her unexpected arrival as the dinghy drew up to shore. Kathleen launched herself from the boat straight into Dominique's welcoming arms.

"Dominique! How good it is to see your dear face again!"

Dominique chuckled, squeezing her tightly in his burly arms before releasing her. "Anyone who can call this scarred face dear is either blind or madly in love with me!"

"I am guilty on both charges!" she declared saucily. She turned to receive Jean's welcoming kiss on her cheek.

"What brings you to Grande Terre, *cherie*?" Jean came straight to the point.

Kathleen's smile melted, leaving her eyes shadowed with sorrow. "I come to ask your help, *mon ami*—yours and Dom's."

Jean's worried eyes met hers and held. "Has this anything to do with Reed?"

Swallowing hard, Kathleen said, "It has everything to do with Reed, Jean. He is missing."

"Missing?" Dominique echoed.

"A month ago I was told that the *Kat-Ann* was lost in a storm off the western coast of Florida. All aboard are assumed drowned. A companion ship searched the area, and two days later came across several bodies, totally unidentifiable from having been so long in the water. They were believed to be crewmen from the *Kat-Ann*, though no one could be sure. A few planks and floating debris were all that could be found of the ship. No firm evidence or certain wreckage from the *Kat-Ann* was found. The government considers the search sufficient and conclusive, and now regards Reed as dead. Because of the war, they cannot spare more ships or time to search further, a search they are positive would be fruitless." Kathleen turned pleading eyes to Jean and Dominique. "I have come to ask you to help me search for Reed. I refuse to believe he is dead! The *Kat-Ann* may be badly damaged and unable to sail. She may have run up on a reef or been blown off course. Any number of things could have kept Reed from returning, but he is *not* dead! My heart tells me he lives, and I will not rest until I find him. Will you help me, Jean? You know that area like the back of your hand. I'll never find him without your aid."

"*Mon Dieu!*" Jean said softly when her speech was ended. "Do you need to ask, *ma petite amie?* Of course we will help you." His warm hazel eyes lingered on her

158

pleading face. "It makes me proud that you have come to me for help, Kathleen. Reed is my dearest friend, and I can do no less. We will turn the islands upside down in our search," he promised. "Come, we shall go to the house and make our plans. Your men can find quarters with mine." His gaze turned to Isabel, standing quietly a little behind Kathleen. "This small one must come with us, obviously," he added.

"I agree," Dominique concurred readily. "Never have I seen so much—uh—so many—curves on such a little package," he stammered.

Kathleen laughed. "I have never known you at a loss for words before, Dominique!" Reminded of her manners, she drew Isabel forward, chuckling as the girl eyed Dominique suspiciously. "Jean, Dominique, may I present Isabel Fernandez, a friend of mine from school-days. Isabel, I am proud to introduce you to two of the best privateers in the world, Monsieurs Jean Lafitte and Dominique You."

Jean stepped forward to kiss her hand gallantly. "Welcome to my island, Señorita Fernandez."

"Thank you, Monsieur Lafitte," Isabel murmured softly, obviously still embarrassed by Dominique's comment.

When Dominique tried to echo his brother's welcome, Isabel hastily withdrew her hand. A look of dismay crossed Dominique's face.

"Oh, Isabel!" Kathleen said. "Do not let Dominique's appearance or talk frighten you. Behind that fierce countenance lies a heart of gold, and the most devoted friend a woman could want. He is just a big pussy cat disguised as a tiger!"

Jean laughed as Dominique turned bright red. "She is

right, of course, but do not tell our enemies this, Señorita.''

Isabel regarded them both dubiously, but allowed Dominique to kiss her hand and to escort her to the house, her hand tucked lightly in the crook of his elbow.

The next day was spent preparing for and planning their search, and the following sunrise revealed three ships leaving Barataria Bay. Jean was taking his own sloop, the *Pride,* Kathleen the *Starbright,* and Dominique was piloting the third. After reaching the most likely area, the three vessels fanned out, each covering a designated area thoroughly. Jean had drawn detailed maps for Kathleen to follow, warning her not to go further than the specific area she was assigned.

''Many of these islands are bases for the most barbarous of pirates, Kathleen,'' he told her.

Kathleen did not take his warning lightly, knowing he was deadly serious. However, recalling her own short term as a piratess, she thought it humorous that he would think to warn her against such men. ''It would not surprise me, Jean, if I were to see a few familiar faces should I encounter one of these pirate's dens,'' she countered wryly. ''I do take your words seriously, however, and I will be careful.''

''Please do, *cherie.*'' His hand reached out to brush her cheek. ''I would not wish any harm to come to you.'' Tenderness was reflected in his hazel eyes, and the ghost of unvoiced feelings from the past.

Bit by bit, they slowly worked their way through chains of islands big and small. There was no sign of Reed or the *Kat-Ann* and her crew. Each evening they met at a preplanned spot. Jean insisted on this, not only to review what they had seen, but because he knew safety lay in numbers. He was taking no chances with Kathleen's safety. Dominique concurred whole-heartedly, but Kathleen felt this was more for Isabel's benefit than hers. Unless she missed her guess, Dominique was quite taken with the petite brunette.

Isabel, for her part, was not quite sure what to make of the burly giant. "He scares me, Caterina," she confessed to Kathleen.

"Isabel, surely you've seen what a gentle giant Dom is," Kathleen scoffed. "He is a big, friendly teddy bear."

"So it seems," Isabel agreed, "but I have learned from experience that appearances can be deceiving. It was a hard lesson to learn; one for which I paid dearly."

"Just because your husband was a beast, does not mean all men are. You said Carlos was handsome and suave at first, later to reveal himself as the swine he truly was."

Isabel nodded silently.

"If it is true that appearances are deceiving, then look at Dominique from that viewpoint. Outwardly he is a huge, fierce pirate—sinister enough to make any maiden swoon with fright, I will grant you. In truth, he is just the opposite; kind, gentle, faithful to the end. If I put my life in his hands, Isabel, I know he would gladly die protecting me."

"But he is so big and muscular," Isabel argued. "It frightens me to think what could happen if I angered him. One swipe of his huge paw, and he could squash my skull like a melon!"

"Isabel, the man cares for you. I can see it in his every look and gesture. His eyes follow you like a forlorn puppy. He'd never hurt you, dearest. I know it."

Isabel shook her head. "I *don't* know, Caterina. I want to like him, but I truly don't know if I can ever fully trust any man again. Dominique's scars are on his face for all to see, but mine are inside, and they are deep.''

"I know, *amiga*. All I ask is that you show him a little kindness now and then. He, too, is my friend, and I hate to see him hurt. He knows nothing of your past trials, and I believe he thinks his size and scars alone cause you to shy away from him. He is aware that he is not a handsome man, and though he never mentions it, he is inwardly very sensitive about his fearsome looks.''

"Oh, dear!'' Isabel sighed miserably. "I had not realized. I don't mean to deliberately hurt his feelings. I just can't help being frightened of him. In future I will try to do better, but I can promise nothing.''

"Time will tell, my friend,'' Kathleen prophesied with a far-away look. "Time may reveal many unexpected turns of events in both our lives.''

Three weeks later, they still had not discovered so much as a chip of paint from the *Kat-Ann*. It was as if she had disappeared into thin air—or the depths of the Gulf. Kathleen was losing her earlier exuberance, becoming more despondent by the day.

It was then Jean decided they should go together to visit his "pirate brethren" to find out if any of them had seen the *Kat-Ann* or heard news of her.

"Will they tell us if they do know anything?'' Kathleen asked skeptically.

"I think they will tell me. We do a lot of business together. I buy their stolen goods and sell them in New Orleans—for a tidy profit, of course—but I pay them a fair price. They will think twice before offending their major buyer.'' Then Jean shrugged. "And what they do not say, we can probably deduce from their actions. Over the years,

I've come to know the value of watching a man's actions, his eyes in particular. It has saved my life many times over.''

Kathleen agreed. ''The primary rule of the best swordsmen in the world—never take your gaze from that of your opponent.'' She smiled, her eyes alight with renewed fervor. ''I should love to spar with you someday, Jean. Few men can give me a competitive duel, but with you it would be a challenge, indeed!''

They headed for a place called Boca Grande, a passage named for its wide mouth. Here, a barbarous pirate, José Gasparilla, had made his stronghold on an island he called Gasparilla Island. He was notorious for having captured a ship and ordering all its crewmen murdered and thrown overboard. Often, women and children met the same fate at his hands, unless they were lucky enough to have a wealthy family to ransom them. Usually he spared only the most beautiful young women, and those worth ransoming. From what Jean told them, Gasparilla was completely without morals, so it came as a surprise to learn that he allowed no harm to come to those ladies whom he hoped to trade back to their families in return for small fortunes. To ensure their safety from his randy crew, he had even built a stockade on a separate island to seclude them. Captiva Island, as it was called, and its hapless prisoners, were guarded only by Gasparilla's oldest and most trusted men.

The other captured women, those young enough and pretty enough to catch Gasparilla's lustful eye, but having no wealthy relatives, met quite another fate. Most of them became Gasparilla's private slaves of pleasure until he tired of them, which he did with amazing regularity. It was also said he had a quick and ungovernable temper, and woe betide the woman who angered him. Rather than beat her, Gasparilla usually beheaded the offender.

Once a new woman had aroused his lust, one of his old harem had to go to make room for the newcomer. The ousted girl was fortunate (or not, depending upon one's viewpoint) to be handed over to his men for their pleasure. Otherwise, she was killed outright.

Gasparilla was a strange blending of merciless beast and learned gentleman. Born into the minor aristrocracy of Spain, he was well educated and even well-mannered when he wished—which was not often. On his island, he had built a fine home for himself, furnishing it lavishly with plundered goods. When at home, he preferred quiet in which to read, rest and love. To assure his peace, he had had his most rowdy men relocate their village to another inner island where they could carouse and not disturb him. Undisputed king of his private paradise, Gasparilla ruled with an indiscriminately bloody sword and an unstable, volatile temperament.

Upon hearing of Gasparilla's reputation, Kathleen was surprised that Jean had included her and Isabel in his plans, and said as much. Jean gave her an amused, if long-suffering look. "Naturally, I thought to suggest it before you took it into your stubborn head to face him alone. Then, too, I think I know you well enough to judge that, had I asked you to stay behind, you would have defied me anyway and come despite the risks. Am I not correct?"

Kathleen had the grace to look properly chastised.

"Thus, I thought it wisest that you accompany us, where I can at least watch over you. Had you gone by your-self, Gasparilla would never have let you leave his island again. Your beauty alone would have been reason enough for him to hold you, but your arrogance and quick tongue would have been the death of you. This way, Gasparilla will see that you are under my protection."

Isabel was concerned. Looking from her own bold attire to Kathleen's she queried. "Do you think Kathleen and I should don our dresses? These breeches are quite revealing. While Kathleen can control her crew, and you your men, there is no sense in stirring up Gasparilla's blood or that of his band of cut-throats."

Jean considered Isabel's suggestion while Kathleen awaited his opinion. "No," he decided. "From what I have seen, Gasparilla prefers delicate, helpless women who will give him little trouble. I think he will be less tempted if the two of you present yourselves as self-willed, strong-minded women. If you are afraid, do not let him see this. Do not deliberately antagonize him, nor let him view you as a challenge to his pride. On the other hand, he must be made to see that you would be quite capable of skewering him if need be. Given that, and the fact that you are in my care, I think he will keep his distance."

"If he wants to live to love another day, he will," Kathleen promised, touching the hilt of her rapier. "Regardless, this trusty blade will not leave my side while we are there."

Gasparilla was everything Jean had said, and more. After identifying themselves, they anchored in the bay and were escorted to his house, where Gasparilla was informed of their arrival. They were seated in his tastefully decorated parlor but a few short minutes before Gasparilla strode in. Nearly as big as Dominique, he dwarfed the room. Kathleen knew immediately that the man regarded himself as a perfect specimen of male supremacy. It was there in the proud tilt of his head, the swagger of his walk, the arrogance of his steely grey eyes. Even his lips seemed molded into a perpetual sneer beneath his full mustache. He obviously liked fine clothing, and wore it well. Taking all this in, Kathleen concluded that, while not ugly, he certainly was not handsome by her standards, and his conceit made him less so.

Kathleen watched as his eyes swept the room, stopping briefly as he assessed the two women in the small group. A sly smile curled his lips and stayed as he addressed Jean.

"Jean Lafitte, what brings you to my island again so soon? We just sold you all our goods not long ago and have little else to trade as yet."

Jean met his look evenly. "We have come on business of another kind, José. It is a matter of grave importance concerning friends of mine."

One bushy brow raised slightly over the cynical grey eyes. "Oh? What has this to do with me?"

"We are trying to locate a missing ship and crew. It is possible you may have seen her in the area or have word of her." Jean was weighing his words carefully so as not to offend Gasparilla. If the man suspected they were accusing him of being involved in the *Kat-Ann*'s disappearance, he would tell them nothing.

The silence was heavy as Gasparilla considered this. Evidently satisfied by Jean's expression, he asked, "What vessel are you looking for—and why?"

Jean explained in detail about the storm and the *Kat-Ann*'s disappearance. "That was nearly two months ago, and still there is no sign of the frigate or my friend. For weeks we have scoured the islands with no success."

"I would need a description of the vessel," Gasparilla told him.

At this point, Jean introduced Kathleen. "This is

166

Kathleen Taylor, Reed's wife and my very dear friend. She can tell you anything you need to know about the *Kat-Ann.*''

The same dark eyebrow rose again in concert with its mate. His gaze swept Kathleen from head to toe, and she bristled at the lecherous look heating his eyes. ''Come now, Jean! What joke is this?''

''No joke, I assure you.'' Kathleen's voice was cool as ice, matching the glacial look in her eyes. ''The *Kat-Ann* is a hundred and seventy foot frigate, weighing out at five hundred tons empty, with a capacity of a thousand tons in her hold. Sleek and fast, she carries a crew of fifty men. She is armed with thirty guns; three twelve-pounders, eleven eighteen-pounders, twelve twenty-four-pounders, and four thirty-two-pounders. Her most distinguishing feature is her figurehead, a figure half-woman and half-cat.'' Kathleen finished listing the *Kat-Ann*'s specifics, her cool green eyes leveled on Gasparilla's bland face.

''How many masts?'' Gasparailla asked.

''Three.'' Kathleen's expression reflected her exasperation. *Everyone* knew a frigate had three masts!

''How many sails on the mainmast?''

''Eight, counting staysails.''

''Is she as fast as Jean's bark, the *Pride*?''

''The *Pride* is a sloop, as you well know,'' Kathleen retorted.

''What is her beam?'' Gasparilla was referring to the frigate's width at the widest point.

''Forty feet.''

''Name her woods.''

''Teak decking, and mahogany planking; solid mahogany helm.''

Gasparilla smiled, a wide, crooked lifting of his lips. ''I

wish I had seen her. If she is half of what you say, she must be quite a vessel."

"The best," Kathleen boasted boldly.

Jean intervened at this point. "Do you recall the storm I mentioned? It must have been quite a blow for that early in the season."

Gasparilla nodded congenially. "It was, indeed. I was out on a run and barely made it back in one piece."

Dominique spoke up. "Could Brew Baker have seen the *Kat-Ann?*" He referred to a fellow pirate based on Bokeelia Island, not far away. Brew had been the one to first introduce Gasparilla to the Lafitte brothers.

"He might have," Gasparilla shrugged. "If so, he hasn't mentioned it to me, but that would not be unusual." Eyeing Kathleen speculatively, he added, "I could send for him. In the meantime, you must accept my hospitality."

Kathleen's level look clashed with his. "To what extent, Señor Gasparilla?" she challenged.

A sly gleam lit his eyes as they traveled shrewdly over Kathleen and Isabel. "After so long at sea, you ladies must be tired, and perhaps longing for a hot bath and a soft bed," he said smoothly. "I can have my servants prepare them at once, as well as a meal more delicious than you have tasted in some time."

"I will live without the frills with no complaint, Señor. The only thing I truly long for is to find my husband as soon as possible." Kathleen's crisp tone assured him she was serious.

"We will fill our water barrels and buy any fresh supplies you have to spare, José," Jean stated, "and we will wait aboard our vessels for Brew's arrival."

Gasparilla's interest was caught. "Yes, my man said you

168

arrived in three ships, only two of which were familiar to us. He said your frigate is a beauty. When did you acquire her?"

"I didn't," Jean replied. "The *Starbright* is Mrs. Taylor's ship. Three vessels can cover a wider area than one."

"Do you have a capable captain and crew, Mrs. Taylor?" Gasparilla asked smoothly. "I would be happy to let you have a few of my men."

Kathleen met him stare for stare. "Thank you, no. I have a realiable crew and the most loyal of captains."

This last comment brought a broad grin from Dominique, duly noted by Gasparilla. Even the petite dark-haired woman, so solemn and quiet so far, had nearly smiled. "You are piloting the lady's ship, Dominique?" he asked.

"No, no," Dominique assured him. "I sailed the third. Captain Taylor handles the helm quite well herself."

Grey eyes widened in astonishment as Gasparilla once more took in the women's unusual attire. His eyes lingered on the rapier adorning Kathleen's curvaceous thigh. "You command the *Starbright*?" he echoed in stunned disbelief.

"I do."

A short laugh barked from his thick throat. "Are you one of those freakish women who thinks she is a man?" he scoffed. "Perhaps your husband was not man enough to satisfy you. Could it be you need a real man to show you your proper place in this world?"

Emerald eyes blazed as Kathleen's hand tightened on the hilt of her rapier. "My husband is all the man I need, Gasparilla, and if you should be tempted to prove otherwise, I would advise you to make your peace with God before you attempt it. This rapier is not for show alone. It is honed to the sharpest edge and is swift to do my bidding. Any man who attempts to take what belongs to Reed alone, will feel the righteous wrath of my blade!''

Jean and Dominique flanked her. ''And I am honor-bound to protect my friend's wife in his absence, José. I do not take my responsibilities lightly,'' said Jean.

''That goes for Miss Fernandez as well,'' Dominique added, a fierce gleam in his black eyes.

Gasparilla laughed dismissively. ''My friends, you take offense for no reason. I have more women than I know what to do with now. Why should I want these two who prefer men's clothing and exhibit such masculine talents?'' But his scornful words did not diminish the hot lust in his eyes as he appraised the feminine curves of the two women before him.

Isabel was hard pressed to hide her shiver of fear, and Kathleen her shudder of disgust. ''Keep that in mind,'' Kathleen suggested sharply. Turning, her long-legged stride carried her swiftly toward the *Starbright*.

''Do you think Gasparilla will try anything?'' Isabel queried anxiously as the two women readied themselves for bed in Kathleen's cabin. They had reluctantly accepted Gasparilla's invitation to supper earlier that evening, where Dominique had jealousy guarded Isabel, as Jean had Kathleen. Following Jean's example, they ate and drank nothing not served from a common platter or sampled by the others. They were taking no chances that Gasparilla might drug them. He was an unscrupulous pirate, after all, and not be be trusted.

"I have no idea," Kathleen responded, "but I think we had better share my quarters tonight, just in case." The two of them crawled into the wide captain's bunk, their rapiers safely at hand beneath the thin sheet. They had previously reviewed a course of action, if neccessary.

Hours later, dozing lightly, Kathleen heard the slight squeak as her cabin door stealthily opened. Nudging Isabel lightly, she felt her friend tense, and knew she was also alert to the intruders.

Two sets of footsteps crept toward the bunk. A sixth sense told Kathleen that a third man stood guarding the door. Just as two knife blades were about to settle upon their respective throats, Kathleen and Isabel reacted simultaneously. Isabel's constant training paid off as her blade found its way neatly between the lower ribs of her assailant. His knife dropped harmlessly to the mattress as he howled and grabbed his side. Concentrating on her own attacker, Kathleen swung her blade upward. Having taken the left side of the bed, it was rather awkward having to bring her blade about in a backhanded move, but she managed it with more success than she'd imagined. The dim light from the porthole reflected off the steel as her sword severed the man's hand completely. Blood spurted everywhere, and the fellow stared in stunned horror as his hand and weapon clunked to the floor.

Alert to the third intruder moving swiftly to their assailants' defense, Kathleen leaped from the bed, her rapier ready. With a few, short, precise strokes, she disarmed him, his cutlass skittering noisily out of his reach.

Summoned by the howls of the wounded men and the clash of swords, several of Kathleen's men now entered the cabin. Swords drawn, they watched as Kathleen rounded on the unarmed offender, her rapier point at his rapidly pulsing throat.

"Now, mate, who sent you?" She prodded him with the tip, drawing a drop of blood. Her freezing glare told him she would give him no quarter.

"Gasparilla," he gasped painfully.

"To kill us or abduct us?"

The man gulped, his Adam's apple bouncing. "We were to bring you to him," he confessed.

"Take them on deck," Kathleen commanded her crewmen. Glancing at her first attacker, clutching his handless arm and trying desperately to stem the flow of blood, she added contemptuously, "Don't forget to retrieve this buffoon's hand from beneath my bed. Throw it to the fish!"

Disregarding their thin nightdresses, Kathleen and Isabel followed the men on deck. There they found Finley gingerly fingering a huge knot on the back of his head. Another crewman nursed a matching lump. Other than that, no one else from her crew had been harmed. Once this was determined, Kathleen turned to the three pirates. "Go back to Gasparilla and take him this message. Tell him we dealt lightly with you. By all rights, I should have your heads! You may also tell him from me, that if he sends any more of his scurvy cut-throats aboard my ship, they will not return alive. He has my promise on this, and I always honor my word."

Just to be sure Gasparilla got her message, Kathleen instructed several of her men to escort the three to Gasparilla's door. Setting new guards, the two women retired, but only after the blood had been cleared from Kathleen's cabin. But Isabel slept fitfully, awakening Kathleen once as she fought the lingering shadows of a blood-filled nightmare.

Chapter 10

The next morning Kathleen, Isabel, Jean, and Dominique marched boldly up to Gasparilla's elaborate house. Gasparilla was wolfing down his breakfast as Kathleen approached the table. With no hesitation, she dumped her bloodstained sheets squarely in the center of the table. Her eyes met his with steely determination, her jaw tight with agitation. "You owe me a set of clean sheets, Gasparilla," she stated grimly.

He nodded, outwardly unperturbed but in his eyes was a new look of admiration and respect. "My apologies, Mrs. Taylor, Miss Fernandez."

To them all, he offered, "Sit down and have breakfast."

"We've eaten," Jean informed him.

"Then share my table and my coffee."

Dominique and the women declined, but Jean surprisingly accepted, saying, "I should like to discuss a certain matter with you, José."

After the other three returned to their ships, leaving Jean and Gasparilla to their discussion, Jean came straight to the point. "If Brew Baker has no news of the *Kat-Ann*, I should like to enlist your aid in finding Reed and his crew. You will be well paid for you help."

Thick brows rising, Gasparilla's look was calculating.

"Will the fascinating Mrs. Taylor be tendering payment, or will you?"

Jean smiled complacently. "I will, Gasparilla—in gold, of course. By now you must be aware that Kathleen does not share her favors. She is sincere in her efforts to find her husband, whom she loves with her whole heart."

"A shame," Gasparilla sighed, "but I must respect her for her faithfulness to the fellow. She is quite a woman, as is her little friend, the *señorita* Fernandez."

"Dominique would gladly kill you if you touched so much as a hair of Isabel's head," Jean warned solemnly.

Gasparilla's smile was sly. "As you would if I were to try to take Kathleen Taylor."

Jean nodded. "She is my friend's wife."

Gasparilla laughed. "Do not try to fool an old fool, Jean Lafitte! You love her. Your eyes follow her constantly. When you think she does not see, there is lust mixed with tenderness in the looks you send her way."

Jean did not bother to deny it. "Yes, I love her," he admitted. "I have loved her since I first set eyes on her five years ago, but she was Reed's wife then, too. I respect Reed and Kathleen too much to do anything that would dishonor our friendship."

"Still, you desire her," Gasparilla insisted. "If her husband can not be found, what then?"

"Then Kathleen will undoubtedly return home to her children."

"She has children?" Gasparilla was surprised.

"Two—a daughter and a son," Jean said.

"And if Captain Taylor is discovered to have drowned after all?" Gasparilla pressed. "Will you take her for your own, then?"

Jean laughed. "No one 'takes' Kathleen, as you put it!"

"If you want her, and Reed is dead, why not take what you want?" Gasparilla could not understand Jean's attitude. "She may fight you, but she'll soon discover who is master."

Jean shook his head, ruefully eyeing the man before him. "You still do not understand, do you, Gasparilla? If Kathleen should ever become mine, it will be because she, too, desires it. I have no wish to force her or crush her magnificent spirit that I admire so much. If—*le bon Dieu* forbid!—Reed should be proven dead, I would not want her to turn to me seeking only sympathy, comfort, or even release. If the day ever arrives when Kathleen can come to me freely and with love in her heart, then and only then will we share our passion. I'll have no ghosts in my bed when I claim her."

Gasparilla shrugged. "Have it your way, Jean. I still say you are a fool, but it is your life."

Brew Baker arrived later that afternoon. The English captain-turned-pirate had not seen the *Kat-Ann* or anyone who may have been a part of her crew. Unable to resist Jean's generous offer of gold, both he and Gasparilla agreed to join the search.

Five days later, as the ships were each cruising their separate areas, three sharp cannon reports resounded in the air, signaling that one of them had located something of note.

Aboard the *Starbright*, Kathleen froze in mid-stride upon hearing the signal. The blood seemed to drain out of her body through the soles of her feet, leaving her cold and pale beneath her summer tan. A terrible trembling attacked her, and she stumbled, sinking in a heap to the deck.

"Oh, God!" she prayed fervently. "Let him be well! Let him be alive!" After all the weeks of searching, it was still a shock to think that within a few minutes she might know his fate at last.

Kathleen started violently as she felt warm arms encircle her shoulders. Looking into Isabel's concerned face, she saw compassion and understanding.

"Isabel, I am so frightened," she whispered, her pale lips barely moving. "Now that the moment may be at hand, I am so awfully scared!"

"I know, Caterina," Isabel crooned soothingly. "I know, *amiga,* but your crew awaits your orders. You must gather your strength and courage about you, and we must go see what has been found."

Above her, Kathleen heard Finley's familiar voice. "Captain?" he queried gently, sympathy coating the single word.

Kathleen swallowed hard, rapidly blinking the moisture from her eyes. "Help me up," she croaked, extending her hand toward him. "Let's be on our way, Finley. We'll learn nothing sitting here worrying. Issue the orders, if you please."

"Will you take the helm?" he asked.

"Aye. At least I will have the wheel to support my watery knees," she joked weakly.

As the *Starbright* started toward the area from which the signal had sounded, Kathleen's heart thudded in her chest, making her breath come unevenly. Equal parts of hope and dread filled her, as well as an uncertain sense of relief that perhaps her suspense would soon be ended one way or another.

It was not to be quite that simple, however. What faced Kathleen upon her arrival was to be the most trying time of her entire life.

Jean and Dominique had arrived just minutes before her to discover what Brew Baker had already found. Their ships rode side by side, guarding their find. As the *Starbright* drew abreast of the *Pride*, Kathleen saw Jean and Dominique standing mutely on deck, their faces shadowed by gloom. The very air seemed to carry the scent of sorrow.

Then she spied the cause of their dismay, and she gasped aloud. Her head spun dizzily, and she feared she might faint as she clutched the wheel for support. There, not twenty feet beneath the crystal surface of the clear waters, lay the battered remains of the once-proud *Kat-Ann*. Held fast by the sharp fingers of a coral reef, she rocked silently with the steady rhythm of the waves, beaten and void of life.

Kathleen slumped over the wheel, her head propped between her hands. Her heart pounded into her throat and head, sending a rush of blood to her brain, and she thought surely she would be sick as nausea assailed her. Pain pierced every part of her body, and she wished then and there for death to claim her, too. Deep, heartrending moans of agony escaped her lips unnoticed as she prayed for an escape from this, her worst nightmare.

She barely noticed the strong fingers prying her grip loose from the wheel. Nor did she hear the whispered, "*Cherie,* come belowdeck, away from prying eyes until you are recovered." Eyes wide open, but blinded by tears, she did not see the torment on Jean's face as he lifted her into his arms and carried her to her cabin. Nothing seemed

179

to penetrate her all-consuming pain.

The wrenching sobs seemed to be coming from someone else. The wetness on her face and in her hair could have been salt spray or rain, for all Kathleen knew. It was as if she stood outside herself, watching the person she once had been, the body she had once occupied. Her limbs and brain felt numb, her skin cold, her heart dead and bloodless. If not for the persistant pain, she might have been dead. A devastating sense of loss engulfed her, even in her shocked state.

Gradually, however, her youthful body reasserted its own will, defying her brain's wish for eternal oblivion. Unconsciously seeking warmth and comfort, she curled like a small child into Jean's embrace, her arms clinging tightly to him. As he caressed her head and back in soothing strokes, she laid her head on his chest, taking comfort in the reassuring beat of his heart beneath her ear. It was as if she needed this sign of life, to hear this steady surge of blood, in order to cling to life herself and withstand the insanity that threatened her. Finally, her eyes swollen and heavy, she fell asleep to the steady drumming of his heart, and awoke sometime later still cradled in his supporting arms. Licking dry, trembling lips, she whispered, "Jean?" Her sorrowful gaze searched his face, finding no ground for hope. "He is really gone, isn't he?"

His chest heaved heavily as he sighed. "It would seem so, *cherie*. We have divers now examining the wreckage for bodies that might be caught inside."

Tears stung her eyes once more. "When they come across one dressed in black shirt and trousers . . ." —here she choked and struggled to go on— "with an onyx ring on his marriage finger . . . it will be Reed."

Jean's arms enfolded her more tightly, trying in vain to

absorb some of her pain into himself, although he had his own share of sorrow to bear for the loss of his old and valued friend.

When darkness fell, the search of the sunken ship was put aside until morning. No one suggested that they depart the area. Instead, they settled gloomily into a fitful rest, awaiting the dark dawn of yet another dreadful day.

By afternoon of the following day, the search of the remains of the *Kat-Ann* was concluded. Several bodies had been found, accounting for about one-third of the original crew—none of them Reed's. The entries in the log book, retrieved in its protective oilcloth enclosure, had been completed up to the day of the storm, telling nothing of what had happened that fateful day.

Obviously, the ship had been blown way off course, coming to rest on the coral reef that had viciously finished the destruction the storm had begun. If the bodies Captain Guthrie had encountered were those of men from the *Kat-Ann*, the sum total of those discovered then and now accounted for only two-thirds of the crew.

Where were the rest? Where was Reed? These questions that echoed and resounded in Kathleen's weary brain and carried her through the endless day and night, drove her to continue her search of the islands. She, Jean, and Dominique were of one accord on this issue. All of them felt led to scour the numerous islands surrounding the wreckage; and all were certain that if Reed were not found on one of them, he must indeed be dead.

The log book, however, did add a few new details. It seemed the prisoner exchange had been accomplished without a hitch. The *Kat-Ann* had traded twenty English prisoners for an equal number of Americans; nineteen men and one woman.

Reed wrote that the woman, Miss Sally Simpson, had been visiting in England when the war broke out. Finding herself on unfriendly soil, she had been frantic to leave the country. When her friends had gone home to Germany, she had tried to cross the border with them, and had gotten caught. A few months in an English prison had been more than enough for the poor girl, and she had been tearfully thankful to be included in the exchange.

In a side note, Reed stated that the young girl reminded him more than a little of Kathleen for some vague reason. Perhaps, he had written, it was her similar build, or her brave determination, he was not sure. There were no other physical similarities, he noted, since Sally Simpson was blonde, blue-eyed, and barely eighteen years of age.

Kathleen, upon reading this personal notation, felt an unreasonable jealousy that Reed should compare her with this stranger, especially in one of the last sentences of the journal. In her heart, she could not help wishing that his last thoughts had been only of her and their children. It hurt to think Reed might have been too preoccupied with saving this girl's life to spare a thought for her, since Miss Simpson's body had not be recovered either. Kathleen hated to picture Reed going to a watery grave wrapped in another woman's arms. Try as she might, she could not shake her morbid, senseless jealousy.

For several more days, they meticulously searched the nearby islands. A few pieces of debris were found washed ashore on one or two. Then the broken dinghy was located on a small beach. Kathleen rowed ashore with the small party of searchers. About a mile inland, they came across a fresh-water pond—and five survivors of the wreckage!

Hope sprang anew as Kathleen recognized three of the sailors from the *Kat-Ann*. The other two were exchanged prisoners. Only one of the crewmen was uninjured. He had been caring for the others as best he could, but with little hope. One man had a broken leg; another had several broken and cracked ribs, now healing. One of the prisoners had a nasty gash in his leg, which had festered badly. Most likely, he would lose the leg. The other American, already weakened by his stay in a British jail, had lapsed into unconsciousness with a raging fever. The remaining sailor had a severed arm and a deep cut across his forehead. His chances of survival were practically non-existent. Four other of their mates had already succumbed to their wounds since washing ashore.

While the wounded men were being tended and gently transferred to the waiting ships, Kathleen and Jean questioned the one sound survivor. The story he told was not encouraging. The storm had been the worst he could recall. Yes, the *Kat-Ann* had been blown off course, but Captain Taylor and all aboard had fought to keep her steady. She had started to break apart after lightning had sent her mainmast crashing through the deck. They had lost a few men overboard then, and more had lost their footing during the course of the storm and gone sliding off where the taffrail had given way. Floundering badly, they somehow managed to stay afloat for a while longer. Then, out of nowhere, they had come upon the reef. The sharp coral had ripped at the crippled ship, tearing a gaping hole in her hull.

With the frigate sinking fast, the remaining men had gone overboard, some in the dinghy and others clinging to barrels and pieces of planking. The sailor recalled clinging to the side of the thrashing dinghy, battered by monstrous waves. As the current pulled them away, the sailor had seen Captain Taylor leap from the foundering ship with the blonde woman slung over his shoulder. A few minutes later, he caught a glimpse of the woman's blonde hair and light-colored dress as she was swept past him. He could not see if her face was out of the water. Nor could he tell if Captain Taylor was with her, for it was too dark. All he could add was that he and the others who had made it to safety on the island had seen neither of them since that night, nor any sign of anyone else. Indeed, it was a miracle to be rescued at all after all this time, and he could not express his gratitude enough.

With renewed hope, they combed the islands for yet another week, but no further survivors were found, though seven more bodies were discovered. Reed and Miss Simpson were not among them. Finally came the day Kathleen had dreaded. They had covered every island any survivors might possibly have washed ashore upon. In fact, they had extended their search beyond what was reasonable. It was time to face the facts. Reed must have drowned. If he were alive, they would have found him by now. Somewhere in the depths of these treacherous sparkling blue waters, his lifeless body lay among the coral-strewn sands, never to be retrieved.

Jean was ready to return to Grande Terre. Gasparilla and Baker had already departed for their respective islands. The injured survivors were improving under the care of the *Pride's* physician, but they needed decent food and calm conditions for their continued recovery.

When Jean suggested to Kathleen that they set course for Barataria Bay, she gazed up at him sadly and shook her head. The pity in his gentle hazel eyes was almost more than she could bear. Isabel, with her constant mothering, was beginning to grate on Kathleen's nerves also.

Just now, Kathleen was blessedly numb, but she realized it was a temporary condition. Something was seething just beneath the surface, waiting to burst forth. A deep anger and terrible grieving was building up within her, and it frightened her. She could sense it, though she could not fully comprehend it, and some inner self warned her that it would not be long before it erupted full-force. When it finally did, she sensed that the force of it would be far more destructive and devastating than anything she had ever experienced.

Kathleen felt an overwhelming urge to get away from everything and everyone. Deep in her soul she felt the need to grieve in peace and solitude, to come to terms with Reed's death and her own feelings without the constant attention and well-meant advice of her sympathetic friends.

Thus, when Jean suggested returning to Grande Terre, Kathleen declined. "You go on, Jean. Take Dominique and Isabel back with you, but I will not be coming."

Jean frowned. "Kathleen, *cherie,* surely you do not intend to continue the search? Surely you realize by now how hopeless it is."

A ghost of a smile touched her lips, but did not begin to reach her eyes. "I am not totally mad yet, Jean. Even I know when I am beaten. Do you need to hear me speak the words? Then I will say it. Reed is dead. I know that, but now I need to accept it, and I need to do it alone."

"I wonder at the wisdom of that," he doubted aloud.

"Wise or not, it is what I must do. I am going to head the *Starbright* out to sea. Just where I shall go or how long I shall be gone, I cannot say. It would please me if you would take Isabel and part of my crew with you. I want a

185

minimum of people with me; just enough to manage the ship.''

"Have you forgotten there is a war on?" Jean reminded her. "What if you encounter a British warship?"

Kathleen shrugged, causing Jean's worry to escalate as he sensed her fatalistic attitude. "I shall contend with that event if and when it should occur," she stated flatly.

"You will come back when you have settled things in your mind?" He was really pressing her for some word that she did not plan to intentionally place herself in harm's way.

She answered vaguely, "When I have come to terms with my loss." Only God could say when or if that would come about.

Isabel, too, feared for Kathleen's safety in her present state of mind. She begged Kathleen not to go, or if she must, to take her along. Kathleen laughed hollowly. "Heavens, Isabel! You would think I had just sold you into slavery! Dominique particularly will take especially good care of you."

"It is not myself I am concerned about," Isabel huffed. Then her voice turned pleading again. "Promise me you will be careful and return safely."

Kathleen's face clouded, and her shoulders slumped. "I can only say I will try, Isabel. Reed vowed that he would return unharmed, and you see what has happened. Promises are nothing but empty words. We are all in the fickle hands of fate."

Jean stood on the deck of the *Pride* watching the *Starbright* carry Kathleen further and further from him, until it was a mere dot on the horizon. He wished he could have locked her safely in her cabin and carried her away with

186

him to Grande Terre whether she wished it or not. A heavy sigh lifted his chest as he admitted he could never have done that to her, no matter how intense his desire.

He understood only too well her wish to be alone just now. Hadn't he, too, experienced that same desire when his beloved wife Rachel had died? Leaving his children with Pierre's wife, he had gone off to lick his wounds in solitary grieving, daring anyone to interrupt his seclusion.

Perhaps better than Kathleen herself at this point, Jean understood what she was going through, and what she had yet to discover within herself. How well he recognized the signs of building anger and frustration she was only now starting to feel! With all his heart, Jean wished he could spare her this private hell, or assure her that it would ease with time. If there were a way to take her pain upon himself, he would gladly do it, but he knew in his soul that this was the one thing she must resolve within herself, and no one could do it for her.

And so he had let her go. He could only wait and pray that Kathleen was as strong as he thought her to be. Too well he knew the temptation to join one's mate in death. The struggle between the forces of life and death could be fierce indeed, and he could only pray that Kathleen would come through this ultimate contest of wills safely. Perhaps that was why God allowed the unreasonable anger to creep in; perhaps it helped to conquer the inevitable deathwish. The rage he had felt after Rachel's death had seemed a strange reaction, at first, and in direct conflict with his terrible grief. The harder he had tried to reject the anger, the stronger it had become, until its blazing fury had given him the release his tears could not. He had raged at the injustice of life and fate. He'd cursed God and man, the painful childbirth that had taken Rachel's life, himself, even his small newborn daughter.

Then, when he had run out of other things to rage at, his anger had turned itself unreasonably on Rachel. She had given birth twice before and never had a problem. Why couldn't she have done that this time? How could she have allowed herself to become pregnant at the worst time in St. Domingue's history, just when they were forced to flee the revolution for their very lives? And why, oh, why, couldn't she have forestalled her labor until they had reached New Orleans? They had been within mere hours of their destination! Most of all, what right had she to die and leave him alone and heartbroken and so lost without her?

Eventually his anger had burned itself out, and he had gone through a less intense period of grieving, achieving a sort of quiet, exhausted acceptance of the inevitable and God's will. That had been nine years ago, and there were still times when his grief seemed as fresh and new as the day she had died, though not often these days. Now his thoughts were of Kathleen and his unrequited love for her —a love that gave, and grew, and asked so little in return.

With a sigh of resignation, Jean turned from the rail. Worried though he was, he could now only have faith in Kathleen's strength to pull her through this hellish trial.

For six days the *Starbright* continued into the very heart of the Gulf, on a more-or-less southwesterly heading, though Kathleen set no specific course. In her grief, she didn't really care where they went or how long they were gone. As far as she was concerned, they could drift aimlessly into eternity as long as they did it in complete solitude.

For the most part, she manned the helm herself, but

there were times when she turned the wheel over to Finley. Then she would spend long hours perched high in the rigging, staring out at the endless blue waters. Her emotions assailed her from every direction, giving her little of the peace she sought. Unlike the calm seas they now traversed, her emotions ran the gamut from anger to despair, frustration to desolation, anxiety to damnation. Tears were her constant companion.

There were many times, high above the deck in her private gloom, when she could so easily have launched herself into the endless depth of the sea below. Her sorrow knew no bounds, her pain no limit. Yet, rising above it all, was an ever-mounting anger. Under the bright tropical sun, it seemed to seethe and fester like an unclean wound.

At last came the day when her wrath rose full and furious to the surface. Alone in the shrouds, Kathleen shrieked at the heavens.

"Damn you, Reed Taylor!" she screamed. "Damn you for leaving me alone like this! You *promised!*" Her voice broke and rose again to blister the skies. "You lousy, lying scum! You *promised* to come home to me! What am I to tell your mother and our children? Shall I tell them you rest below the waves in the arms of some strange woman? If you hadn't tried to save her—if you hadn't been so stupidly gallant—you might be in *my* arms right now!" Her chest heaving with pain, she screamed out her anguish. "You were an excellent captain, Reed. You should have been able to bring your ship through, no matter how vicious the storm, or how high the waves! You should have come home to me! What gave you the *right* to hurt me this way? What gives you the right to lie in peace while I go through this living hell?"

Her words stopped, and she clung limply to the mast, as

if in venting her anger, she had exhausted every ounce of her strength. She felt small and weak and lifeless, but more at peace than she had in weeks. It was as if she had released some of the pain gnawing away at her. Sobbing violently, she slowly descended the mast and crawled away to her bunk to bury herself in the blessed oblivion of sleep.

Dan and Finley stared after her in mutual dismay. It hurt them to see her in such pain when they could do nothing to help. They were limited to seeing to her basic needs and watching over her as closely as she would allow. Each time she climbed into the rigging, or stood defeatedly at the rail staring into the depths below, they tensed with fear. Under this tremendous stress, they knew it would take little to push her over the edge of sanity, on the brink of which she teetered so precariously.

Both had known and loved Kathleen since she was a child. Dan had been like an elderly uncle, patiently teaching her first how to tie knots, and finally how to sail. Kathleen had once gone through a schoolgirl's infatuation for Hal Finley when he was, temporarily at least, her idol.

The two of them had sailed under her command as Emerald, willingly turning pirate simply because she had asked it of them. At her side, they had endured hurricanes and swordfights, fought pirates—and eventually gotten caught. They had sailed and fought at her side, advised her, protected her, worried over her, laughed and cried with her, felt such pride in her they thought they would burst, and watched her mature into the strong, beautiful woman she was today.

In the first year of her marriage, they had seen her suffer and struggle against her love for Reed. They had watched in helpless frustration as Kathleen and Reed had repeatedly, and often deliberately, hurt one another deeply. They'd shared her pain, her anger, and her attempt at revenge. In the past four years, they'd celebrated the lasting love she and Reed had found, and the happy births of their two children. Now they shared her sorrow, but were helpless to lessen her grief.

For the next couple of days, Kathleen was quieter and more subdued than before. It was impossible to tell if she was beginning to accept the fact of Reed's death, or if she was merely falling more deeply into depression.

Kathleen could have told them. With her anger expended, the fight seemed to drain out of her. A strange sense of calm had taken its place, a dreary lassitude that led to dark thoughts of death. She longed to join Reed and put an end to this torment—this awful loneliness. In the turmoil of her mind, she no longer cared if she lived or died. With Reed had gone her reason for existing, her laughter and her sunshine.

It was in this frame of mind that she ordered the sails taken in. The *Starbright* drifted slowly to a rocking halt, bobbing easily on the slight waves. Dan's old heart nearly stopped as he saw Kathleen pull off her boots and stockings and balance herself on the slim railing. He cried out in warning, but neither he nor Finley could reach her before she dived in a perfect arc and plunged far beneath the crystal surface of the water. Tears blurred Dan's vision, and he clutched at Finley's arm in fear. "Oh! She's gone an' done it now, fer sure!"

Finley patted his friend's shoulder in commiseration. "Maybe not. We'll just have to wait and see. It's certain there is not a man among us who can swim as well as Kathleen, so there is no use trying to save her against her will."

The saltwater stung her eyes as Kathleen stroked her way

through sun-sparkled water. It was so beautiful, and so blessedly silent, not the stormy, deadly sea that had claimed her husband's life. She had always loved the sea, sharing a special kinship with it, and now she had come to link its spirit with hers eternally.

Preoccupied with her thoughts and dazzled by the splendor about her, it was several seconds before Kathleen realized that something was not right. The water held an unequaled buoyancy this day. It seemed to bear her up, and as hard as she stroked, she could not swim below a certain depth. Always able to hold her breath for long minutes under water, Kathleen thought surely she had exceeded her limit, yet her lungs were not straining in her chest. Just when she began to feel the familiar pressure and the urge to breathe fresh air, the ocean seemed to lurch and send her bobbing to the surface. There, her lungs reflexively sucked in air, replenishing their supply of oxygen.

Frowning in confusion, Kathleen again dove below the surface; again she could not gain any great depth. But this time she did manage to stay down longer. Her chest ached, her head was beginning to feel light, and bright spots were flickering before her eyes before the sea tossed her spinning to the surface once more.

Kathleen tried five more times to seek welcome oblivion. Once, she went as deep as she could, and deliberately expelled all the air from her lungs, but it was as if someone had tied a line about her and yanked her abruptly to the surface. On her last attempt, darkness was gathering at the edges of her eyes, and her brain was fuzzy for lack of air, when she thought she heard her children calling her.

"What the devil am I doing?" she wondered, sanity

prevailing at last. With a tremendous kick, she stroked for the surface and safety. Sucking in great gulps of air, she thought, "For pity's sake! I can't even drown myself properly!"

Swimming to the side of the ship, she grabbed the line Dan and Finley tossed down to her, and laboriously pulled herself up. A few feet from the deck, her friends each grabbed an arm and hauled her aboard. Flat on her back, Kathleen stared up at them.

"Ye tried t' kill yerself, lass," Dan accused in a wobbly voice.

"Yes, I did, Dan," she confessed weakly, "but I didn't succeed. It seems the sea will not let me make a martyr of myself. She kept spitting me up, time and again. Then, this last time, I heard Katlin and Andrea calling for me . . ." Tears filled her eyes. "I just couldn't ignore their pleading voices begging me to come home. It is not fair that they will grow up not knowing their father. In my heart, I cannot deprive them of their mother, too."

"Thet's the first bit o' sense I've heard ye make lately," he said gruffly, clearing his throat.

The three of them shared a long, silent look of friendship and loyalty. Kathleen held a hand toward Finley. "Give me a hand up, Finley, and let's head this ship for home. We will stop briefly at Grande Terre to pick up Isabel and then it is on to Savannah. I suddenly have a great need to hold my children in my arms!"

Isabel, though she was learning to care a great deal for Dominique, chose to return to Savannah with Kathleen. They were all greatly relieved to see Kathleen once more, having feared she might never return. The joy of seeing her safe, if not yet whole, tempered Jean's disappointment that she was returning immediately to Savannah. He understood her desire to see her children. Then, too, she must inform Kate and Reed's family of the sad results of their search. With all his heart, Jean wanted to keep her on Grande Terre, but he loved her enough to let her go. Time, and the love shared with her children, would perhaps heal her wounds. Maybe then he would see her again, and find a way to open her heart to him.

Chapter 11

The first week of October saw the *Starbright* slip past the British blockade and nestle into her private slip at Savannah's dock. Savannah still had seen no action other than the bother of the blockade. News was eagerly awaited and swiftly passed on. Just now, Andrew Jackson was campaigning against the Creek Indians. The town was celebrating Captain Oliver Perry's brilliant naval victory against the British the previous month, which had effectively freed Lake Erie from enemy hands, and the *Argus*'s resounding victory over the British sloop-of-war, the *Barbadoes,* off Halifax, during which the enemy sloop had been captured and its captain slain.

Kathleen's return was both joyful and sad. After nearly three months away from home, it was wonderful to see her family once again, and to hold her children near. How could they have grown so in the time she had been gone? Alexandrea would turn four this month, her babyhood so swiftly left behind. Even Katlin, now two and a half, seemed surprisingly grown up.

It came as something of a shock to Kathleen to realize how badly it hurt to be around her own son. Katlin resembled his father so exactly that it was impossible to look at him and not think of Reed. When he turned those bright blue eyes on her, or that sparkling crooked grin,

Kathleen wanted to die with the pain.

As much as she loved her sweet boy, Kathleen found herself unconsciously avoiding him. When she realized what she was doing, she deliberately set out to spend more time with him. After all, it was not the child's fault that he was a miniature replica of Reed. It was not his fault that his father had gone off and gotten himself killed. Still, each time she held her son; each time she reached out to brush that errant black lock of hair from his forehead, that crippling lance of pain would pierce her heart. Where once Kathleen had hoped that she might be carrying another child—a last memorial to Reed—she was now thankful that she was not. It was hard enough to be around Katlin.

Andrea was not nearly such a hurtful reminder. Her basic facial features were more Kathleen's than Reed's. Her auburn curls seemed an equal mixture of Kathleen's red-gold tresses and Reed's jet black hair. Even her eyes, that unique and brilliant turquoise—a blend of her father's blue and her mother's green—were still uniquely Andrea's. If her actions sometimes imitated Reed's, or her tastes or temperament aped his, it was, perhaps, less noticeable in a daughter than a son. If Kathleen had thought she was beginning to accept her loss and to work through her sorrow, she still had far to go. Everywhere were reminders of Reed.

Upon hearing Kathleen's sorrowful tale, Mary Taylor was not surprised. It was what she had expected all along, but she had realized that Kathleen needed proof. Having come through the worst of her grieving and adjustment to her son's death, Mary now set about arranging a memorial service. The black crepe and wreath went back on the front door, with no protest from Kathleen this time.

Privately, Kathleen thought she, Isabel, Mary and Susan

all looked like black crows in their mourning dresses, but she could not gather the energy to care. All through the dreary memorial service and the glowing eulogy, she sat like a pale statue, neither weeping nor showing any emotion at all. She felt frozen in her own private hell.

Uncle William and Aunt Barbara had returned from Augusta the previous month. Their sympathetic gestures were almost more than Kathleen could bear. That, plus Mary's sweet, considerate understanding, made her almost wish she had not come home. They loved her, and she them, but their pity was hard to take. If someone was not inadvertently reminding her of Reed, they were stumbling over their tongues trying to remember not to mention him.

Isabel and Kate were the only adults Kathleen could relax and be at ease with at this time. Isabel had finally stopped mothering her, and since she had been with her through the entire voyage, there was no need to explain anything. Isabel had seen it all as it happened.

Kate, on the other hand, had a knack for extracting details almost before Kathleen realized it. Her manner was calm and forthright; and while understanding, she did not eminate the stifling pity Kathleen felt from others. Kathleen knew her elderly grandmother loved her and was there any time Kathleen might need her, but Kate had never been a weak person and she would not encourage her granddaughter to become so.

Kathleen's Uncle William would rather have taken a beating than approach her on the subject of Reed's will, but it had to be done, and the sooner it was accomplished, he decided, the better.

"I didn't even know he'd had one drawn up," Kathleen said in a stunned whisper.

William looked sheepish. "He came to me when he decided to go to war. 'Just in case,' he said."

Kathleen swallowed hard. "Just in case," she echoed.

Clearing his throat, William straightened the papers before him. "Ahem. Now, Kathleen dear, as you may have guessed, Chimera is bequeathed to your son Katlin, under your guidance until he reaches his majority. Generous amounts are specified to be set aside for Andrea's needs and her dowry. There is also a yearly stipend for Mary and for you.

"In addition—and quite unusually I might add—he has left the shipping firm entirely to you." He shook his head in puzzlement, but Kathleen understood completely. Reed was returning to her all that she had brought to him—the shipping company and all the frigates Kathleen's father had left her upon his death.

"Sweet, arrogant scoundrel!" she croaked, choking back a sob. "Heaven forbid he should die in debt to me!"

William looked uncomfortable at the sight of her tears. "Might I ask what you will do with the ships and the firm, Kathleen?"

"Why, I shall run the company myself, with Ted's help, Uncle William," she said without hesitation. "I do hope Ted has not been made to worry over his position with the firm."

"No, no, that hadn't occurred to any of us, dear girl. Our concern was solely for you. We thought perhaps it would be easier on you to sell it and let someone else take the responsibility."

Kathleen laughed rather cynically. "I might be able to sell the ships for a profit to a privateer right now if I wanted, but with the blockade so tight, the shipping industry is not exactly at its height. With all respect,

Uncle, I probably couldn't *give* the firm away right now. No, I'll keep it. I have reliable help. Trade will pick up after the war, and someday my children will inherit it from me.''

A week after she had arrived home, Kathleen ordered all the bedroom furniture removed from the master suite and stored in the attic. It had been decorated to Reed's taste before their marriage in a striking Oriental design of bold reds and blacks. She had always thought the unusual decor suited him so well. Now it was a unique form of torture just to enter the room. His ghost seemed to linger there. Each time she opened the door, she expected to see him standing at the double doors to the veranda, looking out over the plantation, or flung across the wide bed, exuding that fatal, virile charm. The very air still carried the scent of his cologne and cigars. His personal items were still strewn about the room atop the dressers and tables, and his clothes remained in the closets and drawers.

At night, as she lay alone in the immense bed, the room throbbed with the essence of his presence, yet echoed with emptiness. Memories assaulted her all night long, and she replayed in her mind every conversation that had taken place within these walls; every sigh, every kiss, every moan of ecstatic lovemaking that this bed had witnessed.

Kathleen knew that if she did not exorcise his spirit soon, she would go stark, raving mad. That was when she ordered Reed's things stored in the attic. By the time she had finished redecorating, the room looked entirely different, which was her intention. The walls had been painted a deep autumn gold, with a brown and gold patterned Oriental rug and cheery yellow curtains and bedspread. The warm patina of cherry wood welcomed

Kathleen to the moderate-sized tester bed, flanked by cherry nightstands. The matching dresser and armoire were filled soley with her clothing, and against one wall stood her mirrored dressing table. A pair of delicately carved chairs with lemon-colored cushions sat on either side of a small round table. The room reflected only Kathleen's taste. At last she began to sleep decently, though there were still times when she would awake from a deep sleep and swear she had heard Reed's voice or felt his touch. She would still sometimes think she smelled his tangy cologne or cigar, or the musky male scent of his skin.

Reed's private study was another room almost impossible for her to enter. It was so totally masculine and so achingly Reed, with its comfortable leather furniture and gigantic desk. Mementos of Reed's travels lined the walls and tables, and a life-sized portrait of him hung above the fireplace.

For some reason, Kathleen was reluctant to disturb this room. While she did not want it to become a shrine to his memory, she could not find it in her heart to remove his things. What books and records she needed, she transfered to the smaller office behind the main staircase. Then she closed and locked the study door.

The only other item she took was a hand-crafted miniature of the *Kat-Ann,* a birthday gift to Reed from her. It was an exact replica of the ship so dear to both of them, and though she feared she was only prolonging her agony by having it near, she placed it atop the small table in her bedroom. It gave her a strange comfort to see it there—to be able to reach out and touch it in the night. Though she told herself she was being foolish, it was almost like touching a part of Reed in some way.

As time went on, Kathleen's anger, though still there

and very real, was now directed against the British, who had caused Reed's death. Had Reed not felt compelled to defend his country, his life would not have been in danger. Daily she cursed the English. What more could they take from her? Her estate in Ireland now belonged to that poor excuse for a peer, Sir Lawrence Ellerby. They were responsible for the death of her husband. The more she dwelt on it, the angrier she grew. Her wrath became like a canker that ate at her constantly. A fierce desire for revenge was spawned almost without her realizing it, and seemed to nourish itself upon her anger. Bitterness sharpened her tongue and narrowed her tip-tilted green eyes. Her appetite deserted her, and the sharp points of her cheekbones stood out prominently in her thin face.

In desperation, Kathleen immersed herself in running the plantation and shipping line. When she could find no work at home, she took up the reins at Emerald Hill. Kate's sad, wise eyes followed her granddaughter with sorrow and understanding. With the wisdom of her years, she knew Kathleen needed to find peace in her own way, in her own time. She just prayed that the girl would not ruin her health in the process.

It was during this time of restless energy and building resentment that Kathleen brought Reed's black stallion, Titan, to Emerald Hill.

"I can not find the time to excercise him properly," she told Kate. "It breaks my heart to see him confined so much of the time, since no one but Reed and me could ever ride him. He will tolerate no one else on his back, the princely rogue! Besides, I know you will think I am mad, but I think that horse misses Reed every bit as much as I. He stands so forlornly, as though he's awaiting his master's return. I can't bear to see it."

Kate shrugged. "Animals sometimes sense more than people realize. There is nothin' so strange in thet."

A rare smile tugged at Kathleen's lips. "I thought it might cheer him up if we put him with a few of the mares."

"Put him t' stud?" Kate asked, intrigued. Years before, she had sold Titan to Reed. The stallion was part of Emerald Hill's prestigious stock, and therefore of excellent bloodlines. "Aye," she nodded. " 'Tis a wonderful idea!" With a twinkle in her green eyes, she chuckled. "Thet certainly ought t' perk up his—er—spirits alright!"

"You are a leprechaun in a grandmotherly disguise!" Kathleen laughed. "Where is the dignified leader of society hiding behind that outrageous humor of yours?"

Kate smiled benignly, glad to have made Kathleen laugh. It was so extremely rare these days.

Kathleen was conspicuously absent from all social functions that fall. Not only was it inappropriate for a newly widowed woman to go out in society, but Kathleen simply was not interested. Even those few functions she might have gone to, such as the church social and sewing circles, she declined. Sunday mornings found her in the Taylor pew with her two small children, but afterward she returned to Chimera. Often, invitations to Sunday dinner were forthcoming from friends, but aside from an occasional meal at Susan's or Barbara's, she politely refused them all. The only exception she made was to hold a small party for the children in honor of Alexandrea's fourth birthday.

Everyone thought the "young Widow Taylor" was taking her loss extremely hard. They had been used to her ready smile, her tinkling laughter, her vivacious love for life; and it was difficult to compare this thin, withdrawn woman in black with the lively girl she had once been. The life seemed to go out of her with Reed's death; the glow was gone from her once-dazzling emerald eyes. Where formerly she had been the first to flaunt convention, she now seemed content to retreat into her widowhood. If she was a little sharp with well-meaning friends, they understood her deep grief, for they knew how much she and Reed had loved one another.

All the same, there were several of her former suitors who hoped she would soon recover, for when her period of mourning was over, perhaps the lovely widow would once more grant them the favor of her smile—and to some lucky man, perhaps her hand. In the meanwhile, they shook their heads and said, "What a pity! What a shame! All that youth and beauty gone to waste, hidden behind drab widows weeds and tears."

They would have been shocked indeed, to see the lovely Widow Taylor on the anniversary of her beloved husband's birthday. Early in the day, she locked herself in Reed's study, refusing either to come out or open the door to anyone. Della found her lunch tray untouched outside the door.

By late in the afternoon, Isabel and Mary were getting worried. There had been no sound from inside the study for hours, and Kathleen refused to answer their knocks and pleas to come out. Finally, not knowing what else to do, Mary sent for Kate.

Kate had not been inside Chimera for two minutes when the oddest sounds began issuing from behind the study door. Perplexed, the three women went to stand in the hall outside the room. Loud, off-key singing, interspersed with riotous laughter, rent the air.

They looked at one another dumbfounded. Then a wide grin split Kate's features, and she began to chuckle. "Saints alive! The lass is stinkin' drunk!"

"She is *what?*" Mary gasped.

Kate nodded. "Soused t' the gills, if I'm not mistaken, and most likely on Reed's best bourbon."

Isabel leaned against the wall, weak with relief. "Thank God! I was afraid she had hurt herself!"

"Nay, but she'll be hurtin' come tomorrow mornin', I'll wager," said Kate sagely.

Slouched in Reed's favorite chair, Kathleen was sipping from the bottle. When she depleted her repertoire of Irish ballads, she switched to the bawdy tavern songs and chanteys she'd learned from her roughneck crew.

Mary cringed in embarrassment, but Kate and Isabel, at least, saw the humor in the situation. They felt sorry for Kathleen, knowing how hard this particular day was for her, and they knew she would regret her binge the next day. It was humorous until her giddy laughter and raucous singing turned to uncontrollable sobs. The click of the glass from behind the door betrayed her search for yet another bottle of forgetfulness.

"Tryin' t' drown her sorrows, poor darlin'," Kate murmured sadly.

"It doesn't sound as if it is working," Mary sighed.

"It never does for long," Kate supplied.

Kathleen did, indeed, feel dreadful the following day. Her brief moments of forgetfulness had departed with the anesthetizing effects of the liquor. Now she was left with a throbbing head that felt inhabited by a thousand drummers. The high voices of her children pierced her brain like a band of bagpipes, and the light of the day nearly blinded her with its lancing rays. Foul-tasting fuzz coated her tongue, and her stomach lurched at the smell of the mildest of foods.

"Moderation in all things," Mary counciled, as she commiserated with her that morning. Following Kate's advice, she handed Kathleen a small glass of bourbon.

"Ugh!" Kathleen gagged. "I do believe I've had more than enough of this!"

"Kate swears it will help," Mary informed her. "It was your Grandfather Sean's cure for overindulgence—that and a generous helping of fresh air."

That was Kathleen's first venture into the blessed oblivion to be found in strong drink. While she never again indulged to that extent, she did resort to a hefty helping of brandy to relax her nerves before going to bed. Soon she had doubled that amount, as well as increasing her intake of wine at dinner. Before long, her mint julep in the afternoon became two, and sometimes three.

The liquor seemed to ease the pain that was her constant companion, and she soon came to depend on it. Her appetite had diminished, and if she often drank more than she ate, she took little notice. Those persons closest to her noticed, however, and were deeply concerned. Of course, it was a closely guarded secret how much the "young Widow Taylor' drank. It would never do to set the whole of Savannah gossiping.

Thanksgiving came and went without the Taylor family finding much to be thankful about, though if she had thought about it, Kathleen might have been grateful for quite a few things. Her children were healthy, intelligent, energetic youngsters. Grandmother Kate was still active and well at the ripe age of seventy-one. Her family and Isabel were always ready and willing to help her in any way possible. The crops were abundant and being harvested on schedule; and they had been fortunate enough to get them loaded aboard her ships and past the British blockade. They would bring good prices this year. None of her remaining ships had been sunk or permanently damaged. Even the weather had held, affording Kathleen the continued comfort of her daily rides about the countryside. On her palomino stallion, she would gallop about the estate, racing over fields and trails, easing the tensions of both horse and rider. After a breathless run, Kathleen would turn Zeus loose in a meadow and find a secluded spot to nurse her heartache.

More and more often, Kathleen found herself heading Zeus toward the seashore, where she would sit on a knoll or a ledge of rock and stare out upon the endless, restless waters of the Atlantic. As in days past, she was once again experiencing that feeling of unity and closeness with the hidden complexities of the deep. The rhythm of the waves and the constant pull of the tides and currents brought comfort to her soul.

As she had resolved her anger at Reed, so she absolved the sea of its part in his death. She could no longer hold anger in her heart for the two great loves of her life. Here she gained a measure of peace and strength once more, and here her resentment of the British strengthened and grew. The need for avenging Reed's death became a passion, and a litany in her brain. The desire to feel a deck rolling beneath her feet and her rapier in her hand became an immense ache within her. Each time she was drawn to the sea, her yearning to sail and wreak revenge on the British renewed and fed upon itself, until it blocked out all reason and every other emotion.

"I've got to go. *I have to go.*" The phrase repeated itself in her mind until she thought she would go mad.

The restlessness of the sea called to the restlessness in her blood, and Kathleen knew she could not deny its call much longer.

She did manage to resist until the Christmas season was over out of love for her children. The holidays were a trial and torment for her as she recalled past Christmases with Reed. This year there were no special gifts of love from him, nor loving presents from her to him. The holidays lacked luster without his broad, crooked smile to grace them and the sparkle of his blue eyes to lend them merriment. That exact smile and those glittering blue eyes were echoed in Katlin's elfin face, and it was a knife in Kathleen's heart to behold them. Love and resentment; pride and sorrow, warred in her each time she looked at her darling son. She feared the day might come when she might actually despise him for resembling his father so perfectly.

This thought added to her resolve to get away, if only for a while, until the heartbreak eased to a tolerable level. Perhaps once she had sunk a few British ships and sent a few hundred Englishmen to their own watery graves, the score would be even. Maybe then she could learn to live with her memories and not awaken with Reed's name on her lips. Maybe then she could face her small son and not flinch in agony, but see him for himself as well as a living extension of Reed. Perhaps there would actually come a day when she would not weep, or turn a dozen times a day to say something to him, only then to feel his absence tenfold.

Kathleen decided to return to Grande Terre, and made her plans accordingly. Contacting Dan, she had him conceal the *Starbright* in the hidden cove she had used years before. Once again she ordered Dan and Finley to assemble a loyal crew, and to disguise the *Starbright* beneath green paint and sails. She would join Jean as the piratess Emerald, not so much to hide her identity from the world, but from herself. These days, it was extremely painful to be Kathleen Taylor, Mrs. Reed Taylor, or the "young Widow Taylor." Something inside herself cried out to reject this sorrowful person completely; to hide in her other identity. Emerald was bold, beautiful, outrageous in word, dress, and manner. There was nothing she dared not do, no place she dared not go. She was as free as the wind, and bold as brass. Her prowess with ship and rapier was known far and wide, and she had become a legend on the high seas. Kathleen needed to be this free, wild person once again. And she needed her revenge almost more than she needed air to breathe. To this end, she set about transforming herself. From Kate she obtained another batch of black hair dye, and from the depths of her old sea chest, she retrieved the green vest and cut-off trousers that had been Emerald's scandalous attire.

None of her family or Reed's, except for Kate, had ever known of her short reign as Emerald, though they had heard tales of the piratess and marveled at her escapades. She did not tell them now, nor of her plans to return to this identity. She did not mention Grande Terre, or Jean and Dominique to anyone but Isabel and Kate, though the others knew these friends of Reed's by other names. Instead, she told them only that she was going away for a while on one of her ships, asking them to be patient with her. She would return in time. Last, she begged Mary to take good care of her children; to tell them daily that she loved them, and to talk to them often of Reed so they would not forget their father.

Only to Kate and Isabel did she confide the truth. Kate

wearily accepted the inevitable, knowing Kathleen's stubborness well. Isabel promptly told Kathleen that she intended to go along. She, too, would become a pirate and wield her sword alongside Kathleen.

"I wonder if your eagerness stems from a desire for my company, or from a desire to see the devastating Dominique again," Kathleen teased.

Isabel flushed furiously, but refused to rise to the bait. Instead, she packed a bag and prepared to leave with Kathleen.

On the day of their departure, Kathleen stood once more aboard the *Emerald Enchantress,* staring long and hard at her reflection in the mirror. Gone were the sunny red-gold tresses, and in their place hung a heavy curtain of long ebony hair, making her emerald eyes seem brighter. They would be even more so once she acquired a sun-kissed tan on her pale face. The skimpy vest, without a shirt beneath it, gave a tantalizing view of her cleavage, and the short trousers barely covered her buttocks. Comfortably worn black boots rose to her knees. Rapier, pistol, and knife completed her outfit.

Gone was the woeful image that had met her gaze constantly in her mirror at Chimera. Gone was Kathleen—here was Emerald. Welcome, Emerald—beware Britain!

Chapter 12

For months Jean had wondered how Kathleen was managing. He worried about her state of mind, and thought of her constantly. While he hoped to see her again, he never dreamed it would be so soon. Neither did he expect her to arrive as Emerald. When his look-out informed him that the famed green frigate, the *Emerald Enchantress* was entering the bay, he was astonished. Shortly thereafter, the raven-haired beauty greeted him.

"Hello again, Jean," Emerald/Kathleen greeted him, coolly extending her hand.

Gallantly, he bowed, lightly touching his lips to her fingertips. "Welcome, Kathleen—or should I say Emerald? What brings you back to Grande Terre?"

"I have come to join your privateering operation, if you will have me. If not, I shall sail on my own behalf, as I did before," she said boldly. They talked as they walked toward Jean's house, Isabel and Dominque following behind, exchanging their own greetings and bits of news.

"May I ask what led you to this decision, *cherie*? I thought never again to see the *Emerald Enchantress* sail these waters."

She met his gaze directly, fire in her eyes. "Revenge, Jean—purely and simply, revenge. I intend to sink every English vessel I can. They are responsible for Reed's death, and I am going to see that they pay dearly for the grief they have caused me and my children!''

Jean looked slightly baffled. He hoped Kathleen's mind had not become unhinged by grief. ''But, Kathleen, the *Kat-Ann* went down in the storm. The British had no control over that.''

Her eyes spat green flames. ''They had *everything* to do with it! If they had not caused this war, there would have been no exchange of prisoners, and Reed would not have been in the area where the storm occurred.''

''I see.'' Jean nodded his understanding of her feminine logic. ''What I do *not* understand is your appearance once more as Emerald. Why change the *Starbright* back to the *Emerald Enchantress*? As the *Starbright*, she was already legitimately registered as a privateer, which she is not as the *Emerald Enchantress*,'' he pointed out.

''Could you not get me a letter of marque, as you do for your own vessels?'' she countered.

''Easily, but you have evaded the true issue. Why are you hiding yourself behind Emerald's identity once more?'' He was determined to pin her down to an answer.

Her chin went up in defiance, and she answered honestly, ''Because I cannot bear the pain of being Kathleen Taylor, Reed's widow.'' Her eyes closed briefly against her private anguish. ''Do you know, Jean, that I can barely stand the sight of my own son because he looks so much like Reed? I had to get away—away from home, where everything reminds me of Reed—and away from myself and the miserable, drab person I have become.''

She squared her shoulders in a brave gesture that tore at Jean's heart, and forced a smile. ''It is easier to lose myself entirely in her identity. Besides, can you see the proper

212

Widow Taylor prowling the seas and creating havoc with the British fleet? Oh, it would never do—never do at all!" She rolled her expressive eyes heavenward. "Only Emerald can boldly issue her challenges and wield her sword. Only she would dare to wreak her revenge in as bloodthirsty a manner as I intend to do. For I intend to give no quarter, Jean." Her eyes were hard with hatred. "The sea will be a watery coffin for many an Englishman before my soul is satisfied. The British have taken much from me, and I intend to make them pay dearly."

"As well they should," he agreed. "I welcome you into the fold, *cherie*. Welcome to the notorious, if over-rated, society of the Brethren of the Coast!" As if to officially mark her membership, he took her face between his palms and solemnly kissed her on both cheeks.

"Thank you, Jean." Her voice was husky with gratitude. "Thank you for not judging me, as many would do."

He smiled and said nothing, though privately he thought, "Never, my love, could I judge you harshly."

Not everyone was as pleased as Jean and Dominique at having Kathleen and Isabel join their ranks. Though almost all had heard of Emerald, some preferred to think that the piratess's prowess was greatly exaggerated. Then there were those men who simply resented having women claim to be as proficient as they in a traditionally male arena.

There was at least one man who disliked Kathleen's presence for totally personal reasons—Pierre Lafitte. Years ago, he'd sworn vengeance on her for slicing open his sword arm and nearly causing him to lose it. Twice, he had

213

attempted to force his attentions upon her. The second time, Jean and Dominique had prevented him from accomplishing his goal. In fact, they had not only helped Kathleen escape, but had threatened to break every bone in his scurvy body if he ever tried it again.

Now it seemed he would have to put up with her on a permanent basis. Pierre knew how protective Dominique was of her, considering her his adopted sister. Now Dominique had found a second wench to impress; the little Isabel, and Pierre knew Dominique would have his head if he dared harm either of them.

To make matters worse, Pierre had not failed to notice the looks Jean was giving Kathleen when she was not aware of it. Jean was acting like a lovesick pup. No one ever dared take what Jean claimed as his, and these days he had a very proprietary gleam in his eye when it came to Kathleen. As much as Pierre knew his brother cared for him, he also knew Jean would brook no interference here. Whenever Pierre's hatred of Kathleen rose like bile in his throat, he reminded himself that no one crossed swords with Jean and emerged unscathed.

Kathleen's attitude underwent a major change as she projected herself into the bold, free personality that was Emerald. Her eyes flashed with new life, and her skin, quick to turn golden under the sun, took on a glow of vitality. That captivating smile was more in evidence these days, though often tinged with cynicism. Her tinkling laughter joined that of the others more often. Her very stance and walk emanated confidence and determination. Isabel also noted that Kathleen was no longer drinking as she had at Chimera.

Dominique, in a magnanimous gesture—and as an excuse to be in close contact with Isabel—volunteered to act as Kathleen's first gunner. Guessing his amorous intentions, Kathleen accepted his offer. Dominique was one of the best gunners to be had, and Kathleen welcomed him to her crew.

Jean, having never had much contact with Kathleen as Emerald, was at first reluctant to let her go off on her vengeful jaunts alone. Never having seen her in action, he wanted to evaluate her abilities first-hand before he turned her loose without his aid. Therefore, he suggested that their first venture be a joint effort, the *Pride* sailing as consort to the *Enchantress*.

Kathleen had to chuckle to herself at Jean's concern, but if he needed to be convinced, she would not argue the point. It was comforting to know that someone cared so about her safety. Then, too, two vessels against a British sloop-of-war were more assured of victory.

To further raise her spirits, Dominique presented Kathleen with a parrot. His dark eyes sparkling with merriment, he chuckled, "No pirate worth his salt should be without one!"

"Then where is yours, Dom?" she countered saucily.

"Why, I expected you to share old Peg-Leg here with me, of course."

"Peg-Leg?" she echoed. "Where on earth did you acquire this colorful creature, may I ask?" Kathleen was entranced with the bird's bright red, gold, and green plumage.

Dominique's grin was pure deviltry. "I think I will let you guess. Believe me, Peg-Leg will give you plenty of clues in short order."

"Why is he called Peg-Leg?" Isabel asked, eyeing the bird curiously.

Dominique shrugged. "Because he stand on one leg so

much of the time, I suppose.''

''That would stand to reason,'' Jean chuckled dryly. He thought he recognized the bird from a tavern in New Orleans much frequented by rowdy seamen. He was glad Dominique had come up with the idea, but he wished he had been the one to think of it. At any rate, the parrot was sure to be company for Kathleen in her most lonely hours, and he was sure she would appreciate the bird's unusual repertoire of choice words and phrases.

That first night, with Peg-Leg aboard his perch in a corner of her room, Kathleen began to converse with him as she undressed for bed. ''You are a pretty bird,'' she told him.

''*Dirty bird!*'' he squawked.

''*Pretty* bird,'' she corrected.

''*Dirty bird,*'' Peg-Leg repeated.

With a shake of her head and a chuckle, Kathleen completed undressing. Nude, she reached for her nightgown. A lewd whistle split the air, and made her stop stock-still. Her mouth wide open, she whirled on the bird. ''Did you do that?'' she asked him accusingly.

She could have sworn it winked at her. As she turned once more to gather up her nightdress, the bird whistled suggestively once again.

''I'll be switched!'' Kathleen swore in amazement. Tugging her gown over her head, she climbed beneath her bedcovers, giggling gleefully. ''You're right, Peg-Leg. You *are* a dirty bird! Wait until I get my hands on that Dominique!''

January sped by as the *Emerald Enchantress* and the *Pride* traversed the seas, seeking their British prey. Once in a while they would strike a Spanish vessel, primarily for

Jean's benefit. Jean nursed a lifelong hatred of the Spanish, and as he pointed out to Kathleen, it had turned into a very lucrative venture. While there was no profit in attacking British warships, there was much to be gained in carrying off Spanish booty. Kathleen didn't mind, for it helped to pay her crew as well as Jean's.

Their primary objective, however, was English vessels. They encountered their first target just days from Grande Terre. When the British sloop realized she was heading directly toward not one ship, but two, she turned tail and ran. Kathleen and Jean gladly gave chase. The *Emerald Enchantress* being the faster ship, Kathleen swung a wide arc around the enemy sloop, keeping well out of range of her guns, and cut her off from the fore. Meanwhile, Jean closed in from the rear. Thus they both avoided the sloop's dangerous broadside shots, and neatly sandwiched her between them before she could maneuver quickly enough to do any damage.

Kathleen took great pleasure in noting the apprehensive looks as the British saw that both attacking ships flew, not the stars and stripes, but the Jolly Roger. The well-known skull and crossbones had long been a symbol of pirates, and sent fear racing along the stiffest spine.

Rapier at the ready, Kathleen boarded the sloop, Finley close behind. It was her policy, and one she advised her crew to follow, to fight in pairs. In that way, each man had a partner guarding his back. It was a strategy she'd adopted early, and it had served her well.

Bowing to Jean's leadership, she let him deal with the British captain, choosing for herself the quartermaster. The tall, thin man towered over her as she faced him defiantly. Her first advantage was plain to see, as he stared at her obviously feminine form in the calculatedly revealing outfit. After the first shock came the leering, lustful look she had learned to expect.

As she brought up her rapier in challenge, she called clearly, "*En garde!*"

A wide, stupid grin crossed the quartermaster's face. "I'll be! A Frenchie!"

"Wrong, button-brain," she replied caustically. "Now present your weapon, or die like a dog. I care not which."

The man's smile immediately melted into a scowl. "You asked for it," he growled, bringing up his own blade.

The man's expertise with his weapon was practically nonexistent. Within seconds, she had disarmed him, wounding him severely on the thigh.

Her next opponent was little better. It was not until she faced her third Englishman that she was offered any challenge. As she met his first lunge and parried it, a thrill ran through her. Here, at least, was a man who knew one end of a sword from the other. He thrust again, and she skillfully counterparried. A series of graceful sidesteps kept Kathleen safely out of harm's way as she parried his swings and watched for his weaknesses. A quick feint, and she had him lowering his guard. Her blade found his heart with unerring accuracy. It was a clean kill for a worthy opponent.

When the fighting was over, Jean had efficiently taken the captain out of action, and many others lay dead or wounded. The remaining men surrendered fearfully. Even Isabel, in her first actual battle, had held her own, Dominique guarding her fiercely.

With grim satisfaction, Kathleen watched the bodies tossed overboard. Not for one moment did she allow regrets. Instead, she thought of Reed, and felt more than justified. This was the price men paid when they chose to go to war. One did not kiss one's enemy on the cheek and wish him well.

It had been decided that any undamaged vessels they captured would be divided evenly between her and Jean. This first prize would be Jean's, sent to the Grande Terre. The next would be Kathleen's. She had already decided that half of her share of captured ships would be added to her private fleet and sent on to Savannah. The other half she would offer to the government in Reed's memory to help build up the United States Navy.

"Kathleen, I watched you meet your last opponent," Jean stated. "You were excellent! You never took your eyes from his for a moment."

Kathleen calmly nodded. "Thank you, Jean, but your praise is too high when the competition was so poor."

"It was enough for me to see that Dominique and Reed did not exaggerate your skills. No wonder you disarmed Pierre so easily that day long ago."

"Not so long ago that Pierre has forgotten his hatred of me, Jean," she pointed out.

"No, but he will do nothing about it now, *cherie*. True, he is without many morals, but Pierre is not stupid."

"I am not worried. I can defend myself."

"Where do we go from here?" Jean asked, including her in the decision. "Why don't you show me where you hid the *Emerald Enchantress* when you were stalking Reed so diligently?"

Kathleen laughed up at him. "Jean, a lady never tells all her secrets," she teased.

An answering light made his hazel eyes glow with an emotion more than mere pride. For a moment, they stood before one another as a man and a woman, and Kathleen felt the pull of his charm. For the first time in months, she felt like a woman, if just for a few seconds, and it confused her. She saw the desire flare in Jean's eyes, and her reaction was totally feminine. Wordlessly, he was telling her she was beautiful and desirable.

For a moment she stood mesmerized by his heated gaze. Then she turned from him in confusion and shame. There had been a time after she had first met Jean, when Kathleen had recognized the immediate attraction between them. She had admitted then that if she had not been so madly in love with Reed, she might have been drawn to Jean's dynamic masculinity.

Now Reed was dead, but it was much too soon for her to be able to acknowledge any feelings for Jean. Loneliness was creating this ache within her, and her traitorous body wanted to be held close in strong arms. Kathleen told herself to ignore the physical desires welling up within herself for the first time in many months. Guilt that she was feeling these things rose up in her and stained her cheeks a bright pink. Though Reed no longer stood between her and Jean, his memory was sweet, and his loss far too bitter as yet. Reed did not stand between them, but his ghost did.

Jean saw the confusion on her face as she turned from him, and cursed himself for allowing his desire to be so obvious. He knew it was too soon, and he hoped he hadn't frightened her. He did not want to set her running from him just when he was hoping to lure her nearer little by little. Hope rose as he recalled that tiny spark of answering desire she had involuntarily shown. With patience, she might yet be his.

He reached out to brush an inky curl from her hot cheeks. "*Cherie,* you have not answered my question. Will you show me your secret hideaway?"

Gathering her wits and her nerve, she faced him once more. "Of course, Jean," she answered steadily. "There is no great cause for secrecy now; no reason you should not know of it."

They sailed to the southern tip of Florida, to the area called the Florida Cayes—or Keys, as the Americans were prone to say. Here, amid moss-draped islands, Kathleen showed Jean her favorite hiding place, a small bower in which a ship could remain completely unnoticed while able to secretly observe a goodly area round about. It was superbly located to view one of the primary passes into the Gulf, a route heavily traveled by ships voyaging to and from Louisiana and Mexico.

Jean was duly impressed. "You chose very well, *petite.* No wonder you always seemed to catch Reed unaware. You had only to wait and let him come to you."

"As we have only to wait, like spiders in a web, to catch the unsuspecting British," she stated grimly.

This they did, capturing three English vessels in as many days. Two of the British ships were badly damaged in the fray, and were sunk. The third Kathleen sent to Grande Terre, later to be sailed to Savannah.

While awaiting their prey, there was much time for leisure. The friends passed the time with amiable talk and challenging card games. This suited Jean well, as it threw Kathleen more intimately into his company. Dominique was of a similar opinion, getting to know Isabel better each day.

As time went by, Kathleen was becoming quite attached to the outrageous parrot. The bawdy bird followed her everywhere, spouting epithets and choice phrases. It soon became apparent that Peg-Leg had a taste for rum. He was also hopelessly addicted to fresh scones when he could get them. When forced to eat dry biscuits instead, he complained loudly. He could say his name, and after hearing Dan address Kathleen often enough, Peg-Leg soon began calling her ''Cap'n Kat.'' An incorrigible flirt, he was constantly winking and whistling and squawking, ''Kiss me, sweet!'' His extensive vocabulary included many salty phrases learned from the sailors who had frequented the tavern. ''Blow me down!'' and ''Shiver me timbers!'' were two of his favorite sayings. He was a colorful bird in more ways than one, and provided Kathleen with many a laugh. Peg-Leg had several modes of transportation, none of which included much exertion of flying. Often he could be seen traversing the deck atop Dom's arm or Finley's hat, when he was not perched on Kathleen's shoulder. Even Dan sometimes grudgingly allowed the bird to ride on his head. Peg-Leg's prime target was often the ship's cat—it was riotous to see the poor, befrazzled cat streak by, Peg-Leg clinging victoriously to its back, squawking and pecking with glee.

At first Isabel wanted nothing to do with Kathleen's ludicrous pet, but Peg-Leg gradually won her over. ''He's a crazy bird, but he *is* entertaining,'' she admitted. ''However, I am glad he is yours and not mine. Invariably he says something embarrassing at just the wrong time!''

Kathleen finally convinced Jean into letting her sail the *Emerald Enchantress* from their hidden bower for brief scouting forays. When she encountered a British vessel, she would make sure the *Enchantress* was seen, then turn tail and run, the English in hot pursuit. She led them straight back to Jean, where she, Jean and their crews would jointly pounce. After half a dozen ships were taken in this area, the privateers wisely decided to move on. Even the British, as dense as they could be at times, were sure to send a convoy sooner or later to investigate the disappearance of several of their fleet. As experienced as the crews of the *Pride* and the *Enchantress* were, they were not so foolhardy as to face a number of British vessels at once.

They wandered up the western Florida coast toward Mobile and New Orleans, where they harassed the British blockade along the southern coastline. When they sighted a ship by itself, either the *Pride* or the *Enchantress* would try to lure the enemy further out to sea and attack in force. This worked well, netting them three ships—until they lured a lone British sloop into the open, only to be discovered by a second British warship as they were attacking the first. Suddenly the British outnumbered them by half again their crew.

Jean, his eyes bright with the light of battle, turned to Kathleen. "Well, *ma petite piratess*, shall we make a run for it or stand and fight?"

"I'll never run from an English dog if I stand the slightest chance of beating him! We shall fight, *mon capitaine!*"

And fight they did. This time Jean stood at her back, and they cut a wide swath through the enemy swarm. The thrill of combat sang in her veins as her rapier flashed in the sunlight, scoring strike after strike. Her eyes sparkled like polished gemstones, and her throaty laughter rang out in chorus with the clash of steel meeting steel.

Triumph lent impetus to her blade even when her arm grew weary under the weight of her sword.

Kathleen was at her finest that day. Her nimble feet and agile moves were both graceful and deadly, and the sword in her hand seemed directly propelled by her brain, reacting instantly to its commands without the slightest hesitation. She could see the surprise on her opponents' faces when they first found themselves squared off against a woman, and sensed their initial reluctance to fight a female; but her flashing blade soon convinced them that they were fighting for their lives. This delicate-appearing creature fought like a man, and had no qualms about sending her blade into their flesh. A few of the men she faced threw out coarse comments, but she remained unruffled by their obvious baiting. Her shrewd eyes assessed them contemptuously, and her laughter rang clear as she threw herself into the business of defeating them. Kathleen was enjoying herself thoroughly. A few of her opponents were worthy of her skills, issuing just the challenge she needed to keep her senses sharp. She and Jean were a striking pair to behold. Their finesse was marvelous, and their success was an inspiration to their fellow crewmen.

Isabel, always under Dominique's watchful eye, was gaining confidence in her own abilities and displaying excellent swordsmanship. Her courage and daring made up for any skills she had yet to master, and her mind flew as fast as her feet and her sword. Her spirits were undaunted as she fought with fierce determination. Dominique's pride in her knew no bounds as he fought beside this vivacious pixie who had stolen his heart.

By the end of the battle, both English ships were theirs,

though one was too badly damaged to salvage. Only three of their own men were wounded, none seriously. A victory celebration was definitely in order.

Chapter 13

After this triumphant bout, they headed back to Grande Terre, where they left their ships and boarded pirogues for a trip to New Orleans.

The two women decided that the journey called for wearing dresses. Certainly they could not traverse the streets of New Orleans in their sailing togs. For the first time in months, Kathleen regretted having to wear mourning garb, but she had brought with her only two black dresses. Telling herself that her widow's weeds did not fit Emerald's flamboyant image, Kathleen promised herself a new gown or two from the elite establishments of this famed city.

The one blot on their adventure was that Pierre had decided to go along, supposedly to see his children and wife. While Pierre did visit with his family, too often he chose to accompany the others—mainly to annoy Kathleen, she was sure. In front of his brothers, he was unfailingly polite, but at opportune moments he would make barbed comments to Kathleen, and she could feel his hatred simmering under the smooth surface of his deceptive smile. At such times, Kathleen drew comfort from the feel of the dagger strapped securely to her thigh beneath her skirts.

It seemed Jean knew nearly everyone in New Orleans,

and everyone knew him. Most of the French and Creole population adored him, as well as some of the American inhabitants, though a few, including Governor Claiborne, distrusted and publicly maligned him. As they toured the city, Kathleen saw first-hand evidence of the governor's enmity. On nearly every city block was displayed a "wanted" poster. Governor Claiborne had posted a reward of five hundred dollars for the capture and arrest of Jean Lafitte.

Immediately alarmed, Kathleen turned to him. "Jean, we must go back to Grande Terre!" She reached out to lay her hand upon his sleeve. "I would never have come if I had known you were endangering yourself. You could be arrested at any second!"

Had he been in actual danger, Jean could not have cared at that moment. It would have been a small price to pay to see Kathleen's concern for him, and to feel her delicate fingers curled about his arm. His own hand moved to cover Kathleen's; hers seemed to burn like a brand through his shirt and set his blood racing.

"I thank you for your concern, *cherie,* but do not upset yourself. Those notices mean nothing, I assure you. It was a ploy that failed, for I roam the city freely and no one bothers to turn me in. As you see, the citizenry of New Orleans love me. I bring the goods they want so badly through the British blockade, and they would hate to do without their luxuries." Jean waved to a merchant as their carriage rolled slowly past a store.

Dominique laughed. "Yes, and see there!" He pointed to a notice on a nearby fence. "Jean has his own ways of dealing with the illustrious governor."

Upon reading the sign, Kathleen burst out laughing. Jean had posted bills of his own, offering a reward of

228

fifteen hundred dollars for the capture and delivery of Governor Claiborne to him at Grande Terre. "I do not believe this!" she gasped in amazed delight. "Jean, you have a wicked sense of humor!"

"It is a game we play, the governor and I," Jean explained with a grin. "So far I am ahead, and Claiborne is pulling his hair out."

Jean took them shopping, refusing to let either Kathleen or Isabel pay for any dresses and accessories they bought. "Jean," Kathleen complained prettily, "you are making me feel like a kept woman!"

Though he knew she was teasing, a note of seriousness tinged his answering comment. "Would that be so terrible, *cherie*?"

Their eyes locked in a private moment of communication, until Kathleen tore her gaze from his and turned away, blushing uncomfortably.

Being set loose among the shops of New Orleans was like the best of Christmas wishes. Beautiful lacy gowns adorned the windows; lovely, delicate parasols in the sheerest of fabrics were irresistible; satin slippers and reticules in every shade imaginable beckoned.

"This is heavenly," Isabel sighed rapturously, sniffing at yet another scent in the exclusive perfume shop they had discovered. "I can't recall when I last had so much fun!" Isabel, over the past year, had shed so much of her reserve that the vivacious raven-haired young woman now resembled the girl Kathleen had first known. But there was a maturity about her that only added to her charm. Isabel's dark eyes sometimes reflected hard-earned self-respect and painful secrets, even while they flashed with renewed life and laughter. Isabel's recovery was nearly complete; however, Kathleen's had barely begun.

It was unthinkable to be in New Orleans and not visit her dear friend Eleonore. Eleonore was delighted to see her, inviting both Kathleen and Isabel to stay with her while they were in town. Kathleen was torn between her desire to be with Eleonore and an unwarranted feeling of disloyalty to her friend because of Jean's obvious admiration for herself. Not for the world would she cause pain to Eleonore, wittingly or otherwise.

Seated over tea in Eleonore's parlor, the three women conversed. "I am so sorry for your loss, Kathleen," Eleonore sympathized. "You loved one another so much! I can only guess at the pain you feel."

Kathleen shook her head in sudden despair, her eyes filling with tears. "Eleonore, I can not imagine anything hurting more. For a long time I refused to believe it was true. I was so *sure* Reed was still alive—I spent months searching for him, and not until we discovered the wreckage of the *Kat-Ann* did I accept the reality of his death."

Eleonore nodded in understanding. "Jean told me; and now you are back at sea, once again the famed Emerald. Why?" Eleonore was one of the few who had known about Kathleen's adventures as Emerald years before. Though Eleonore had been Jean's lover at the time, she had applauded Kathleen's escapades, and aided her in numerous ways.

"Revenge," Kathleen answered shortly. "What else? Revenge against the British for causing this war in the first place; this war that took Reed from me forever!"

Eleonore sighed sadly. "I, too, am awaiting the end of the war, so that I might sail once again for France. For months a great homesickness has assailed me. I would give anything to be home again on French soil."

"It is my turn to ask why, Eleonore? New Orleans could nearly be a city in France—so much of its culture is here. The architecture, the language and customs, the people, all reflect their French heritage."

"True," Eleonore agreed, "but it is not the same. In ways, it only makes me more homesick, reminding me of what I miss."

Kathleen hesitated, then asked, "How much of this homesickness has to do with Jean? Did he break your heart badly?"

Eleonore laughed softly. "Ah, Kathleen! How can I explain to you, who were so desperately in love with Reed, how different it was between Jean and me? Yes, I loved Jean, and he loved me in his way, but it was never as it was with you and Reed. From the start, we knew our affair was a temporary thing. We shared our lives and our passions with none of the usual jealousies of lovers. It was a time when each of us needed the comfort and companionship the other offered. We were friends as well as lovers. Now the spark of passion has faded, but the friendship lives on. It was an exciting interlude, and since it has ended, neither of us has regrets. We enjoyed what we shared; we shall treasure the memories; and we meet and part as dear friends, now and always."

"But you were so good for each other—so special together," Kathleen argued.

Eleonore shook her head, her gentle brown eyes holding Kathleen's. "Jean and I both need more than the other can give. It is better this way. Jean cannot give me what I desire."

231

"What is that, Eleonore?"

"I want to go home to France, where I hope to find a husband on my own social level—perhaps a count or a marquis." Eleonore's face took on a dreamy look. "You can not imagine how I have missed being a part of that elite circle of society at court! There is a special excitement and intrigue that is particularly addictive. I love it."

"It is distinctly lacking here, I must agree," Isabel put in. "These Americans take democracy very much to heart. In many ways, that is good, but there is a certain grandeur missing."

"Quite so, Isabel," Eleonore affirmed, "and besides Versailles, there is a special splendor unique to Paris. How I long to walk its streets again; to shop with old friends and stop at a little *café* for *croissants* and coffee when we are done; to visit the *galaries*."

"And catch the eye of some very eligible bachelor?" Kathleen teased.

"But of course!" Eleonore declared. "Before I am too old, I wish to have children." Her eyes became dreamy. "We shall have a townhouse in Paris for the social season, and the rest of the year we shall spend in our country chalet raising babies and grapes. My husband will adore me, and we shall be very happy."

"I hope your dream comes true, my friend," Kathleen said sincerely. "I shall miss you when you leave."

"As I shall miss you," Eleonore returned. "We have shared so much. We shall write, as we have since you went with Reed to Savannah. The letters will take just a little longer to reach their destination. You must come and visit me in France. We will sit up late into the night after everyone else has retired, and share memories that only the two of us could guess at, *n'est-ce pas?*"

Kathleen nodded, and Eleonore added with a laugh, "And when I am an old woman, I will take my grand-children on my lap and tell them tales of pirates and the wild adventures I have known in younger years, and they will wonder if their *grand'mère* really did all those amazing things or is merely addled in her old age!" With an odd gleam in her expressive eyes, Eleonore continued, "I will especially tell them of a certain piratess and the men who loved her, both as Kathleen with the flaming red hair and flashing green eyes, and as Emerald with her midnight tresses flying in the ocean breeze." After a small pause, she said softly, "Jean loves you, Kathleen. I can see it in his face when he looks at you."

Kathleen swallowed hard. "I do not *want* him to love me, Eleonore. I do not want to hurt him—and I don't want to hurt you."

"You wouldn't be hurting me," Eleonore insisted. "On the contrary, it would make me very happy to see you and Jean together. You see, Jean needs a strong woman who shares his love for the adventurous life. You would be perfect for him!"

Tears glistened in Kathleen's eyes. "Don't match-make, Eleonore," she choked. "It is too soon. It may always be too soon, loving Reed as I have."

"Perhaps *now* is too soon, but you are a young woman. You have many years ahead of you, and there is no reason all of them have to be empty—or filled only with memories of happier times. Do not close your heart and mind to loving again, Kathleen," Eleonore counseled. "Your children need a father to guide them, and you need a man in your life; someone to fill your days and hold you in the long, dark hours of the night. Jean could be that man. There has been a spark between you from the first. I believe it is still there, beneath your pain.''

Kathleen groaned in dismay, covering her face with her hands. "Is it so obvious, Eleonore? When Reed was alive, it was so easy to ignore this attraction. Now, so soon after Reed's death, I hate myself when I feel the pull of Jean's charm. I choke on my guilt, yet I feel drawn to him against my will. And Jean is becoming increasingly obvious about his feelings for me. He is kind and gentle, and was so helpful in my search for Reed . . . his patience amazes me.''

"The man adores you," Isabel corrected. "His devotion increases daily. It is plain to anyone who has eyes that the man is totally enthralled by you. Eleonore is not the only one to notice this.''

"Then it should come as no surprise to you when I say that Dominique is equally entranced by *you*, Isabel," Kathleen countered. "Are you ready to return his love?''

Isabel frowned. "I am not sure, but that is not the point.''

Kathleen disagreed. "It amounts to the same thing, Isabel. Jean no longer bothers to conceal his emotions for me. Sometimes, my heart tells me one thing, and my body another.''

"Your conscience is too active," Isabel stated. "Reed is dead, while you and Jean are both very much alive and attracted to one another. There is nothing wrong in that.''

"Isabel is right," Eleonore added. "You last saw Reed in early May. That was nine months ago. Your official period of mourning will end shortly, and no one would condemn you for starting life anew and loving again. You are so young, and it is natural to reach out for love and joy.''

"I didn't learn of Reed's disappearance until July," Kathleen pointed out. "Besides, Reed was the great love of my life. Surely I could never love Jean as I did Reed, and I could not cheat Jean that way. It would not be fair to him at all."

"Has it ever occurred to you that you could love Jean perhaps *differently* than you loved Reed?" Eleonore suggested gently. "Perhaps it would not be with all the wonder of first love, but with the warmth of a tender, abiding sharing. Each love is unique, bringing its own excitement and splendor. This I tell you from experience, my friend. It is possible to love more than once in a lifetime; deeply, wholly, and wonderfully."

"I do not want to think if it now," Kathleen said firmly. "All this talk of loves lost and found is depressing and confusing. Let us talk of something else." Her eyes brightened suddenly as she set her mind on a different tack. "Better yet, let's put on our prettiest new gowns and go to the theatre, just the three of us!"

"Ah, yes," Eleonore sighed appreciatively, as Isabel nodded vigorously. "Let us go tempt the gentlemen of New Orleans until they are out of their minds with desire for the three most elusive women to be found anywhere!"

They raised their teacups in smiling salute to one another. "To New Orleans' three *femmes fatales!*" Kathleen's eyes sparkled once more. "Long may they reign!"

Isabel added her own wicked merriment. "To beauty, charm, and feminine wiles. Long may they triumph!"

"Amen!" laughed Eleonore.

One incident alone marred Kathleen's introduction to

New Orleans. Quite by chance, she happened upon a jeweler's establishment while strolling with Jean one afternoon. The display in the window, small as it was, was enough to draw her attention to its fine workmanship. Intrigued, she wandered into the shop to see more of the merchandise, Jean at her side.

"Monsieur Lafitte! How nice to see you!" the jeweler greeted him effusively.

"Mr. Lovit, how is business these days?"

The man shook his head dismally. "Slow, as it will probably remain until the blockade is lifted."

"We are trying our best to encourage the British to go home," Jean told him. "A few blockade runners are still getting through."

Mr. Lovit suddenly brightened. "That reminds me— your friend, Captain Taylor from Savannah, has not been in to pick up the last necklace I made for him. Would you tell him it is ready, when you see him? I thought he had said he wanted it in time for Christmas, but I must have been mistaken."

Kathleen grabbed for the counter as her knees threatened to give way beneath her. A strangled cry alerted the jeweler to her paper-white face, as Jean's strong arms went about her.

"*Cherie*, take a deep breath. I am here." Jean's soothing voice was the only reality that registered through the shock she was feeling.

"Can I get your lady something?" Mr. Lovit offered hastily. "A chair? A glass of water?"

"The necklace . . ." Kathleen gasped.

"What?" Jean barely heard her words.

Taking a deep breath, Kathleen blurted, "The necklace, Jean. Tell him I want it."

The jeweler had heard her request. "Oh, but madame, this necklace is not for sale! It is for Captain Taylor's wife —made especially!"

Jean's arms tightened about Kathleen, as if to support her against the impact of his next words. "Mr. Lovit, Captain Taylor died last spring. This lady was his wife. The necklace was meant for her. Please bring it."

"Oh, dear!" the man exclaimed, thoroughly distressed. "I am so sorry, madame! I will bring it right away!" He scurried off to the back room.

Kathleen was battling tears and gulping great lungsful of air. "Kathleen, *cherie,* do you wish to sit down?" Jean suggested.

Suddenly she turned into his embrace, her face hidden against his shirt front. "Oh, Jean!" she whimpered. "Please hold me. Just hold me!"

With a tenderness that would have amazed his enemies, Jean complied. "As long as you will let me," he whispered so low that she thought she must have imagined the words.

The necklace the jeweler brought forth was an exquisitely designed collar of intricately carved ivory. Between the top and bottom bands of beads lay three carved letters spelling the word KAT. On each side of the name were three delicately detailed frigates. When worn, the name would be centered on her throat, the ships riding in silhouette against her skin. Since they were first married, Reed had been bringing home necklaces such as this for her. They had become Kathleen's own distinctive symbol, each different in design, but each fashioned as a collar to fit snugly about her throat. Upon presenting Kathleen with the first, Reed had jokingly commented that every green-eyed "Kat" should have a collar, and over the years he had ordered many from this very jeweler.

Now, as she lightly touched the beautiful crafted ivory, Kathleen trembled. "It feels so strange, Jean, to know that Reed ordered this for me so long ago. It seems ironic that his last gift should by symbolic of ships, don't you think? Do you suppose he somehow felt that something would go wrong? Could he have had a premonition of doom?"

"I think you are imagining more than you should," Jean counciled. "Reed knew your love of ships and the sea. That is all there is to it."

"You are probably right," she said on a sigh. "Still, it makes one wonder . . . "

Turning to the jeweler, she asked, "How much do I owe you?"

Still embarrassed, and looking quite pained, the man answered, "Your husband paid in advance, Mrs. Taylor. The necklace is yours."

Later, Kathleen would ponder whether the man had told her the truth, or had merely let her have the necklace out of pity. She even entertained the possibility that Jean might have gone back later and paid the jeweler, but she never asked him. Either way, she cherished this final gift from Reed, despite the fresh pain it brought.

With Jean as escort, and sometimes Eleonore, Isabel, and Dominique, Kathleen saw much of New Orleans in those few days. They went shopping, to the theatre, visited Jean's warehouses, and even attended a couple of dinner parties. As luck would have it, Governor Claiborne was also invited to one of the parties.

From the moment Jean arrived, Kathleen on his arm,

the tension rose, until the very air seemed to vibrate. Behind exaggeratedly polite facades, Jean and Claiborne dueled verbally, pointed remarks finding their targets more and more often. Fortunately, the other guests were used to this, and tended to ignore it. Certainly, it was no secret that the two men disliked one another.

Shortly after their arrival, the governor openly inspected Kathleen, his eyes roving appreciatively, if speculatively, from her raven head to her satin-clad feet. Having cast aside her mourning, she was wearing a magnificent emerald satin gown, with a daringly low neckline. Her midnight tresses were swept up onto the crown of her head, to fall in a profusion of artfully careless curls. About her throat, the ivory collar rested as possessively as a lover's hand.

Kathleen saw the admiration in Claiborne's eyes—as well as the disdain he could not quite hide.

With a sidelong glance at Jean, Claiborne commented slyly, "Where is Eleonore this evening, Lafitte? Could this beauty on your arm be the reason we have seen less of you these days?"

Kathleen felt the muscles of Jean's arm beneath her hand tighten, but he answered lightly, "This curiosity about my life never fails to amaze me. It seems almost that others know more about what I do than I—or they think they do."

Claiborne's attention centered on Kathleen. "You have not introduced us, Jean." His fingers came up to lightly stroke the ivory letters on her necklace. "Kat, is it?"

"Caterina," Kathleen supplied tightly, standing her ground. This man raised her hackles, and she deliberately used Isabel's Spanish version of her name. Her eyes swept the man before her with a disdain equal to his.

"Caterina Emeraude," Jean said, adding the French word for Emerald. This bit of private humor set Kathleen's eyes glimmering with laughter, and curved her lips upward in a beguiling smile.

"Caterina, may I present our esteemed governor, William Claiborne." Jean completed the introductions.

The governor bent low over her hand, kissing her fingertips. "You must be a newcomer to our fair city. I do not recall ever having seen you before, and I am sure I could not have forgotten someone as attractive as you."

Kathleen extracted her hand as unobtrusively as possible. "This is my first visit to New Orleans," she replied coolly.

"I hope you are enjoying your stay," Claiborne persisted. "Where are you from?"

Kathleen's chilly gaze speared him. "If I wished you to know, I would have volunteered the information, Governor," she told him with regal scorn.

Claiborne glared at her, his voice raised to carry to the ears of the other guests. "Gossip has it that you are Jean Lafitte's new light-o'-love, madam."

Several people gasped at Claiborne's ungentlemanly conduct, and Jean nearly leaped at Claiborne's throat, but Kathleen's hand, firmly on his arm, held him back. Flaming emerald eyes met Claiborne's challenging look squarely, and she managed a careless shrug. "I rarely put much stock in gossip, Mister Claiborne. Wagging tongues reflect the dull minds of those with unexciting lives and little imagination. I am much to busy to be bothered with the opinions of small-minded persons.''

Amidst the indrawn breaths of the fascinated on-lookers, Kathleen stared victoriously at the red-faced governor.

Jean's delighted laughter rang out clearly in the silence surrounding her words. ''Aptly put, *cherie,*'' he chuckled, leading her away from the irate, speech-less governor.

Thus it was that Kathleen discovered herself believed to be Jean's latest mistress. Governor Claiborne and his sycophants seemed to be the only ones to berate her, however, as most of the people she met were friendly and outgoing. No one else dared question her relationship with Jean, and many simply did not care. They accepted her as she appeared to be, a beautiful, intelligent, well-mannered lady of obvious refinement. Her ready wit and enchanting smile endeared her to them, and her quick mind and reserved demeanor earned their respect.

While she did not bother to refute the gossip about herself and Jean, neither did she do anything to fuel it. Knowing they would believe what they wished, she doubted there was much she could actually do about it. If she protested too loudly, it would only make people believe the tale all the more, so Kathleen went about as if none of it disturbed her in the least.

Actually, she was very upset. Not that she gave a whit what the citizens of New Orleans thought, for she might never meet any of them again. For herself and her own most private feelings, she was deeply concerned, however. That old, deeply buried attraction toward Jean was coming more and more to the fore. There was no denying that she found him extremely handsome. His old-world charm was tremendously hard to resist, particularly when it was combined with his devil-may-care attitude. She had seen him in the role of the cultured gentleman and that of the daring corsair, and admired him in both. His unsurpassed expertise with sword and ship had won her undying respect.

All this she could admit, and not find fault with. What troubled her now were her own feelings and longings rising to the surface—her own reactions to Jean's disturbing presence. At times, she would turn to find his eyes on her, hot with desire, and her heart would leap in response to the urgent message in his eyes. His hand would reach for hers, and the contact would set her nerves tingling until her hands would actually tremble. If his arm brushed her breast, her skin would feel seared. His tender smile would bring an answering curve to her lips, his devilish humor set her laughing. His arm about her shoulders or waist was comforting and disturbing at the same time, confounding her further.

She and Jean had so much in common. At odd moments, Kathleen felt she had known him forever, and at others, not at all, especially when he was silently imploring her to become a part of his life. Not by spoken word or overbearing advances did he press his suit, but she felt his ever-present desire—exactly as he intended.

While Kathleen held him off with one hand, a part of her wondered what he would be like as a lover. For these thoughts, she berated herself severely, constantly reminding herself how deeply she and Reed had loved one another, how much they had shared. With shame, she told herself that a woman so recently widowed as she should not be entertaining thoughts and feelings of this sort toward another man. It was too soon. It was too much. Oh, Lord, it was so confusing—so tempting—so wrong—so increasingly hard to resist!

Chapter 14

Kathleen was under a great deal of pressure, and her nerves drew taut. Torn between an attraction she could not deny yet did not want to give in to, and an irresistible longing to be held in the arms of a man who cherished her, she wavered between despair, shame, and an uncontrollable desire she heartily wished would dissolve.

The strain of constantly fighting her conflicting feelings led her to be much more bold and daring when they at last returned to sea. It was as if she were daring death to claim her, laughing in the face of Fate, tempting the dark spirits to touch her. In her outrageous fearlessness, it was as though she were thumbing her nose at danger and flirting with death in the most impudent manner possible.

It made Jean cringe to watch her. She took the most outlandish chances, sometimes deliberately letting her guard down in battle, then fending off her enemy's sword scant seconds before his blade could find its mark. Her defiant laughter, quite unlike its usual merry tinkle, would dance across the waves, causing gooseflesh to rise on many a neck. Her feet were nimble, her body fluid, her emerald eyes fever-bright as her rapier flashed. Not a movement was wasted, not one foe spared.

Word of the bold piratess was once again spreading across the Gulf and Caribbean. Tales of her prowess and daring circulated throughout the islands and along the coasts. That she gave no quarter was certain. Fellow pirates admired her, many jealous of her skills and awed by her fierce vengeance. All feared her, even those few who dared to dispute some of the most amazing of the tales about her. None wished to be on the receiving end of her anger and her swift, singing blade. Some had begun calling her the Angel of Vengeance; the Enchantress of Death.

Even Pierre, in his intense malevolence, had to admire Kathleen's courage and skill, however grudgingly. Her extreme daring drew a reluctant regard even from her most implacable enemy, though Pierre took care to conceal his admiration lest she sense a weakness in him and taunt him for it.

Jean and Kathleen were becoming the most notorious and feared marauders of the seas. Their monumental success lay, not solely in their famed mastery of fighting skills, but their varied and innovative methods of capturing enemy vessels. They never concentrated their efforts in any one area for long, thus lessening the chances of their own capture.

As the weeks wore on, the ease of their success made Kathleen even more daring. Dominique and Jean were horrified when she decided that while the *Pride* and the *Emerald Enchantress* would remain hidden, she would dress in a revealing cut gown and launch out alone in the dinghy, pretending to be the only survivor of a shipwreck. Kathleen played her part to perfection, but the dinghy had drifted further away from her hidden frigate than she had calculated, and the British sloop that ''rescued'' her nearly made off with her on board before Jean and Kathleen's crew could arrive in the very nick of time.

On the heels of that escapade, she and Isabel hatched an

equally dubious scheme. This time, Isabel was to be the lure. Gowned in a torn, bedraggled dress, she was to pose as a lone woman marooned on an island. Standing on an open stretch of beach, she would be easily spotted (though the two ships concealed nearby would not). When a vessel dropped anchor to save her, the *Pride* and *Enchantress* would rush out and capture their prize, with no danger to Isabel at all. This ploy worked so well that they used it several times afterward, though Isabel complained that it took her out of the thick of the action. This suited Dominique quite nicely. Though he had to admit that Isabel could protect herself well, and fought as well as many men, he found his heart lodged in his throat each time she faced an armed opponent. The very thought of her being harmed caused the blood to curdle in his veins. Wisely, he kept his worries to himself, enduring the pains of the damned in his own private hell. As Isabel strove to improve her abilities and prove her worth, he loomed protectively over her like a burly watchdog, silently daring anyone to harm the woman he loved.

Isabel was softening in her attitude toward Dominique. On the rare occasions when he was not guarding her back, she missed his powerful presence. Since she had come to understand how gentle he was with Kathleen and with her, she had ceased to notice his ugly scars, seeing only the tender man behind the fierce countenance. Beneath his rollicking sense of humor, she discovered a sensitive, intelligent gentleman. By no means ready to let down her guard completely, Isabel was nonetheless beginning to admire the gentle giant who so openly offered his heart and his friendship.

While they were yet at sea, St. Valentine's Day arrived. Kathleen was totally unaware of the date, until she awoke to find a note and a small gift on the pillow beside her head. The gift proved to be a twenty-dollar goldpiece strung on a gold chain. The note contained a beautiful poem, painstakingly authored by Jean, which conveyed his feelings for her, while not being too flowery in tone. Kathleen was both touched and dismayed. She spent a long while writing him a note to thank him for his thoughtfulness, at the same time trying not to encourage his attentions, nor to hurt his feelings.

St. Valentine did not forget Isabel, either. From Dominique she received a book of sonnets. On the foreword page, in Dominique's large scrawl, there read simply, "To my dearest Isabel—Always, Dominique—February 14, 1814."

Their encounters at sea were not always handily won victories. A few times, they nearly ran headlong into neatly set British traps. Immediately before these near-disasters, Kathleen always felt unnaturally uneasy, as did several of the others. Especially sensitive to invisible warnings in the air, Peg-Leg would hop irritably about, unable to settle on a perch. He would squawk and flap his wings, his tail feathers drooping pitifully. As soon as Kathleen became aware of the relationship between his unusual behavior and the occurence of a hidden trap, she came to rely on the parrot as an advance warning system. Peg-Leg and his antics served her crew well, saving their skins several times. Never again did any of the crew complain that the bird was a nuisance. Rather, he became their good-luck charm.

Not long after the middle of the month, a monumental change came about quite by chance, in the middle of a fierce battle with the crew of a Spanish brigantine. The crew were well-trained in defense and determined to defend their cargo. Kathleen had just defeated her expert challenger, when a sword came skittering across the deck to land at her feet. As she glanced up, she heard a triumphant cry in Spanish, and immediately knew one of her own men was in danger. The sight that met her eyes was a jolt, indeed. Pierre's gaze left his lost weapon to cling to hers for a fraction of a second. In that single, brief glance, Kathleen and Pierre measured the situation and one another. Then Pierre's attention was forced back to the armed enemy before him. Despite his slovenly appearance, Pierre was still fast on his feet. Nimbly he eluded his opponent's thrust, dancing gracefully out of reach of the sharp blade.

For mere seconds, Kathleen debated with herself. Now was her opportunity to be rid of Pierre's threatening presence forever. She could simply let the Spaniard take care of the problem, and no one could point the finger of blame. Even as she thought this, her conscience told her that if she let Pierre die, she could never face Jean or Dominique again. Regardless of his faults, they still loved their brother.

Swiftly, she bent and retrieved the weapon at her feet. Timing her moment, she called out sharply, "Pierre!" The sword left her hand before the single word was completed, sailing through the air toward the man who most wished to see her dead. Pierre caught the weapon deftly, immediately swinging into action. Minutes later, his opponent lay dying on the deck.

The battle was soon over. As Kathleen stood assessing the situation, Pierre approached her. "You saved my life. Why?" he stated boldly.

"Is this your way of thanking me?" Kathleen inquired dryly, meeting his gaze.

"Yes, I am grateful, but I am also wondering why you did it. Certainly, I never expected you to come to my aid."

"If you are saying you did not deserve my help, I agree with you," she snapped.

Pierre smiled. "*Touché*, Madam Piratess. The fact remains, you saved my life regardless of our differences these past years. I cannot honestly say I would have done the same for you."

Kathleen laughed harshly. "I may live to regret it."

But Pierre disagreed. "No! You have placed me in your debt, and I find myself in the position of having to repay you."

"What are you saying, Pierre?"

"You need not fear me any longer. My anger has spent itself."

Again, she laughed. "At the risk of reviving it once more, I must tell you I have *never* feared you, Pierre."

Pierre shrugged nonchalantly. "So you say. Still, I think it is time we become friends."

Kathleen eyed him skeptically. "Just what does being 'friends' entail, Pierre? I seem to recall a time when your desire to be 'friends' resulted in near-rape and a duel with Reed that nearly cost his life!"

Pierre waved a broad hand. "That is the past." Then he smiled ruefully. "Perhaps I was a bit overzealous, but my brothers would have my head if I tried the same thing now —particularly Jean. Besides, I no longer see you in the same light as I did then. I was judging you by the same measure as the other women I had come to know about the island at that time. After you nearly destroyed my sword arm, I was determined to see you pay for my pain."

"You brought it on yourself when you tried to stab Reed in the back," Kathleen reminded him.

"I did not look at it like that then," he admitted.

"And now?" she insisted.

Again he shrugged. "Now is too late to concern myself with the right or wrong of past deeds. Today I offer you my friendship—nothing more. I wish to forget the hatred between us and fight together as allies against a common enemy."

"Forgive me if it is difficult for me to trust your words, Pierre," she said dryly.

"I shall prove that you can trust me," Pierre insisted. "I owe you my life, and it is not a debt I take lightly. From this day, I shall fight at your side and join my brothers in seeing that no harm befalls you." He offered his hand. "Friends and allies?" he proposed.

For long seconds she stared at the proffered hand. Then she looked him straight in the eye. Gone was the usual glare of hatred and lust. His hazel eyes reflected only an honest, genuine gratitude that rang true. Slowly her hand met his strong grasp. "Friends and allies," she repeated, then added for good measure, "Do not give me reason to regret this decision, Pierre Lafitte, or you need not fear your brothers. There will be little left for them to do after I have finished with you!"

"I will keep it uppermost in my mind," he said with a wide grin, then sobered. "But you need not worry. When Pierre gives his word, he keeps it."

Later, Dominique cornered her. "What was all that between you and Pierre earlier, Kathleen? He wasn't giving you trouble, was he?"

Kathleen grinned. "No, my friend. In fact, Pierre has decided that we should bury our animosity and join forces. He offered me his friendship."

Kathleen enjoyed the amazed look that crossed

Dominique's features, knowing the feeling well. "Friends?" he echoed.

"So he says."

"Why?" Dominique demanded, a deep frown creasing his tanned forehead.

Kathleen chuckled. "I suppose it has a lot to do with the fact that I saved his worthless hide this afternoon."

"Why?"

She laughed outright. "Is that the only word you are capable of, Dominique?" she asked.

"It is just that this turn-about is so sudden," Dominique explained, shaking his head.

"Which? My saving Pierre's life, or Pierre wanting to make amends?"

"Both!" Dominique exclaimed.

"Well, to ease you confusion, I must confess I helped Pierre only because he is your brother, and I could face neither you nor Jean if I deliberately let him be killed," Kathleen told him. "Now I must hope it was not a mistake on my part. Pierre swears he will prove that I can rely on him."

Dominique mulled this over. "I, too, have doubts, but once Pierre swears his allegiance, he is fiercely loyal. I fear you are stuck with him, *cherie*. He will defend you to the death."

"Yes—but mine or his?" Kathleen wondered aloud.

"Time will tell," Dominique said. He lounged against the ship's rail, eyeing Kathleen speculatively. "Speaking of time, *ma petite amie*, how long are you going to leave Jean dangling? He is very much in love with you. I have not seen him so taken with anyone since his wife Rachel."

Kathleen groaned. "Everyone seems determined to

throw me into Jean's arms! The world is full of match-makers these days—even you, Dominique!''

"Don't you care for him at all?" Dominique asked gently.

Kathleen sighed and leaned her elbows on the top rail, staring deeply into the waters below. At length, she spoke. "Yes, Dominique, I care for Jean, but I have no right to do so. Guilt and shame are eating me alive!''

"Because of Reed?" he asked.

Kathleen nodded. "I feel I am being unfaithful to Reed, even though he is forever gone from me. Others tell me I am foolish to go on feeling this way, but I cannot seem to help myself. I loved him so much!''

Dominique's arm came comfortingly about her shoulders. "I know you did, little sister. What you are feeling is entirely normal, but you cannot let it destroy the rest of your life. You seem to forget that Reed and Jean were the closest of friends. Do you honestly think Reed could condemn you for finding love again with his best friend? Reed loved you, and he was like a brother to Jean. Would he not wish for both of you the happiness you deserve?''

Tears swam in her emerald eyes. "I don't know, Dominique! It seems I know very little these days—except that I am thoroughly confused. It just seems too soon.''

"Perhaps time is the remedy to this dilemma also,'' Dominique suggested. Then he laughed mirthlessly. "I am hoping it will solve my own problems with Isabel, as well.''

"There is always room for hope, Dominique, and with patience you can win Isabel, I think,'' Kathleen said.

"As Jean will win you?" he asked.

"I don't know. I just do not know. There is so much to consider, and I need time to think."

From that day on, Pierre became one of Kathleen's most staunch defenders. Even Jean was surprised at the loyalty his brother displayed. It soon became apparent to everyone that this was not merely a passing fancy. He took his debt to her very seriously, and devoted all his considerable energies proving his trust and friendship. Kathleen could not have shaken him loose from her shadow if she had wished to. Now that she was finally assured that Pierre's offer of friendship was not a trick, and that he had overcome his lust and desire for revenge, she found herself growing to like him a little. His loyalty was admirable, his laughter contagious, and his cock-of-the-walk attitude amusing, though he hid his intelligence beneath a slovenly facade. While Jean maintained the image of a gentleman privateer, Pierre preferred the role of ruthless pirate, playing the part to perfection, and loving it.

After a month at sea, they decided it was time to return to Grande Terre to allow Jean to catch up on business there. The island was every bit as beautiful as Kathleen remembered it. Vividly colored flowers and birds delighted the eye, and delicate butterflies flitted among the blossoms and greenery. Soft sea breezes wafted floral and tangy ocean scents. Puffy white clouds dotted the brilliant blue sky, and the sun sent down its blessings nearly every day. If Eden was half as lovely as this tropical paradise, Kathleen thought Adam and Eve must have deeply regretted losing it. For the first time since Reed's death, Kathleen was fully appreciative of the beauty about her. It was a spectacular place, indeed—one she had come to love during her short stay here with Reed just after their wedding. With the overpowering beauty came the pain of remembrance; but it was a bittersweet pain, and she bore it gladly. With poignant heartache, she recalled their time together in this tropical paradise so right for young lovers.

Passing the tavern and warehouses on the docks, she remembered how she had found Reed with Rosita and been so blindly jealous. At the slave arena, she stood imagining the night it had been transformed for the fiesta, and she had entranced Reed by dancing for him. Walking by the bay, she remembered Reed's amazement when she had rescued the beached dolphin and frolicked with it in the water.

Nearly everywhere on the island, sweet memories assaulted her, but most of all along the sandy shore where she and Reed had often strolled on sun-dappled days and moonlit nights. Her heart yearned for him so in this idyllic heaven of bright colors, soft scents, and balmy breezes, that Kathleen almost fancied Reed alongside her. Often she felt that if she should turn suddenly, she would find him there; tall, dark, and so achingly handsome, his blue eyes out-sparkling the sea. . . . Lying on the sun-warmed sand, she could almost feel his presence as she vividly recalled their lovemaking on this very spot. If she closed her eyes, she could feel his touch, his lips blending with the light caress of the sea breeze; hear his deep voice and loving laughter over the chatter of the birds. It was both torment and joy as she relived her precious memories one by one and made Reed come alive once more.

Unlike her first visit to Grande Terre with Reed, this time Kathleen resided in Jean's house instead of one of the cottages nearby. His home was large, airy, and comfortable. Though not overly opulent, it was decorated with taste and a sense of understated dignity that seemed a perfect reflection of its owner. The furnishings were of the finest quality, with several notable paintings and *objets d'art* casually displayed. One look was enough to tell anyone that Jean's wealth had been used to provide comfort and a warm, welcoming atmosphere.

If Jean's self-indulgence was obvious anywhere, it was in the private gardens behind his house. There, between carefully tended flowers and hedges, was the most fantastic collection of statues to be found anywhere. All were representations of sea gods and goddesses, and Kathleen had been thoroughly enchanted with them from the first moment she had set eyes upon them. Now she was at leisure once more to study them to her heart's content, and when she tired of that, there was the rest of the entrancing island to fill her senses with its soothing balm.

Once Kathleen was accustomed to the idea of being Jean's guest, she relaxed and began to enjoy herself. Jean was propriety itself, the perfect model of the gracious host. In no way did he attempt to take advantage of the close proximity of their living arrangements, or his position of absolute power on the island. Unobtrusively, he saw to it that all Kathleen's needs were met, her slightest wish anticipated, but otherwise he assumed an attitude of watchful, hopeful waiting.

The third day of their much-deserved indolence was interrupted by the abrupt arrival of a special courier. They were just sitting down to the midday meal when the lookouts sounded the alarm, sending a message that two British warships were anchored just outside the mouth of Barataria Bay. A dinghy with a lone messenger was on his way into the Bay at this moment.

Everyone was instantly alert, but Jean had an idea what

the courier would have to say. "I have been approached twice before by the British," he told Kathleen. "They wish to form an alliance with me and my men against the Americans. If they can enlist my aid, their way will be clear to attack New Orleans and close off the Mississippi River completely to all trade. From there they could control the western front all along the Mississippi, from New Orleans practically to Canada."

"What have you told them, Jean?" Kathleen inquired curiously.

"So far, we have been playing a game of cat and mouse, both sides very cautious. I have tried to warn Governor Claiborne of the imminent threat of British attack, but the stubborn jackass will not take anything I tell him under serious advisement. Meanwhile, I continue to entertain the British envoys, hoping they will relax their guard enough to reveal some of their plans and provide us with time to defend New Orleans against them."

The messenger arrived with a request that Jean receive two naval officers of His Majesty's Royal Navy. Jean wrote a note of reply, granting the interview and inviting the gentlemen to dine with him later that evening.

"Let them cool their heels for a few hours," he said cheerfully. "After all, they are here to ask favors of me, and it is never wise to appear too eager to please."

"Your policies of negotiation intrigue me, Jean. I get the distinct impression there is much I could learn from you," Kathleen responded, her eyes bright with admiration and approval.

"Someday I would love to teach you all I know, *cherie*," he answered, watching her blush as she absorbed the dual meaning of his words.

"Shall we dress for dinner?" Isabel inserted into the

awkward silence.

Jean's attention never wavered from Kathleen's face. "No. I should like to see their reactions when they find themselves confronted with two bold and beauteous female pirates. That should shock them to the soles of their very proper English boots, don't you agree?"

Kathleen's eyes sparkled in answering deviltry. "Shall I dredge up my convincing British accent while I am about it?" she suggested, her nose tilted into the air.

"Quite so, my dear," Jean laughed, aping her accent.

Kathleen and Jean were standing at the open veranda doors when the British officers arrived. A servant showed the two men into Jean's spacious salon. As Jean left her side, the guests took note of her presence for the first time, and stopped stock-still in a momentary lapse of protocol. Forgetting their manners, and apparently stunned speechless, they stared openly, taking in the astounding sight before them.

Kathleen stood proudly before their avid inspection, the bold piratess Emerald in all her glory. She laughed inwardly as their disbelieving eyes took in her brief green vest, the front lacings creating enticing shadows in the cleft between her breasts. The matching breeches barely covered her bottom, revealing long shapely legs encased in high black boots. Her rapier hung ready at her side, suspended by a wide sash tied about her hips. At length, their eyes retraced their route, taking in the gleaming black mane streaming in abundant waves to her waist, the huge golden earrings resting near each sunkissed cheek, the perfection of her delicate features. Finally their gaze met her tip-tilted emerald eyes, sparkling with haughty daring. One fine dark eyebrow arched in wordless challenge as she raised her wine glass in a saucy salute.

"*Ahem!*" Jean cleared his throat loudly, drawing the men's attention to himself at last. A smile twitched his lips as he shot Kathleen a quick glance. "I realize Emerald can quite take one's breath away at first meeting, but I shall be glad to introduce you when you have sufficiently recovered."

Stepping forward, he offered his outstretched hand to one of the men. "Captain Percy, it is my pleasure to greet you again." His glance slid questioningly to the other officer, a stout stern-looking older man.

Percy hastened to perform his duty. "Mr. Lafitte, may I present Admiral Lowe of His Majesty's Royal Navy."

Jean chuckled and said dryly, "Ah, the last time we met, you came accompanied by a colonel—this time, an admiral. Should I consider this a compliment or a threat, I wonder? Just how badly do you want my services?"

"That is what we have come to discuss with you, Lafitte," the admiral stated gruffly. His gaze cut to Kathleen, watching nearby. "Privately," he added in a gratingly superior tone, his lips curling in distaste.

Deliberately, Jean let a silence fall before he spoke quietly and firmly. "Gentlemen, may I present Emerald, one of the finest captains on the sea, and my partner." (He stressed the word "partner.") "Anything you wish to discuss with me, you may say to her also." With these words, Jean set the tone of the evening, leaving no doubt in the admiral's mind just who was in charge not only on the seas, but in Lafitte's home.

"Yes, well, that is certainly your right, Lafitte," Admiral Lowe backed down reluctantly, "but you needn't pretend that this—uh—*woman* is anything more than your doxy." The man laughed curtly, nostrils distended disdainfully. "Who would actually believe she is a sea captain?"

"Who, indeed, but half the population of the Caribbean?" Kathleen put in, a sneer curving her lips.

The admiral stiffened upon being addressed by this outlandish creature. As though she were not present, he continued to Jean, "Tell me, Lafitte, which of your vessels does she command?"

"None of them," Jean answered. Before the admiral's superior "Aha!" could be heard, Jean went on, "She has her own fleet, the most noted of which is the *Emerald Enchantress.*"

Captain Percy's eyebrows rose at this, and his gaze swung swiftly to meet Kathleen's.

"You seem to have heard of me, Captain Percy," she purred.

His eyes narrowed as he admitted as much. "Your name is bandied about in every port tavern from here to Barbados. It *is* you they tout so tirelessly, is it not?" he questioned.

"The one and only," came her bold answer.

Admiral Lowe was frowning. "Word has it you are a pirate," he accused.

Kathleen gave him her cat smile. "Word has it correctly," she taunted silkily.

Jean laughed. "Gentlemen, you are two of the few to ever face Emerald, the famed and ruthless piratess, who will live to speak of it!"

Captain Percy was eyeing her speculatively. "Could it be," he ventured, "that this—er—*lady* could be responsible for the losses we have been incurring lately in the Gulf?"

Kathleen met his piercing look unwaveringly. "Why

should I bother, Captain Percy?'' she countered smoothly. ''What would be the profit in attacking a British warship? Shrewd businesswoman that I am, I am well aware that it is more lucrative to waylay a Spanish vessel bearing gold, or a Portuguese frigate, or even an American cargo ship.'' She smiled sweetly. ''Surely none of your men have blamed *me* for their misadventures?''

''None of the vessels in question have produced a single survivor,'' Percy replied grimly.

''Oh, my!'' Kathleen's eyes widened dramatically. ''You certainly have had severe losses then, haven't you?'' she taunted.

Isabel's appearance at dinner created another brief stir. ''Another pirate captain?'' Admiral Lowe jeered, glowering at Isabel's form-fitting trousers and full-sleeved shirt clinging seductively to her pert breasts.

''Heavens! I'll never be a captain!'' Isabel exclaimed brightly. ''I do not know the first thing about sailing a ship!''

''The truth at last!'' Captain Percy muttered.

''Isabel is one of my crew, gentlemen,'' Kathleen proceeded to enlighten them. ''Do not let her small stature fool you. She has taken many a man out of action with her swift sword.''

''They must have been poor swordsmen then,'' Lowe decided aloud.

''Yes, they were, actually,'' Isabel agreed with an impish smile, her dark eyes twinkling.

''I thought the same of many of my own opponents,'' Kathleen admitted, recalling some of the bumbling Britons she had faced.

The meal concluded, the officers presented their offer, again attempting to get Jean to agree to their proposition.

"You and your men would be an invaluable asset to us, as you must know," Lowe said.

"We figured that out by ourselves," Pierre inserted.

"Your knowledge of the bayous and backwater ways would aid the British cause a good deal," Percy added.

"Without which, you and your men could flounder forever in the swamps," Isabel pointed out serenely.

"If the gators, snakes, and swamp fever didn't finish you off—not to mention the quicksand," Dominique added with a wicked grin.

"Your point is taken," Lowe replied coolly. "We would like to enlist your aid; for which you will be amply rewarded, Mr. Lafitte." He directed his words to Jean.

Jean silently lit a cheroot. "Ahem—yes." Admiral Lowe cleared his throat loudly. "Well, now, I have been instructed to inform you, that should you agree to fight with us against these upstart Americans, we are prepared to offer you the governorship of the Louisiana territory, including New Orleans and the surrounding area."

"Oh, Lord!" Kathleen hooted before she could stop herself. "Wouldn't old Claiborne have an apoplectic fit if he could hear this!"

Jean chuckled indulgently at her humor. "Emerald, you are a very wicked *petite chatte.*" His admonishment sounded curiously like a caress.

"How is that?" Lowe inquired.

"A little cat—a kitten," Pierre translated with a broad grin, "with sharp claws and eyes that see in the dark."

The two men stayed late, and Jean plied them with liquor and fine cigars in an effort to loosen their tongues. Kathleen and Isabel did their best to get the stiff British officers to relax and let down their guard a bit. By the evening's end, despite themselves, the Englishmen had revealed a good deal of information about the size and whereabouts of their ships though nothing as specific as the privateers would have wished. For his part, Jean agreed to consider their offer, telling them he would require more time to think about it.

When the British had returned to their ship, Jean turned to his brothers and the two women. "It is time we return to New Orleans and try once again to convince our mule-headed governor that a British attack is inevitable. I can only hope he is ready to listen to reason this time!"

Chapter 15

While Kathleen and Isabel visited Eleonore again, the Lafitte brothers went to see Governor Claiborne. As in the past, the governor scoffed at their warnings, Claiborne loudly proclaiming them all worthless pirates, and again threatening to have them all arrested at the slightest provocation. The Lafittes left his office shaking their heads in dismay. If Claiborne did not relent soon, New Orleans would not have sufficient time to prepare for the attack. The city would fall like a ripe peach into the hands of the British.

At this time, a visitor to New Orleans would never have guessed there was a war in progress. The city vibrated with excitement and gaiety in preparation for the annual Mardi Gras Celebration. It took a bit of persuasion to convince Kathleen to remain for the festivities. Her mind kept going back to the times she and Reed had donned costumes for Savannah's annual St. Patrick's Day fete and their New Year's Eve balls.

"The holidays are the worst," she confided to Eleonore. "Each month seems to hold some significant date that stabs at my heart like a lance, reminding me that Reed shared these times with me." Tears coursed slowly down her cheeks, and she closed her eyes to stem the flow, burying her face despondently in her hands.

"The first year is bound to be the worst," Eleonore agreed, "but it will soon be past. Next Christmas, and those thereafter, you will build new memories of times with your children, and it will hurt less with each passing year."

"Perhaps you are right, but my memories are so precious, so sweet, that I do not really know if I *want* them to fade. At times, I can barely stand the pain, but along with the heartache comes the remembrance of a love so wonderful that I cling fiercely to it, as if to experience it all again and have Reed close to me, if only in my heart."

"It is only natural, Kathleen, but someday you must put aside your old dreams and reach out for new ones. To waste yourself on faded memories is a shame, when a new love stands waiting in the shadow of your pain—waiting for you to turn and recognize him, to accept the love he offers."

"Jean," Kathleen sighed tearfully.

"Jean," Eleonore nodded.

Kathleen looked sadly at her friend. "I don't want to hurt him, Eleonore."

"At this point, he is so taken with you that I suspect he would be satisifed with whatever affection you could spare."

"That would not be fair to him," Kathleen argued.

Eleonore shrugged. "Who is to say what is fair? Perhaps a love affair with a man like Jean is just what you need to bring you back to life. You might even surprise yourself."

In the end, Kathleen succumbed to her friends' entreaties, and stayed to experience Mardi Gras in New Orleans. She told herself she was doing it for them;

especially for Isabel, who'd had so little fun and frivolity in recent years.

There was a hint of spring in the early March air here in this southern port city, and it lent an added air of exuberance to the revelry. The streets were crowded with lively celebrants, all eager for this final outbreak of levity before entering the somber season of Lent. The entire city was awash with color, every hue of the rainbow exhibited in the vivid costumes seen everywhere. Throngs clogged the streets, people jostling one another cheerfully, joyful shouts rising in a cacophony of voices.

"This is fun! I am glad you talked me into staying," Kathleen admitted to Jean, her eyes bright in her flushed face as they sat at a table at an outdoor café, watching the passing parade.

Jean reached across and took her hand in his, pleased beyond measure when she did not retrieve it, but let it lie soft and warm within his. Kathleen let her eyes travel over his outfit. Jean looked extremely handsome in an elaborate pirate costume, chosen to complement hers as Emerald. A plumed hat sat jauntily on his head, below which a black patch covered his left eye. His white silk shirt was open at the neck, a silver medallion gleaming against the mat of hair on his chest. Over the shirt he wore a short green vest which matched the snug trousers tucked into shiny black boots. A waist sash completed his outfit, and secured his rapier at his side.

For her part, Kathleen wore her usual piratess attire of short green breeches and vest. For propriety's sake, she had donned a white silk blouse beneath the vest, the full, billowing sleeves fluttering in the breeze. Her sleek midnight tresses stood out in sharp relief against the white of her blouse, and her eyes glowed. The gold coin Jean had given her hung about her neck, nestling between her breasts, and winking between the lacings of her vest.

"I believe you chose that pirate costume, not so much as a match to mine, as to torment Governor Claiborne," Kathleen teased him.

"*Ma petite chatte*, my beautiful kitten, you have a naughty mind," Jean scolded with a laugh. "You are quite correct, however, when you say that our dear governor will disapprove. No doubt, we shall see him tonight at the ball."

"And you love to antagonize him, Jean. Admit it," she urged, wagging a slim finger at him.

Jean shrugged. "Perhaps I do enjoy adding fuel to the fire from time to time. His superior attitude annoys me, and to take him down a peg or two adds spice to our confrontations."

That evening, they attended a ball for the elite of New Orleans society. Eleonore and her escort, René Robinault, had made certain they all gained entrance to this select affair, even Dominique and Pierre. They made quite an impressive group. Eleonore and René had chosen to appear as a cortesan and courtier, resplendent in bejeweled attire. Pierre, because of his short stature, made a very believable Napoleon, his wife Francoise representing his former empress Josephine at his side.

Much to Kathleen's surprise, when Dominique had suggested that he and Isabel portray a Spanish don and his lady, Isabel had agreed without protest. Obviously, her painful experiences at her husband's hands were fading rapidly. Dominique looked splendid in his black jacket and trousers trimmed in silver thread. Isabel resembled a tiny, beautifully dressed doll, her dark hair pulled up and held by a high ornate comb and draped with a delicate lace mantilla. She looked lovely and fragile next to Dominique's towering bulk.

If Kathleen was feeling a little guilty at enjoying the evening's festivities, she quickly buried her reservations. Surely she deserved a bit of frivolity, a touch of happiness admist her sadness. The evening stretched before her, a brief respite from thoughts of loss and revenge. The atmosphere was jolly, filled with laughter and lighthearted enjoyment. The music was heavenly, the companionship the finest, the dancing divine. Wine flowed in sparkling abudance, and Kathleen's goblet was never empty.

Soon she was caught up in the festive mood. She relaxed for the first time in months, allowing herself to be soothed by the music and the feel of strong male arms enfolding her possessively as they danced. Surrounded by her friends, she laughed and joked and let down her protective guard.

Toward midnight, Kathleen guessed she was a little tipsy from the amount of wine she had consumed, though she had eaten well from the buffet tables. She clung giddily to Jean as he whirled her about the dance floor. Her head was spinning, and she was laughing at everything. The beautiful ballroom had taken on an added glow, and Kathleen's eyes sparkled like genuine emeralds in her happy face. When Jean drew her nearer, their thighs brushing and their bodies touching, she melted against him willingly. His warm breath fanned her hair and tickled her ear as he whispered sweet French phrases of love. As if her will was no longer her own, she shivered and cuddled closer. Chills of desire, so long denied, raced up her spine as Jean's fingers traced her backbone. Kathleen's eyelashes fluttered closed, and she swallowed a moan as her bones turned to jelly and her knees threatened to give way. Only Jean's strong arms kept her from crumpling at his feet.

As if from a distance, she heard him say, "Let me take you home with me, *cherie*. Let us have this night together —a magical night of fantasy and love."

Wordlessly she nodded her assent, incapable of withstanding his charm on this enchanted night.

The carriage ride was short, doing little to clear her wine-fogged head, and soon Jean was leading her up the stairs of his townhouse and into his bedroom. Little of the resplendent furnishings registered as he drew her with him to the side of the big bed.

Slowly, Jean proceeded to undress her, taking his time over lacings and ties, savoring each part of her body revealed to him. By the light of the single lamp burning by the bedside, he viewed the woman before him, his eyes caressing what his hands would soon possess.

"*Magnifique!*" he whispered reverently, his hazel eyes glowing. "You are, without doubt, the most beautiful woman I have ever seen!"

A dreamy smile curved her lips, and her body leaned into his of its own accord, her mouth raised to receive his kiss. His lips tasted hers, gently at first, as if sipping the rarest of wines; and then more boldly, staking their claim to her mouth. Her lips parted beneath the demand of his, their tongues meeting and mingling as the kiss deepened.

Placing her gently upon the bed, Jean's lips left hers reluctantly for the time it took him to discard his own clothing. Then he was beside her, their naked bodies touching and burning as he enfolded her in his embrace and joined their lips once more.

The heated demand of his lips took Kathleen's breath,

and she felt herself slipping helplessly into that deep abyss where passion ruled the senses. For mere seconds, she fought the feeling, then let herself succumb to his sweet persuasion. Her hands reached out to touch, and then caress, the hard male contours of his body. Her fingers combed sensuously through that mat of curls covering his chest, her palms measuring its width, her fingertips learning the feel of her lover. Across his shoulders and onto his back, her hands continued, there to clutch tightly and draw him nearer to her.

Kathleen's skin quivered beneath Jean's expert touch. At first he merely stroked the length of her, from shoulder to thigh. Then, satisfied with what he had discovered there, his long, lean fingers came up to cup one perfect breast, causing Kathleen to gasp at the emotion this act evoked in her. Her breast swelled to his touch, as if to encourage his fondling, the nipple standing out pertly, pouting for his attention.

Jean did not ignore the signals her body was giving him. His mouth left hers to trail sweet kisses along her throat and shoulder, working its way inevitably nearer, until his hot, moist mouth finally closed upon its prize. Again Kathleen gasped, and her body arched itself into his, as if by his command.

"Sweet," he murmured softly, "so sweet; like the ambrosia of the gods." As his mouth and tongue tantalized her breast, his hand trailed a path of fire across her smooth abdomen, and slid beneath her thighs to explore the moist warmth awaiting there. "You were made for love, *ma cherie, ma beauté*," he said softly. "You are truly a goddess."

Kathleen's head tossed slightly in denial. "I am but a woman, Jean—a mere woman," she sighed, catching her breath at what his hands and mouth were doing to her. Her fingers untangled themselves from his hair to dance down his body. There she found the hot length of him that lay branding her thigh like a hot spear, and she gave him pleasure for pleasure.

Finally he rose above her, and through the passion-induced mist that clouded her mind, she felt the heat of him against her. She arched toward him, her body aching for his ultimate possession.

"Kathleen," Jean groaned, his hands gently encasing her face. "Look at me. Tell me who it is that is about to make love to you!" His voice trembled, not only with immense desire held barely in check, but with the fear that she might mistake him for Reed.

Her lashes fluttered open to reveal passion-glazed eyes, their color deepened almost to jade. "Jean—you are—Jean . . ."

At her answer, Jean's breath expelled from his lungs at the same time his body plunged into hers. Her startled gasp melted into sighs, as his driving movements set her senses spinning and her silkin skin pressing against his in a quest for glory. When he was sure she had found her release, Jean joined her there, both trembling in the aftermath of their headlong flight.

Tranquility invaded the very marrow of Kathleen's bones, and her eyelids refused to lift at her command. Smiling at her sleepy struggles, Jean drew her within the curve of his arm, her head pillowed sweetly on his shoulder. "Sleep, my little sweetheart. The morning is already near." With a contented sigh, he joined her in sated slumber.

Kathleen woke slowly, reluctant to give up the sweet

dream that held her in thrall. It seemed so real that she could actually feel the heavy arm thrown across her waist, the warmth of a long male body. In that state halfway between waking and sleeping, Kathleen believed she was back in Chimera, waking next to Reed in their wide bed. She stretched contentedly, fully relaxed—until Jean's sleepy voice cut through her thoughts.

"Be still, *cherie*. I am not ready as yet to join in the activities of the day."

Immediately she froze, her eyes widening and her breath catching in her throat as drowsiness fled before reality. A dismayed gasp escaped her constricted throat as the truth invaded, destroying her peace of mind. Jean, having felt her stiffen and heard her gasp, flipped her onto her back. Propped on his elbow, he stared into her startled green eyes. Kathleen closed her lids against his penetrating gaze and the morning light that stabbed at her eyes, sending shafts of pain through her head. Her full lips trembled, and tears squeezed past the corners of her lids. Vivid memories of the night before came flooding back with amazing clarity. "What have I done?" she moaned, not meaning to say the words aloud.

Giving her a rough shake, Jean said gruffly, "Open your eyes, Kathleen." When she did so, he continued. "You remember what we did last night." It was more a statement of fact than a question.

"Yes," she whispered reluctantly.

"You came with me willingly. I did not force you."

"I know." She tried to turn her face from his heated gaze, but he held her chin with strong fingers.

"If you know, then you can erase that look of regret and dismay from your face and your eyes." His voice had hardened, and his jaw was clenched in something very like anger. "It is too late for regrets, *ma cherie*, too late to wish you had not chosen to live as a whole woman again. What is done, is done. You must now come to terms with it. Last night you were alive and aglow in my arms. You held back nothing from me. You were warm and exciting, and more than willing to serve my pleasures and claim your own."

His stark words brought a flush of shame to her face. She wanted to hear no more. Closing her eyes, she groaned, "Please, Jean!"

"Please don't tell you what you know to be the truth? Please don't remind you what a wanton witch you became when I took you at last? Please make love with you again and share the rapture once more?"

"No!" she shrieked, her hands flying up to cover her ears.

His hands left her face to ensnare her wrists and pin them to either side of her head. "Yes!" he stated hoarsely, as his warm lips swooped down to capture hers in a kiss of devastating insistency.

The harsh reality of the morning could not lessen the sharp thrill that shot through her at his touch. Just when her arms were released to curve of their own volition about his neck, she did not know, nor did she care. Kathleen was lost in the world of intense sensual delight that Jean wove about them. His knowing hands charted her body until it tingled and trembled beneath his caresses. All the while, he showered her fevered skin with kisses, mesmerizing her with sweet phrases and words of love.

Afterward, Kathleen had to face herself truthfully, as well as Jean. A deep sigh shook her frame as he raised himself up to look into her face. "Deny what we have shared, if you dare," he prompted. "Deny that you are mine—that you belong to me."

"I cannot," she whispered defeatedly. "I haven't strength enough to fight you and myself as well, Jean." Kathleen swallowed hard. "That is not to say I am pleased with myself, however. Regardless of all your persuasive arguments, I am filled with guilt and shame right now; and I am angry—angry at myself for allowing this to happen, and for feeling so guilty afterward." She turned sorrowful eyes to his face. "Most of all, I am saddened that I cannot tell you I love you, Jean. I care for you. You are very dear to me, but my heart is not mine to give. It died when we located the wreck of the *Kat-Ann*. You excite me, and my body yearns for yours, even as I speak, but I cannot offer more." Her huge eyes searched his features, reluctant to see the hurt there, but she found only understanding, and a hint of steely determination.

"That will suffice for now, *cherie*. The rest will come in time." He planted a kiss on the tip of her nose.

"I don't want to hurt you, Jean."

"Let me worry about that." Then he chuckled and raised himself off the bed. "Besides, it is a little too late for warnings of pain, *ma petite chatte*, after your sharp nails have torn my back to shreds." He turned to let her view the raised ridges her fingernails had scored on his smooth skin.

"Oh, Jean," she cried. "What can I say?"

His sharp gaze swung on her again. "You can tell me you understand how it will be between us from now on. There is no going back from here—only forward. Having tasted of your sweetness, I cannot let you go."

"As long as you do not ask for more than I can give, Jean," she conceded.

He nodded. "We are agreed, then. You are my woman, if only for mutual sensual pleasure; and I am your *amoureux,* your lover, and your friend."

Jean needed a few days to catch up on business at his New Orleans warehouse, so they stayed a while in town. When Kathleen would have stayed with Eleonore, Jean vetoed the idea, personally seeing that her few things were transferred to the house.

"Everyone is well aware by now where you spent Tuesday night," he told her.

"Even so," she argued, "there is no sense in confirming their suspicions. It is none of their affair."

Jean laughed at her. "When has public opinion ever mattered to you, Kathleen? Haven't you always been the one to flaunt convention and damn the consequences?"

"Yes, but . . ." she began.

"No buts! You shall stay with me."

He was just as adamant that she must accept the extravagant gifts he bought her. When she demured, he simply said, "Let me pamper you. It pleases me to do so." Put that way, how could she refuse?

These small concessions she made, but Jean was also wise enough to respect her as his equal and treat her thus. Together they planned future strategies. When Kathleen insisted she would rather go to the warehouse with him than stay at home or go shopping, he gladly accepted her company. Often he asked her advice on business matters. They went driving together, took their meals together, went out to dinner parties and other gatherings as a pair. Their friends accepted their new relationship without comment, and in doing so, greatly eased Kathleen's anxieties. Others who might have voiced another opinion feared Jean's famed skill with his sword too much to say anything.

Not for the first time in her life, Kathleen found herself in a situation over which she had little control; and as always before, it bothered her. She could accept her bodily urges and the intense pleasure she received from Jean's loving, especially after the active lovelife she and Reed had shared and the long abstinence she had enforced upon herself. What she could not obliterate was a severe feeling of infidelity. It did not make sense, under the circumstances, but it clung to her like a persistent shadow. Yet another part of her grieved that she could not love Jean as she had Reed. In truth, if admitted only to herself, she feared to love Jean in this way, even were it possible. To do so would make her vulnerable to the same pain she had known when she had accepted the fact of Reed's death. She had lived through hell once—a second loss would surely kill her. Kathleen, who feared almost nothing, was afraid to risk her heart again.

Jean realized Kathleen's struggles. He knew that each night he held her in his arms, he held only that part of her which she could not help but give. His male pride was soothed by her cries of ecstasy, knowing he gave her pleasure, but he craved more. Kathleen was generous when she came to his bed. He could not fault her there. Still, he wanted her full surrender, and prayed that one day she would come to love him as he loved her—with all her heart. Each day, he fell more under her spell, and each day he hoped that soon he could ask her to be his wife, and hear her say yes.

When the returned to Grande Terre, they went to work

readying their ships for another excursion. The hulls were being scraped and re-tarred, sails repaired, and line replaced. Fresh stores were laid in, and everything prepared for a long sea voyage.

Now they shared his house, his room, his bed. Everything he owned, he considered hers also. He strove to keep the mood of their relationship light, for her sake. They laughed and joked and played together. They swam in the bay, splashing and dunking one another like carefree children. There were sunlit picnics on the island, exotic flowers for her hair, and long walks hand-in-hand along the beach at sunset. At evening, they sat and talked on the gallery overlooking the garden as the cool sea breeze wafted soft island scents and sounds their way. And each night, he took her into his bed and delighted her with the mastery and glory of his love, holding her in his arms as they drifted off to sleep.

One evening after supper, they began a serious discussion on the art of fencing. Soon their talk became a heated debate on various movements and counterattacks. While they agreed on many points, they soon realized they had many differences, each preferring his own style.

"I have been fighting since you were a child, Kathleen. Please believe I know what I am talking about!" said Jean.

"Jean, I am not reputing your skill. Your swordsmanship is legendary. I am merely suggesting that my way might be better in certain circumstances. Allow me the respect of listening to my views. Just because I am female, does not make me witless!"

Jean sighed. "I believe we are at a stalemate."

"Then prove me wrong, and I will concede," she said.

His hazel eyes narrowed on her face. "What are you suggesting?"

"That we pit our skills and individual styles against one another in a fair contest," Kathleen answered calmly.

"And who will call the duel?" he asked dubiously.

"We shall. First blood shall judge the winner." At his frown, she added, "A mere scratch at most, Jean."

"The thought of harming you makes me cringe, *cherie*," he admitted.

Kathleen threw him a jaunty grin. "Then I shall win the match!"

"You may try," he countered with a wry smile. Her outrageous idea was beginning to appeal to him. "Shall we set stakes?"

"By all means. Do you want my next captured ship?" she offered.

Jean's smile widened wickedly. "Oh, nothing so crass as that. If I win, you shall be my slave for an evening." His eyes glittered. "You shall serve me food and drink, light my cigars, and see to my every comfort."

"Oh?" Kathleen was intrigued in spite of herself.

"*Oui*. It would particularly delight me to have you draw my bath and bathe me, then give me a massage with warm spiced oils. And when I am fully relaxed, you can make love to me as I desire."

"Agreed," she said huskily, her green eyes glowing like a cat's. "And if *I* win, you shall do the same for me. You shall wash my hair and brush it dry after you bathe me. Then I wish you to soften my skin with sweet oils, and make love to me, doing all the things you know drive me wild."

Jean lifted a wine glass and handed it to her, taking up his own and proposing a toast. "To a good fight; winner take all!"

Kathleen's goblet clinked against his, her laughter

mingling with the chime of the glass. "May the best one win!"

They met the next afternoon in the music room. Jean had ordered all the furnishings moved to one end, creating a large, empty area in which to maneuver. He had also ordered everyone out of the house, warning them to stay away until he gave the word. They did as he said, though Jean had not explained his reasons. Kathleen felt he had done this to ensure that neither would be embarrassed over losing. His thoughtfulness touched her. The others need never know of this private duel—or the outcome.

They took a few minutes to inspect their weapons. As Kathleen stood flexing her wrists and elbows, Jean asked, "Would you like a practice round?"

Kathleen shook her head, smiling. "Thank you, no." She tugged on her gloves and lifted her rapier. "Ready when you are!"

They squared off in the traditional stance, though Kathleen knew that once the match was under way, formality would be left by the wayside. Their eyes locked, and Kathleen's soft *"en garde"* announced the start of action.

As she had planned, Kathleen let Jean take the offensive at first, parrying his first light thrusts. Gradually, the tempo of his attack increased, and she felt the strength behind his blows. They circled like dancers, warily measuring one another's abilities and reactions, ever watchful of an opening. Kathleen was careful to keep her guard up, but try as she might, she could spot no flaw in Jean's attack. He was a master at the art; this would surely be the most challenging duel she had ever fought.

At length, they'd felt one another out long enough, and the bout began in earnest. It took all Kathleen's concentration and strength to ward off Jean's swift lunges and powerful strokes. For a few minutes she did nothing but parry his thrusts, blocking him at every turn. When the moment felt right, she swiftly turned the tables, assuming the offensive herself. This was where she felt most confident, and it showed in her decisive lunges and skillful feints. A glimmer of respect glowed in Jean's eyes as he silently acknowledged her expertise.

For a quarter of an hour they fought steadily, the offensive changing sides several times, neither gaining the advantage they sought. Kathleen's arm ached and her rapier seemed to weigh two tons. Her wrist felt as if it would snap under the strain each time she parried one of Jean's expert blows. Round and round they went, thrusting, parrying and counter-parrying, feinting and side-stepping, lunging, recovering, and leaping out of the way of a lightning attack. Their blades whistled in the still room, and sang as they sliced through the air. The clash of steel on steel rang loudly in their ears. Their eyes never wavered from one another's.

Kathleen was tiring quickly under Jean's ruthless onslaught, but she dared not let him see her weakness. One unguarded moment, one faltering step, would tell him the contest was his for the taking.

Kathleen feinted to one side, bringing her rapier about to block his move. Accurately, he counter-parried, forcing her blade aside. So swiftly she barely saw it coming, his blade caught the lowest lacing of her vest, slicing neatly through it. Only her lightning reflexes saved her from feeling the prick of his swordtip on her skin.

For just a fraction of a second, Jean's eyes flickered downward to the portion of alabaster breast exposed by the severed lacing. It was all the time Kathleen needed. Before his gaze could return to hers and register her intention, she brought her rapier up and inward as hard and fast as she could, putting all her strength and weight into the blow. The edge of her blade caught his just below the hilt, jarring it loose from his hand and sending it skittering across the floor out of his reach. Like a cat stalking her prey, she took longer than she needed to bring her blade about. Then, with a flourish and a victorious smile lighting her emerald eyes, she touched the tip of her rapier to his chest where his open shirt exposed the skin below his throat. With a slight flick of the wrist, she lightly pricked his skin. One drop of crimson blood welled up ðn the surface. Softly, regret mixed with respect and triumph, she breathed a single word—*"Touché."*

Following his initial expression of disbelief, a slow smile spread across Jean's face. "*Cherie,* you are the first in many years to defeat me at my own game. I congratulate you. Your skill is matched only by your beauty."

Kathleen returned his smile. "Thank you, Jean. If I didn't know you better, I would swear you gave the match away. If you hadn't lost concentration for a moment, you would have won. I was tiring quickly."

Jean chuckled wryly. "The perils of facing an opponent as exquisitely formed as you, my dear. I simply could not help myself!"

"I am sorry, Jean," she told him sincerely. "I feel almost as if I had cheated, playing on my femininity to win the match."

With a shrug, Jean replied philosophically, "*C'est la vie,* Kathleen. *Le bon dieu,* in his infinite wisdom, has given us different strengths and weaknesses. To man he gives a muscled back and strong arms—and a weakness for beautiful women. To woman he gives soft curves and feminine wiles to lure man to do her bidding. It is up to each man and woman to decide when and where it benefits us to use these gifts He has bestowed so benevolently, and to guard against our weaknesses.

"The moment my eyes strayed, I realized my mistake. It was my fault alone—you won the match fairly. I concede defeat without rancor, and with much respect for your skill. You have given me one of the best contests I have ever known. We should spar again sometime, if only to sharpen my wits and keep me on my toes."

"You, too, are probably the toughest opponent I'll ever face," Kathleen admitted. "I will gladly offer you a rematch, but only after I have recovered my strength."

"Beware, *ma petite piratesse,*" Jean warned, his hazel eyes twinkling merrily. "I will not fall for the same trick twice!"

"Then you'd best keep your blade from my lacings," Kathleen admonished saucily, "and your mind on the business at hand instead of my body."

Her tinkling laughter burst forth, joined by his hearty chuckle. "I shall try," he promised, "but it will not be easy."

Kathleen sighed luxuriously as Jean drew the brush through her freshly washed hair. True to the terms of their wager, he had shampooed and bathed her. As his slippery hands had soaped her body, lingering where her desire was strongest, the cleansing had quickly become sweet torment. Now, while he dried her hair to an ebony lustre, Jean turned even the act of drawing the brush through her silken tresses into a sensual exercise that heightened her desire.

Their eyes met in the mirror, his hot with promises of

delights to come, hers wide and wondrous with the feelings he inspired. Bending, he kissed the exposed flesh of her neck and shoulder, gently biting at the sensitive cord just below the surface. Her quick quiver transferred itself to his lips, and he smiled lazily.

Gently, he drew her to her feet. "Come, *chatte*, my beautiful little cat. Lie down on the bed and I will soothe your tired muscles and make you purr beneath my fingertips."

"It sounds heavenly," she agreed contentedly.

It was heaven and hell combined. The oil lent an especially sensuous quality to his gliding touch. Her skin seemed unusually sensitive this evening, and Jean's hands were both soothing and erotic in their play along her body. He took great pains to ensure that not one inch of her was left untouched; not one spot that was not endlessly craving his caress.

In the end, she was writhing helplessly beneath him, begging him to take her, arching her body against his. When at last he complied, she was mindless with desire, his to command—a wild creature tamed only by his touch of fire.

Chapter 16

Once again Kathleen, Jean and their crews scoured the seas in search of British warships. They hunted them down like dogs, making certain there were no survivors to carry tales back to the enemy. They were ruthless, merciless, giving no quarter. Kathleen's mission was one of fierce revenge, always uppermost in her mind.

Jean had hoped that once Kathleen became his mistress, she would cease to take such reckless chances, but he was doomed to disappointment. If anything, she became even more daring. It was as if she were atoning for some sin, taking out her guilt on her hapless foes. She was like one pursued by a personal demon, trying to exorcise it with intense physical action and her singing sword. The Enchantress of Death was on a rampage, making her presence felt and feared on the seas. A whirlwind of seemingly limitless energy and resourcefulness, her goal seemed to be to sink every ship the British ill-advisedly put in her path, or die trying.

By day, Kathleen was commanding and decisive, deftly manning the helm or slaying her enemies. Each night, she hung up her sword and became the sweet angel of Jean's dreams. There was but one thing she refused him—her heart. As the weeks wore on and Kathleen did not show any signs of the love he craved, Jean began to despair. As willingly as she came to him, as generous as she was as a lover, an anger started to grow in him. How could she treat his feelings so lightly? True, he had agreed to accept her on her terms, but he was beginning to find them increasingly hard to abide by. How long could he stand the knowledge that she did not love him before he reached his limits? Jean felt caught in a trap, and could find no solution to his problem. He was not ready to give up hope, but he knew that if he pressed the issue now, Kathleen would run from him like a frightened doe from a hunter.

Kathleen's parrot, Peg-Leg, was another thorn in Jean's side. The crazy bird was so accustomed by now to sharing Kathleen's quarters, that he refused to be removed when Jean took up residence in Kathleen's cabin aboard the *Enchantress*. On the first evening, they were preparing for bed, and Kathleen had just removed her vest, when from the corner of the room a raucous voice screeched, "Fry me feathers!"

Taken by surprise, Jean nearly leapt to the rafters. "*Mon dieu!*" he swore. "That silly bird startled me out of ten years of my life!"

When Kathleen had stopped laughing, she apologized. "I forgot to warn you about Peg-Leg. He has rather taken over my boudoir. We have spent many a lonely night together."

Jean eyed the bird spitefully. "As your nights are no longer lonely, he can find other quarters in which to perch, *n'est-ce pas?*"

"Oh, let him stay, Jean. He is perfectly harmless, and he is used to my room. You'll soon become accustomed to him—you'll hardly notice he is here."

"Somehow I doubt that," Jean muttered, "but we shall see."

They proceeded to undress, and just as Kathleen was climbing into bed, Peg-Leg let out a long, low whistle.

Jean cocked an eyebrow in Kathleen's direction. "You were saying?" he commented wryly.

Kathleen shrugged, and grinned. "Ask Dominique where Peg-Leg picked up all his bad habits. He's a dirty bird."

From his perch in the corner, Peg-Leg squawked, "*Pretty* bird! *Pretty* bird!"

Kathleen frowned at him. "Make up your mind, will you?"

For a while, everything quieted down, and soon Jean and Kathleen were absorbed in lovemaking. Suddenly Jean felt a familiar tingling along his spine—that same signal that always alerted him in battle that someone was watching him, planning an attack. Whipping about, he met two beady eyes and a sharp, curved beak. Peg-Leg was interestedly viewing their activities from a beam directly above Kathleen's bunk.

Kathleen watched in gleeful amusement as Jean let out a roar of outrage and swung his fist at the inquisitive bird. Peg-Leg scuttled out of the way just in time for Jean's hand to connect with the beam with a resounding *thwack*. Another bellow split the air, this one of pain.

Biting her lip to control her laughter, Kathleen rose to kneel beside Jean, carefully examining his hand. Luckily for Peg-Leg, she found no broken bones. Jean's hand and pride were both bruised, but neither seriously.

"Jean" she remonstrated, "you might have broken your hand!"

"I was trying to break his beak!" Jean ground out. "If I wanted an audience, I would charge admission!"

"Now *there's* a novel idea," Kathleen laughed, tongue-in-cheek.

"Kathleen," Jean growled in warning, "I am trying to keep hold of my temper, and I must tell you, I am losing ground very quickly. Would you be so kind as to do something about that feathered voyeur, before I eliminate him permanently?"

"Very well," Kathleen soothed. "I will put him in his cage. Perhaps with a cover over him, he'll go to sleep."

"With any luck, he will suffocate!" Jean grumbled.

Peg-Leg had returned to his perch, and as Kathleen lifted him into his cage, he squawked, "Mercy me! Mercy me!"

Quickly she tossed a cloth over the cage. "Will you pipe down, you dumb bird?" she whispered. "Don't you know you're about to become parrot stew?"

Thereafter, Kathleen put the bird in his cage each night and covered him. Usually, Peg-Leg grouched a few minutes and went to sleep. But when occasionally she forgot, Peg-Leg would remind her with a lewd whistle or a crusty comment. A croak of "Kiss me, lovey!" or "On guard!" would bring a glare from Jean, and send Kathleen scurrying to cover the bird for the night. Sometimes the feisty parrot would eavesdrop as Jean was showering Kathleen with words of love and adoration. Kathleen would double up with suppressed laughter as the parrot mimicked Jean's words, or squawked a sour "*Bilge!*" as if telling Jean that all his pretty poetic phrases were just so much nonsense.

Once, in the middle of a particularly passionate moment, Peg-Leg, still wide awake, squawked. "Step lively, mate!" Kathleen collapsed with giggles, completely destroying the romantic mood.

Jean was livid. "Either you find a way to keep that pesky

pile of feathers quiet, or I will truss him up and feed him to the sharks mouthful by mouthful!'' he warned. ''Then I will do the same to Dominique for giving him to you in the first place—after I strangle my beloved brother!''

Kathleen resorted to stiffer measures. Since the parrot kept everyone else awake squawking and throwing a fuss if she tried to house him overnight anywhere else, she finally stuffed his cage into her armoire each night. There he could neither see nor hear what went on in the room, and after a few choice curses, he would tuck his head under his wing and sulk himself to sleep. The problem was solved to Jean's satisfaction, Kathleen's relief, and Peg-Leg's salvation.

As the end of March approached, so did Katlin's third birthday, and Kathleen found herself in a dilemma. Should she take time away from her venture and sail up to Savannah? The loving, motherly part of her desperately wanted to see her daughter and be with her son on his special day; yet warning bells went off inside her head at the very thought. Could she stand seeing the miniature Reed just as she was starting to enjoy life again? Was it time—or was it too soon—to go home again? Would seeing Katlin destroy her precarious happiness and bring her loss fresh to her heart with aching intensity just as it was beginning to fade?

Ten days before Katlin's birthday, Kathleen made her decision. By way of a captured British brig she was sending to Savannah, she sent a letter to her Grandmother Kate, in which she asked Kate to give her love to Katlin. Also, she sent money and instructions for Kate to purchase a pony and cart as Kathleen's gift to her son. ''Tell him his Mama misses him and loves him very much,'' she wrote. ''Wish him a happy birthday for me. Tell him I hope he likes his gift, and I will be home soon to see him drive his pony cart. Give both my darlings a hug and kiss for me, and tell them not to forget me until I get home." Then she added, "I am finally starting to adjust and accept what Fate has dealt me, but I am not certain I can face Katlin just yet. The pain has lessened, and I fear renewing it. It is like waking from a bad dream, and I dare not think about the dream, or it might come back to haunt me again. I feel I am not strong enough to return to Chimera just yet.

"Isabel has helped me so much. You would not recognize her now. The shy, fearful creature has been replaced by a confident, happy woman.

"All my friends have been wonderful, Gram, but Jean most of all. He has drawn me out of my misery into the light of day again. Joy and laughter are his gifts to me. He has dried my tears with his healing love. I only wish I could return his feelings. Our mutual love for Reed is both a bond between us and a gap that separates us. Jean's generous nature and selflessness heal and chafe at the same time. His attentions make me feel both happy and guilty, and I am helpless to know what to do. He would be so easy to love, Gram, but love brings so much pain, and I have had my fill of pain. In that, I am a coward. I would rather face a dozen foes, than risk that kind of pain again."

Dominique, in a fit of pique and despair over Isabel's apparent reluctance to return his love, decided early in April that it was time to go off by himself for a while. Assembling his own crew, he sailed off on the *Tigre* to work out his problems and frustrations away from Isabel's disturbing presence.

Isabel suddenly found herself missing Dominique

tremendously. Without his constant presence, life seemed empty, and her days ten times as long as before. Her confidence waned and her concentration flagged without his protective bulk next to her in battle. She moped about the ship, lost without his teasing humor, his infectious laughter, his tender looks of adoration.

Kathleen watched her friend in silent commiseration, for who was she to advise anyone else about love? She could sense Jean's growing frustration with their own situation, yet she could not bring herself to reveal her feelings, for she did not understand them herself. She could not promise him anything at this point, so she kept silent. Meanwhile, his discontent was becoming more evident, though he did not voice his disappointment. They continued as lovers and partners in piracy.

So busy were they that Kathleen's birthday would have slipped by unnoticed had it not been for old Dan Shanahan's remarkable memory. Between them, he, Finley, Isabel and Jean put together a surprise party for her. Their carefully laid plans almost fell through at the last minute, for the seas were unusually rough that day, and the ship's cook had a devil of a time trying to bake a decent cake aboard the pitching vessel. Then, late in the afternoon, they encountered a British ship that led them a merry chase and gave them tough opposition once they had boarded her.

It was dark by the time the battle was finished, and everyone was tired and dirty. "All I want now is a quick wash and a good night's rest," Kathleen told Jean wearily.

Had it not been her birthday, Jean would have readily agreed, but everyone had gone to great pains to prepare this small celebration. "You must have something to eat, *cherie*," he advised her. "Go clean up and meet us for dinner. Isabel is in need of cheer, and I believe Finley mentioned that he had a few things to discuss with you."

"Let's hope cook has something nourishing to offer. I could eat a horse, I am so hungry!" she said as she plodded to her cabin.

Cook not only had a hot meal of steaming stew and biscuits, but he had also managed an applesauce cake and rice pudding. Kathleen, who had completely forgotten her own birthday, was surprised and pleased that her companions had remembered. After the delicious dinner, she opened her few gifts. Finley had given her polished shark's teeth, which she decided to have fashioned into a pendant and earbobs. From Isabel, there was a new silk sash. Dan had obviously been planning ahead for weeks, to have finished the whittled carving of a parrot, easily recognized as Peg-Leg. Jean, too, had a gift for her, which he said he would give to her in the privacy of their quarters.

Later, he presented her with a small package which fit neatly into the palm of Kathleen's hand. In her heart, she knew what it contained before she began to untie the ribbon. Her hesitancy showed in her troubled green eyes and trembling fingers.

"Jean, if this is what I suspect it is . . ." she whispered.

His hands came up to cradle her face, his eyes sincere as he said, "It is a gift, Kathleen—nothing more. If you only wear it in friendship, I will try to understand, but you must know how I feel about you. Someday I hope you will wear it for the purpose for which I originally purchased it."

He helped her to unwrap the small box and lift the lid. Inside, lay a beautiful white gold ring, the center stone of which was a sparkling marquise-cut diamond, encircled by small, perfect aquarmarines.

"Oh, Jean!" Her eyes flew up to meet his. "It is beautiful, but . . ."

"Think of it only as a birthday present for the time being," he interrupted, as he slid it onto the third finger of her right hand.

It fit perfectly; Kathleen suspected he had bought it from the same jeweler Reed had frequented. Tears sprang to her eyes. "Jean, I know I am hurting you, and that is the last thing I wish to do. Please be patient with me a while longer until I can sort out my thoughts and feelings."

His hand brushed her hair back from her face. "What else can I do for you, my Kathleen?"

Her hesitancy melted beneath his caress. "Hold me, Jean," she murmured as she slid into his welcoming arms. "Make love to me!"

Near Easter, feeling they had earned a short respite from their labors, Kathleen and her fellow pirates returned to Grande Terre, where an unpleasant surprise awaited them on Jean's island. Dominique lay seriously wounded, Charles in attendance. Near Santa Cruz, Dominique had encountered a Spanish warship, and the battle had gone badly. The *Tigre* was damaged, but the crew had managed to escape and limp home with their injured. Charles had been summoned from New Orleans to tend the wounded, and was there when Jean, Pierre and Kathleen arrived with Isabel.

"How is he, Charles?" Jean asked when the good doctor finally emerged from Dominique's room.

Charles shook his head. "It could be worse, Jean. Dominique took a ball through the shoulder, which would not have been so serious if attended immediately. But infection has set in, and that is our primary problem now. His fever is high, and he is often delirious."

"Will he live?" Isabel asked fearfully, her voice small.

"I think so," Charles answered, "but his attitude worries me. He does not seem concerned with recovering." Turning to Jean, he inquired, "Has he been worrying about something lately? Is there anything you can suggest to revive his will to live?"

Jean leveled a thoughtful look in Isabel's direction. "I have an idea what is bothering Dominique—but the answer is not mine to give."

Isabel bit her lip and turned red under his direct gaze. "I want to see him, if I may," she said finally.

Kathleen released the breath she had been holding. "Do you want me to come with you, Isabel?" she offered.

"No." Isabel shook her dark head. "This is something I must do alone. It should have been done long ago, but I was too stubborn to see it." Her velvet eyes filled with tears. "Now it may be too late!"

It was two long and worrisome days before Dominique's fever broke, and another twelve hours before he awoke to a bright spring morning. Isabel stayed with him nearly all that time, letting Kathleen or Jean relieve her for short periods only. In those hours Isabel spent with Dominique, she talked to him, even when she was not sure he could hear or understand, begging him to get well, and promising that they would talk things over as soon as he was able. Though Dominique did not waken, or give any indication that he heard her, Charles said he now seemed to be struggling to throw off the infection.

When he finally awoke, fever-free and lucid at last, the first thing he saw was Isabel's face above his. As he struggled to speak, she hushed him with a gentle finger on his dry lips. "Save your strength, Dominique. We will talk later." Tears of joy made her eyes sparkle like gems. "Welcome back. I have missed you."

"Love you," he croaked out drowsily.

Isabel smiled shyly. "I love you, too, Dominique, but you have to get well before we speak of that." She started to rise from his bedside. "I'll go tell Jean and Pierre you are awake. And Charles is here from New Orleans."

Dominique spoke through cracked lips. "Come back?" he asked, grabbing at her hand.

Isabel's smile widened. "Yes, I will be back, you great bear! In fact, you will probably be tired of seeing me by the time you are well again."

"Never," he whispered.

Kathleen and Jean stayed a week at Grande Terre, until Charles assured them that Dominique would completely recover. Jean's birthday happened to fall at the end of that time, and Kathleen wanted to be sure it was especially festive, to make up for all the worry Jean had been through these past days. Pierre had revealed to her the date, and helped to arrange a special, quiet dinner in honor of the occasion. It was also Pierre who ushered everyone else out of the way shortly after dinner, leaving Kathleen and Jean alone.

"Do you recall the wager we made on our duel a while back?" Kathleen asked, feeding Jean a fig and letting her finger trace his lips provocatively.

They were seated outside on the gallery, watching the dark sea in the distance and the moonlight playing on the waves.

Jean nipped at the pad of her finger with his teeth. "Yes, my little tease, I remember."

Kathleen smiled a half-smile. "Do you remember what you wanted, had you won?"

"It would be hard to forget," he said quietly. "Why?"

"Because, my dear," she purred, as she urged him out of his chair, "that is exactly what you are about to receive as your birthday gift from me!" At his stunned look, she said softly, "Come. Your bath awaits, and your slave is eager to serve you in all the ways that please you most."

It was a night that Jean would carry in his memory forevermore. His most magnificent fantasies of Kathleen fell far short of the reality of this mystical night of love. She was bold—she was shy. She was goddess and nymph. She was his to command, in all but her heart. Could he have commanded her to love him and made it so, Jean would have done so, but he knew he could not force her feelings. Still, for this one night, they shared a rare magic, and as the morning sun peeked over the horizon, they fell into a deep sleep of satiated exhaustion.

When the *Emerald Enchantress* and the *Pride* sailed once more, Isabel stayed behind to nurse Dominique. All went well, and the weather was unusually free of storms. They followed their usual pattern of attacking British ships at random and quickly veering off in another direction in search of their next victim. Then, on the first day of May, a storm hit—several in fact, each of a different and volatile nature. It was a day fraught with problems. First, it marked Kathleen and Reed's wedding anniversary, and Kathleen was in a foul, depressed mood from her first waking breath. She was surly and withdrawn to the point that Jean itched to shake her out of her silent, private musings. She spent a good part of the morning perched high in the rigging, suffering alone and ignoring everyone and everything.

If they had not sighted a British frigate, Kathleen might have stayed there all day. Instead, she was forced to climb down and lead her crew in the fight. The battle this day was more intense than most, or so it seemed to Kathleen. A storm was moving in, and Kathleen wanted to end the conflict as quickly as possible, but it seemed destined to be a long, drawn-out fight. Kathleen's opponents were particularly skilled, and her concentration was not at its best. All these factors combined against her. Kathleen could not have said what happened exactly—one moment she was parrying a blow, and the next, she was lying flat on her back, staring up at her opponent from the deck. Just in the nick of time, she rolled out of the path of his blade as it came slicing toward her. A sharp pain in her left arm told her she was wounded, but she had no time to be concerned. Leaping to her feet, she brought her rapier hard about as she rose, catching her enemy off-guard with her swift recovery. Her blade entered just below his ribcage and sliced upward through his lung to his heart.

Jean was angry as he watched the ship's doctor bandage Kathleen's arm. The gash was neither deep nor severe, though it might leave a small scar as a reminder.

"You can not mean to go back on deck in this storm, Kathleen," Jean railed at her. "Finley is capable of manning the wheel in your place. Isn't it enough that you let your memories interfere with your concentration today and nearly got yourself killed? Do you need to try a second time by braving this gale with a wounded arm?"

Kathleen's temper flared to match his, her eyes flashing fire. The doctor escaped before her retort singed the air.

"This is my ship, Jean, and I will do as I damned well please! Besides which, I do not need your permission to be pensive on the anniversary of my marriage to a man I love and miss more than you can imagine!"

"It nearly cost you your life, you little fool!" he roared, wincing inwardly at her words.

"That is my concern!" she retorted.

Jean's face closed into a hard mask. "It is, indeed," he stated coldly. With that, he proceeded to collect his belongings from the cabin.

Stunned, it took several seconds for his actions to register. "What are you doing?" Kathleen demanded.

Jean swung about to glare at her, his eyes hard. "I am tired of doing all the caring, Kathleen. I am tired of giving everything, and getting nothing in return from you but the gift of your body. The woman I love nearly got killed today—thinking of another man, I might add—and she tells me it is none of my concern! I would say it is past time for me to stop beating my head on a stone wall, don't you agree?"

Kathleen was shaking inside, whether from anger or the day's events, she did not know. All she did know was that Jean was leaving, and she had to stop him. Her hand went out to him imploringly. "Jean, please! Don't go! I'm sorry. We will talk!"

"We can talk later, perhaps, when we are both more reasonable," he stated firmly. "Do not look so stricken, *cherie*. I will be in the next cabin. The storm is too severe for me to return to the *Pride* tonight."

"But Jean, I need you," she argued tearfully. "This entire day has been miserable from beginning to end! My head is aching, my arm is throbbing, I am tired, wet, hungry, and I can not even think straight. Now this! I do

298

not want to fight with you, Jean. What I want most is to creep into the comfort of your arms and forget today ever happened.''

Jean shook his head and sighed. ''No, Kathleen. Not this time. What *I* need must come first this time. For my own sanity's sake, I must refuse you. I have reached the limit of my patience. I can no longer go on taking your body without your heart. I need more from you than that. There are times I could swear there are three persons in our bed—you, me, and Reed. I refuse to share you with a ghost any longer!''

Jean headed for the door, leaving her standing as if rooted to the floor. He glanced over his shoulder, noting her pale face. ''When you can come to me and tell me that you love me, I will listen, Kathleen. When you can assure me that you have laid Reed's ghost to rest and I need not compete with his memory in your heart, then we will talk, but not before.'' He closed the door softly behind him, leaving her in stunned silence, staring at the door through a mist of tears.

Kathleen stood at the helm of the frigate, her hands clenched tightly to the wheel. Her thoughts were as turbulent as the storm about her. Long, wet strands of ebony hair whipped about in the wind, occasionally robbing her of what little vision the driving rain had not already obliterated. Salt spray and rain mingled with the tears streaming unchecked down her cheeks. The gash on her arm throbbed as she strained to control the lurching ship and guide it through the immense waves. Lightning speared the sky continuously with white jagged bolts of light that seemed to launch themselves with fierce intent into the sea surrounding the *Emerald Enchantress*. The constant rumble of thunder deafened her to all but the roar of the storm, the thud of the frigate slamming against the waves, and the wind whining in her ears.

Kathleen winced involuntarily as lightning hit close off the starboard bow, and again, seconds later, slightly astern. The heavens seemed to be toying with the frigate in a terrorizing game of touch and run. This was a seaman's nightmare—to be caught up in a storm of this intensity, watching for the next devastating bolt to come tearing through the rigging or strike with deadly accuracy at a mast. This frail wooden vessel was the only thing standing between a sailor and a raging sea, waiting to claim him with yawning jaws.

"Damn! Damn! *Damn!*" Kathleen swore, but her curses were more directed toward her personal dilemma than the storm she fought. Her thoughts were on Jean. "I am going to lose him if I do not make up my mind soon," she worried, gnawing at her lower lip.

Her temper flared briefly. "Three short weeks ago, Jean said he would give me time. Evidently, my time is up, according to what he said earlier this evening. It's not fair!" Fresh tears ran their course from lashes to jaw. Her chin wobbled precariously.

Kathleen sighed defeatedly. "Why can't I decide what to do? Why do I hesitate?" Her mind ticked off known facts. "Jean loves me. Reed is dead. I love Jean . . ." Kathleen's eyes widened at this last thought, her mind stunned at what her heart had inserted into her mental listing. "I love Jean," she repeated aloud, slowly, thoughtfully, as if testing the flavor of the words on her tongue. It felt right. It tasted of truth. No wonder she had gone so unresistingly into his arms and his bed! Her heart must have known all along what her mind refused to accept.

Even after admitting this to herself, Kathleen's eyes squeezed shut in distress. "Still, the idea of it scares me simple!" she screamed silently. "To put my heart into Jean's keeping frightens me. It requires a faith and trust on my part that I am not sure I possess since Reed's death. There is so much more to be considered than the fact that we love one another. Do I have the courage to take a chance on love again—to dare to think that Jean and I could have a future together? Could I give my children into his care?"

Her thoughts raced round and round in her weary mind, always coming back to the one basic fact. "Yes. I love Jean. Not as I loved Reed, but differently, as Eleonore had said. Now, what do I do about it? How much am I willing to risk?"

Caught up in her thoughts, and in managing the ship, it was a while before Kathleen noticed Jean standing on the main deck below, leaning against the mast and silently watching her. Even through the slashing rain, the intensity of his gaze seared her. Jean stepped toward her. At the very moment he started forward, a vicious streak of lightning split the night sky, arcing with all the accuracy of a perfectly aimed arrow toward the mast under which Jean had moved. The white light was blinding, leaving only the ears to register the sharp *crack* as the mast split.

"*Jean!*" Kathleen screamed as canvas, line, and beams came crashing toward the deck—and Jean. She saw the spar hit him, and he fell, to be shrouded immediately in the folds of the sails.

Abandoning the helm to the hands of Fate, Kathleen ran for the ladder. At the corner of the sterncastle, she collided with Finley coming on deck. Together they raced to Jean's aid. With no one to guide her, the *Emerald*

Enchantress lurched and bucked against the waves. The stench of charred wood was heavy and frightening, as others joined in to help. Above the raging storm, Kathleen shouted, ''Jean is hurt!''

She lost her footing as the frigate lunged sideways. ''Finley! Take the wheel!'' She struggled up and fought her way through tangled lines and sails toward where Jean had fallen. Just as she neared the spot, a wave caught the ship broadside, making her list dangerously, and Kathleen lost her footing.

It was then she spotted Jean. Unconscious, his face deathly pale, he was sliding across the deck toward the rail, limbs ensnared in tangled lines. Before she could regain her feet, she saw him slide beneath the rail, pulling line and sail with him into the boiling dark waters far below.

Stark terror held her in its grip. Then, with an anguished cry, she tore off her boots and flung herself into the savage sea after him.

Chapter 17

An inky blackness encased her as Kathleen dove beneath the waves. It was terrifying in its absolute lack of light and sound, and for a moment, Kathleen almost succumbed to the fear that threatened to engulf her. Fighting her disorientation, she swam blindly through the water. Here, below the churning surface, the water was calmer, buffeting her only slightly as Kathleen headed in what she prayed was the right direction.

Relying solely on her instincts, she sensed a disturbance in the course she had chosen—a presence somewhere nearby. Her outstretched hand touched the tangled lines of the broken mast. Following the line and floating sails deeper, she prayed she would find Jean before it was too late.

After what seemed centuries, her fingertips brushed against cool flesh. "Oh, God!" her mind shrieked, as her hands worked frantically to free him from the rope and sail. "Don't let him be dead!" She yanked viciously at the wet hemp, dragging yards of canvas out of her way, until, at last, she had Jean free. Her lungs were on fire and her head pounding for want of air as she wrapped her arms about his chest. With a strength born of desperation, she lunged for the surface.

As she clawed her way upward, Jean in tow, she defied

the sea that might have claimed them both. "No!" she screamed silently. "I won't let you have him! Not Jean, too! *Not Jean, too!*"

At last they broke the surface, and now the huge waves buffeted them about, making it difficult for Kathleen to keep Jean's head above water. They had surfaced near the ship, and Kathleen struggled to grab the line Dan threw to her. This she tied under Jean's arms, about his chest. As several crewmen pulled Jean aboard, Kathleen labored up the knotted lines of the broken mast. Near the rail, she felt hands grab her roughly, hauling her the rest of the way to the deck.

On hands and knees, Kathleen gulped mouthsful of air. Her weary body wanted desperately to collapse in a heap, but she had to find out Jean's condition. She dragged herself to where several sailors knelt around him.

Jean lay on his stomach, unconscious and still. "He's not breathin'," she heard Dan murmur.

Rage alone dictated her actions then—rage at the sea and the storm, and the injustice of life that would take a second man from her just when she had discovered her love for him. Wanting to strike back at the world, she struck her fists instead against Jean's broad, wet back. Again and again her fists pounded; and finally, when her abused hands would no longer form fists, she aimed her weak blows with the flat of her hands. "Not again!" she screamed over and over. "*Not again!*"

Pity lined the tired faces of her crew as they watched Kathleen vent her fury and pain. No one paid any attention to Jean—until suddenly he began to choke.

"What the . . ." Dan looked on in amazement, then hastened to stem Kathleen's blows. "Cap'n K! Stop! He's alive! He's chokin', but he's breathin'! Quit beatin' on him so he can catch his breath!''

While the men aided Jean in expelling the water from his lungs, and brought the ship's doctor to see what other injuries he had sustained before they attempted to move him, Kathleen sat back in shock and disbelieving joy. She was incapable of speech. Sitting huddled on the rain-washed deck, rocking mutely back and forth, her eyes never left Jean's bedraggled form. Tears streamed down her face, and sobs shook her body as she prayed, and hoped, and watched a miracle unfold before her eyes. Now that Jean was alive and relatively safe, all the strength seeped out of her, and all she could do was weep great tears of relief and joy.

The doctor examined Jean and found only a large bump on the back of his head. "You will have one devil of a headache for a few days, and you might have blurred vision or nausea, maybe a little dizziness," he told him. "I want you to stay in bed for a few days and take it easy. No swordfights, no excessive activity, and no excitement. That spar hit you a pretty good blow, but after a few days' rest, you should be fine.''

Kathleen put him to bed with tender, loving care—in her bunk. Jean had not the strength to put up much resistance, beyond a groggy "This is ridiculous! Fussy old sawbones!''

Kathleen, herself weary to the bone, slid carefully in next to him. "Ssh, Jean. You are not to get excited, my love. Save what little breath I knocked back into you, and go to sleep.''

"Did you mean it?'' he asked softly.

"Mean what?''

"Did you mean it when you called me your love, or did you merely mean your lover?"

Kathleen smiled in the dark. "I meant it, *mon amour*." More softly, and in a voice filled with wonder, she said, "I love you, Jean. I love you, and it scares me witless. I thought I would die when I saw you slide overboard!"

As if he had just realized it, he said in awe, "You dived in after me! That is what all the men were talking about!"

"Of course I did!" she retorted sharply. "You didn't expect me to just stand there and do nothing, did you? What was I supposed to do, weep and watch you drown?"

"Don't be sassy!" he barked back. "I am just saying it was a risk I would never have asked you to take."

"You didn't ask. I made the decision on my own. Instead of growling, you should be thanking me!"

Jean groaned. "I am grateful." After a short pause, he asked, "Why are we bickering? We are both alive, in love, and together. We are two of the most fortunate beings on earth."

"I know," Kathleen whispered past the lump in her throat. She cradled him close. "Oh, Jean! When I think how close I came to losing you, just when I had finally admitted to myself that I love you. You might have died before I got the chance to tell you!"

"You decided this before the accident?" he asked quietly.

"Yes. I realized it before I noticed you on deck. Then I couldn't wait to tell you, and suddenly lightning struck the mast and the world fell apart."

"What about Reed?"

Kathleen made no reply.

"Do you still love him?" Jean persisted.

"Of course I do! I will always love him, Jean, but that

has nothing to do with my love for you. I have finally come to realize that what Eleonore told me is true—It is possible to love more than one man; each in a different way.''

"Eleonore told you that?'' he wanted to know. "When?''

"A couple of months ago—the first time you took me to New Orleans. It was then she told me it would make her happy if we could find love between us. I was afraid she would be hurt by it, but she assured me otherwise.''

"Eleonore is a wonderful woman,'' Jean agreed sleepily.

"And you are a wonderful man, but we are both tired and need our rest. We can talk more when you are rested.''

"Tell me again that you love me,'' Jean requested. "I want to fall asleep with the sound of your sweet voice saying those precious words.''

"I love you,'' Kathleen murmured softly. "I love you, Jean Lafitte.''

They were only a day's sail from Grande Terre by morning, so they decided to return to Jean's base for repairs. During the time it took for a new mast to be fitted on the *Emerald Enchantress*, Jean rested and visited Dominique, who was recovering nicely from his wounds, thanks to Isabel's tender care.

Pierre decided this would be a good time for him to take a short trip to his home in New Orleans to see his wife and children. He had not returned by the time they wished to sail again, so they left without him. Dominique agreed to tell Pierre that they would return in a few weeks, and he could rejoin them then if he wished. Dominique and Isabel would take charge of things on Grande Terre until then, as Dominique was still unfit for travel or warfare, and Isabel would not leave his side.

The weather was beautiful, perfect for sailing. The shock of the storm and Jean's near-fatal accident soon wore off. Jean had secretly harbored the fear that Kathleen's confession of love had been prompted by all that had occurred that terrible night. Now, with each day that passed, he grew more confident. It was a dream come true, and Jean reveled in it.

As for Kathleen, now that she had made her decision, she blossomed like a spring flower in sunlight. Her joy was evident in her ready smile, a smile that heightened the green of her eyes to the color of a new leaf, and added a glow to her cheeks. She laughed more, and was much more relaxed than in days past.

When Jean asked her to marry him, Kathleen accepted, but they agreed it was best put off until the war was over. Then they would travel to Savannah, and Kathleen's children could meet Jean and become accustomed to the idea of a new father. This would give Jean and Kathleen time to decide where they wanted to live, and what to do about Chimera and Jean's privateering base at Grande Terre.

The Gulf waters shimmered like a dark jewel beneath the star-studded night sky and the moon shone brightly, a huge silver crescent. A balmy breeze blew softly, as if blessing them, as Kathleen and Jean stood at the ship's rail and gazed at the wondrous beauty about them.

"I love the sea like this," Kathleen sighed, leaning back against Jean's supporting chest. "I love her in all her moods, but especially this way. It is as if she is dressed in her finest black velvet gown, with diamonds sprinkled over it."

Jean chuckled, his chest vibrating with the sound. "I shall try not to be jealous, *cherie.*"

Kathleen turned in his embrace, and looked deeply into his clear hazel eyes. "No need for jealousy, my darling. I still love you best." Her fingers feathered into his thick brown hair, while her hands cradled his face between her palms.

"Now and always?" he whispered into her hair.

A shiver danced up her spine at his words, an unknown fear that she could not fathom. Reasoning to herself that she was probably still cautious in the face of so much happiness, she answered softly, "As long as the fates allow."

"You are shivering. Let's go inside. I shall warm you with my love."

"Poor Peg-Leg!" Kathleen laughed. "He has a long night in the closet ahead of him!"

There was a poignancy in their loving this night, for some reason. It touched both of them, as if neither could quite believe their good fortune. Kathleen clung to him as if afraid he would disappear at any moment. Kathleen knew how quickly joy could be taken away. It made their time together all the more precious. Jean seemed especially tender this evening, as if aware that life was too unpredictable to count on unending blessings.

Jean's lips worshipped her; his hands charting her body as if to commit each curve to memory; as if he felt that she might be taken from him at any time, and he needed to remember each small detail to perfection. He loved her tenderly and thoroughly, bringing her body to a quivering, molten mass of desire beneath his touch. Her sharp cries of delight and low murmurings stirred his passions as never before.

309

Jean's whispered endearments, his hands on her hot, craving flesh, held Kathleen spellbound in a web of desire, as waves of pleasure swelled over her. When he moved over her, uniting them in the final act of love, her body melted beneath his. They were like leaves caught up in a whirlpool, spinning ever faster until they were at last sucked into the center and drowned in a devastating current of ecstasy—yet Kathleen could not prevent the thought that bolted unbidden into her mind: "This moment will never come again. Time is slipping through my fingers like grains of sand, forever gone and irretrievable." A sob caught in her throat, and she held Jean tightly to her, his head clasped close to her heart.

His fingers found the moisture over her temples. "Why are you weeping, *petite*? What strange mood holds you tonight?" he whispered softly against her breast.

"Oh, Jean," she sighed tearfully. "Surely you feel it too, this heart-rending sadness?"

"*Oui,* I too feel a certain uneasiness, as if we tempt destiny with our joy," he admitted, "but let us not weave a cloud of doom where only sunshine exists. Let us enjoy to the limits all the love we are allowed to share. No matter what tomorrow brings, let us exult in one another now."

As if in precious promise, he made love to her again, driving all the shadows and fears from her heart and mind, leaving only the sweetness of his love to color her dreams.

Kathleen awoke the next morning in the cradle of Jean's arms. Again they made delicious, languorous love, taking time to satisfy one another's needs, savoring the delight and rapture to the fullest.

Content and replete, Kathleen went lazily about her business aboard ship. Satisfied to drift aimlessly through the crystal waters of the sunlit Gulf, she felt no immediate need to hunt down enemy vessels this day. Her urge for vengeance seemed suddenly spent.

The first half of the day was idyllic—sunshine, warm breezes, a picnic lunch for two on the afterdeck. A school of dolphins even appeared to entertain them with their grace and playful antics. Laughter and love lulled them into rare peace of mind.

Just past midday, that peace was abruptly interrupted. They had inadvertently crossed paths with a British warship on the prowl.

Jean heaved himself to his feet, pulling Kathleen up after him. "I knew this was too good to last," he groaned.

That same peculiar shiver tingled along Kathleen's spine at Jean's words. Throwing off the feeling, she shrugged lightly. "It is back to work for us, *mon amour,*" she teased with a smile. "We needed something to sharpen our dulled wits anyway."

Jean swatted her bottom affectionately. "Speak for yourself, my dear." Her fingers played with the diamond and aquamarine ring now resting on her engagement finger. She had only the previous week replaced her emerald wedding ring from Reed.

The *Pride* and the *Emerald Enchantress* worked in perfect concert to approach the enemy vessel. The British, upon being confronted with two ships, decided to turn tail and run, attempting to avoid a confrontation. The two privateers gave chase, and the race was on.

In high spirits, Jean and Kathleen were enjoying the game. Knowing full well that they could overtake the British vessel at any time, they toyed with it as a cat teases a mouse. When at length they tired of the game, they moved swiftly to close the gap. In short order, they had outmaneuvered the heavier ship and flanked her on both

311

sides, effectively hemming her in.

In a move perfected by repetition, Kathleen grabbed a boarding line and swung herself gracefully aboard the enemy ship, her rapier at the ready. Jean landed softly at her side, prepared to fight in tandem with her, each guarding the other's back. They immediately launched into the fray, blades flashing in the sunlight.

As was their usual pattern, Jean faced off against the ship's captain, while Kathleen took on the quartermaster. With an ease that was ridiculous, as well as enviable, she defeated her opponent handily with a last quick feint and a smooth thrust. As Jean, too, had finished off his foe, they went on to match wits and blades with yet another pair of hapless victims while their crew efficiently rounded up the remaining Britons.

Busy dealing with her latest adversary, Kathleen took no note of the tall, bearded man standing near Finley, avidly watching her every move. Her full concentration was on the burly seaman before her, anticipating his actions almost before he'd thought of them himself. Her gaze never flickered from his, even when she heard Jean's choked gasp behind her. Moving swiftly to block a heavy blow, she called over her shoulder, "Jean, are you wounded?"

Jean's voice sounded strangely strangled as he answered, "Do not concern yourself, *cherie*. I am in no danger."

With nimble, fluid motions, she dispatched her enemy with three neatly executed strokes. Immediately she turned to locate Jean.

What she found completely disconcerted her. Never before had she witnessed such pain and anguish in a human face, such regretful sorrow in a pair of eyes. "Jean!" she cried out in alarm. "What is it?" Her eyes were anxiously scanning his body in search of a wound, but found nothing.

His arms opened wordlessly, and she flew into them, her eyes searching his. Jean's embrace was bone-crushing and full of tension. A heavy sigh shook his chest as he pressed her to him, holding her head against his pounding heart. "My little sweetheart!" he groaned into her midnight hair. For her ears only, he whispered in hushed torment, "Always remember how much I love you! Promise me you will not forget the love we shared!"

Fear and confusion tore at her, and she raised her head to gaze into his face. "Jean, what is the matter? Are you hurt?"

His hands gripped the sides of her head. "More than you will ever know," he murmured, then said grimly, "Brace yourself, *cherie*, for the most immense shock of your life." Without further warning, he turned her about in his arms.

Had she received a rapier thrust to the heart, Kathleen could not have been more stunned. At the sight before her, she stiffened, incapable of movement. Her breath left her chest in a rush; her head went suddenly light with dizziness; her rapier slid with a clatter from her lifeless hand. Her mouth went dry and her knees weak, and had it not been for Jean's supporting arms, she would have crumpled to the deck.

There, before her disbelieving eyes, in the flesh and very much alive, stood Reed.

Shaking her head slowly back and forth in denial of the vision before her, Kathleen tried to back away, but Jean's form prevented this. Her eyes wide with bewilderment, she whimpered pathetically. "This cannot be real!" Her voice rose in hysteria. "This is a cruel, brutal joke! A

313

ghost! Jean! Make it go away!'' She turned to hide her face against his protective chest.

Reed started forward, and then stopped, his brow furrowed in confusion over Kathleen's reaction. Naturally, he had expected her to be shocked, but nothing like this! He hesitated, not knowing what to do, not wanting to add to her hysteria, and at the same time appalled by the obvious intimacy between his wife and best friend. What had been going on in his absence? And why had she resumed her role as Emerald?

Jean's hand clamped about Kathleen's upper arms, and he thrust her roughly away from him. ''Kathleen!'' he shouted over her screams. ''Kathleen! This is real! It *is* happening! Reed is here and he's alive!'' He shook her until her teeth nearly rattled in her head. Finally, in desperation, he slapped her face smartly. As she stared up at him, dazed, he said more softly, ''Face it, *cherie,* and deal with it.''

''Oh, my God!'' she sighed heavily, clinging to Jean's arm as she turned once more to face her long-lost husband. A multitude of emotions mingled within her as she stared at him—shock, surprise, lingering disbelief, along with the rebirth of long buried hopes—wonder, anger and hurt at his year-long disappearance, relief—and finally, love.

A separate part of her mind was cataloging the changes in him. He was thinner, a bit haggard. His beard needed trimming . . . Then, finally, when she found the courage, her gaze rose to meet his. Those sky-blue eyes looked out at her from a dearly familiar face. Along with his confusion at her odd reaction, his eyes reflected a cool anger, held in check by obvious effort as he watched her collect her wits.

''This is not exactly the reunion I had envisioned all these endless months, Kat,'' he stated gruffly.

314

As if hearing his voice again had broken the spell that had held her motionless. Kathleen gave a glad cry and launched herself at him, tears streaming down her face. "Oh, Reed! Reed! If this is a dream, don't let me wake up!"

He gathered her close in his arms, enclosing her in a fierce embrace that lifted her off her feet. "Kat! Aah, love, you feel so good! It has been so long!" he groaned. His lips melded themselves to hers in a hungry, starving kiss that threatened to steal her breath from her body. Her joyous tears wet both their cheeks, but neither noticed nor cared. For timeless moments, his mouth devoured hers, reacquainting itself with the taste and shape of her, quenching that first fierce need. Then, as the kiss lengthened, her lips softened beneath his, inviting the tender caresses she remembered so well; the lingering exploration of lips that clung and promised untold wonders.

"This is more what I had in mind," he murmured.

"I love you. I love you so much," she sighed against his lips.

With reluctance, his lips left hers at last, and he drew slightly apart from her, his eyes devouring her features as if to assure himself that she was truly here with him. "I love you, too, kitten," he answered softly.

"Reed, I missed you so!" she cried, her arms still linked about his neck, afraid he might disappear if she released him.

"For a while, you had me doubting that," he commented wryly, slicing a questioning look at Jean. Taking a deep breath, he sighed with relief. "I have so many questions! How are Andrea and Katlin? Is everything at Chimera alright? And what on earth are you

315

doing here?''

''They are fine—everything is fine! I'll wager I have twice as many questions as you!'' Her eyes shone like emeralds, and she gulped back a sob. ''Where on earth have you *been* all these months?'' she exclaimed. ''My God, Reed! We have all thought you were dead for nearly a year now!''

A frown creased his sun-browned forehead, and his narrowed gaze swept from Kathleen to Jean in quick assessment. ''What! Why would you have thought that?'' he asked in amazement.

Jean at last stepped in. ''The government sent a courier to Savannah last June to break the news to Kathleen and your family,'' he explained. ''Captain Guthrie reported you missing and presumed drowned after the storm your ship encountered in May.'' After a short hesitation, he offered his hand in belated greeting to his old friend. ''Naturally, we are delighted to find you are alive after all.''

''I wonder,'' Reed muttered low, taking Jean's hand with some reluctance. ''Somehow, I got the impression you were less than thrilled to see me, Jean.''

''It was an unexpected surprise,'' Jean answered smoothly. ''Of course, now that you realize that we believed you drowned, you can better understand Kathleen's shock at suddenly seeing you standing before her.''

Kathleen's eyes closed briefly, then opened to fasten on Reed's face. ''I thought I was seeing a ghost at first,'' she said softly. ''For a few moments, I believed I had finally lost my mind and gone completely mad. I am still not positive this is really happening.'' But hope shone brightly in her emerald eyes, and she reached out a hand to touch his face, as if to reassure herself of his actual presence.

Doubt and building frustration clouded Reed's face. "Did any of you think to search for me?" he asked harshly.

"Search for you!" Kathleen screeched, her anger instantly fired by his accusing glare. "We searched the entire Gulf, and then some! For months we combed the seas and every island we came across! We moved heaven and earth, enlisted the aid of pirates when the government refused to help, and never gave up hope, even after we found the remains of the *Kat-Ann* on that damnable reef! Only when we found a couple of survivors, months after the storm, and heard one tell of seeing you dive from the sinking ship into the sea, never to be seen again, did we finally begin to accept the fact that you were dead." Then, recalling the question that had plagued for her months, she screamed at him, "Where in Hades *were* you?"

"On one of those God-forsaken islands you neglected to search!" he roared back. "Exactly where I have been up until three days ago, when this British warship happened to spot us!" His eyes flashed blue flames at her.

"Don't you scream at me, Reed Taylor!" she retorted hotly. "Have you any idea of the hell I have been through? Do you realize that I was so devastated by your death that I could barely stand the sight of our own son, because he resembles you so strongly? Does it matter to you that I could not sleep without the blessed oblivion of liquor to dull my mind, that I very nearly became an alcoholic idiot as a result?"

"Sweetheart, I'm sorry . . ." Reed swore, becoming gradually aware of the agony she had suffered.

Kathleen barely heard his words as she continued ranting. "Do you care that I needed to escape the agonizing memories so badly that I could not face myself in the mirror—could not look upon the tear-ravaged woman I had become? That I finally resorted to the only refuge I could find—my beloved sea? That I had to bury myself in the image of Emerald because I could no longer stand the heartbreak of being the Widow Taylor?'' Her tirade finally wound down, leaving her shaken and trembling.

Reed's face had softened, but now his eyes skimmed her brief outfit. ''Is that why you are disguised again as Emerald, sailing your famous green frigate?''

Kathleen nodded. ''Yes, for that and other reasons—among them the desire for revenge. I felt driven to avenge your death, and I set out to sink as many British vessels as I could, and send as many Englishmen as possible to a watery grave. Jean, Dominique, Isabel, and all our crewmen have joined me on my crusade against the British. Even Pierre and I have buried our differences and joined forces.''

Reed's gaze fell again on Jean's face. ''That is quite a tale, but I feel there is much more you have not yet said.''

Before anyone could reply, a loud screeching drew their attention. All eyes turned toward the sound, to find a seaman leading a struggling young woman across the deck. Her blonde hair was streaming over her face, and she was kicking and clawing for all she was worth.

''I found this one hiding under a bunk in one of the cabins,'' the seaman explained. ''She's lucky we discovered her before we fired the ship.''

The petite blonde's startled gaze flitted from face to face, but when she spotted Reed, she wrenched herself from the man's hold and threw herself headlong into Reed's arms. ''Oh, darling!'' she wailed. ''Don't let these savages hurt me! Save me!''

Reed patted the girl awkwardly. "It is all right, Sally. We are safe now."

Kathleen's eyes met Reed's over the top of the little blonde's head, and her face hardened into a mask of stony fury. Her emerald eyes blazed in her pale face, her cheeks twin spots of high color. "There is more than one person present with some explaining to do, it seems, Captain Taylor." Her voice was icy, her words clipped.

Twisting her head about, young Sally surveyed Kathleen from head to toe, her pale blue eyes taking in Kathleen's unusual attire. "Who is *she?*" she whined.

Before Reed could reply, Kathleen said sharply, "I am Emerald, captain of the *Emerald Enchantress,* and one of the most feared pirates on the seas." After a pregnant pause, she added, "I eat little girls like you for breakfast, and if they are not tasty enough, I toss them overboard to the fish!"

For the first time since Reed's sudden appearance, Jean laughed. "Emerald," he said, stressing the name heavily, "is it truly necessary to frighten the poor girl to death?" As he spoke, his eyes flashed a silent message to Reed and those crewmen standing nearby. His look clearly warned that it would not be wise to reveal Kathleen's true identity at the moment.

Kathleen chuckled without humor. "That would depend on what her relationship is to Captain Taylor," she drawled.

Sally's eyes widened, and once more, before Reed could speak, she blurted, "He is my fiancé! We plan to be married soon."

It was all Kathleen could manage not to stagger at the girl's announcement. To give her a moment to compose herself, Jean interceded, his words coming at the same

319

time as Reed's. "I can explain. Sally is . . ."

"It would seem congratulations are in order, Miss . . ." Jean's voice trailed off.

"Sally Simpson," the girl offered.

At last Kathleen found her tongue. "As far as I know, bigamy is considered a crime. I am sure Captain Taylor's *wife* will be delighted to hear your news, Miss Simpson," she snapped. "Your fiancé also has two small children— or weren't you aware of that? Did the dear captain neglect to inform you of his family?" Her words dripped venom, and her eyes seared the girl and Reed in the same all-encompassing glare.

"This is ridiculous! If you would only listen . . ." Reed began, only to be cut short again by Sally.

"Oh, he told me everything about himself!" the girl announced brightly. "As soon as possible, he is going to divorce his wife and marry me!" she assured them.

Reed groaned at the fire in Kathleen's eyes at this added bit of news. "That is not precisely correct," Reed put in hastily.

Kathleen's smile was more of a sneer. "I gather that you and Miss Simpson did more than collect seashells during your extended stay in that island paradise of yours," she hissed.

"Now Ka . . ." Reed began.

"*Captain* to you," she snarled, cutting him short before he pronounced her name.

Anger suffused Reed's face. "*Captain!*" he barked. "Tell me how I am to ascertain how faithful my dear wife has been during my absence!"

"At least *she* had the excuse of thinking you were dead all this time!" she shot back. "What excuse will *you* offer?"

Reed's eyes narrowed to icy slits. "As long as we are getting so personal, perhaps you could tell me the extent of your relationship with my dear friend Jean." His gaze traveled accusingly from Kathleen to Jean.

At this point, Jean deemed it prudent to intercede. "As much as I hate to interrupt this enlighting conversation, might I point out that the sun is dipping low over the horizon, and we still have business to finish here." To Kathleen, he said, "It is your turn to claim the vessel, if you wish."

Kathleen's stomach lurched at the thought of keeping the ship that had just brought so much upheaval into her life. "I would not have this ship on a bet! Take it for yourself, or fire it, Jean!"

Jean was of the same opinion as Kathleen. Within a few hours, this vessel had brought Reed back into their lives, and torn Kathleen from Jean's arms forever. He knew he had lost the woman he would love for the rest of his life. To his quartermaster, he ordered tersely, "Sink it!"

Kathleen turned from them. "I have my work to attend to," she announced, grabbing at a boarding line.

Behind her, she heard Reed say, "Come, Sally. I will help you board the *Enchantress.*"

Kathleen whirled on him, her face furious. "I will not have that woman aboard my ship!" she announced.

"*Your* ship?" he roared.

"Yes, *my* ship!" she snarled. "The *Emerald Enchantress* has always been my ship, whether in my father's name or any other! She has always been mine! She always has been, and always will be *mine!*"

"The young woman can come aboard the *Pride,* if you wish," Jean offered smoothly.

"Fine!" Kathleen snapped. "Or she can swim home, or

321

go down with this ship! I don't care which! But I will *not* have her aboard the *Enchantress!*''

''And I refuse to venture aboard the *Pride!*'' Reed stated firmly. ''What do you have to say to that, my dear Emerald?'' he sneered.

Kathleen leveled a fire-filled glare at him. ''You, Captain Taylor, can go where you damned well please!''

With that, she swung smoothly aboard her frigate, leaving the others to make the arrangements.

Chapter 18

A short while later, Reed boarded the *Emerald Enchantress,* minus Miss Sally Simpson, who had wisely chosen to travel with Jean on the *Pride*. He found Kathleen perched high in the shrouds, Finley manning the helm in her stead.

Reed climbed to within shouting distance of her. "I am taking over command of the *Enchantress,*" he announced loudly.

"Try it, and I'll slit your bloody throat!" came her reply. At the moment, she felt entirely capable of it.

"Damn it, Kat!" he roared. "If you had allowed Sally to board, we could sail directly for Savannah and get things straightened out on the way!"

"Ha!" A short, sharp laugh shot down to him. "*That* would certainly stand Savannah on its ear! It is not every day such a notorious vessel as the *Enchantress* docks at her port!" Kathleen leaned over to peer down at him. "In case you haven't noticed, this frigate is *green,* sails and all, and there is not another like her on the seas. Add to that the fact that for the last few months the piratess Emerald has been on a ruthless rampage, and earned quite an infamous reputation." Her voice lowered to a throaty purr. "Do you really want all the world to know that your wife is a blood-thirsty pirate, Captain Taylor? If so, then by all means, sail for Savannah immediately—but without your doxy!''

Reed gritted his teeth, striving for a measure of calm. ''I take it we are headed for Grande Terre?'' he asked.

''Quite right!'' she shot back. ''There we will pick up Isabel, and you can choose from any number of captured British vessels the one you wish to sail to Savannah, unless you prefer to wait until the *Enchantress* can be turned back into the *Starbright* once more.''

''I do not intend to spend any more time on my former friend's island than necessary,'' Reed grated.

''You have no call to bear a grudge against Jean,'' Kathleen called down. ''If you recall, everyone thought you were dead until an hour ago!. If anyone is guilty in this mess, it is *you!*''

''I am a man, not a monk!'' he yelled back. ''We were marooned together for a *year,* for God's sake! What did you expect?''

''Too much, obviously,'' she snapped. ''I should have remembered that you cannot abstain for longer than two weeks without causing yourself extreme anguish! Yet, while you expected *me* to remain faithful, the same rules do not apply to *you!*''

Reed's temper exploded. ''Did you, or did you not, have an affair with Jean?'' he demanded loudly.

''If I did, I would never admit it to you now!'' she screamed in reply. ''Wonder about it until the day you die, but I will never tell you!''

''Are you going to stay up there forever?'' Reed called up much later.

''That is a distinct possibility,'' she fired back.

''You have missed your supper.''

Kathleen laughed humorlessly. "Would it surprise you if I said my appetite had fallen off drastically?"

"Not really," Reed sighed wearily. Trying to avoid touchy subjects, he asked, "What is all this about captured vessels at Grande Terre? I do not want to borrow one of Jean's ships."

"They aren't Jean's. They are mine," Kathleen informed him. "Half of all the worthy prizes we captured became mine, according to my agreement with Jean when we joined forces. In fact, besides the three now at Grande Terre, I have sent half a dozen to the government in Washington in your memory, and at least that number have been added to the shipping firm in Savannah."

Reed whistled his amazement. "Good God, Kat! Were you trying to wipe out the entire British navy single-handedly?"

"Yes!" she hissed. "I had assumed I owed them that much for destroying my life. God have mercy on my soul for all the men I have killed trying to avenge your death—and you were not even dead!" An anguished laugh became a groan.

As another thought occurred to her, she said, "The only ship we have lost in this entire war has been the *Kat-Ann*. I couldn't believe my own eyes when I saw her shattered remains! How the devil did you manage that, Reed Taylor? You should have been able to bring the *Kat-Ann* through any storm without much damage, yet there she lies, broken and battered—the pride of my father's fleet—my mother's namesake!" She broke off with an angry sob.

"I certainly didn't run up on that reef purposely, you little fool!" he retorted. "Do you think I enjoyed being stranded on that island for an entire year?"

Kathleen laughed tersely. "I am sure Miss Simpson eased your misery immensely!"

"As Jean eased yours?" he shot back.

Stony silence was her only response.

Kathleen's heart was aching. Her head was spinning, flooding with thousands of fragmented thoughts and feelings. Within one short afternoon, her entire world had turned upside down once again. "Oh, Reed," she moaned to herself, laying her head on her folded arms. "Did you return only to bring me pain? What am I to do?"

After the initial shock, glorious joy had poured through her. Reed was alive! Her beloved was safe in her arms! The sea had not swallowed him up for all eternity! It was a miracle!

Then Kathleen had remembered Jean, and Sally Simpson had introduced a new twist to the tangled maze Kathleen suddenly found herself in.

Now, as she sat high in the shrouds, she was more miserable and more confused than she had been since Reed had been reported missing. "Jean," she sobbed, "I never meant to hurt you!"

Her heart was torn in two and the pain was nearly unbearable. Kathleen wished she could disappear in a puff of smoke—simply cease to exist. Her thoughts spun round and round in a ceaseless circle, with no solutions in sight. On the one hand, she was deliriously happy that Reed was alive. It was the answer to her prayers, the thing she had longed for all those endless months. Even now, she knew she would be returning with him to Chimera and their children. She needed to be near him; to see him, hear him, touch him—to believe in his existence.

Kathleen was beginning to believe that joy generally

came hand-in-hand with sorrow. There was a price to be paid for extreme happiness. One must earn it through tears. She hurt for herself, for Jean, even for Reed. She knew he had envisioned a more joyous reunion. To finally get off that island, which must have been hell even with the fair Miss Simpson there, and find his wife involved with another man, and that man his best friend! Kathleen had no doubt how much that must have hurt Reed. She was filled with the same agony, inflicted by Sally Simpson's blunt announcement. While Kathleen could discount some of the blonde's words as an effort to save herself from an uncertain fate, the fact remained that Reed had been unfaithful. He had even admitted as much.

How much had he come to care for the younger woman, Kathleen wondered? A year was an awfully long time to spend alone together. Was he in love with her? She certainly was beautiful, even after all that time on the island. And she was young; no more than eighteen. . . .

Then there was Jean. Fresh tears came to Kathleen's eyes just thinking of him. What must he be feeling now? Her gaze searched out the dark shape of the *Pride* against the night sky. Jean had pulled her back from the edge of insanity. He had taught her to live again—and to love. He had become a vital part of her life, and she loved him dearly—yet she loved Reed more. Reed *was* her life; the very air she breathed; her heart, her soul, her blood. It was a wound to her heart to think of leaving Jean, but to lose Reed a second time would be to die inside.

It grieved Kathleen that circumstances had rent the fabric of the beautiful friendship between Reed and Jean. They had loved one another like brothers, and now they were on opposite sides, with Kathleen standing between them. Would their friendship ever be mended? Could anyone win in this crazy war of love and possession? By law, she belonged to Reed, yet a part of her would always be Jean's. Technically, Kathleen had committed adultery, yet she could not feel guilt. She had finally forgiven herself, believing Reed lost to her forever. She had gone to Jean with love in her heart, though she would die before admitting this to Reed. What good would it do any of them? It would only cause more grief, and would ensure that Jean and Reed would never be friends again. Kathleen was glad she had had the presence of mind to remove Jean's things from her cabin before hiding away in the shrouds.

Interwoven through Kathleen's mingled pain and joy was a gnawing anger. While she had unwittingly been unfaithful to her supposedly drowned husband, Reed had gone into his affair with full knowledge of his infidelity. He had burst back into her life today without warning, a spectre resurrected, expecting Kathleen to welcome him with open arms regardless of his indiscretions. Within minutes, he had reverted to his old demanding, possessive arrogant self.

Miss Sally Simpson was another matter, indeed! Kathleen did not need to be a soothsayer to forecast trouble ahead from that quarter. That pale blonde hair and those cool blue eyes would attract any man, let alone a virile man on a deserted island! Kathleen had noticed that, though petite, the young woman had a well-proportioned figure.

"Why couldn't she have been old and ugly, with wrinkles and warts?" Kathleen groaned. "She even has a pretty face and straight teeth!"

It was evident that Sally Simpson was greatly attracted to Reed. She'd had him to herself for a year, and would not give him up easily, whether Reed was married or not. The girl meant trouble in more ways than one! Beneath that helpless, charming facade, Kathleen sensed a shrewd mind and a calculating nature. Possessing these same qualities herself, she could easily recognize them in her rival.

Kathleen grimaced, seeing her own jealousy for what it was. " 'Meow,' said one cat to the other," she mocked sarcastically. Still, beyond her justified reasons for disliking the girl, Kathleen's enmity went further. There was something about Miss Simpson that did not quite ring true; something Kathleen could not quite identify, but that told her that Sally was not what she appeared to be. Her instincts told her that Sally was a ruthless little manipulator beneath that clever disguise of sweet femininity, an unscrupulous type who would use any means to achieve her goal, unless Kathleen missed her guess. Kathleen's natural wariness told her she would be a fool to underestimate little Sally Simpson.

With that in mind, it was imperative that Sally never connect Emerald's identity with that of Reed's wife. The woman would have no compunctions about using that handy bit of information to her best advantage, Kathleen was sure. It would pay to be very careful, indeed, if Sally Simpson was to be around for any length of time. It was Kathleen's devout hope that upon reaching Savannah, Miss Simpson would travel on to other parts without delay, but Kathleen sincerely doubted this would be the case. The woman seemed too much the tenacious type to give up so easily.

Kathleen's lids drooped over sleepy, tear-laden eyes. "I am so tired," she thought hazily, "so weary of battling my thoughts and feelings!" Too much had happened too quickly, and now her body was insisting she rest. Her eyes blinked shut heavily once, twice—and suddenly it was too much of an effort to open them.

When she almost toppled off her precarious perch, Kathleen decided to climb down. She descended slowly, her limbs stiff from hours of immobility, and made her way slowly to her quarters. There she stopped, noticing the thin line of light showing from beneath the door. Reed must be in her cabin! As she hesitated, debating whether to go in search of another place to sleep, or to get clean clothes from her quarters first, she heard Reed's voice.

"Come in, Kat. Don't cower in the passageway all night," he growled.

Her hand found the doorlatch, and she marched into the room, slamming the door behind her. "I have never cowered in my life, Reed Taylor!" Her gaze narrowed on him, comfortably reclining on her bunk, his boots off and his shirt half unbuttoned. "I see you have made yourself at home in my cabin."

"Where else would I spend my first night reunited with my loving wife?" he asked innocently.

Heading for her sea chest, Kathleen said, "I am really not up to a lengthy argument with you tonight, Reed. I just want to be by myself. If you won't sleep elsewhere, I will."

An agitated squawk from the corner of the room drew her attention. There, in his cloth-covered cage, sat a disgruntled Peg-Leg. "What have you done to Peg-Leg?" she demanded.

As she reached to uncover the cage, Reed barked, "Let him be. He was being a nuisance, so I covered him up." Reed examined his left hand critically. "The rotten bird pecked me!"

330

A reluctant smile tugged at Kathleen's lips. "Just shows what an excellent judge of character he is!" she retorted smartly, returning to take clean clothes from her chest.

"Kat," Reed's drawl held a confident, leisurely quality. "If you think you can reach that door before I do, you are welcome to try, but I will warn you now that you will not be leaving this cabin until we get a few matters settled between us."

Mentally measuring the distance to the door, and considering Reed's deceptively relaxed pose, Kathleen knew she had made a foolish mistake in entering the cabin in the first place. She closed her eyes with a weary sigh. "All right, Reed. Tired as I am, I suppose you will give me no rest until we do. Let's talk." She walked to her desk and sat warily on the edge of it. The sheath of her sword clinked noisily against the desk, and out of habit, she removed her weapons and laid them down. Then, tense and nervous, she faced her husband.

Reed was watching her, a thoughtful expression on his face. "It is difficult to think of you as Kathleen, with your hair dark. I keep wanting to call you Emerald." His tone turned reflective. "All that time on the island, I kept picturing you at Chimera with our son and daughter, your copper hair flying in the breeze, your emerald eyes bright with laughter . . ."

A wobbly, wistful smile touched her lips. "Whenever you came to mind, I kept forgetting you had grown that mustache and beard. I'd only seen it the last time you were home . . ." All her unvoiced agony was reflected in her eyes.

Reed's gaze found hers and held it. Softly, as if afraid his words would break the spell that held them, he said,

"You will be going back to Chimera with me, Kat?" It was half-question, half-statement.

Pushing herself away from the desk, Kathleen crossed to the porthole. She stood looking out at the dark, starlit night, her arms wound about her waist as if to contain her pain. She nodded, her eyes closed tightly. "Yes," she whispered at last. Her glossy black hair fell forward to shield her face as she bowed her head. Her teeth caught at her lower lip to stifle a sob that would not be held back. Tears rolled down her face as she stood in abject misery.

Quiet as a cougar, Reed slipped up behind her. Until his hands clamped about her arms, she was unaware of his approach. Whirling her about to face him, his face was now a hard mask of bitter fury. "Tears, my sweet?" he asked scornfully. "Tears for your lost love, perhaps?"

Mutely, she shook her head in denial. How could she explain that she was crying for all of them—for love gained and lost; for a world made mad by one ironic twist of fate?

Angered by her quiet sobbing, he shook her hard. "Don't lie to me!" he ground out through gritted teeth. With an oath, he threw her from him, to land half across the bunk.

Amazement held her there as he stalked across the small space separating them. His long legs caged hers between them as he bent forward, his hands delving into her hair to hold her gaze to his. "Tell me about you and Jean," he growled, his eyes twin blazes of blue flame. His thumbs reached down to press against her throat. "Tell me before I strangle you!"

Kathleen glared back, too angry to be frightened. "Are we to exchange confidences now, Reed?" she asked tartly. "Are you as willing to tell me about your experiences with your island playmate?" Despite the telling tick in his jaw that denoted his anger, she goaded him further. "Did you employ your caveman tactics with her, too?"

Reed sneered down at her, his face dark and sardonic. "It was never necessary with Sally," he answered spitefully.

Kathleen struggled to keep the hurt from showing on her face. "How convenient for you!" she sniped.

"Quite," he snapped. "Now it is your turn. How accommodating were you to Jean? Did you show him your famous temper, or did you tempt him with honeyed lips?" His fingers tightened, pulling at her hair.

"Go to hell, Reed Taylor!" she hissed.

"I probably shall, my love, but I shall take you with me." His lips lowered to within a hair's breadth of hers. "You see, my lovely, wanton wife, you belong to me, and what I own, I don't give up," he whispered menacingly. "Neither do I share my prize possessions!"

"I am not your slave, or your horse, or . . ."

He cut her angry retort short. "But you are mine!" he snarled, his lips claiming hers in a devastating demonstration of his mastery. She fought him silently, her lips caught in the vise of his. His fingers freed her hair to loosen the lacing of her vest, and he quickly drew it from about her wriggling torso. With deft motions, he stripped her breeches from her, then held her bucking body to the bed as he wrestled out of his own clothing, ignoring her screeching oaths.

His body came back over hers, hot and hard against her silken skin. His mouth reclaimed hers with demanding authority, forcing her lips to part beneath his to receive his questing tongue. Calloused fingers held her jaw, preventing her from biting him.

A muted scream of rage gurgled in her throat. *Damn*

him, anyway! He *always* did this to her! He always found a way to make her forget everything but his touch! She wanted to stay angry at him now—or did she? Long-buried fires were flickering slowly to life under his knowing caresses, and Kathleen found herself fighting a losing battle, both with Reed and with herself. Through a daze of tears and confusion, she heard him murmur, "Don't fight me, kitten." Before she could respond, he spoke again, and his voice held a gentle note of pain and pleading. "Please don't fight me, love. I've dreamed too long of this moment."

His soft admission was her undoing. With a final whimper of defeat, her body softened beneath his, her lips accepting his kiss greedily. Her body yearned toward his, reminding her that she had long been without his touch and had craved it endlessly, even in Jean's arms. . . .

She was lost. Lost in a world filled only with Reed and the desires he was stroking in her hungry body. Mindlessly, she called his name again and again. Exactly when he released her, she knew not, but her arms had found their way about his neck, locking him to her in desperate need. Just when she thought she would die for wanting him, he claimed her totally. It was as if they had both found a long-lost piece to a treasured puzzle. Kathleen's breath caught in her throat, only to be returned as Reed groaned a sigh into her mouth. Then he was moving within her, and her hands were caressing his back and buttocks in urgent strokes. Passion flowed between them, and a rainbow of glorious colors swam before her closed lids, colors Kathleen had not dared dream of seeing again. The rapture built to unbearable limits, then broke, showering them with blinding ecstasy that blurred the brilliant hues into a kaleidoscope of swirling colors and emotions.

Kathleen lay quiet beneath him, trying to sort out the myriad emotions that swept over her, trying to pinpoint the exact moments she had surrendered her pride to him in exchange for passion. Deep inside, a voice cried out in protest, bringing forward all the lingering hurt and anger so easily shoved aside moments earlier.

When at length he moved to her side, she turned from him, showing him her back, tears stinging at her lids. Immediately, she found herself facing him once more, as he flipped her back around. "Don't pull away from me, Kathleen," he said. "It will do you no good to try to ignore me. I am here to stay, so you had best get used to it." His brow lifted over measuring blue eyes. "You are mine, sugar, body and soul, and I will never let you go again." After a significant pause, he added softly, but determinedly, "I'll never give you up to him!"

At his announcement, a part of Kathleen rejoiced, while yet another part of her mourned in silence.

In the golden glow of early dawn, Reed made love to her again. With slow, easy caresses, he drew Kathleen to awareness. In her sleep-fogged state, she was easy prey to his kisses, aware only of her love and long-buried need for this man who claimed her as his own. Even before her mind had cleared, she recognized the taste of his lips, the texture of his skin beneath her fingertips. As desire flared at his touch, there was no thought of resisting him, no place for hurt or anger in this golden moment.

As his hands wandered familiar paths, Kathleen returned his kisses hungrily, greedily claiming her due. When his lips left hers to sear their way down her throat, she tilted her head to give him easy access to points of pleasure, and when his mouth found the rosy peak of her breast, he found it aroused and pouting for his touch. A throaty moan escaped her parted lips as he suckled, and deep inside she felt a tingling of heightened desire. Her fingers laced into his midnight hair, as much to steady her rioting emotions as to encourage his gentle teasing.

A cry of protest when his lips left her breast, was replaced by an exclamation of rapture as he trailed feathery kisses across her abdomen to the silken triangle of her womanhood. He held her wriggling hips with strong, calloused hands as his mouth worked its magic, and soon she was crying out in delight, begging him to complete their union.

A sigh of intense pleasure greeted him as he met her request, thrusting deeply into her moist warmth. "Love me, kitten," he groaned.

"I do, darling," she replied on a sigh. "I do, Reed!"

Whispered words of love drowned them, even as they cascaded over a bounding waterfall into a calmer, sunlit pool of repletion. As they lay quietly entwined, their breath and heartbeats slowly returning to normal, Kathleen knew she was totally his once more. In surrendering her body so wholly, she had handed Reed her soul. Regardless of the anguish it might bring her, no matter what lay ahead, there was no turning back. The passion they once had shared was still there, and though they were like strangers in some ways, they would find their way forward together, fitting together the broken bits of their lives, and perhaps finding a love stronger than ever in the process. She hoped so. With all her heart, Kathleen hoped they could resolve their differences and revive all the trust and love they had once held so dear.

Feeling oddly shy and unsure of herself, Kathleen stood

at the helm later that morning. When Reed came to stand behind her, she was amazed to find herself blushing like a bride.

"Do you want me to take over for a while?" he asked. His arms came about her, and his hands closed over hers on the wheel. As his fingers curled about hers, he lifted her left hand to his lips.

Unconscious of his frown, she answered, "If you wish."

His fingers nearly squeezed the blood from hers as he grasped her hand and brought it before her face. "*What the hell is this?*" he thundered.

Kathleen jumped involuntarily. A guilty flush stained her cheeks as she stared at the diamond and aquamarine ring Jean had given her. "It is—a—a ring," she stammered stupidly.

"*I know that!*" he roared. "What I want to know is where it came from, who gave it to you, and what it is doing where *my* ring should be!"

Dismay choked her until she could barely speak. "Jean gave it to me—on my birthday," she murmured.

"And you wear it on your left hand in place of your wedding ring?" he demanded. "Don't play me for a fool, Kat! Tell me all of it!"

Kathleen swallowed hard. "We were engaged." Her words were the barest of whispers, yet he heard.

Reed's breath came out in a rush, as if he had received a blow to the stomach. "*Damn!*" A world of pain echoed in his voice. "Damn him! Damn you!"

Disregarding the fact that Kathleen was steering the frigate, Reed wrenched the offending ring from her finger, and with one mighty heave, tossed it overboard into the foaming sea.

A cry of dismay tore from her, and her hand reached out of its own accord, as if to recall the jewel from the ocean depths. "No! Oh, Reed!" she wailed. "Why did you have to do that? I would have given it back to him! I forgot I had it on! I forgot all about it!"

His long fingers dug into her shoulders, his face blazing with anger. "Just as you forgot me, Kathleen? So quickly —so easily?"

Her eyes widened in surprised denial. "I never forgot you!"

He ignored her protest. "You replaced my ring with his, and he took my place in your life—but no longer! I will have no other man's mark on you, no other man's symbol on your finger while I make love to you. I will kill you myself before I see you in his arms again!"

With precise motions, he took her emerald wedding ring from her right hand and replaced it on the proper finger. "Never," he ground out, "*never* take this ring off again!"

"Reed, I swear to you, it has been but two weeks that I wore Jean's ring in place of yours. We thought you were dead!" Her eyes reflected her agony, tears swimming in their emerald depths.

"If you ever remove that ring again, you will *wish* I was dead—or that you were!" he threatened darkly. "Never again will any man claim what is mine!" As if to prove his words, his mouth covered hers in a hard, possessive kiss meant to dominate. Only when her lips softened in sub- mission did he raise his head from hers. "Say it, Kat," he commanded. "Whose woman are you?"

"I am yours, Reed," she whispered softly. "Always yours." With tears blurring her vision, and an ache in her

338

heart, she yielded her lips to his once more.

A short time later, Kathleen once again retreated to her private perch high in the shrouds. There she sat, contemplating her future and all the problems she faced. It was there that Reed found her.

"Hiding again?" he suggested wryly.

"Just thinking," she said with a shrug.

"You know, Kat, I am heartily sick of having you disappear up here each time you want to escape me. It is time you learned that this particular ploy will no longer work."

Kathleen frowned. "What do you mean by that?"

"Precisely this," he said, clamping hold of her leg with a firm hand.

His motion caused her to tilt toward him, and her hands flew out to catch at his shoulders. "Reed!" she shrieked. "What are you doing?"

As his broad shoulders took her weight, he shifted his hold. In one, smooth, unexpected movement, he slung her across his shoulder, face down, her bottom near his bearded cheek.

"*Reed!* For God's sake! You'll get us both killed!" she screamed. "Put me down!"

One hand clinging to the mast, and the other holding onto her thighs, Reed nipped at her bare leg with sharp teeth. At her outraged screech, he ordered, "Be still and stop wriggling!"

Steadily, if awkwardly, he began to descend the mast. Kathleen closed her eyes against the swaying deck far below. "This is insane!" she gulped.

Reed laughed his devilish laugh. "Insane it may be, but I mean to get you off of this mast and keep you off. No more running off to hide in your private world of clouds and daydreams. No more secluded refuge where I cannot reach you. Wherever you hide, I'll find you and drag you back again. There will be no reprieves and no escapes any more.''

When his feet finally touched the deck, he still did not release her. Feeling much safer now, Kathleen's temper flared. Beating on his back with her fists, she raged at him. "Put me down, you brute!''

He had the nerve to laugh at her. "Settle down, Kat! You are making a spectacle of yourself!''

"Oh, you swine! You mad beast!'' she shrieked. "You are purposely demeaning me before my crew, and I will never forgive you for this!''

"What a shame!'' he taunted with a chuckle that vibrated through her ribs. "I am severely wounded, Kat!''

"I'll show you wounded,'' she snarled ominously. Seconds later, her teeth sank into the flesh of his back.

His surprise yelp of pain was followed by a smart slap to her bottom.

"*Yeow!*'' she yelled, releasing her teeth from his skin. Kathleen subsided in silent mortification until they had gained the privacy of their quarters. There, Reed tossed her unceremoniously upon the bunk.

"You hit me!'' she declared heatedly.

Hands on his hips, Reed glared down at her. "Yes, and you bit me. Nasty actions bring nasty returns. Remember that in future!'' With that, he stalked to the door. "And stay off that mast, unless you want a repeat of this morning's demonstration!'' he warned in parting.

Her outraged screech of impotent fury followed him out the door. Reed's answering laughter only increased her anger and humiliation to the point of exasperated tears and useless oaths. "Impudent, overbearing, son-of-a-skunk!" she wailed.

Chapter 19

Supper that evening would have been a silent affair, but Reed began questioning Kathleen about Chimera, and she told him what she knew of friends and relations. From Finley, Reed had gotten news of the war. Now he wanted to know of things closer to home.

"How long has it been since you have seen Katlin and Andrea?" he asked.

Kathleen hesitated, knowing her answer would displease him. "Four months," she admitted sheepishly.

"Four months!" he exclaimed. "Do you mean to say that our son just spent his third birthday with neither parent there?"

Kathleen's chin rose in defiance. "I sent instructions to Kate to buy a pony and cart as my gift to him, and to tell both of them that I would be home soon."

Reed was having none of it. "Gifts do not take the place of a mother's love!"

"Drat it all, Reed!" Her eyes begged him to understand. "Don't you see? Katlin is your spitting image! I couldn't bear to look at him and be reminded at every turn just how much I had lost. I tried—believe me, I tried—but my heart broke each time I looked at him." Tears sparkled and her lips trembled as she recalled the agony of separating herself from her children. "It wasn't easy to leave them, but it was the only solution I could find at the time."

Reed could only begin to imagine what it had been like for her. "Was it that bad, kitten?" he asked softly, his eyes searching her face.

"It was hell," she whispered simply. "Pure hell!"

Another discussion that could not be avoided concerned Sally Simpson, and the need to get Emerald out of the picture and return Kathleen to her natural role without raising Sally's suspicions. Even Reed had to agree that it was best to keep Emerald's true identity a secret between them.

"We will exchange ships at Grande Terre, and have the *Enchantress* returned to Savannah when she has been transformed into the *Starbright* once more. That, at least, takes care of one problem," Reed said.

"I don't see why we can't leave Miss Simpson at Grande Terre or New Orleans. She is certainly able to find her way from there." Kathleen wanted nothing more to do with the little blonde, but Reed felt responsible for her.

"Don't be spiteful, Kat," he advised. "She was a passenger aboard the *Kat-Ann*, and as the captain, I have a responsibility to see her to a safe, accessible port. At least from Savannah she can travel overland, and not risk further dangers at sea."

"Just where is her destination?"

"She was headed for Washington. I believe she has an uncle there. Our problem now," Reed continued, returning to their original discussion, "is how to bring my wife on the scene and retire Emerald gracefully. I do not suppose you want to spend the entire voyage to Savannah hidden in the cabin."

"Not on a bet!" Kathleen declared, envisioning Sally clinging adoringly to Reed, while she sat huddled below-deck.

"Well, then, have you anything to suggest?" Reed prompted.

Kathleen thought a moment. "First of all, we must see that Sally gains little information from the residents of Grande Terre. One word from any of them, and it would destroy all our efforts at secrecy. Also, if Isabel returns to Savannah with us, Miss Simpson must not get a good look at her either."

Reed noticed the doubt in Kathleen's tone. "Why wouldn't Isabel want to go home with us?"

"Isabel and Dominique are quite taken with one another," Kathleen explained with a smile. "When Dominique was wounded a few weeks back, Isabel elected to stay behind and nurse him back to health. I am not sure what she will want to do now."

Reed's brow wrinkled in disgust. "What the devil is Jean doing—growing passion flowers on the island?"

"I thought we were discussing our dilemma," Kathleen reminded him curtly.

"By all means, continue." Reed waved a hand in sarcastic apology.

"I was saying that Miss Simpson needs to be kept occupied so she is not tempted to wander about on her own."

Now Reed smiled, a bit devilishly. "I could undertake that mission," he volunteered.

"I'm sure you could," Kathleen snapped.

"Jealous, kitten?" he taunted, his teeth flashing in a grin.

"When pigs fly!" she lied.

Reed raised a skeptical brow, but merely said, "Go on with your plan."

"I could sail the *Enchantress* out of Barataria Bay, and anchor her in a nearby inlet, letting everyone assume Emerald has gone on another mission. Isabel could come along. If we could arrange to be picked up by pirogue, we could return the next day and you could meet your wife at the dock."

Reed shook his head. "That is fine, as far as it goes, but it would still give the impression that you are in close association with Jean's operation."

Kathleen agreed, and after a few minutes of concentration, she finally hit on a workable solution. "Suppose you found out that Isabel and I were visiting New Orleans just now, staying with friends? Quite a coincidence, I will grant you, but who is to dispute the possibility? Naturally, you would send someone for us. Miss Simpson would assume that we have traveled from New Orleans to Grande Terre at your request."

Reed mulled this over thoughtfully. "Yes, I think it will work," he said at last. "It will take teamwork and good timing, but it seems plausible."

So it was decided. Reed would see to informing Jean of their plans. Jean would alert his men, and Reed would keep Sally occupied while Kathleen went about the actual work of the deception. Kathleen was not thrilled by Reed's part in the plan, but she kept her annoyance to herself for now, in the fervent hope that Miss Simpson would soon be out of their lives.

The next day brought a final encounter at sea before reaching the seclusion of Grande Terre. Mid-morning the *Enchantress* crossed the path of a Spanish barkentine, heavily loaded and riding low and heavy in the water. She was easy prey, and too good to forfeit. Kathleen's eyes sparkled with anticipation. She had been aching for a good fight for days, ever since Reed's reappearance and meeting Sally Simpson. The tension had been building within her —a swift attack and a hearty swordfight would greatly relieve it.

Reed could not fail to see the excitement on Kathleen's face. "You are itching for one last victory, aren't you?" he said, grinning and shaking his head in mock dismay.

"Yes," she admitted without reserve. "I want that ship! Every once in a while, we take a Spanish vessel. It keeps the crews well paid, since there is little profit in attacking British warships. One last haul would fill the men's pockets before heading home again."

"And perhaps provide a few baubles for a greedy piratess in the bargain?" Reed suggested.

Kathleen laughed, her spirits high. "That, too."

"Signal Jean for the attack, and let's go to it, then," Reed said. "I could use a little practice after all those months without a sword in my hand." He, too, was getting caught up in Kathleen's excitement, and the desire for physical action. He hoped his sword arm hadn't lost its skill.

The chase was short, the two faster vessels closing in swiftly. The Spaniards were not eager to part with their precious cargo, however, and the fighting began in earnest. Swords flashed in the sun, and the melee was loud and fierce as the outnumbered Spanish fought for their ship and their lives. This time, Kathleen fought at Reed's back, and though her attention was focused on her worthy opponent, her ear was tuned to the sounds of fighting behind her. Realizing how long Reed had been away from combat, she was wary lest he be wounded.

Reed was handling the challenge with ease, and enjoying every moment. A wide grin split his face, and a devilish glint lit his eyes, as he parried and counterparried his enemy's moves. Hearing Kathleen's cry of victory behind him, he quickly finished his own match, and they went in search of further action.

Kathleen's color was high, and she felt more alive than she had in days. Observing her, Reed admitted a reluctant admiration. As Emerald, Kathleen was stunning to behold; her dark hair flying about her, her rapier singing in the air. Her face held a bold confidence, a defiant challenge echoed in her brilliant eyes. Her husky laughter matched her daring mood. She was magnificent! She was in her element! She was his! Even while he preferred her as Kathleen, Reed's heart expanded with pride that this marvelous, bold creature belonged to him.

In the end, the barkentine was theirs. Since neither she nor Jean had claimed the British warship, this ship counted as Kathleen's. As she went about the business of securing the captured ship and investigating the cargo, Reed slipped away to talk to Jean about their plans upon reaching Grande Terre. The Spanish vessel abounded in treasures worthy of a king. The hold was filled with gold, silver, jewels, and finely wrought items of great beauty and worth.

In one particular crate, Kathleen came upon platters and plates, goblets and dinnerware, all of solid gold and encrusted with jewels of every description. As she inspected a beautiful chalice, she suddenly knew what she wanted to do with it. Finding Dan, she gave her instructions, swearing him to absolute secrecy.

When she joined Reed on deck, he was brusquely concluding his business with Jean. Before she could speak a greeting, Reed was hurrying her aboard the *Emerald Enchantress*, but not before Jean's sharp gaze had noted the absence of his ring on her hand, replaced now by the emerald. His eyes flew to her face, taking in the passion-bruised lips still swollen from Reed's lovemaking that morning. Kathleen flinched visibly at the hurt reflected on Jean's face, and wordlessly begged for his understanding.

Jean made his way slowly toward his cabin. He wished he could vent his agony in anger, but he could not. He had read the apology on Kathleen's features, and he understood Reed's anger. After discussing their plans, Reed had abruptly asked Jean if he and Kathleen had been lovers. Evidently, Kathleen had not told him, and Jean knew her well enough to doubt she ever would. Jean had simply told Reed he would have to ask his wife. He did not want to make things more difficult for Kathleen. Lose her though he must, he could not begrudge her. He had seen her agony when she believed Reed dead; he had held her while she sobbed until the tears would no longer flow. He loved her enough to let her go and wish her happiness, though his own pain was immense.

The moment he opened his cabin door, Jean saw the chalice on his desk. There it sat in golden splendor, its jewels sparkling in all the glorious colors of the rainbow. He had never seen a goblet so beautiful, and he knew immediately who had sent it, and why. It was a shining symbol of Kathleen's love—a love never again to be voiced aloud. It was an apology; a mute plea for forgiveness. It was also a final farewell, a gift to remember her by forever.

There, in the privacy of his solitary cabin, Jean Lafitte,

the notorious privateer, the most feared pirate of his time, broke down and cried for the love he had lost, and would never find again.

Immediately upon their arrival at Grande Terre, Reed went aboard the *Pride* to check on Sally. While the others dallied purposely, Jean went ashore, to warn the islanders to silence, and to inform Dominique and Isabel of the details of Reed's reappearance. Kathleen remained aboard the *Emerald Enchantress*, awaiting Isabel.

Before long, disguised as a sailor, Isabel arrived, carrying a loaded knapsack. She had also brought dresses for herself and Kathleen, and the special herbal soap Kathleen used to remove the black dye from her hair.

With much commotion, and noisy farewells, Emerald set sail out of Barataria Bay, in full view of everyone. The famed piratess and her notorious green frigate were apparently headed for the high seas once more.

Once out of sight, Kathleen swung the ship about and put in at a small secluded inlet Jean had designated. The evening was spent with the two women catching up on one another's news, and returning Kathleen's hair to its natural red-gold state.

"I nearly fainted when Jean told us Reed was alive after all!" Isabel proclaimed.

"I nearly died of shock where I stood. I thought my mind had finally come unhinged and I was seeing a ghost!" Kathleen finished telling Isabel about her first encounter with Reed. "I swear to you, Isabel, I never want another such shock as long as I live! It is a wonder my hair didn't turn white instantly!"

"I don't think I am going to like this Simpson

woman." Isabel's delicate nose turned up at the thought, though she had yet to meet Reed's lover.

"You can always stay here with Dominique," Kathleen offered. "I know you two are in love."

Isabel nodded. "Yes, we are, but until the war is over, Dominique will by busy, and I cannot desert you when you need me. You stood by me when no one else would, and I shall do the same for you. Something tells me this Miss Simpson will not easily give Reed up."

"I am afraid you may be right," Kathleen sighed, "and things are difficult enough between Reed and me just now."

Isabel frowned. "Does Reed know you and Jean were lovers? Can he possibly blame you, when all of us thought he was dead?"

Kathleen laughed ruefully. "Reed strongly suspects the truth, though I have not admitted it—and yes, he does indeed blame both Jean and me."

"That is preposterous!" Isabel exclaimed heatedly. "He has had his own lover all this time, with no excuse whatsoever!"

"Yes, but what is sauce for the gander is *not* necessarily sauce for the goose in Reed's book," Kathleen responded with irony. "He is as hurt and angry as I am, and I am very much afraid he will never forgive Jean."

"Poor Jean," Isabel murmured. "He loves you so. This must be terrible for him."

Kathleen's face clouded. "I feel so awful, hurting him this way. I love him, too, and I ache for all of us."

"There is nothing else you can do," Isabel comforted. "You are Reed's wife, and you must return with him to Savannah and your children."

"I know, but Jean does not deserve to have this happen to him. Why is life so unfair to the nicest people, Isabel? Why do the good get hurt, while the evil prosper?"

Isabel shrugged. "We can only do our best and struggle on."

At noon the next day, Kathleen and Isabel made their grand entrance on Grande Terre. Since this was supposed to be her first glimpse of her beloved husband in a year, Kathleen played her part to perfection. Alighting from the boat, she stood staring at Reed with disbelieving eyes. Then, when his arms opened wide to receive her, she rushed into his embrace, skirts and copper hair flying.

"My God, Kat!" Reed groaned aloud, crushing her to him. Then, in a whisper, he added, "I had forgotten what a superb actress you can be."

Stung by his sarcasm, tears rose to her eyes, adding an element of reality to her performance as she pulled back to gaze at him. Only Reed noticed the anger and the glint of promised retaliation lurking there. "I can't believe this is happening!" Kathleen sighed rapturously. "It is too wonderful!" Then, without warning, she executed a perfect swoon, falling limply into his arms.

Isabel, standing quietly next to Dominique all this time, concealed a giggle with an exclamation of dismay.

Reed, stunned by Kathleen's actions, barely managed to catch her, as the others, including Sally Simpson, looked on. Muffling an oath, he swung Kathleen into his arms, and headed for the house. "You will pay for this, my sweet," he promised in her ear.

"So will you," she murmured back, hiding a smile against his shirt front.

While waiting for their vessel to be readied and stores

laid in, Kathleen and Reed played the part of newly reunited husband and wife. They were constantly together, touching and gazing into one another's eyes, completely ignoring everyone and everything around them.

Kathleen took immense satisfaction at the stormy look on Miss Simpson's face, but felt terrible about the hurt reflected on Jean's. In order to escape Jean's pained looks, (and in the process anger Sally further), Kathleen suggested that she and Reed take a private walk along the beach. Reed readily agreed, for he wanted Kathleen's last recollections of Grande Terre filled with memories of him, not of Jean.

Together they walked along the sandy beach. Bright sunlight danced on the aqua waves and white sand, dazzling their eyes and turning Kathleen's red-gold tresses to shining copper. Birds chattered and butterflies flittered from flower to exotic flower. The light breeze sent the heady scent of hundreds of blossoms their way. Palm fronds swayed, creating a whispering music of their own. Knowing she would never see this tropical paradise again, Kathleen drank in the sights and sounds as deeply as she could, storing mental images to take back to Savannah. "God created a masterpiece when he made Grande Terre," she said reverently. "Another Garden of Eden." They had stopped in a perfect spot; a small glade of fragrant, brilliant flowers beneath the shade of a palm tree. A few yards away, the sea glistened, and the waves splashed rhythmically against the shore.

Here, in this secluded place, it was easy to imagine they were alone on the island. A spell seemed to be weaving itself about them. Reed gazed deeply into the endless emerald depths of her eyes, his own now sapphire pools of desire. "Do you suppose Adam and Eve made love on beds of tropical flowers?" he murmured, clasping her body close to his, his hands skimming her curves.

Kathleen raised her lips to nearly touch his. "I don't know, but *we* will, won't we?" she whispered seductively, her breath fanning his lips.

For answer, his mouth claimed hers in a kiss of sweet torment, his hands pushing her dress from her shoulders, while hers tore at his shirt.

There, amidst the sunlight and flowers, birds and butterflies fluttering about them, they came together in dazzling passion. For a few absolutely perfect minutes, the world was theirs in all its beauty and glory, their problems forgotten as ecstasy claimed them.

They left on the evening tide. Reed's wife, now recovered from her first shock, was obviously dismayed at having discovered her husband had spent the past year of his life secluded on an island with another woman. Kathleen's disdain was very genuine. She and Isabel pointedly ignored Miss Simpson, putting Reed in an awkward situation and raising his hackles in the process.

"Surely you didn't expect this to be a pleasant voyage," Kathleen jibed.

"You could at least be polite to her," Reed countered gruffly.

Kathleen's eyes flashed. "I will not acknowledge your doxy in any way," she said. "I will not speak to her, look at her, and I certainly shall not entertain her! You have done quite enough of that in the past twelve months!" Gone was the sweet emotion of that afternoon, washed away by Sally's presence aboard ship. Kathleen marched away, leaving Reed to stew in a broth of his own making.

A problem arose when Reed attempted to make love to Kathleen that night. Resigned to having to occupy the same quarters with him, Kathleen was still determined to exercise her will. "I refuse to make love with you while your mistress is just across the passageway," she stated firmly. "I have had just about all I can take of both of you!"

"Is that so?" Reed ground out, his temper straining at its last threads. "Let's just see about that!" he growled, pinning her to the sheets.

It was their old test of wills, one Kathleen was doomed to lose. At first she fought him, determined for once not to let him arouse her passions against her will; but as his lips played masterfully over hers, and his hands skillfully found all those points of exquisite pleasure, she found herself weakening. Flames of passion were coursing through her, turning her blood to molten lava.

Kathleen's lips molded to his, as demanding now as were his, her body arching to meet his hot flesh as his body covered hers. "Damn you, Reed Taylor!" she moaned in reluctant surrender. "*Damn* you for doing this to me!"

His triumphant laugh echoed in her ears, as together they spun helplessly into that wondrous world of rapture.

Afterward, he pulled her to his side, stroking her soft bright hair. "You are a copper-haired spitfire, whether in anger or passion," he murmured into her hair. "My own adorable kitten with sharp, slashing claws—but I will forgive you."

"I shan't forgive you," she retorted, stung by embarrassment at her traitorous body, "for taking what I did not want to give."

"Ah, but love, you know it is always like this with us. You can no more help yourself, than I can stop desiring

355

you. It will always be this way between us, Kat,'' he said
softly.

The next couple of days were a trial to everyone.
Simpering Sally Simpson clung to Reed like a barnacle to a
ship's hull, as though Kathleen did not exist. Kathleen's
temper escalated several notches with each reccurrence. As
for Reed, he seemed to be enjoying the game. Though
Kathleen suspected he was doing his best to arouse her
jealousy, she could not stem the rising anger or the ache
inside each time she saw the two of them together. With
Isabel's aid, she managed to maintain a cool, indifferent
manner, difficult though it was. Even in the privacy of
their cabin, she strove to hide her feelings. It would not do
to let Reed know how deeply he was hurting her. Her pride
would not give him that satisfaction. It was bad enough
that she betrayed herself in his embrace each night,
unwillingly yielding to his passions and her own, clinging
to him and calling out his name at the height of her
rapture.

At one point, Reed came upon her as Kathleen was
gazing longingly up into the high shrouds of the
mainmast. ''Don't even think of it, Kat,'' he warned.
''I'd haul you down from there so fast your head would
spin. Then I would blister your bottom until you couldn't
sit for a week.''

Throwing him a spiteful glare, she answered, ''You
would, brute that you are!'' and stalked off in a huff.

But it was when Reed casually informed Kathleen that
he had invited Miss Simpson to Chimera to recover from
her ordeal before traveling on, that the feathers really flew.

''You did *what*?'' Kathleen shrieked, flying into an
immediate rage. ''Oh, no! Definitely not, Reed! It is bad
enough having to put up with her aboard ship! I refuse to

have her at Chimera. Enough is quite enough!"

Reed's face darkened with an answering anger. "She will come as I say she will!" he shouted back. "Chimera may be your home as well, but I am still master there!"

"Lord of all he surveys!" Kathleen quipped sarcastically. "And how will you explain her to your mother, pray tell?"

"That will not be a problem, if you would be more cooperative, Kathleen." At her outraged look, he continued, "There are several secrets I am sure you would not care to have known about yourself. What would Mother think if she knew you had been carrying on with Jean?"

"You have no proof of that, Reed!"

"I need no proof. You may have thought that I would forgive and forget, but it is not as easy as all that. You may deny it all you want, but I know you and Jean were lovers."

"You know less than nothing!" Kathleen faced him defiantly.

His face hardened in stubborn determination. "I know that Sally is coming to Chimera with us—and I know you will accept it. I also know that I am tired of your belligerence and your hostile attitude. Next to you, Sally is an angel."

Kathleen snorted. "A *fallen* angel," she reminded him. "Sullied and used."

"No worse than you, my dear wife," he shot back, "and perhaps better. The more hateful you become, the better Sally's impetuous fabrication sounds. Perhaps I really ought to consider divorcing you and marrying the sweet Miss Simpson. What would you do then, my pet?"

Kathleen blanched at his words, but stood her ground.

"I would go to my grandmother, of course. Kate could hardly refuse to take me in."

Reed's look was bitter, and his next words sliced like knives into her heart. "You would go alone, Kathleen, without Katlin and Andrea. I would never let you take our children with you, and you would never see them again."

Kathleen's face crumpled at his deliberate cruelty. "You wouldn't!" she cried. "Besides, what would your family say if you were to divorce me? They would never stand for it. You would estrange yourself from them forever."

Reed's crooked smile was demonic, and his eyes flashed blue fires of revenge. "I am sure they would understand if I told them of your adventures as Emerald, and your affair with Jean Lafitte. How could they blame me for not wanting a piratess for a wife and the mother of my children? Could they condemn me for ridding myself of my 'widow', who so quickly flew into the arms of another man?"

"That is blackmail, Reed!" Kathleen sank quickly into a chair before her knees gave way beneath her.

"True," Reed drawled. "If you recall, you once blackmailed me into keeping our marriage a secret; threatening to tell the world that I was a pirate! How does it feel now that the shoe is on the other foot, my dear?"

The thought of losing Reed and her children forever was unbearable. That Reed might actually cast her aside in favor of the insipid Miss Simpson made Kathleen nauseous. White-faced, she raised enormous green eyes to his. "What do you want, Reed?" she whispered in defeat.

"I want you to settle down and behave as a wife should; to become a model mother—the very picture of decorum.

I want a sweet, obedient wife, not a screeching shrew! Learn to control that nasty temper and sharp tongue of yours, or pay the price, Kathleen. I am tired of being at odds with you. You either mend your ways, or by God, I'll carry out my threats. And don't think, even then, I would let you go running back to Jean. I would see you dead first!''

Under the weight of Reed's threats, the remaining days aboard ship were agony for Kathleen. Forced to accept his edicts, she curbed her tongue and temper. Only Isabel heard her wild ravings.

"Surely he would never go so far!" Isabel exclaimed.

"At this point, he could do anything, and it would not surprise me," Kathleen replied tearfully.

Isabel was as furious as Kathleen. "He is a heartless, unforgiving beast!" she proclaimed. She got no argument from Kathleen. "He intends to see you pay for your happiness with Jean, even though he was with another woman for a year! Men! I swear they have no conscience or sense at all! Does he really mean to install his mistress in the same house as his wife?"

"Evidently," Kathleen moaned. "He is out to humiliate me in every way he can think of, and he has made damned sure I can do nothing about it."

"We'll see about that," Isabel promised, not elaborating on her thoughts.

Although Kathleen could not force herself to be congenial to Sally Simpson, she did nothing to antagonize Reed further. While Isabel shot darts across the table at them with dark eyes, Kathleen struggled not to choke on each mouthful of food. Not by word or glance did she object when Sally clung blatantly to Reed's side much of the day.

Kathleen had stopped trying to resist Reed's lovemaking, but she continued to silently condemn both herself and Reed when she inevitably succumbed to blind passion in his arms each night. It was as if she lost all self-control at his touch. Only while he slept, holding her tightly to his side with strong arms, did she let down her guard. There, in the protective darkness of the late night, Kathleen wept bitter tears. If, in order to keep Reed and her children, she had to humble herself and become his obedient slave, she would. If there was no other way, she would grovel at his feet, though every cell in her body cried out in protest, urging her to find another way out of her predicament.

The sky was just lightening to the pearl-grey of dawn as their vessel slipped quietly into dock at Savannah. As they prepared to debark, Reed took Kathleen's arm in his. She started to pull away, and his hand clamped over hers in instant anger. His cool blue eyes resembled chips of ice, as he stared down into her face, daring her to defy him.

"You are walking a fine line, Kathleen," he warned ominously, causing chills to dance up her spine. "Don't cross it, my love."

Chapter 20

Their arrival in Savannah caused quite a stir. Everyone was stunned to see Reed returned, as it were, from a watery grave. Kathleen managed to present the image of a deliriously happy wife, reunited with her beloved husband. She even pretended a rather frosty solicitude for Sally Simpson, whose adventures enthralled the Bakers. By the time they were ready to leave for Chimera, Kathleen thought her face would crack from the perpetual smile she kept plastered there. The smile never quite reached her shadowed eyes, however.

Susan was ecstatic at her brother's safe return, as was Ted. Ted babbled on about how bereaved Reed's friends and family were on learning of his presumed death, and how inconsolable Kathleen had been. He raved about her courage and determination to find him, lauding Kathleen's spirit and refusal to give up hope against all odds.

Reed raised a skeptical black brow in Kathleen's direction. "How admirable and touchingly loyal!" he said, with hidden disdain. "That's my loving Kathleen."

Susan insisted upon being present when Mary Taylor discovered her son was alive and well, so they all piled into the Bakers' carriage for the trip to Chimera, and Kathleen found herself crushed next to her husband's former mistress in the crowded carriage.

"Would you be so kind as to remove your elbow from my ribcage, Miss Simpson?" she asked coolly, earning a sharp look from Reed that Susan was quick to catch.

"Is anything wrong, Kathleen?" she asked solicitously. "You have been so quiet this morning." Susan's grey eyes scanned Kathleen's pale face, noting the violet shadows beneath emerald eyes that lacked their normal glow.

"I'm just tired, Susan," came the subdued reply. "It was a wearisome journey."

"To say the least," Isabel put in meaningfully, shooting a dark look at Reed.

If not for Susan, it would have been a silent ride. Ignoring or unaware of the friction between Kathleen and Sally, she chattered gaily about friends and events in Savannah these past months, then turned to her brother, asking him to elaborate on his experiences.

As Reed told of the shipwreck, the months spent on the deserted island, their rescue by the British and then by Jean, and his reunion with Kathleen, Kathleen silently noted the omissions in his tale. Reed glossed over his time on the island with only the lovely blonde for company; to hear his version, one would think they were as innocent as babes, and Kathleen dared not contradict him.

Sally sat demurely next to Kathleen, her blue eyes wide in her guileless face. When Reed had finished speaking, she added adoringly, "He is being gallant and gentlemanly, but in reality, he saved my life. I would not be here today if not for Reed's care all those long months. He was truly wonderful!"

Kathleen thought she might be sick.

Susan's puzzled gaze traveled swiftly between her brother and the young blonde, and she suddenly knew that Reed was not telling all. She glanced then at Kathleen, who nearly winced at the pity in Susan's grey eyes.

Evidently, Susan wasn't the only one not buying Reed's and Sally's tale, for suddenly from his cage at Kathleen's feet, Peg-Leg squawked a loud "Bilge!"

The bird's raucous statement captured everyone's attention. "Where on earth did you find such an unlikely pet, Kathy?" Ted asked.

Kathleen laughed nervously. "Peg-Leg comes from New Orleans, where he formerly resided in a tavern. His vocabulary is outrageous, and his manners are atrocious, but I have become quite attached to the noisy rascal."

"He also has a nasty habit of biting," Reed said darkly, rubbing the scar on his thumb.

"Only people he finds offensive," Kathleen responded sweetly.

Mary Taylor nearly swooned upon seeing her long-lost son. Joyous tears poured down her cheeks, and she flung herself into his arms as if she would never let him go. As Reed poured out the story of his adventures once again, Mary would reach out now and then to touch his sleeve or stroke his bearded face, to assure herself that he was really here and not a figment of her imagination.

"We should have believed Kathleen all along," she admitted with a tremulous sigh. "She refused to accept that you were dead. Even when we finally forced her to admit it, she was reluctant. The poor girl was practically destroyed!"

Under other circumstances, Sally Simpson's introduction and cool reception from Reed's family would have caused Kathleen to gloat openly. Mary, though polite, was obviously wondering exactly what had gone on between her son and the little blonde during those long, lonely months. Susan, usually so bubbly and outgoing, was decidedly reserved toward the young visitor. Both mother and sister, aware of Reed's trigger temper, wisely kept their own council, but it was plain that they were on Kathleen's side.

Reed's reunion with his children was the one truly perfect moment of the day. Rosy-cheeked and bleary-eyed from their naps, they came trotting down the stairs behind Della. After one brief, astonished look, Andrea launched herself full-force into Reed's open arms. Katlin, just turned three the end of March, was less sure of this bearded stranger, preferring his mother's comfort first. As Kathleen gathered him close, kissing his dark, damp baby curls, her eyes met Reed's above Katlin's head. It was a poignant moment of shared love and joy.

"Katlin, my love," she murmured graciously, "go kiss Daddy hello."

Katlin gazed up at her with puzzled blue eyes, so exactly like his father's, that Kathleen's heart contracted in her chest. "Go on, sweetheart," she urged.

Obediently, he slid off her lap and crossed cautiously to his father's side, his eyes wide with wonder. "Daddy?" he asked, not knowing quite what to make of this tall dark man who was almost a stranger.

Reed set Andrea to one side, and the little girl bounced over to embrace her mother. Reed held out his arms. "Katlin. Son," he croaked, his voice gruff with emotion. Katlin walked hesitantly into his father's embrace, to be pulled immediately onto Reed's lap. After gravely touching the bearded face near his, Katlin smiled. "Daddy," he crooned, cuddling contentedly against his father's broad chest, and sticking his thumb in his mouth.

Reed's eyes glistened as he held his son close to his heart. "It is so good to be home," he said hoarsely, choking back a sob of joy.

Sally's reaction to meeting the children was both stilted and over-effusive. "What darlings!" she cooed, with nearly believable sincerity. Directing her attentions to Andrea, she said, "You must be Alexandrea. Your father has told me all about you. You certainly are a little beauty!"

Andrea stared back, unimpressed. "I know it," she replied with pert confidence.

Taken aback, Sally turned to Katlin. "Now *here* is a boy after his father's heart!" she exclaimed a bit too brightly. "I suppose everyone tells you that you look exactly like your papa."

Katlin frowned, clutching at Reed's shirt and nursing his thumb.

"Katlin," his father directed gently, "say hello to Miss Simpson."

Thus prompted, Katlin popped his thumb out of his mouth, offering the same wet hand to Sally in manly imitation of a handshake. "Lo, Miss Simpleton," he muttered.

Kathleen almost choked on suppressed laughter. Sally Simpson gasped in offended disbelief, while Reed sent a black look in Kathleen's direction, his gaze pinning her to her place. Kathleen's slanted green eyes widened innocently as she struggled to maintain her composure, while behind her, Isabel giggled audibly. Several chuckles were quickly quelled by Reed's glare at each member of his family.

His blue eyes narrowed suspiciously, as Mary put in hastily, "Children will say the oddest things!"

"Yes," Susan added helpfully. "Teddy is constantly embarrassing me to death! I just never know what he is going to say next."

Her comment served to ease the tension, and the incident passed without further remark.

A surprise awaited Reed when he entered the bedroom to change for dinner, to find the room completely changed from the last time he had left it.

"What the devil?" he exclaimed in bafflement. "Kat! Get up here!" he roared from the head of the stairs.

Racing up the staircase, Kathleen could not imagine what had upset Reed, until she saw his face as he viewed the room.

"Oh, my goodness!" she gasped, clamping a hand over her mouth. "I had completely forgotten! I redecorated!"

"I can see that," he drawled, amused at her reaction. "Can you tell me what you did with my clothes?"

"In the attic," she blurted.

"Fine. Might we retrieve them so that I can dress for dinner?"

"I will see to it right away," she promised, heading out the door in search of one of the house servants. Then she popped her head back in, her teeth worrying at her lower lip as she hesitated.

"Yes? Have you forgotten something?" he asked.

"Reed, do you want the room changed back to the way it was?"

Eyeing his surroundings critically, he considered this. "That won't be necessary. Just add another dresser and an armoire for my things, and if you exchange one of those delicate chairs for a deep, comfortable one, the room will accommodate us both. In fact, I rather like what you have done with it. I was getting tired of the old decor.''

"I'm glad.'' Kathleen breathed a silent sigh of relief that the room, at least, pleased him. She had not looked forward to redecorating again.

"Of course the bed is a bit smaller than our old one, but that won't bother me at all. And I can be reasonably sure no one else has shared this one with you,'' he added bitingly.

Kathleen's good mood dissolved. With a glare, she stamped out of the room.

The next day, Kathleen rode over to Emerald Hill to visit her grandmother. It dismayed Kathleen to see how much Kate seemed to have aged in the last few months. Much of the older woman's fabled vitality was missing, and her once-brilliant copper hair was now completely white. Even the sparkling emerald eyes seemed dimmer now, but her mind was still alert and her wit sharp. After their loving reunion, she sensed that Kathleen was troubled, and soon her granddaughter was spilling out the entire tangled tale.

"Well, lass, when ye get yerself into a mess, ye certainly make it a good one!'' Kate said, shaking her head sadly. "I wish I could help ye, but I can't. Only ye and Reed can set things straight b'tween ye. 'Tis a shame!''

"I know, Gram. It would not be so bad if that Simpson creature would be on her way, but I have a feeling she won't be leaving very soon. She's making herself right at home!''

"From the sound o' it, she's set her cap fer Reed. Ye'd better stand yer ground and watch out fer thet gal,'' Kate advised.

"Oh, I shall, for all the good it will do me,'' Kathleen

sighed. "Reed certainly has me over a barrel this time."

Kate patted Kathleen's hand soothingly. "We'll think o' somthin', lass. Don't ye fret."

It was to prove a long and disastrous summer. Reed was kept busy tending to matters both on the plantation and at the shipping office in Savannah. While he regularly sent his ships on privateering missions, he was now too occupied to take voyages of his own. After a year's absence, there was much that needed his attention.

Indeed, everyone was very busy, with the exception of Sally Simpson, who was left much of the time to herself. Susan returned to her family and home in Savannah. Aunt Barbara and Uncle William, after a short visit to Chimera to welcome Reed and Kathleen, went to Augusta for a few months' stay with Amy and her family. Mary helped Kathleen manage the household at Chimera as did Isabel, which gave Kathleen freedom to help Kate at Emerald Hill, and to learn more of the horse breeding trade. Every spare minute she devoted to Katlin and Andrea.

There were the usual multitude of social activities—parties, balls, and picnics. Reed's miraculous return from the dead only increased his popularity, and the Taylors found themselves invited to all the major functions. Kathleen managed the time to visit her dressmaker and order a new summer wardrobe for herself and Isabel, and the two women made it a shopping spree to remember, taking great glee in handing Reed the bills for their extravagant expenditures. Some of Kathleen's pleasure evaporated when she discovered several of Sally's clothing bills on Reed's desk, also. Kathleen tried to tell herself it was no more than she had expected, but it hurt, nevertheless.

Chimera, large as it was, was too small to house both Kathleen and Sally Simpson, but Sally was in no hurry to move on. Each day was a supreme trial to Kathleen's patience. At least twice a day she was forced to sit down to a meal at the same table with Reed's former mistress. Kathleen could barely force the food past her lips, and most days she managed to lunch with Kate at Emerald Hill.

When her duties did not occupy her time, Kathleen took long rides on her stallion. Away they would fly, racing across the fields. It was one way of relieving her pent-up tensions. For a while, astride Zeus, she could forget her problems, and revel in the feel of the powerful animal beneath her and the wind streaming through her shining, unbound hair.

Once in a while, Reed would join her. It seemed the only time they were truly at peace with one another, perhaps because they rarely talked then. They rode in silent companionship, enjoying the brisk pace and sharing their love for the land. When they did speak, it was of Reed's work, his plans for Chimera, or Kathleen's progress in her study of horse breeding.

But most of the time, they lived in a state of armed truce. Reed had changed drastically from the loving, teasing husband Kathleen once had known. He had become more adept than ever at wounding with sharp words or a dark glare from those steely eyes. It was apparent to Kathleen that his suspicions about her and Jean were still eating away at him, making him hateful and giving neither of them much joy or peace.

Reed seemed to take a special pleasure in taunting Kathleen, as if he were deliberately pushing her to the limit of her patience. Then, just as she was about to explode in angry words, he would casually remind her of all she stood to lose. Lately, he had taken to insinuating he did not care for her any longer; that the only reason he didn't cast her aside was because his family adored her, and for the children's sake. In that same vein, he always managed to stress that Kathleen was still his wife, and therefore his property and subservient to his will.

Kathleen felt like a mouse cornered by a huge cat. The constant strain was telling on her. The shadows beneath her eyes were becoming more pronounced, and Kathleen, who rarely wept, many times found herself rushing away to cry in secret.

To add to Kathleen's misery, Reed was openly gallant to Sally Simpson, often taking time out of his busy day to be with her. So obvious were his attentions that it almost seemed as if he were courting her. Though he dutifully escorted Kathleen to the social functions they attended, he spent much of his time entertaining Miss Simpson, and before long, the entire county was abuzz with gossip about Reed and his attractive houseguest.

Of course, this made Sally unbearably smug. While largely ignored by the rest of the Taylor household, she found ample opportunity to needle Kathleen. At first, she did so unobtrusively, or when she found Kathleen alone, but as time went on and Reed did not rush to Kathleen's defense, Sally became more bold and blatant in her vindictiveness and her flirtation with Reed.

Catty comments at the dinner table were one thing; private confrontations were quite another.

"When are you going to realize that Reed no longer cares for you?" Sally would say. "Why don't you give in gracefully?"

Rather than lose her temper, Kathleen learned to deal

with Sally with cool disdain. "My dear, you have been in the sun too long," she countered smoothly. "It addles the brain, and I must warn you, it does horrid things to your complexion."

Sally especially delighted in taunting Kathleen with the year she had spent on that deserted island with Reed. "We had a lot of time to get to know one another, you know. We became very close." Then Sally would sigh adoringly. "Reed is *so* muscular; his strength and endurance amaze me. And he is such an *attentive* lover!"

Kathleen forced a carefree laugh. "Who else did he have to impress with his prowess all those months?" she pointed out with deliberate spite. Outwardly, Kathleen took Sally's taunting in stride; inside, she was bleeding.

"Then how do you account for Reed's attentions toward me now, Kathleen?" the girl countered. "We spend a great deal of time together, while you are off doing whatever it is you do all day. Surely you realize we do more than chat."

Kathleen smiled mockingly. "And surely *you* realize whose bed he prefers each night."

Sally chose to ignore that remark. "All Savannah knows of Reed's feelings for me. How can you go on humiliating yourself this way?" she asked with feigned pity.

Slanted emerald eyes narrowed, but Kathleen's reply was cool. "*I* wear his wedding ring. *You* are whispered about in every parlor, Sally, and the comments are not kind."

Her face suffused with the heat of angry frustration, Sally announced, "I will win him in the end!"

Kathleen shook her head in mock sympathy. "Do not delude yourself, little girl. Throughout the ages, men have toyed with their mistresses, but they rarely divorce their wives for them. Why buy the cow when the milk is free? You would be very foolish to take him seriously. Reed is playing with you, Sally, in a cruel game for his own private amusement.''

Dealing with Sally was one thing, dealing with Reed quite another. Here, Kathleen had to tread carefully, and it was increasingly difficult. During the day, she could ignore his indifference but at night, alone in their bedroom, it was impossible to deflect his vindictive attacks. In public, he treated Kathleen with cool deference and courtesy, but behind closed doors, the polite veneer was stripped away.

Reed was obsessed with the need to dominate her and bend her to his will. It was as if he were compelled to obliterate all traces of Jean's touch, to defile any sweet memories of him that Kathleen might still hold dear.

Kathleen's subdued behaviour these days had forced Reed to wonder if her unsmiling face and haunted eyes had more to do with losing Jean as her lover than with his own actions. Jealousy drove him to retaliate by lavishing more time and attention on Sally; he knew it would hurt Kathleen to believe that Sally continued to be his mistress, though that was not the case. While he knew that Sally would willingly assume that role, hoping eventually to win him as her husband, Reed had not touched the girl since their rescue. His heart still belonged to the copper-haired vixen with the flashing green eyes, Reed admitted to himself, and as long as he loved Kathleen, no other woman could lay claim to him.

Still, driven by some inner demon he could not control, Reed continued to torment Kathleen as the certainty of her love for Jean tormented him. He shrugged off twinges of conscience when she would tearfully ask, ''Why are you doing this, Reed? What more do you want? I am trying to please you in every way I know, and still it is not enough. I do not know what else to do!''

"You might try ceasing to mourn your lost lover," he suggested cruelly.

"If you are referring to Jean, it is you who keeps reminding me of him," she pointed out. "Rarely a day passes that you do not bring up his name.''

Her words were true, and both knew it. Reed flayed her with his suspicions at every turn, trying to wring a confession of guilt that Kathleen would rather die than give, realizing that to do so would only inflame Reed's anger further. She would have given anything if her brief affair with Jean had never happened, considering the grief it had caused all three of them.

Even while making love to her, Reed could not let the matter rest. As his hands roamed her body, he would ask, "Did Jean caress you this way, Kathleen? Did he know to touch you here? Did he find this spot on your shoulder that drives you wild? Did his hands make you mad with passion, as mine do?''

Kathleen's fervent denials only seemed to spur him to greater lengths. Time and again, he took her to the edge of rapture, only to make her beg for the ultimate ecstasy. He took a demonic delight in humiliating her, often requiring her to acknowledge her subjugation to him before satisfying her needs.

"Who do you belong to, Kathleen?" he would demand. "Who rules your heart and body?''

Caught in the bondage of her need for him, she would admit, "You do, Reed." And then she would weep.

Not understanding the reasons behind Reed's actions, Mary eventually took her son to task. "While I realize that you are a grown man, I feel compelled as your mother to tell you that you have been behaving abominably!" she remonstrated. "You have been treating Kathleen horribly, and flaunting that—that *hussy*—in everyone's face, including mine. I do not mind telling you that I do not appreciate your dragging the Taylor name through the mud! Just why Kathleen tolerates such abuse from you, I can not begin to guess!"

"And I do not appreciate your interference, Mother," Reed replied stiffly. "What goes on between Kat and myself is solely our business!"

Never had her son spoken to her in such a manner. Mary's temper, hardly ever in evidence, rose at this. "Not when you have made it a public matter by your own actions!" she countered. "Why are you behaving like this? If you would just explain, perhaps I could understand and help in some way."

"I will deal with it in my own way, thank you. If you do not care for the way things are at Chimera, you can always stay with Susan for a while."

Hurt by her son's sharp words, Mary retorted, "If not for Kathleen, I would do just that, but I will not desert her while you are treating her so poorly!"

Reed shrugged negligently. "Stay then, but kindly keep your well-meant meddling to yourself, Mother."

During this trying time, Isabel was Kathleen's salvation. The little brunette pulled Kathleen out of her well of self-pity and made her laugh again. Through Isabel, Kathleen managed to retain her equilibrium and gain a better view of her situation. Her natural high spirits began to revive despite the oppression of Reed's tyranny. Once it had been Kathleen who had led Isabel into joining her in outrageous girlish pranks at their boarding school. Now it was Isabel who suggested delightfully inventive means to aggravate Sally Simpson no end. If they could make Sally uncomfortable enough, perhaps the woman would leave. Together, they set out to make Sally's life at Chimera as miserable as possible. Readily persuaded into participating, Kathleen soon thought up innovative ideas of her own to add to the list, always making certain beforehand that Reed would not be able to place the blame at her doorstep.

Their first major triumph was when they were all invited by one of their neighbors to a foxhunt. Aware that Sally did not ride well, the two companions in deviltry decided to make sure that Miss Simpson did not enjoy her outing. While Kathleen kept a sharp lookout, Isabel loosened the cinch on the saddle of Sally's mount.

Sally's sole reason for agreeing to ride was her wish to please Reed. She perched stiffly on the saddle, obviously unsure of herself and her horse.

"Relax, Sally," they heard Reed say. "I have seen to it that you have the gentlest mount in the stables. Once you set your mind to it, you are going to enjoy yourself." (Unluckily for Sally, he did not think to check the cinch a second time.)

Sally's weak smile lacked certainty. As her horse sailed over the first jump, her saddle slipped sideways a little, but amid the chaos, her stifled cry of dismay went unnoticed. It was near the second jump that disaster occurred. Her horse, aware of the inexperienced rider on his back, decided at the last second to skirt the jump rather than take it. As he swerved, the saddle slid further, tipping Sally headlong into a puddle of muddy water.

Cantering along behind her, Isabel and Kathleen exploded in mirth. As Sally raised herself slowly out of the

375

mire, Isabel cried, "Oh, my! She looks just like a big chocolate bon-bon!"

Kathleen, as she breezed past, saluted her rival with a rousing, "Tally ho!" She hadn't laughed so hard in months.

Laughter was a precious commodity during these trying weeks, and Kathleen greedily grabbed at every chance for enjoying herself. Reed certainly did not strive to amuse her. At barbecues, he left Kathleen to fend for herself, aiding Sally in filling her plate and finding a shady spot to sit. When there was dancing, he twirled the pink-cheeked blonde across the floor, rarely deigning to dance with Kathleen. Kathleen, however, did not lack for dance partners of her own, which of course irritated Reed no end. Kathleen surrounded herself with her own throng of male admirers who hung avidly on her every word.

At riding events, Kathleen's expertise always made Sally look awkward and inept. Turning the tables on Reed, Kathleen began ignoring him. At picnics, she laughed with her friends, played with her children, and bestowed her attentions on the most handsome swains Savannah had to offer. The gentlemen knew Kathleen was only enjoying their company in the most proper sense, but they basked in the glow of her smiles, entranced by her beauty and wit. Kathleen was always circumspect enough to avoid causing gossip, but she enjoyed seeing the scowl on Reed's face when he saw her enjoying herself despite his lack of attention.

One afternoon, when a certain lucky chap was elected to pair off with Kathleen in a game of croquet, Reed became surly. Observing the young man with his arms about Kathleen, aiding her in a difficult shot, Reed promptly deserted Sally's side. With a few sharp words to the fellow in question, Reed took his place. Over Kathleen's shoulder, his hands clenched over hers on the wooden mallet, Reed growled, "You are making a spectacle of yourself!"

Serenely unruffled, Kathleen replied sweetly, "Just following your lead, darling. If the head of the Taylor household may make a fool of himself over a bit of fluff, how are the rest of us supposed to act?"

Kathleen and Isabel enlisted the eager aid of other family members in ousting their unwelcome guest. Upon learning that Sally was dreadfully allergic to strawberries, Mary made her famous fruit punch, making certain the unwary blonde did not divine the ingredients—which were, after all, a treasured family secret. Before the evening was over, Sally had broken out in the most brilliantly bright red hives any of them had ever witnessed. For three glorious days, they were free of her presence, as Sally huddled miserably in her suite, crying her baby-blue eyes red until they resembled twin American flags.

Even Andrea and Katlin had decided that "Miss Simpleton" was fair game. Sally would not soon forget the afternoon Andrea danced merrily into the parlor at tea-time with a plate of chocolate cookies—neither would the rest of them. Her turquoise eyes shining brightly, Andrea presented the plate to Sally with her best curtsy, giving an adorable imitation of a perfect lady acting as hostess to a favored guest. "Would you care for a cookie with your tea, Miss Thimpthon?" she lisped prettily.

Delighted at the child's first attempt at friendship, Sally accepted. At the first bite, her face became mottled, and she grabbed hastily for her napkin. Coughing and choking, she spat the entire mess into the cloth, dabbing at her tongue in the most indelicate fashion.

"What is wrong, Sally?" Reed asked concernedly. As she continued to choke and gasp, he shouted, "For heaven's sake, what is it?"

Finally catching her breath, Sally shrieked, "That obnoxious brat! She gave me a *mud pie!* If she was my child, I'd slap her silly!"

Not pleased with his daughter's behavior, Reed nevertheless did not take kindly to Sally's harsh words. "She is *not* your child," he stated stonily. Turning to Kathleen, he directed, "Kat, take Andrea to her room. I will see to her there."

Andrea was sent to her bed early for her playful prank, but she was not spanked.

A few days later, Katlin had his turn. Ear-splitting shrieks brought Reed running from his study to the veranda, where a pale, shaken Sally sat trembling in a chair, waving her arms about like a demented windmill. Kathleen stood nearby, comforting her weeping little son, Katlin's dark head buried in her skirts.

"Why is it that every time I think I am going to get some work done, this place erupts into havoc?" Reed complained loudly. "What happened this time?"

Sally threw herself out of her chair and into Reed's arms. "Oh, it was *awful!*" she wailed.

Reed unwound Sally's arms from about his neck and set her roughly aside. "My God, woman! Stop that yowling! You sound like a cat with its tail caught in a door!"

Sally's weeping reduced itself to an irritating series of hiccups. Katlin still sheltered in his mother's skirts, was quiet now, and Reed could tell by the look on Kathleen's face that she was holding back laughter with great effort. Her emerald eyes shone like many-faceted gems in bright sunlight.

"What is wrong with Katlin?" Reed barked.

"Miss Simpson scared Harry and slapped Katlin's face," said Kathleen demurely.

Katlin peeked at his father. "It's all right, though, now. Mama slapped her back, and Harry will be fine. Mama said so."

Reed rolled his eyes toward the heavens. "We will take care of who slapped whom in a moment. Right now, though I dread to ask—who is Harry?"

"Not who—*what*," Kathleen corrected. "He is Katlin's new pet."

Feeling much safer now, Katlin brought his hand out from behind Kathleen's skirts. With a proud smile, he held up his pet snake, all two and a half slithering feet of him. "Do you like him, Daddy?"

Sally let out another round of deafening squeals, and Reed was tempted to slap her himself, though he now understood the problem.

Seeing the stormclouds gathering over Reed's brow, Kathleen nudged Katlin toward the door. "Perhaps you had better take Harry back to the garden for his lunch," she suggested.

She would have escaped with him, but Reed stopped her with a glare. "Kathleen, start at the beginning, and don't leave out anything," he ordered sternly.

Dutifully, she told him how Katlin had generously decided to share his precious new pet with Miss Simpson. "The poor boy had no idea she would become so upset over a harmless garden snake!" Kathleen huffed. "Then, not satisfied that she had scared both Katlin and Harry half witless with her screaming, she had the audacity to slap Katlin across the face." Kathleen's eyes snapped with anger now. "I am here to tell you that no one slaps my son and gets away with it!'' she declared righteously. ''I slapped her back, alright, and I'll do worse than that if she ever lays a hand on either of my children again!''

Reed watched as Kathleen marched into the house, her chin and shoulders set in that old familiar stubborn stance. In that moment he smiled, thinking he had never seen her so beautiful as now—defending her children with magnificent motherly indignation. He also smiled at the memory of the picture Katlin had made, standing there proudly with Harry held out for display.

''What are you grinning at?'' Sally snapped irritably.

''Oh, shut up!'' Reed directed sharply. ''You are beginning to be more trouble than you are worth, Miss Simpson! Furthermore,'' he added, ''if you ever slap anyone here again, I will hit you myself!'' With that, he stalked back to his study, leaving Sally to sulk in solitary misery.

Chapter 21

June had given way to July, and Sally was still in residence at Chimera. She had redeemed herself in Reed's eyes by reversing her tactics, and becoming sickeningly sweet toward everyone. Her excuse for her previous behavior was a severe case of nerves brought on by her harrowing adventures, which she swore she was over now.

Though Sally had recovered from her strange malady, Kathleen was experiencing some all too familiar symptoms of her own. Each morning, soon upon waking, she made a mad dash for the slop bucket, only to lose her breakfast in like fashion an hour later. By noon, she was fine, except for her swollen, tender breasts and a tendency toward tears.

Kathleen was certain she was pregnant. What she could not be positive about was who had fathered her babe—Reed or Jean. Upon frantic reflection, her last monthly flow had been two weeks before Reed's unexpected return. She had been intimate with both men since then, and it was impossible to guess which of them was responsible for her current condition.

For a while, Kathleen kept her news to herself, telling only Isabel and Kate, the two people she knew would understand and not condemn her.

"Reed will have fits!" Isabel predicted. "And just when

he seemed to be softening toward you, and seeing Sally for what she is!''

Kate, too, had dour feelings about Reed's reaction. ''I have t' agree with Isabel, lass. Yer timin' couldn't be worse! If only there was some way t' be certain who the father is!''

''What are you going to do, Kathleen?'' Isabel asked.

''Before or after I hang myself?'' Kathleen inquired bitterly.

''What? Would you actually go to that length to spare Reed the trouble?'' Isabel teased, bringing a reluctant smile to Kathleen's lips.

''No, I suppose not,'' she admitted wryly. ''I have never taken the easy way out of anything. Still, I think I had better wait to break my news to him. Miss Simpson, thank God, is planning a trip to Washington soon. I will tell him once she is gone.''

''So we're finally t' be rid o' that nuisance! Good riddance!'' Kate exclaimed.

''I should be so fortunate! No,'' Kathleen explained, ''she is not going for good. She says she will be back within a fortnight.''

''Is she going to see her uncle?'' Isabel asked. ''Maybe he will talk her into staying with him.''

Kathleen frowned. ''If you ask me, there *is* no uncle. Why she is going, I can not say, but all is not as it seems with our sweet Miss Simpson. The other day, I walked into my bedroom to find her rifling through Reed's dresser drawers. When I asked her what she was doing in our bedroom, she gave some lame excuse about looking for a clean handkerchief. Naturally, I ordered her out, thinking she was up to some jealous mischief. Then, just yesterday, I caught her going through the papers in Reed's desk in his private study. This time, she told me Reed had sent her to get some account books for him."

"Did ye ask Reed about it?" Kate inquired.

"Yes, and he knew nothing about it. I also mentioned finding her in our bedroom. When I suggested that something strange was going on, Reed laughed, saying she was just letting her curiosity get the better of her. He also thought my jealousy was coloring my judgment."

"What nonsense! I wouldn't trust the little snip any further than I could throw her!" Isabel retorted.

"There is definitely more here than meets the eye, but Reed refused to see it. I tried to warn him to keep watch and take care what he says around her, but he did not seem to take me seriously. All he agreed to do was to speak to her about her snooping."

If Kathleen had not been so worried over telling Reed about her baby, she would have looked forward to Sally's departure. She might even have devised some last prank to see Sally on her way and tempt the girl not to return, but Kathleen's mind was occupied with her own problems.

Thus, it was left to Peg-Leg to provide more mischief. The parrot had been relegated to the sunporch since arriving at Chimera. As this was where the family ate breakfast on hot summer mornings and often took refreshments in the afternoon, he still had plenty of company, but Reed had refused to let Peg-Leg take up residence in their bedroom.

The morning of Sally's departure, they were all breakfasting together in the sunlit room. As usual, everyone except Reed was ignoring the girl. Peg-Leg was more talkative than normal, and Sally was chattering away about her plans. Mary, nursing a headache, and tired of hearing both of them, suddenly suggested tartly, "Since the two of you never stop talking, why don't you and the parrot wear each other's ears off and give me a rest!''

Reed, after one startled look at his usually serene mother, laughed. "A good suggestion! Peg-Leg!" he called to the bird in the corner, "Say hello to Sally!"

"Sally? Sally?" the parrot squawked in reply. Then, out of the blue, he started to sing. "Whiskey Sal! Quite a gal! For a shilling, she'll be willing!"

Stunned silence followed the bird's little ditty. Reed was the first to react, spitting his mouthful of hot coffee in a spray across the table in an effort to keep from choking. Sally's indignant gasp was barely heard, as Isabel and Mary dissolved in helpless laughter. Try as she might, Kathleen could not hold back, and soon she was laughing as hard as the other two, tears of mirth pouring down her face.

"What a horrid, hateful bird!" Sally shrieked in outrage. Sally's exclamation set the other three women into worse fits of uncontrollable giggles. "Reed! *Do* something!" Sally wailed.

What Reed did next was not what Sally had in mind at all. His mouth had begun to twitch at the corners. Now, in the face of Sally's helpless plea, he lost control entirely. A series of deep chuckles escalated into rolling laughter that shook his entire frame. He laughed until his sides ached, and still he could not stop. It didn't help that Peg-Leg, delighted over the success of his song, kept chanting the offending lyrics in the background.

At last, when all of them were too weak to catch their breath, they looked around to find Sally gone from the room. With order finally restored, each drew a deep breath of relief, but dared not look at one another for fear of another outbreak of hilarity.

Just as Kathleen dared a peek in Reed's direction, Peg-

Leg piped up loudly. "Bless me bones! Tweak me beak! What a mess!'"

A definite snicker escaped Mary's lips, setting off a chain reaction that almost sent them rolling off their chairs, as peals of laughter echoed through the house.

"In case it should ever present a problem again, does Katlin have any other pets like Harry?" Reed drawled, a smile tugging at his lips. He and Kathleen were on the back veranda several days later, lingering over a sherry before dinner, and waiting for the others to come down and for Kate to arrive.

Kathleen smoothed her skirts, hiding a smile of her own. "He has a pet frog called Croaker, and until recently, a mouse named Tiny. Unfortunately, Harry ate Tiny for lunch one day."

Reed laughed. "How did Katlin take that?"

"Oh, he was quite put out with Harry for a while." Kathleen bit her lip on a chuckle, her eyes sparkling with mirth. "He wanted to throttle Harry, but he had trouble locating the poor snake's neck."

Reed's dark head went back as he enjoyed the joke. "That would be difficult. I believe the boy takes after you in his choice of pets. That blasted parrot of yours is a terror! I've lost count of the times I have been tempted to wring *his* neck and toss him into a stew pot. His latest antics were almost too much."

"I will admit, his vocabulary is unusual, and his timing atrocious," Kathleen agreed. "At least Harry is the silent type."

Reed suddenly sobered. "I do hope Katlin does not go about picking up any snake he encounters. Has anyone instructed him about the more dangerous variety, and

385

warned him to avoid them?''

Kathleen's face tightened in agitation. ''Of course we have, Reed! Obviously, your opinion of me as a mother leaves much to be desired!''

''Now, Kat, apart from your time away from them, you know I have always considered you a wonderful mother.''

''I'm glad,'' she blurted, ''because I am expecting another child. I'm pregnant.''

Reed looked as if she had hit him with a barn door. It took him several seconds to gather his wits. ''When?''

Kathleen whispered, ''Sometime in February, if my calculations are correct.'' Watching his frown darken as he tabulated the timing in his mind, she asked defensively, ''Aren't you going to ask whose child it is? That is your usual pattern, if I recall.''

''Actually, that was my next question,'' he said, his quiet tone frightening her more than if he had screamed at her. His eyes blazed in his face as he glared at her. ''I'm waiting for an answer.''

Gathering her courage, she called his bluff. ''It is yours, naturally.''

Now he exploded. ''Naturally? *Naturally!*'' he roared, toppling his chair over as he leaped to his feet to tower over her. ''Woman, I can count, and I am not a moron! What makes you so sure this child is mine?''

''What makes you think it is not?'' she countered.

''Damn it, Kat! You and I both know what went on between you and Jean!''

''*I* know. *You* are just guessing!'' she snapped.

Reed let out a roar of frustrated rage. ''I ought to break your neck!'' he raged.

At this point, Mary called down from an upstairs window. ''What is going on down there? For heaven's sake, you are screaming like a couple of banshees! Kate can probably hear you at Emerald Hill!''

But Kate had already arrived. She stood framed in the doorway. ''Kate heard it all,'' she said softly, gaining their attention. ''Keep it up, Reed,'' Kate stated with dignified anger, ''and Kathleen'll lose this babe, jest as she lost yer first. Think about it. Think how ye would feel, having killed an innocent child in the womb. It happened once b'fore, when yer jealousy overruled yer good sense!''

Reed glowered at Kate. ''*Then*, the child was mine. This time, there is definite reason for doubt.''

Kate stood firm. ''Even if thet were so, there is an even chance thet the babe is yers. Do ye want t' risk endangerin' the life o' one o' yer own offspring, and thet o' its mother?''

Reed ground his teeth together so hard that Kate heard it from where she stood. His face was dark with fury, and his hands were clenched into tight fists at his sides. He scowled down at his wife. ''You have until the babe is born, Kathleen. If the child resembles Jean in any way, I shall throw both of you out of this house, and you will never set eyes on either Katlin or Andrea again!'' he warned. ''In the meantime, you will continue to abide my rules. You will be a demure and obedient wife, doing my bidding and seeing to my comforts as a proper wife should. Do I make myself perfectly clear?''

''Clear as crystal,'' Kathleen answered evenly, with an answering glare of her own.

With a last glare at the two of them, grandmother and granddaughter, Reed stormed off the veranda. ''Tell Mother I will be home when she sees me!'' Minutes later, they heard him racing down the drive on his big black stallion, he and Titan hell bent on destruction.

* * *

It was three days before Reed returned, red-eyed, unkempt, and horribly hung-over. His clothes, badly wrinkled, were mute testimony that he had worn the same outfit the entire time. Grunting an unintelligible greeting to his mother, he stumbled off to bed, where he promptly passed out and slept for eighteen hours. Upon waking, he bathed, ate, and threw himself into his work about the plantation, more surly and uncommunicative than ever.

Mary was distraught, but there was little she could do, since neither Kathleen nor Reed seemed willing to explain their latest row. In view of Kathleen's condition, she suspected the unborn child had something to do with the problem, but she could not understand why that should be. Reed adored his other two children, and had been thrilled at the prospect of their birth. Perplexed, Mary shook her head in bewilderment and kept her thoughts to herself. When they wanted her advice, they would ask for it. Until then, she would not meddle.

It seemed Sally had no sooner left then she was back again, adding to the already disastrous tension at Chimera. She had evidently forgotten her anger at Reed, and forgiven him for laughing at Peg-Leg's nasty little song. Isabel, now doubly protective of Kathleen, took every opportunity to annoy the girl and keep her out of Kathleen's way. For the most part, at least within Reed's hearing, Sally was behaving herself. Upon learning of Kathleen's pregnancy, however, the girl went into a private snit, obviously displeased and perturbed at this turn of events. Only Reed's cool attitude toward Kathleen gave Sally continued hope.

Reed, infuriated by the thought that Kathleen might be carrying Jean's child, redoubled his attentions toward

Sally. Purely out of revenge, and to hurt Kathleen, he courted the girl openly though only he and Sally knew that the relationship stopped short of actual intimacy.

Kathleen was miserable. Added to the discomfort of morning sickness, the weather was oppressingly hot and humid. Too, she was convinced he was continuing his affair with Sally, though he still made love to Kathleen nearly every night. Despite his rage at her, he still desired Kathleen, and until her pregnancy prohibited lovemaking, he intended to have her.

"I fail to see why you insist on carrying out this charade, when you can barely stand the sight of me," she declared tersely. "Doesn't Miss Simpson satisfy your needs?"

"I am a man of varied tastes, my pet," Reed drawled, trailing long fingers up her inner thigh, "and as long as I am paying for your keep, I intend to have my rewards."

"You are a devil of the first degree!" Kathleen snapped, biting back a gasp as his wandering fingers found their mark.

Reed chuckled, accurately reading her reaction to his caresses. His dark head lowered to her breast. "I never did like being thought second rate in anything," he replied, just before capturing the puckered nipple between his teeth.

Kathleen sucked in her breath sharply as the fires coursed through her, the aching need building in her body.

"Tell me what you want, Kat," he prompted, as her body arched into his. "Say the words!"

Already drowning in desire, she moaned, "I want you, Reed. I need you to make love to me!"

With his hands and his mouth, he tempted her, drawing her ever near that peak of ecstasy, but never to the summit. In desperation, she clutched at him, raking his shoulders with sharp nails. "Now!" she cried. "Love me now!"

He did. With all the skill at his command, his body possessed hers, urging her to follow where he led. As one, they reached for the sun on golden wings, grasping for that elusive final rapture, that unequaled total glory, until they held it shining in their grasp.

"I despise you, Reed Taylor," she murmured as he pulled her close. "There are times I thoroughly despise you."

"Ah, but you do it so uniquely, kitten," he chuckled, "and you purr so adorably while you are about it."

It was the last comment that prompted Kathleen to wear the ivory collar with the carved ships and the letters KAT at dinner the next evening, the necklace she had found in New Orleans; the one Reed had ordered and never picked up. She had not worn it since Reed's return. In fact, he was totally unaware that she possessed it.

Reed spotted it the moment she stepped into the room. Gulping down his mouthful of sherry, he rasped, "Where did you get that necklace, Kat?"

"From the jeweler in New Orleans who made it for you," she replied softly, her eyes watching how his caressed her throat. "At the time, I thought it was your final gift to me. I treasured it as I have no other."

"It is beautiful," he breathed, his gaze traveling from the necklace to her face, framed by waves of copper-gold hair. "*You* are beautiful. It suits you as it would no other woman on earth."

His admiring gaze drew her to him, until their bodies were but a breath apart. "Kiss me," she implored on a whisper. "Hold me."

His arms enfolded her, molding her to him as his lips covered hers in a kiss full of all the wonder and tenderness that had been missing from their encounters for so long. So lovely and adoring was it, that tears misted the long lashes that fanned Kathleen's cheeks, and she returned his kiss with all the longing and love in her aching heart. Her fingers buried themselves in his ebony hair, and she felt him delve through her shining tresses to hold her lips to his.

It was thus that Sally found them when she entered the parlor. Her dismayed gasp shattered the fragile web of tenderness they had spun about them. Reed drew back, his eyes assuming the cool glint so hatefully familiar to Kathleen these days; the gentle moment passed as if it had never been.

The summer festivities continued, and Kathleen buried herself in activities to ease the pain in her heart. Because of her delicate condition, Reed forbade her to ride, or to do anything strenuous that might harm her or the baby. Still, there was plenty to occupy her time.

As the days passed, Sally was once again reverting to type, and thoroughly unpleasant type it was. Isabel and Kathleen decided it was time to take the girl down a notch or two; a few lessons in humility were long overdue.

One day, as Kathleen and Isabel sat talking to Kate, the older woman complained, "I have got t' mix up another batch o' hair rinse. Every time I run out o' it, my hair feels like someone starched it!"

Isabel answered absently, "Sally is always raving about a special mixture she must use for her fine blonde hair to make it manageable."

Kathleen looked from one woman to the other. Her lips began to twitch, and her eyes to sparkle with devilry. Kate knew that look well. "And what fine piece o' mischief are ye thinkin' up now?" she demanded.

"Oh, I have just had the most deliciously evil idea!" Kathleen crowed. "I wonder what would happen if someone put starch in Sally's special rinse?"

" 'Twould probably come out stiff as a board," Kate chuckled dryly.

Isabel laughed. "That would be a sight to see!"

It was a sight, indeed! Sally, having just washed her hair, came running down the stairs, screaming for Reed. Mary came dashing from the parlor, nearly colliding with Kathleen and Isabel. "What do you suppose the problem is this time?" Mary muttered. Then, "Oh, my stars!" she cried, as she caught sight of Sally.

Even Kathleen and Isabel, prepared as they were, were impressed by their handiwork. "Saints preserve us!" Kathleen exclaimed softly. Sally's once beautiful blonde hair stood out stiffly in every direction, giving her a striking resemblance to a scarecrow. Framing her livid face were a row of short, scorched stubs, where she had evidently tried to correct the damage with a curling iron.

"*You* did this! *You* did this!" Sally raved, pointing a finger at Kathleen accusingly. "I know it was you!"

"Whatever are you talking about?" Kathleen asked innocently. "I have not been within ten feet of you all day."

"I can attest to that!" Isabel supplied. "Kathleen never touched a—a—hair on your head!" She burst out laughing. "Or what is left of it!" she choked out.

The mid-August thunder storm was the worst Savannah had seen in years. Rain poured in torrents from heavy black clouds. The wind roared in from the ocean, tearing down fences, blowing shingles off roofs like pieces of paper, even uprooting huge old trees as if they were twigs. Thunder rumbled down the valleys like the roar of an enraged bear, and blinding lightning sent jagged white spears of fire to earth with frightening vengeance.

The livestock went wild with fear, and Kathleen had spent several arduous hours at Kate's trying to help settle the crazed, high-strung horses. Then she had driven home in the carriage, fighting her own horses every step of the way, and getting thoroughly drenched.

When at last she dragged herself in the door at Chimera, and collapsed in a heap on the first chair she came to, Reed was livid. "You crazy fool!" he roared. "You haven't got the sense God gave a gnat! Were you deliberately trying to get yourself killed?"

"Would you have cared, Reed?" she asked wearily. He certainly had not acted lately as if it would have bothered him.

"*Cared!*" he yelled. "I was half out of my mind wondering if you were lying trampled and bleeding on the road somewhere, or face down in a water-filled ditch! Don't you ever make me worry like that again!" Kathleen's teeth, already chattering from her wild ride and soaked clothes, rattled in her head as he shook her soundly.

Luckily, Mary came to her rescue. With Isabel's help, she soon had Kathleen tucked snugly into bed after a hot bath, a good rub-down, and a bowl of warm broth.

Perhaps it was the storm resounding so furiously outside the window, sending bright shafts of light into the darkened room. Perhaps it was her wild flight through the rain, and her weary muscles protesting their overuse. Whatever it was, Kathleen dreamed of that terrible storm aboard the *Emerald Enchantress* the night Jean had almost drowned. Again she relived the terror of seeing the spear of lightning strike the mast beneath which Jean stood. With frightening clarity, she watched the canvas come crashing down upon him as she tried frantically to reach him. Through rain and tears, she saw Jean washed overboard as she stood helpless. Arms outstretched, and sobbing in terror, she cried out his name again and again, trying in vain to call him back from the boiling waves.

From afar, she heard her own name being called. The sound came gradually clearer; it was Reed's voice, strong and angry.

"Damn it, Kat! Wake up!" he shouted, once again shaking her heartily.

Kathleen's eyes flew open to meet Reed's furious face. "It is about time you woke up!" he snarled, tossing her back against her damp pillow. "If I'd had to hear you call for Jean one more time, I might have strangled you!"

Still groggy, Kathleen wiped at her wet cheeks, gazing up at Reed in disconcerted wonderment. "I was dreaming . . ." she muttered in confusion.

"Obviously!" he snapped.

"It was awful!"

Reed laughed harshly.

"It was a nightmare," she whispered.

"I don't want to hear about your dreams of your lover, Kathleen," Reed growled.

"You don't understand! I dreamed Jean was drowning! The storm—the lightning—!" Her hand reached out for Reed's arm, but he jerked away sharply.

"I said I don't want to hear it!" he barked.

"Please, Reed! It is not what you think!"

He whirled on her, his face a dark mask of anger. "I will

tell you what I think, Mrs. Taylor." He nearly spat the words at her. "I think I have been a fool to worry about you; to let you get under my skin. But no more, dear wife! No more! I am finished caring what happens to you, and wondering what goes on in that devious little brain of yours!"

"Reed!"

"Not another word, Kathleen," he warned. "Not one more word, or I won't be responsible for my actions!" She watched in silent misery as he slammed out of the bedroom.

The August heat did little to ward off the chilly atmosphere at Chimera in the following days. Reed had reverted to his overbearing, antagonistic ways, and Kathleen tried to shield herself from the cold anger reflected in his eyes, eyes that stared at her like two frozen lakes, without a whit of warmth.

Only one thing helped, even while it hurt. Since the night of the storm, Reed had not slept with Kathleen. She discovered that he had been retiring to a spare room just down the hall. Unfortunately, due to servants' gossip, everyone else was soon aware of this fact as well, including Sally, who made the most of the situation.

"Problems in the marriage bed?" Sally questioned brightly one morning. "I can hardly say that I am surprised."

Kathleen's eyes narrowed dangerously, but she held her tongue, determined not to give vent to her irritation.

Sally straightened her skirts, and fussed with the bow at her trim waist. "In a few months, you will have no waistline at all, will you, Mrs. Taylor? You will be swollen and awkward. You must be already unattractive to Reed!" With a vindictive look, she added, "He is all mine now, and I shall do everything in my power to satisfy his manly needs. It will be a long time, if ever, before he requires your attentions again. You might try warm milk at bedtime to help you sleep.''

"And you might try *this!*" Kathleen snapped, tossing a spoon smartly into Sally's lap.

The girl raised pale eyebrows. "Whatever for?"

Kathleen scowled. "I hate to see you dig your grave so slowly with your loose tongue. Use the spoon and speed up the job, Miss Simpson!"

Isabel, who had witnessed the exchange, shook her head ruefully as Kathleen swept from the breakfast room. "You really aren't very smart, are you, dear?" she said to Sally. Following her friend, she advised, "I would take care, if I were you. In fact, if I were in your place, I would leave Chimera as soon as possible. I would run as fast and far as I could, were I you!"

Sally smiled superciliously. "No one can force me to leave as long as Reed wants me here."

Isabel raised one dark brow. "Never say I did not warn you, Miss Simpson. You are out of your class when you challenge Mrs. Taylor, and you will live to rue the day you tried, mark my words!"

Sally was to recall Isabel's warning many times over, as her life at Chimera became a series of unexplainable accidents and incidents. No one ever knew how the pincushion happened to appear on her chair seconds before she sat down, causing her untold pain and embarrassment; or how that odious toad found its way into her bedsheets; or who put the itching powder in her corset. Then, just as the discomfort of the itching powder receded, Sally somehow came into contact with a patch of poison ivy and spent another two weeks covered with blotches and welts.

She knew Kathleen was behind all of this, but the beautiful mistress of Chimera calmly denied it, and went on about her business as usual. When Sally at last dared to confront Reed, and demanded that he do something about his wife, he grew impatient. "I have more important things to do than to intercede in your petty squabbles, Sally. If you are unhappy here, you are free to leave."

"But you *know* she is being deliberately hateful!" Sally whined, turning wide blue eyes up to his.

"I suspect you are right," Reed answered, casting a shrewd look at the small blonde. "I am also aware that you have been deliberately antagonizing everyone. If you can't hold your own in a battle of wits with Kathleen, don't come crying to me for help. I am far too busy to be bothered with the nonsense of foolish women."

In honor of Kate's seventy-second birthday, Kathleen organized an elaborate dinner party at Chimera. All of Kate's many friends from the neighboring plantations were invited, and it was one of the grandest parties of the summer. The ballroom had been opened, the gardens and greenhouses raided for the most perfect flowers, and the verandas bedecked with lanterns and decorations. Kathleen went out of her way to insure the success of this occasion. In the face of her grandmother's failing health, she was afraid Kate might not survive to see another year.

There was no way to exclude Sally from the festivities. During the preparations, Kathleen feared that she was letting herself in for a lot of undue humiliation, and her anxieties did not prove groundless. While barely civil to his own wife, Reed showered attention on Sally. For her part, Sally clung to him closer than bark to a tree, and Reed seemed to bask in the glow of Sally's untempered adoration.

"That is disgusting!" Susan snorted, watching Sally fawn on her brother. "And Reed is lapping it up like a cat at a bowl of cream!"

Catching a glimpse of Kathleen's proud, tense face, Ted agreed. "I feel so sorry for Kathleen! What the devil is wrong with Reed these days, Sue? You would think Kathleen had committed a crime, the way he treats her now, and they were such a perfect couple before his disappearance."

Susan shook her dark head. "Whatever the problem, Miss Simpson's presence is not making matters any better. The longer she stays, the worse things get. Mother is at her wit's end with both Reed and his little houseguest!"

Kathleen was seething. The longer she watched Sally simper at Reed's side, the angrier she became. That Reed was enjoying the twit's attention was obvious to all. The fact that she was helpless to do anything about it made her rage inside, while she bravely smiled and chatted with her guests and ignored their sympathetic looks as best she could.

Dinner was particularly trying, with Kathleen seated at one end of the immense table, and Reed at the other, Sally on his left, a blonde vision in pale blue ruffles and lace. All through the meal, Kathleen watched the girl monopolize Reed's attention, laughing gaily and hanging on his every word. Kathleen would have given anything to see one of the servants pour hot gravy down Sally's revealing bodice, as well as onto Reed's lap.

Later, Kathleen was dancing with a neighboring planter, when a collective gasp from her guests drew her attention toward the refreshment table. Her eyes grew wide at the sight of Sally staring down in horror at her ruffled gown which was stained from bodice to hem with pink champagne punch.

Kathleen's gaze traveled from Sally to Reed, who stood gaping in open-mouthed amazement like everyone else. Then, as Susan reached up delicately to pluck a strawberry out of Sally's decolletage, his face darkened like thunderclouds.

In the silent room, Susan's voice rang clear as she crooned, "Oh, dear! How *dreadfully* clumsy of me! The ladle just slipped right out of my hand! And it was so *full!*"

"*Susan!*" Reed roared.

Beside him, Sally reacted with a squeal of rage. Seizing a cup of punch from the table, she flung it at Susan, who, ducked nimbly behind Reed's broad back. The liquid hit Reed square in the face, then dripped to stain his snowy-white shirt in streaks of pink.

"*Susan!*" Reed roared again, blinking and wiping at his face.

"Don't shout at me, brother dear!" Susan said sternly. "*I'm* not the one who just threw punch all over you!"

"You started this fiasco," he growled.

"Honestly, Reed!" Susan stamped her daintily slippered foot in frustration. "You would think I had done it on *purpose!*"

"Didn't you?" He glared glacial daggers at her.

"I tripped," Susan declared innocently. "When I reached out to steady myself, I bumped into Miss Simpson, and I'm afraid the ladle just spilled punch all over her lovely dress!''

Reed wiped at his shirt front with his handkerchief. ''In that case, you owe Sally an apology.''

''Oh, no!'' Susan balked suddenly. ''That woman was aiming for me when she tossed that cupful of punch! That makes us quite even!'' For the first time anyone could recall, Susan not only stood up to her older brother; she walked away from him in defiance.

Sally, thoroughly mortified, fled to her room in tears; and Reed stomped off to change clothes and wash.

To her credit, Kathleen contained her glee and managed to restore order and calm to the party, though her emerald eyes gleamed with suppressed laughter. Kate declared it the finest birthday party she had ever had.

By the time Reed returned downstairs, everyone was once again enjoying themselves—with the exception of Sally, who remained in her room for the rest of the evening. Seeing Kathleen once more surrounded by her admirers, and without Sally to devote himself to, Reed spent the remaining hours at his wife's side.

Because many of their guests had been invited to spend the night at Chimera, Kathleen suddenly found her husband once more sharing her bed. Unsure of how to react, Kathleen battled an unfamiliar shyness and a reluctance to undress before him made her fingers fumble at the buttons of her gown. She was about to call a servant to help her undo those fastenings she could not reach, when Reed stepped up behind her. ''Don't be so stubborn, Kat. If you need help, say so.'' As her back was bared to him, he kissed her shoulder, running his fingertips along the exposed ridge of her spine, and feeling he shiver at his touch.

''You are exquisite! Your skin is like warm, smooth

satin," he murmured. Pulling the pins from her hair, he let it tumble in wild profusion down her back and across her shoulders. "If Eve was half the beauty you are, it is no wonder Adam couldn't resist her and was doomed!" He turned her to face him, his hand pushing her gown from her body to fall in a silken heap on the floor.

"Do you feel doomed, too, Reed?" Kathleen whispered, drowning in the fierce blue gaze that held hers.

"Yes, damn you, I do!" he admitted with reluctant intensity. "As much as I try to hold myself away from you, I am still drawn to you. You've woven your web of desire well, my own venomous temptress, and as much as I long to, I cannot break free of it!" As if to punish her for making him want her, his lips took hers in a crushing kiss that bruised as well as burned.

As her knees gave way beneath her, Kathleen felt Reed's arms slip behind her knees, and he carried her easily to the bed. Trembling with her own awakened desired, Kathleen watched as Reed removed his clothing, and finally, the rest of hers.

He took her with hunger and passion and impatience, cursing both himself and her. Their coming together was wild and wanton. After a brief respite, he made love to her again, and yet again before dawn streaked the sky with gold. And each time, he felt himself more bound to this green-eyed vixen who had bewitched him. Each time, he lost a little more of himself to her, and his agitation and smouldering jealousy of Jean dissolved proportionately. When at last he drew her, exhausted, into his arms, he held her gently to him, stroking her hair tenderly as she slept.

Chapter 22

The last week of August all Savannah was shocked and appalled as they learned of the British attack on Washington. The English, under General Ross, had captured the city easily in a surprise attack, burning both the Capitol and the White House.

Reed immediately made ready to go to the capital and set sail the first of September. Sally, who had begged to accompany him to see if her uncle was alright, sailed with him. While Kathleen was glad to be rid of her, something about Sally's concern for her "uncle" did not ring true. She was almost certain Sally had business of another sort in Washington—perhaps British business. When she warned Reed to be careful and keep a sharp eye on Sally's movements, Reed first laughed at her, and then became angry.

"Haven't you done enough to the poor girl, Kat," he chided. "Now you try to convince me she is a British spy!"

" 'Poor girl' my foot!" she snapped. "It is not impossible!"

"It is highly improbable, and the lengths to which your jealousy drives you amazes me!"

"If you can not tell the difference between jealousy and concern, then I pity you, Reed," she told him shortly. "You deserve whatever befalls you!" On that discordant note, they parted.

Reed was gone for three weeks. Without Sally's disruptive influence, peace reigned at Chimera, though the women worried over the welfare of their country and of Reed. During his absence, Kathleen launched into a whirlwind of activity. The house was given a thorough cleaning and put in order for fall a bit early. Crops were being harvested, and foodstuffs being preserved for winter. With the help of Mary and Isabel, Kathleen also saw to the cleaning and harvesting of Emerald Hill for her grandmother, whose health was failing at an alarming rate.

Kathleen was now a full four months along in her term, and she felt the need to set things in order before she became too ungainly. Her morning sickness had passed, and she glowed with health. Her pregnancy was barely noticeable, partially due to some clever alterations in her gowns by her talented seamstress, who had already begun to sew a winter wardrobe to accommodate Kathleen's burgeoning figure.

When Reed returned, unfortunately so did Sally. He brought news of the British attack on Baltimore, the twelfth of September. This time, however, the enemy had been routed by a successful defense organized by Senator Smith. Reed had participated in the counter attack launched from Fort Henry, and the British had turned back in defeat, retreating down Chesapeake Bay to the blockade lines.

Sally's return emphasized her single-minded determination to have Reed for her own no matter what the cost. She delighted in taunting Kathleen about the time she had spent alone with Reed on the short jaunt to Washington. Sally's lies cut Kathleen deeply, but she hid her anguish behind an unruffled calm.

Privately, she told Isabel, "The woman is either incredibly dense or incredibly sure of herself! Either way, it is obvious that stiffer measures are called for, or Miss Sally Simpson will be an albatross forever about my neck. It is bad enough having to deal with this pregnancy, and Reed's threats if the child resembles Jean. I simply must be rid of that witch before my baby is born! If not, I fear I may lose Reed for good." Kathleen sighed, laying a protective hand over the slight mound of her stomach. Whatever other confusion she felt, she already loved this child, regardless who had fathered it. She hoped fervently it would prove to be Reed's babe, but should it be Jean's, she would still love and care for it. As it grew within her, she prayed for its health and safe birth. Her body shielded and nourished it, and Kathleen had a strong protective maternal instinct. Son or daughter, Reed's or Jean's, this child was *hers*. She would protect it from all harm; with her life if necessary. This babe would not feel unwanted or unloved, regardless of what was revealed upon its arrival into this chaotic household.

One morning, barely past dawn, Kathleen was up and about, seeing to breakfast preparations. Some sixth sense had nagged her awake early, and she felt a need to go to Emerald Hill as soon as possible.

"Miz Taylor! Miz Taylor!" Milly, one of the house-maids, came running into the kitchen, her eyes wide with alarm. "Come quick!"

Kathleen followed the girl. "What is it, Milly?" she asked with apprehension.

"A rider jest come from Em'rald Hill. Miz Kate is bad sick! She callin' fo' ya."

Kathleen stopped short, the color draining from her

face. With effort, she collected her wits, forcing back the dizziness threatening to overcome her. "Tell him to ride back and tell Gram I am on my way," she instructed Milly. Turning on her heel, she dashed for the stable.

Kathleen had Zeus saddled, and one foot in the stirrup when Reed caught her. "Kat!" he cried, pulling her away from the stallion. "Get away from that horse!"

Frantic, Kathleen fought him, kicking and screaming. "Let me go! Let me go!" His hands were like bands of steel about her arms as she struggled against him in her need to rush to Kate.

"Kat! Listen to me! The horses are being hitched to the buggy. I will drive you to Kate's!" He drew her to his chest, and held her tightly, feeling her tremble violently against him. "Honey, I will take you to Emerald Hill myself, but I will not let you risk your life galloping across the fields on that stallion."

"Oh, Reed!" Kathleen gulped on a sob. "She is dying!"

"I know, sweet. I know." His arms crushed her to him protectively.

Reed drove the horses as fast as he dared. The house was morbidly quiet when they arrived, the servants wide-eyed and tearful as they passed them on their way to Kate's room.

Kate lay propped up on several pillows, obviously struggling for every breath she drew. Her face was ashen, and her eyes dulled with pain. "Kathleen," she wheezed, reaching out weakly for her granddaughter.

"Oh, Gram!" Kathleen cried, gently taking her grandmother's hand. Tears clouded her vision as she fell to her knees at the bedside. She was dimly aware of Reed coming up behind her, laying his hands on her shoulders, silently lending her his strength.

Weak as she was, Kate stroked Kathleen's bright disheveled hair. "Ah, me pretty colleen," Kate sighed. "Don't fret so." She stopped to catch her breath. " 'Tis time fer me t' go and join me darlin' Sean, but I had t' see ye one last time b'fore I went."

Kathleen clutched Kate's frail hand, weeping uncontrollably.

"Don't try to talk, Kate," Reed said gently, gazing tenderly at the old lady he had come to love and admire so greatly over the years. "Don't worry yourself over Kathleen. She will be fine. I will see to it."

The old green eyes twinkled momentarily. "I know ye will," Kate gasped, "or I'll haunt ye forever!' "

"Don't go, Gram," Kathleen begged. "I need you."

Kate's head wobbled weakly from side to side in denial. "No, lass. Ye're fine and strong; a true O'Reilly. Don't fash yerself. Ye'll be fine, as Reed says. I've seen t' thet." These last words made little sense to Reed or Kathleen, as Kate gasped and gathered strength to speak once more. " 'Tis glad I am we've had these last years t'gether. I love ye, lass. Remember me . . ."

"Always, Gram," Kathleen sobbed. "Always. I love you, too."

Her strength depleted, Kate spoke no more. Sinking back on her pillows, she fought for each tortured breath, while Kathleen's heart broke at the sound of her grandmother's struggles. Reed's eyes misted at the sight of granddaughter and grandmother, so much alike, sharing this last moment together. He would have given his own life to ease their pain.

It was perhaps a quarter of an hour later when Reed realized he no longer heard Kate's tormented wheezing over Kathleen's quiet sobs. Gently, he pried Kathleen's fingers loose from her grandmother's. "It is over, Kathleen. She is gone."

"No! No! I won't let her!" Kathleen wailed. She tried and failed to reclaim Kate's hand, as Reed drew her to her feet.

"Oh, God, Reed! What will I do without her?" She sought the shelter of his embrace, clinging desperately to his warm, solid form, burying her head against his broad chest.

For precious moments, he held her while she wept, sharing her deep grief. At length, he picked her up and carried her to the parlor, laying her on the divan. After issuing orders to the servants, he sent a messenger to Chimera, asking his mother and Isabel to come and stay with Kathleen. He knew they would see to the necessary arrangements, and comfort Kathleen in her loss. He felt so damned useless, so helpless.

Kathleen went through the next two days in a daze. Kate was laid out in the parlor, and the door draped in black crepe, as friends and neighbors paid condolence calls. Kathleen refused to leave Emerald Hill until after the funeral, muttering something about not leaving Kate alone. She stayed in an upstairs bedroom, though she slept very little. Often, Reed awoke to find her side of the bed empty, and to hear her wandering through the house. After a while, he would go to her, leading her weary body back to bed, and holding her while she wept. He worried what the strain might do to her and the child she carried.

Mary returned to Chimera and the children, and Isabel stayed at Emerald Hill with Reed and Kathleen, doing what she needed to maintain order. The day of the funeral was inappropriately bright and sunny. Kate was laid to rest next to Sean O'Reilly, the two graves lying companionably side by side beneath the huge old oak a short distance from the house. All around them, the meadows of Emerald Hill spread out in verdant splendor, as green as the land from which they had come.

Throughout the funeral and the days preceding it, Reed stayed close to Kathleen's side. The depth of her grief dismayed him. He had never seen her like this before, and it made him wonder if she had mourned him with such intensity when he had been believed dead.

From somewhere deep within Kathleen managed to draw enough strength to present a fairly calm front to visitors, but her eyes were rarely dry, her face swollen and red from crying. At odd times, she would disappear, and Reed would find her hiding away, sobbing her heart out alone. She let her grief flow freely, wailing out her pain like a wounded animal. It tore at Reed's heart to see her this way, to hear her cries in the night, to see her shoulders shake with the force of her wrenching sobs.

Shaking his head sadly, he confided to his mother, ''She eats so little; and she is taking Kate's death so hard! I am afraid she will make herself ill.''

Mary, suffering her own sorrow over her dear departed friend, and still miffed at her son's irrational behavior, was impatient with him. ''Your worry over your wife is touching, Reed, after the way you have treated her these past months! However, Kathleen's grief now is mild compared to her reaction when you were assumed dead. I have never seen any human mourn more deeply than she did then.'' Mary sighed deeply. ''You are right to worry, son. This cannot be good for her in her delicate condition, but we must have faith that all will be well. Perhaps it is best for her to vent her grief, instead of leaving it to fester inside. Help her to release all her sorrow now, that she may heal more quickly.''

His mother's words gave Reed food for thought. Was there any truth to the idea that the more a person mourned at first, the more completely they recovered? Could this possibly explain why she had given herself to another man barely a year after she had thought him dead, or was Reed merely looking for a plausible excuse for her actions?

Still, there was the matter of the child she carried. There was every possibility it could be Jean's, and Reed could not bear that thought. Time and the birth of the child would tell, and only then would Reed know if he could forgive Kathleen.

Reed's eyes scanned the groups of mourners clustered about Emerald Hill. Refreshments had been served, and soon people would be departing, returning to their own homes. His gaze failed to find Kathleen among them, her red-gold hair veiled in black, yet still a beacon in the bright afternoon sunlight. Going in search of her, he finally located a servant who had seen her quietly slip away.

"Suh, Miz Kafleen done took de buggy."

"Did she say where she was going?"

"No suh, but she headed in de direction ob yo place."

Somehow, Reed doubted that Kathleen was at Chimera. For one thing, Sally was there. For another, he had a strong feeling that Kathleen would seek the comfort of the sea, as had always been her habit in past times of stress. If she headed west, as the servant said, she would not be headed for the coast, but for Savannah, and more than likely one of the frigates docked there.

A hard hour's ride found Reed pulling his lathered horse to a halt at the docks. His sharp eye noted the absence of the *Starbright,* Kathleen's favorite ship, and he cursed the fate that had placed the ship in port at this time. Spotting Dan's figure on the docks, Reed headed at a lope to intercept the older man.

"Where is she, Dan? Where is Kathleen? She is out on that damned ship, isn't she?"

"Yep, Cap'n," Dan acknowledged dourly. "Left 'bout half an hour ago. Should ha' cleared the mouth o' the river by now."

"Damn it, man!" Reed roared, beside himself. "Why did you let her go? She is in no condition to be out on the seas now!"

Dan eyed Reed in disgust, and spat a long string of tobacco juice into the water before he answered. "Ain't nothin' stoppin' thet woman when she sets her head t' somethin', Cap'n. Ye should know thet better than any o' us by now. 'Sides, how far can she go without a crew?"

Reed stared at Dan, agape. "She took the *Starbright* out alone?" He could scarcely believe even Kathleen would dare such a thing!

"Thet she did, but I wouldn't worry none. 'Tis my guess she's headed fer thet cove we used t' hide the *Enchantress* thet first year. Thet lass isn't fool enough t' do nuthin' harmful t' the bairn. She jest needs the feel o' a deck under her feet t' ease her misery some."

Reed had ridden Titan nearly to his limit by the time he reached the cove, following Dan's directions. Sure enough, there was the *Starbright,* safely anchored in the hidden bay, the current lapping gently against her hull.

Dismounting and pulling off his boots, Reed muttered, "Damn fool woman!" The refreshingly cool water did not chill his temper as he swam out and hoisted himself aboard.

The first place he looked for her, out of habit, was in the rigging. With a mixture of relief and anxiety, he failed to find her there. Neither was she anywhere on deck. When he did locate her, his anger melted. Kathleen was in the captain's cabin, sound asleep on the bunk. Her face was tear-streaked, and about her shoulders she clutched one of Kate's favorite shawls.

Quietly, Reed tiptoed from the cabin. Swimming back to shore, he untied his horse, looped the reins over his neck, and slapped him sharply on the rump, sending him galloping for home. Titan would most likely reach Chimera long before they would. Then Reed went back to the *Starbright* and waited.

It was full dark when Kathleen awoke at last. Her first feeling of calm was disrupted as she immediately sensed another presence in the small cabin. Sitting upright with a jerk, she asked nervously, "Who is here?" How she wished she'd had wits enough to have a weapon handy, but she had been too distressed to think of it earlier.

She saw the glow of a cheroot, and smelled the smoke as the intruder exhaled. "Relax, Kat. It's me." Relief flooded her as she instantly recognized Reed's deep voice.

Brushing her tangled hair from her face, she lay back with a weary sigh. "How did you find me?"

"Dan." His short answer gave her no hint as to Reed's mood, but Kathleen was too tired to care.

"Go back to sleep," he told her quietly. "Chimera can survive without us till morning."

Somehow, Kathleen felt he was not as angry as she had

412

expected, and she dared to ask, her voice quavering with tears of grief once more, "Hold me, Reed. Please come and hold me. I wanted to be alone for a while, but now I need to feel your strength surrounding me."

For a time, he held her, letting her cry and kissing the salty tears from her cheeks. At some point, she began to return his caresses, and a measure of needful demand registered in her kisses as she claimed his lips with hers. With trembling hands, she pushed at his clothing, until he willingly removed it to allow her full reign as her fingertips roamed his body, setting fire to his flesh with her knowing touch.

At her urging, he undressed her, following the path of his hands with his mouth until she cried out in longing. As his body merged with hers, she sighed out his name. She set the rhythm of their lovemaking and when their rapture broke, it was as if they had stepped into the midst of a magnificent rainbow after a summer storm.

When Kate's will was read, her oblique statement about seeing to Kathleen's welfare suddenly came clear. It was obvious that Kate was determined, even beyond the grave, to shield Kathleen from any harm that might befall her. The old lady had willed Emerald Hill to Katlin, with Kathleen as administrator and manager until he was of age. It was specifically stated that Reed was to have no say in matters at Emerald Hill.

Kathleen was both pleased and embarrassed; and Reed was clearly angry. It was clearly understood that if he wanted Katlin to inherit Kate's estate, he would have to remain married to Kathleen, like it or not. No longer could he hold the threat of divorce over Kathleen's head to insure her compliant behavior. In fact, Kate had neatly turned the tables on Reed. Not only did Kathleen now have a safe haven to retreat to if she so desired, but the will stated in absolute terms that if the conditions were not adhered to, the entire estate would go to—of all people—Dominique You!

Reed could not believe Kate's audacity. The wily old woman had certainly set the thumbscrews to him! Reed nearly choked on his impotent rage. Since Kate had met Dominique only briefly, Reed could see only one reason why she would make him her heir by default—revenge against Reed for his treatment of her beloved granddaughter. Kate knew, that under present circumstances, Reed would rather die than have any of the Lafitte clan as neighbors. Either he must abide by the terms Kate had set, or have Dominique and Jean practically living on his doorstep.

Isabel was the only person at Chimera to take full delight in Kate's directives and Reed's predicament. Totally understanding Kate's reasoning, she also had to chuckle at the woman's wisdom and sense of humor. Kate had succeeded where everyone else had failed—she had taken the reins from Reed's hands, and placed them in Kathleen's, which put Sally Simpson at a distinct disadvantage, if not entirely out of the picture. When Kathleen's baby was born, if it was obviously Jean's, Kathleen could take refuge at Emerald Hill; and Reed could not take her older children from her unless he wanted to risk having Jean and Dominique residing close to Chimera. What a marvelous turn-about!

Reed was in a black mood. He growled at everyone for days, and buried himself in his work in a concentrated effort to avoid all of them. Even Sally, distraught over the implications of the will, felt the biting edge of his anger.

414

Under the circumstances, it was assumed she would give up and leave Chimera at last, but the stubborn wench stayed on.

"Will nothing drive her away?" Kathleen moaned in dismay. Since Kate's will had been read, Reed had been almost impossible to live with, let alone having to put up with Sally, too. Reed was back to being hateful and rude, all traces of tenderness eclipsed by his vile temper, and Kathleen almost wished Kate had not provided for her future welfare. Yet a small voice whispered that the worst could be still to come, and Kathleen might one day be heartily grateful for her grandmother's concern.

The first warm October days passed, with little improvement in Reed's mood. Toward the middle of the month, when Kathleen estimated herself to be a full five months into her pregnancy, she felt the baby move for the first time.

She and Reed were alone in their room, dressing for dinner, when it happened. Kathleen's mouth formed a round O, and her eyes grew wide with wonder, as she placed both hands upon her protruding stomach. She must have made some small sound, for Reed stopped in the act of tucking his shirt into his trousers and stared at her intently.

"What is it, Kat? Is something wrong?" he questioned with a frown.

"What? Oh, no, everything is just as it should be," she sighed. Eyes full of awe, she smiled and reached for his hand. "The baby just moved, Reed. Come feel it.'

Reed jerked back as if burned, a dark scowl drawing his brows together. "No thank you, little mother. I will leave that pleasure completely to you this time around," he drawled sarcastically.

Kathleen turned away, rapidly blinking back the tears she was too proud to let him see.

The incident marked the end of their lovemaking. From that moment on, Reed shared her bed, but he did not touch her. Kathleen told herself it did not matter, for it was time for them to halt such intimacies for the baby's sake anyway. Still, it pained her that as her belly grew, so did Reed's rejection of her. If he woke to find her snuggled next to him in the night, he promptly untangled her limbs from his, and turned his back.

Taking full advantage of the state of things, Sally was, if possible, more impossible than ever; and Reed seemed to take savage delight in tormenting Kathleen by paying special attention to the blonde once more.

Kathleen was certain she had never been more miserable. "Surely things can get no worse," she moaned. As if voicing the thought aloud had tilted the scales of fate a notch further in the wrong direction, the very next afternoon, who should suddenly appear on the scene but Dominique You. "Oh, God!" Kathleen groaned, dropping weakly into a chair as Isabel flew out the door to throw herself happily into his warm embrace.

Kathleen knew that Dominique's unannounced arrival would send Reed's temper soaring to new heights, so it was fortunate that he was away in the fields when Dominique appeared. Between them, Isabel and Kathleen quickly outlined the events of the last few months, and heard from Dominique what had been happening on Grande Terre and in New Orleans. A letter from Kate's attorney had been sent to Dominique in New Orleans, and this, among other things, had prompted his journey to Savannah. "I would have come sooner," he explained, casting a loving look at Isabel, "but as soon as you had left, word came from New Orleans that Governor Claiborne had arrested Pierre. Jean went immediately to see to his release, but Claiborne held Pierre without bail, and it was just last month that he was freed.''

''Claiborne held him for *four months* before letting him go?'' Kathleen asked.

Dominique grinned. ''Not exactly, *petite*. Eleonore's brother, the good Dr. Charles, finally came to our aid. He claimed Pierre had cholera, and bribed a frightened jailer into turning his back while Charles helped Pierre to escape.''

''It was all a trick then?'' Isabel questioned. ''Pierre is alright?''

''No,'' Dominique shook his head, ''Pierre does not have cholera, but he is very ill. Charles says he will recover soon, but the chill, dampness and poor food for such a length of time left Pierre with a deep, hacking cough that he cannot get rid of. He is as weak as a newborn kitten. Francoise is caring for him in New Orleans.''

''What else has happened?'' Isabel wanted to know.

''The British came again in early September to talk to Jean about joining forces with them . . .''

''And again, Claiborne refused to listen when Jean tried to warn him, I suppose,'' Kathleen interjected.

''Worse than that,'' Dominique answered glumly. ''Claiborne sent troops to Grande Terre to destroy our base of operation.''

''What!'' the women chorused.

Dominique nodded. ''On September sixteenth, the schooner *Carolina*, under Commander Patterson, arrived at Grande Terre carrying the infantry troops of Colonel Ross. We had just enough warning for Jean to get most of the ships loaded with goods and out of the bay before they

417

arrived. Jean refused to fire so much as a warning shot.''

"What happened then?" Kathleen asked.

"While Jean took the ships and anchored them at Isle Derniére, setting up a new camp, I and my crew set fire to the remaining goods and all the buildings on Grande Terre. Naturally, I was arrested. That is how I came to be in New Orleans when the lawyer's letter arrived, telling me about the death of Madame Kate.''

Kathleen sat stunned at the news. In her mind, she could see Jean's magnificent house with all the fine furnishings, and the beautiful gardens with those precious, invaluable statues she held so dear. Tears stung her eyes. "Oh, Dominique! I am so sorry! I know it was necessary to destroy it all so the troops could not have the pleasure of looting and ruining everything, but to think of that beautiful house and fabulous garden all gone! Jean must be in despair!''

Dominique shrugged, then stared at her meaningfully. "They were only objects, *cherie*. One can live with their loss. What hurts more is to arrive and find you with child, obviously well along in your term." One dark, shaggy eyebrow raised in question. "Am I correct in thinking the child is Jean's?''

"That is a question many of us would like to know the answer to," Kathleen sighed.

Isabel said, "It is impossible to know whether Jean or Reed fathered this child, Dominique. Though Kathleen has never admitted her affair with Jean, Reed also questions the babe's parentage. Only the child's birth will say for sure, and Reed is convinced it will resemble Jean. He theatened to divorce Kathleen and keep Katlin and Andrea from her if this happens. Kate knew this, and that is why she made her will the way she did—to protect

418

Kathleen from Reed's jealous rage.''

"What a tangle!" Dominique exclaimed. "My poor Kathleen! I am so sorry . . ."

Kathleen smiled wanly. "And so am I, Dom. But you must see why you cannot stay at Chimera. Reed would probably murder us all!"

It was arranged that Isabel and Dominique would stay at Emerald Hill during Dominique's visit. As much as she longed to be with Dominique, Isabel was awash with guilt at leaving Kathleen to face Reed's anger alone. Kathleen feigned indifference. "He will either kill me, or he won't," she joked weakly. "Go on, Isabel. Do not waste time worrying over me, when you can be happy with the man you love."

Reed's reaction went beyond anger, bordering on insanity. He ranted and raved and threatened and roared until everyone on Chimera ran for cover. "Has Dominique come to look over his future property?" he bellowed. "Well, you can tell him for me that snowballs will fly in Hell before he gets his grubby hands on Emerald Hill!"

"Dominique came to see Isabel," Kathleen told him wearily. "You might recall that they are in love, and planning to marry after the war."

"How sweet! How cozy!" Reed growled sarcastically. "The two of them had better plan on living elsewhere, then."

"I am sure they will," Kathleen sighed.

"I suppose Dominique brought you word from Jean. Could he be your liaison in planning a tryst with your pirate lover?" Reed stopped ranting long enough to glare at Kathleen's swollen stomach. Then he laughed tersely. "Bad timing, my dear! Even Jean would not dare touch you now!"

Kathleen flinched at his words. "Reed, don't be this way! Please!"

Reed grasped her arms in a hard grip, his blue eyes blazing. "If Dominique came to see Isabel, then let them be together, but *you* stay completely away from Emerald Hill until he has gone. Do you understand?"

"Reed! This is ridiculous! Dominique is our friend, and Jean and I are not in communication with one another, nor do we plan to be!"

"Then stay away from Emerald Hill, and I might believe you," he growled. "You do want me to believe you, don't you, Kat?"

"Yes!" she murmured, trying to hold back her tears.

For the first time in weeks, he kissed her, a cruel demanding kiss meant to hurt and dominate. As he walked away, Kat touched her bruised lips and dashed the tears from her emerald eyes. "I do want you to believe me, Reed," she whispered tearfully, "and I want you to love me again as you once did—as I still love you, with all my heart."

Chapter 23

Dominique stayed at Emerald Hill for a week, and true to her word, Kathleen did not see him during that time. Once, Dominique rode over to Chimera with Isabel to try to talk to Reed, but Reed sent him on his way, refusing to have anything to do with his old friend.

During this week, Reed watched Kathleen like a hawk. When she tried to slip out of bed late one night, Kathleen suddenly found her wrist in the iron clasp of his big hand. "Where do you think you are going at this hour?" he growled.

Kathleen sighed in exasperation. "Sweet heavens, Reed! I am big with child, and if you don't mind, I need to visit the water closet—now!"

Had there been enough light in the room, she might have seen the sheepish look on his face as he released her.

Knowing Kathleen's staunch defender was fully occupied at Emerald Hill, Sally made a great display of throwing herself at Reed. While she oozed charm in Reed's presence, she spat venom in his absence, ridiculing Kathleen's misshapen form at every opportunity. Kathleen held her ground, difficult though it was.

"You know, Miss Simpson, the day will come when I am going to publicly humiliate you so badly that you will run from Chimera—and Reed—as fast as your little legs will carry you," Kathleen promised sweetly.

"You have already tried that, Kathleen, and failed," Sally cooed confidently.

A wicked gleam lit Kathleen's green eyes, and her tinkling laugh sent chills along Sally's spine. "No, Sally Simpson. When I really try, I will get results!"

October officially began the social season in Savannah, and though Reed had not offered to escort Kathleen to any of the functions, he had already taken Sally to town several times in the first two weeks. To Kathleen, it was the last straw. When Dominique left to return to New Orleans, and Isabel was once more free to help her, Kathleen decided to move to Emerald Hill until her child was born.

One afternoon when Reed and Sally were out, Kathleen ordered the servants to pack up her belongings and those of Katlin and Andrea, took Peg-Leg and Isabel, and left. That evening, just as they were sitting down to dinner at Emerald Hill, Reed came bursting through the door.

"What is the meaning of this, Kathleen Taylor?" he stormed.

"Why, Reed! How nice of you to come calling on our first evening in residence," Kathleen countered.

He strode up to her and clamped a hand over her wrist. "Get your things! You are coming home!"

Kathleen matched him glare for glare, her Irish temper on the rise. "Take your hand off me, before I carve it off at the wrist!" she snarled, her eyes snapping with emerald fire.

Suddenly faced with her famed stubbornness and anger after months of living with a greatly subdued wife, Reed blinked in surprise and released her. Catching him off guard, Kathleen continued her attack. "I have decided to stay at Emerald Hill, Reed. Isabel and the children will be living here with me. You and your mistress can have the run of Chimera, for all I care, but I refuse to put up with your abominable behavior any longer, and I will not subject my children to such debauchery!''

''What in blue blazes are you talking about?'' he roared.

''I am referring to that spiteful blonde viper you have been bedding at every turn!'' she shouted back. ''I am talking about the way you flaunt your affair under my very nose and before all of Savannah! You have humiliated me in every way possible! You have stood calmly by while that witch scorned me in my own home! Well, I am tired of it, and I have found a new home—away from you and away from her!''

''I am still your husband, Kat! That gives me some authority, and the right to insist that you move back home.''

''Tell that to Kate's lawyer, and see how far you get!'' she shot back. It felt good to stand straight and tall with pride, after months of groveling.

Reed tried another tack. ''Have you thought how this will look to your friends and the good citizens of Savannah? Do you know how they will talk about a woman who leaves her husband? You won't be able to hold your head up in town.''

Kathleen stared at him, dumbfounded that he would dare to mention public opinion. ''What kind of mule-headed imbecile are you? There is not one person in Savannah who hasn't already been scandalized because of your actions! Most of them do not even bother to hide their pity for me and scorn for you! If I go into town tomorrow, I will be able to hold my head as high as I do now—perhaps even higher now that I have regained my self-respect. My friends will understand, and no doubt applaud my actions. They, and all the rest of Savannah, have wondered how long I would put up with you and that floozy flaunting yourselves all over town and in our own home.''

Reed was furious, and getting desperate now. "I could tell them you are carrying another man's child, and I threw you out," he threatened.

Kathleen only laughed. "And humiliate yourself in the same stroke? I doubt it, Reed. Besides, what would you say, if, when the child is born, it has *your* coloring and features? Do you dare to chance it?''

Reed glared at her. "Damn it, Kat! I want you to come home and stop this foolishness!''

Kathleen shook her head, her anger swiftly turning to weary sorrow. "No, Reed," she answered quietly. "I am sick to death of being humiliated. I will take no more abuse from you and that trollop. I am tired of being made to pay for something that was not my fault.''

Her sudden change of mood confused him, causing him to issue what he considered the ultimate concession. "Would you change your mind if I consider sending Sally packing?''

Kathleen shook her head. "I am sorry, Reed. A few weeks ago, that might have meant a great deal, but I am tired of fighting with you. It hurts too much to see the scorn on your face each time you look at me; to feel you turn away from me when I reach out to you. I am tired, and I need some peace of mind if I am to have a healthy, happy baby.''

Her refusal angered him anew. "So help me God, Kathleen, if that child turns out to be Jean's, I will find a way to break you! Perhaps it *is* best if you remain here until the baby is born. That way, I will be spared the trouble of tossing you out again on your blasted bottom!'' With one last glare, he left her to her newfound pride and her ever-ready tears.

Unable to budge Kathleen, Reed took to visiting Emerald Hall often in the following days, on the pretext of seeing Katlin and Andrea. Kathleen feared he was actually looking for a means to get back at her for leaving Chimera. Looking down at her ever-enlarging belly, she was disinclined to believe he might actually be missing her. Still, Kathleen was seeing more of Reed now than when they had lived in the same house.

Visiting Emerald Hill also meant putting up with Peg-Leg and Isabel, and Reed could not decide which of Kathleen's constant companions irritated him more. Here, Kathleen let the arrogant parrot have the run of the house, and the bird seemed to delight in tormenting Reed whenever he came by.

''Blast it, Kat!'' Reed growled, swatting at the pesky parrot and brushing crumbs out of his black hair. ''Can't you control that bloody bird?''

Kathleen laughed, something she was doing more of these days in the calmer realm of her new home. ''Peg-Leg is a law unto himself.''

''Still, there should be limits! He followed me to the outhouse the last time I was inspecting the stables. I didn't even realize he was in there with me, until he screeched, 'Drop me drawers!'! He nearly scared me to death!''

Peals of laughter escaped her, and she clapped a hand over her mouth, to no avail.

''It is not funny!'' Reed retorted. ''I jumped so when he startled me, that I hit my head on the wall. If I could have caught him, I'd have dropped him down the hole and slammed the lid!''

Peg-Leg tried to light on Reed's head again, and Reed swung at him. ''Sticks and stones! Sticks and stones!'' the parrot chanted.

''One of these days, Kat, I am going to yank his feathers out one by one!'' he warned. ''Maybe when he's naked the little buzzard will learn to keep his beak shut!''

''You will have to catch him first,'' she chuckled, ''and Peg-Leg can be very elusive. Besides, if I ever see you sporting so much as one wisp of his colorful plumage, you will answer to me, Reed Taylor. I happen to adore that parrot!''

Reed's birthday, the thirteenth of November, presented a problem. Previously, Kathleen had arranged a celebration, inviting friends and neighbors to dinner at Chimera. Now that she was living apart from him, and with Sally Simpson still residing at Chimera, this seemed inappropriate, to say the least.

Susan provided the solution. ''Why don't we rent a hall in Savannah. Then none of us have to entertain that hussy in our homes, Kathleen won't feel like an intruder in her own house, and we can all leave when we want.''

As much as it aggravated her, Kathleen agreed, detesting the fact that Sally was still disrupting her life. It annoyed her further to find that Sally was using Kathleen's own favorite seamstress to have a special gown made for the occasion. Six months pregnant, Kathleen felt huge and ungainly. As Mrs. Fitz pinned and measured and tucked in an effort to disguise Kathleen's bulging shape, Kathleen fumed.

''Any particular color of fabric you would prefer, Mrs. Taylor?'' the seamstress asked through a mouthful of pins.

"Definitely not any shade of orange," Kathleen stated decisively. "As lovely as that rust gown was, I felt like a pumpkin in it."

"Might I suggest a taffeta, perhaps? The material is stiff, and would hang away from your body, rather than cling to it as satin does."

Mrs. Fitz brought out a bolt of midnight blue taffeta, shimmering with delicate silver threads. "If you like this, I could cut it so that it would disguise your condition fairly well."

Kathleen smiled gratefully. "Mrs. Fitz, you are a wizard with needle and thread!"

The woman nodded, pleased with the compliment. "Since you first came to Savannah, my business has tripled. Everyone wants to be gowned as fashionably as the beautiful Mrs. Taylor. Any time I can be of service to you, it is my pleasure."

"You could ruin Miss Simpson's gown," Kathleen murmured, almost to herself.

Mrs. Fitz's eyes widened in surprise. "Are you serious?" she asked.

Kathleen stared at the seamstress. Finally she nodded slowly and a mischievous smile touched her lips. "Yes, I believe I am *quite* serious!"

"Have you decided on a gift for Reed's birthday, Kathleen?" Isabel asked several days later.

"I have had it for months," Kathleen admitted.

"Let me guess," Isabel laughed. "You are giving him Peg-Leg!"

"Surely you jest! That would be condemning the poor bird to the stewpot!" Kathleen said. "No, not Peg-Leg.

427

Do you recall my telling you about all the fabulous treasures we took from that last Spanish vessel we captured?''

Isabel nodded, and Kathleen continued, ''Among these, I found a magnificent rapier, with jewels imbedded in the guard. It is surely one of a kind, and I thought of Reed the moment I saw it.''

Isabel shrugged. ''Well, if worse comes to worst, you can always run him through in style!'' she suggested dryly.

Before the party, Kathleen vowed to keep a tight rein on her temper and maintain a calm, dignified demeanor before their friends. Her place was at her husband's side on his special day. If anyone should feel unwelcome, it ought to be Sally. Kathleen was determined to put an end to Sally's mischief once and for all. If everything worked as she had planned, this would be Sally's last evening in Savannah.

On his natal day, Reed was feeling content and almost benevolent. Under the circumstances, he was surprised that Kathleen had planned a party at all, and positively astonished when she arrived bearing a brightly wrapped and peculiarly shaped gift.

She looked spectacular this evening, serene and confident. As she removed her cloak, Reed let his eyes rove over her figure. If he didn't know better, he would hardly guess she was expecting a child. The blue gown was stunning, the high-waisted design almost magically disguising her pregnancy. Caught up on the crown of her head, the long red-gold hair shone in copper splendor, giving her the regal look of a queen. Reed had never seen a woman look more enticing while carrying a child. Others might appear tired or dowdy or clumsy, but Kathleen always glowed with vital energy. As he watched her smile and greet their friends, he felt himself tighten with unfulfilled desire. With a soft curse, he turned his attention elsewhere, straining to bring his lustful body under control.

The dinner was delicious and relaxed, with good food and excellent wines from Chimera's cellars to celebrate Reed's thirty-two years. To his amazement, Kat seemed to go out of her way this evening to hide her malevolence toward Sally. Several times, he caught Sally deliberately baiting Kathleen, but his beautiful wife kept her temper and ignored Sally's taunting with cool disdain. Beside Kathleen's ripe beauty, Sally's prettiness paled significantly. Reed admitted to himself that he only permitted Sally to stay on in order to retaliate against Kathleen, but even he became agitated when Sally took it upon herself to belittle his wife. He could barely stomach the girl by now, and he certainly was not about to entangle himself further with the greedy wench. As soon as she ceased to be useful to him, he would send Miss Sally Simpson packing.

A small orchestra had been hired to provide dinner music and to oblige those who wished to dance afterward. Several couples were waltzing, and others milling about in pleasant conversation as Reed opened his gifts. As in the past, he had opened those from Katlin and Andrea earlier, at home in the nursery. When he opened Kathleen's present, the magnificence of the sword stunned him. That, combined with the open look of love on Kathleen's face, made Reed feel unworthy.

After opening the other gifts, Reed extended his hand toward Kathleen, wanting his first dance of the evening with his wife. Sally stood watching in mute fury, a tight, angry expression pinching her features into ugliness. The hall was crowded, and someone behind her jostled Sally. She felt a slight tug on her dress, and suddenly to her horror and everyone's utter amazement, the skirt of the gown slid swiftly and silently to the floor, leaving her standing in her bodice and bloomers. Even the musicians had stopped playing to gawk. With a strangled cry, Sally bent to retrieve her skirt. The slippery material eluded her shaking fingers, and when she finally did manage to clutch it, blushing to the roots of her hair, Sally peered about her in panic, wailing in despair. Thoroughly mortified, she wanted to melt into the floor boards, but she was frozen to the spot. She could not seem to budge, let alone run for cover. She looked around at all the eyes staring at her and heard the gasps and whispers of the crowd. These were Kathleen's friends, but surely there was one among them who would take pity on her. Where was Reed? Why didn't someone come to her rescue?

Reed was almost too shocked to move at first. He stood as open-mouthed as everyone else. When his brain finally did start to function, he knew Kathleen had had a hand in this disaster.

Aware that he must do something to aid Sally, Reed removed his jacket and started toward her. Smothered chuckles and titters made his own ears burn, and he could only imagine what Sally must be feeling.

Behind him, he heard one of his friends comment, "Well, now we are all aware of what Reed has been familiar with for some time!"

Another man answered, "Doesn't look that great to me. Personally, I've seen better along the waterfront!"

Another said, "Why would anyone bother with that, when he has Kathleen, I ask you?"

Reed had almost reached the quivering girl, when Kathleen's voice rang out crisp and clear, stopping him in his tracks. "Happy Birthday, Reed!" she chirped, her emerald eyes flashing. "I know how you *love* surprises!" With a marvelously wicked laugh, she added, "I do believe everything has been unwrapped now!"

He watched in angry disbelief, his ears ringing with the laughter of the guests, as Kathleen swept by him, exiting the hall with a grand flourish.

Sally was on her way by mid-morning of the following day. Reed didn't know where she was headed, nor did he care. He was profoundly relieved to see her go. Now, perhaps, he could regain the respect of his friends. Without Sally's nagging presence, he might be able to pull his life into order again. Sally had served her purpose— until Reed had made the mistake of once again under-estimating his wife. He was not sorry to see Sally go. She had been a thorn in his side for much too long, and he considered himself well rid of her. He was only sorry he had not sent her away sooner.

Kathleen was of a similiar opinion when she learned of Sally's departure. While she knew that Sally was only a symptom to the larger problem between herself and Reed, she was one factor Kathleen was glad to see eliminated. If only the rest of her dilemma could be resolved as success-fully!

Thanksgiving was traditionally strictly a family affair, and Susan was hosting the festivities this year. Ted's family as well as the Taylors were invited, with all their children, numbering six by now. There were Reed and Kathleen's two, Susan and Ted's two, and Martin and Amy had produced a baby daughter in addition to their son. Isabel attended, as she had since coming to Chimera, but Kate's presence was sadly missed; her loss was felt by everyone,

431

but most of all by Kathleen. This was the first holiday since Kate's death.

Tradition and pride decreed that Kathleen attend, though she dreaded it. In the ten days since Sally's departure, Kathleen had not seen Reed. He had come to Emerald Hill several times to see the children, but Kathleen had deliberately avoided him. She knew it was cowardice, but as much as she berated herself, she simply could not face him. Through Isabel, he had sent a message asking her to return to Chimera. Not yet ready to tackle the problem awaiting her there, Kathleen declined, saying she considered it best to wait until after the baby was born.

It was a quiet, subdued gathering on Thanksgiving Day. Kathleen and Reed, though polite to one another, had difficulty in finding things to say. Too much had happened to them in the past months, and they were awkward and ill at ease with one another. Both were glad when the tense day was over; especially Reed, since for the first time in his memory, he felt like a pariah in his own family, all of whom blamed him and him alone for the continuing estrangement between himself and Kathleen.

On his visits to Emerald Hill, Kathleen no longer avoided him, but she rarely entered the conversation willingly, or joined him in playing with Katlin and Andrea. Once in a while, Reed would deliberately goad her into an argument, but their encounters lacked the old intensity. Kathleen was determined to await the birth of her baby before seriously considering a relationship of any kind with him.

It was in the midst of this war of wills that a message arrived for Reed the end of the first week in December. It was a summons from General Jackson, requesting that Reed and several of his ships come immediately to New

Orleans, to aid in the defense against the British.

On his way to Savannah, Reed stopped by Emerald Hill to say goodbye. Upon hearing his news, Kathleen was visibly upset for the first time in days.

"I have to go, Kat," he told her.

"But Reed, if you leave now, you will most certainly miss Christmas with the children!" she cried.

"I have no choice. Besides, it won't be the first Christmas I have missed," he reflected bitterly.

Kathleen's face clouded over. "No, but it will be the second consecutive Christmas you will have been away," she reminded him tartly.

"It can't be helped, Kat," he repeated sharply. Then bitterness overcame him, and he taunted, "Don't worry. I will be back in plenty of time for the baby's birth; and if I see your old lover while I am there, I will send him your greetings."

"Do that!" she snapped back.

Taking her completely by surprise, Reed caught her into his arms and kissed her. What began as a demanding brand of possession soon became a searching, longing kiss of farewell. "Take care of yourself and the children, Kat," he murmured, prying his lips from hers.

"Return home safely, Reed," she whispered; and he swore that for just a moment he saw tears sparkling in her emerald eyes as he rode away.

Chapter 24

A week later, Reed arrived in the chaos that was New Orleans. Always a bustling port city, it was now preparing for the inevitable British attack. Jackson's soldiers were much in evidence—and a rag-tag crew they were. Jackson had driven them hard to reach New Orleans. They were well-seasoned, but tired, some of them ill from traveling through rain and swamps, with inadequate food and rest. General Jackson himself was unwell, but the gruff military man refused to succumb to his illness, ignoring spells of dizziness and feverish chills.

"Captain Taylor, glad you could make it," Jackson greeted Reed.

"Did I have much choice, sir?" Reed answered.

"None," Jackson replied, his eyes twinkling with humor. "But you might have arrived too late to do us any good, which would have distressed me more than I can say. How many ships did you manage to bring?" Jackson pounded a fist on his desk in agitation. "Damn! It is a shame there is no way to get them on up to New Orleans on the Mississippi, but the British have us bottled up tighter than a miser's whiskey jug."

Reed frowned. "There were only four frigates in port when I got your message. The others were out on privateering missions."

Jackson shrugged. "That is four more than we had before. Where did you anchor?"

"I started to put in at Barataria Bay, but after seeing the destruction there, I went on to another island nearby. What the devil went on?"

Jackson snorted. "That fool Claiborne can't see his nose in front of his face! He sent troops three months ago to wipe out Lafitte's outfit. The jackass nearly had me believing that Lafitte was a British spy, as well as a pirate. It wasn't until yesterday that I discovered Lafitte has been trying to warn Claiborne about the British for months now; and Claiborne, through some personal grudge with the Lafittes, chose to ignore him. If he had taken Lafitte's advice, we'd now have the troops and ammunitions we need so badly."

"Are things that bad, General?" Reed's eyebrows rose in question.

"Son, if the British knew how desperate we are for men and ammunition, they would storm this place tonight and walk away with New Orleans and the entire Mississippi River in their pocket. The only breastworks we have are those we've managed to throw up since my troops arrived. The only stores are those I've ordered laid by. Only the men I brought with me are trained for battle. Hell! I'm surprised Claiborne didn't just send the British an engraved invitation and be done with it!"

"Shall I send one of my vessels back up the coast to collect arms? We could ferry them up the back bayous to New Orleans."

The general considered this. "You could try, but just send one. I doubt there will be time for them to get back before the British strike. In the meantime, I can use every pair of hands you can supply to help dig more breastworks.''

There was a knock on the general's door. At his answer, a lieutenant came in, saluted, and announced, ''Jean Lafitte here to see you, sir.''

Jackson nodded. ''I've been expecting him. Send him in.''

Reed's immediate desire was to leave, but Jackson motioned for him to stay, and there was little he could do but obey and prepare himself to come face to face with Jean.

Jean saluted smartly. ''General Jackson,'' he greeted. Then he started in surprise as he spied Reed. ''Hello, Reed. I didn't expect to see you here.''

Jackson looked from Jean to Reed. ''You know each other?''

Reed hesitated, then admitted, ''Yes. How are you, Jean?''

''I've been better,'' Jean replied, ''but today I have come to offer General Jackson my aid.''

''What sort of aid, Lafitte?'' Jackson asked.

''I offer you my services, and that of my men. Unlike the sheltered citizens of New Orleans, my men know how to fight. They know the area around New Orleans, and the routes through the swamps. They want a chance to prove their loyalty to America, as do I.''

A speculative gleam entered the general's eyes. ''How many men are you talking about?''

Jean gave an eloquent shrug. ''Fifty—eighty—perhaps a hundred. It depends on how many I need to maintain my new base and my ships. Naturally, I would gladly offer the use of a few of my vessels also, but only with my own crews in charge.''

While the general mulled this over, Reed put in, ''Why would you do this, Jean, after Claiborne routed you out of Grande Terre?''

Jean leveled his hazel gaze at Reed. ''Because I am an American,'' he declared proudly, ''and I want to help defend my adopted country. Once before in my life, I have had to flee my home, leaving all I cherished behind. Never again do I want to see that happen. Besides,'' he added with a wry grin, ''you know how I have always detested the English.''

''Your men would have to supply their own guns and ammunition,'' Jackson said.

Jean chuckled. ''Yes, I have heard your arms depot is sadly lacking. Perhaps I could be of assistance there, also.''

Fully alert now, Jackson leaned forward. ''Sit down, Lafitte, and let's get down to particulars.''

In the end, both Jackson and Jean were well pleased. The same could not be said of Reed. Jean had agreed to provide much-needed arms and ammunition from his private warehouses and stockpiles on his island retreat. The U.S. government would later repay him in full, General Jackson had promised. Jean and his men would help fight against the British, lending the use of ships and crews, if needed. He would also aid in drawing up maps of waterways through the swamps, and oversee lines of defense in these areas. In return, Jackson would see that Claiborne sent a letter to the President, asking for amnesty for the Lafittes and any of Jean's men who had been declared pirates.

For his part, Jackson had ordered Reed to help govern all of Jean's projects, as well as a few others, and to report back to the general on the progress made. While Reed might have objected to the assignment, Jackson said, "Time is short, Captain Taylor, and while I get the feeling you and Lafitte are not on the best of terms, personal animosities must be set aside. You have admitted to knowing those swamps nearly as well as he, and that makes you the best man for the job. You are the only one qualified to maintain order between his men and the regulars. I know I can depend on you to do what is needed."

There was no way Reed could refuse, though the thought of having to work hand-in-glove with Jean set his teeth on edge. Of all the idiotic turns of events! To find himself forced into close association with his rival, the very man whose child Kat might be carrying! If he and Jean did not manage to kill one another before this war was over, it would be a miracle!

As Reed and Jean left Jackson's office together, Jean commented, "Well, *mon ami*, it will be like old times fighting together again, eh?"

"We are no longer friends, Jean, and not likely to be again," Reed snarled. "If not for General Jackson, I would call you out."

Jean looked amused. "You would challenge me to a duel?"

Reed nodded. "With none of your crew there to knife me in the back after I'd killed you," he sneered.

Jean's eyes saddened. "I am sorry it has come to this between two friends such as we. I bear you no ill will, Reed."

"I can not say the same for you, and I am surprised you can feel that way," Reed said sarcastically. "Have you found you did not really love my wife after all?"

Jean sighed. "I love Kathleen very much. I always shall, but she belonged to you first, and it is you she loves above

439

all else. Knowing this, what chance did I have to claim her?''

Reed stopped walking, shooting a glare at Jean. "You would have done well to recall that sooner, Jean. As it is, I would sooner shoot you than look at you. Only circumstances and the general's orders may prevent it.''

The warnings of British attack took on fresh meaning when the English entered Lake Borgne the next day. General Jackson immediately declared New Orleans under martial law. No one entered or left the city without his approval, and under his watchful eye, defense measures were stepped up to a feverish pace. All available men labored day and night digging entrenchments outside the city. The women were busy, rolling lengths of bandages and readying food and supplies in case of a long seige.

Reed worked with a vengeance, taking out his frustrations in hard physical labor. Arms were brought from Jean's new base, and ammunition from his private warehouses, and distributed in varied locations, so that if one was destroyed, the others would be saved. The ships were deployed to strategic areas, and lookouts posted. Jean's men, and many of Reed's, were deployed in and around the swamps.

Throughout the hectic activity, Reed did his best to ignore Jean's presence as much as possible. Whenever they could not avoid one another, the very air seemed to vibrate with the tension. Hatred and rage flared from Reed's eyes whenever Jean passed by. Sharp words were exchanged on both sides, and it was only a matter of time before it all came to a head.

As their captains continued to quarrel and glare at one another, the men started to choose sides. No matter that they had sailed with and known the others for years, developing mutual respect and exchanging tales over many a keg of rum; now they were adversaries, and feelings ran high.

Dominique tried to put a stop to it. "Look at you," he pointed out derisively to Reed and Jean, "acting like two schoolboys! Fine examples you are setting for your men! Most of them are ripe for a fight, just waiting for either of you to give the signal. We have more important things to do than fight each other!"

"My brother is right, Reed," Jean agreed.

Though Reed could see the truth of Dominique's words, he said, "Perhaps, but once this battle with the British is over, nothing would give me more pleasure than to beat you to a bloody pulp, Jean."

"Why don't you challenge him to a duel of swords, Reed?" Pierre suggested sneeringly. "Or perhaps you hate to admit that Jean is the better swordsman." Then as an added jab, he taunted, "Kathleen bested Jean once, in a test of skills. Can you do less than your wife, and still hold your head high?"

"What exactly do you mean by that?" Reed's eyes narrowed. "How did Kat beat Jean? When?"

"It was on Grande Terre," Pierre responded with spiteful glee. "None of us were supposed to be aware of it, but Dominique saw it all. Kathleen challenged Jean to a test of swords, and she was *magnifique!*"

"She actually defeated Jean?" Reed was incredulous. He knew Kathleen was skilled—he had fallen prey to her expertise many times—but to defeat the renowned Jean Lafitte . . . !

"I must admit that she did." Jean nodded. "She is one of the most proficient swordsmen in the world."

"I can not refute that fact. The little Irish witch is just full of surprising unladylike talents—one of which appears to be collecting lovers!" growled Reed.

Exploding in righteous anger, Jean leapt for Reed's throat. "You despicable bastard!" he roared. "That woman mourned you! She wept tears of anguish! She took monumental risks with her life because she did not care to live since she thought you had died!"

Reed's fist flew into Jean's face. "Yet she tumbled into your bed fast enough!" He grunted as Jean countered with a blow to Reed's stomach.

They broke apart momentarily, and Jean retorted, "While you were counting seashells along the shore with Miss Simpson?"

Reed tackled Jean, and they both fell to the ground. "Keep your nose out of matters that do not concern you," Reed ground out, trying to pin Jean's body beneath his.

For several minutes the two men wrestled, each striking telling blows, but neither gaining the advantage. At length, they pulled back and regained their footing, circling one another carefully. "If Miss Simpson is not my business," Jean panted, "perhaps Kathleen is, if you believe the child she carries may be mine."

The matter was now in the open.

"I suppose Dominique told you that," Reed surmised, squinting malevolently at Jean and waiting for an opening in Jean's defense.

"He told me everything Isabel had to say of the way you have treated Kathleen," Jean said.

They moved at the same time, fists flying, pounding at one another mercilessly. Reed's knuckles connected with Jean's nose, and blood spurted. Through Reed's guard, Jean struck a blow, and Reed thought he felt one of his ribs crack. Again they fell, grappling on the ground.

"Isabel should mind her own affairs!" Reed huffed.

"She is right to be concerned," Jean grated through clenched teeth. "If you do not care for Kathleen any longer, I would gladly have her back, without qualms over whose child she bears." Jean rolled away.

Blind with rage, Reed grabbed for Jean, flipping him to his back, and wedging a husky arm against Jean's throat. "I'll kill you both before I let her come to you!" he roared.

Jean kneed him in the groin, breaking Reed's hold and leaping to his feet. "That is the trouble with you, Reed," he wheezed, as Reed, too, labored to his feet. "You lead with your temper instead of your brain. If Kathleen truly wanted to be with me, nothing could stop her. Think about it!"

Reed lunged, his weight carrying them both down once more. By the time Dominique and Pierre pulled them apart, they were both struggling for breath and barely conscious.

Jean glared at Reed through a badly swelling left eye. "You are a fool, Reed! Kathleen loves you more than you deserve!"

"That still doesn't settle the issue of the child," Reed muttered past a split lip, trying vainly to throw Dominique off and get at Jean once more.

"If you loved her enough, you would see her side of things, and it would not matter!" Jean spat, trying to rid his tongue of the taste of blood. "You do not deserve that woman, Reed! Your own pride and stupidity are blinding you to her worth!"

Reinforcements finally arrived when General Coffee and

443

General Carroll appeared with their troops. Three days before Christmas, the British crossed Lake Borgne under cover of night, and by early dawn of December twenty-third, emerged on an evacuated plantation just eight miles below New Orleans.

Putting aside their personal rancor, Jean and Reed united behind Jackson to lead an unexpected attack on the British before they could regroup and move further toward the city. They charged the plantation, routing the English just as the schooner, the *U.S. Carolina,* barraged the shore and their boats. The British beat a hasty retreat, and though everyone knew it was but a temporary reprieve, it raised their spirits.

In the next few days, the Americans worked to finish building their entrenchments and the embankments for their cannon. Though Reed's resentment threatened to erupt, and Jean's animosity flared, both men managed to keep their tempers under control.

In a tiny tent, with mud oozing beneath its sides, Reed sat on his cot and thought of home. It was Christmas Eve, and he wondered what Kathleen and the children were doing. Were they all at church, attending Christmas Eve services? Was Kathleen staying in town for the holidays with Susan or her Aunt Barbara? Reed rubbed at his forehead wearily. Damn, he wished he was home! Even an argument with Kathleen would be preferable to this aching loneliness. How dear her sharp words and tart tongue seemed just now! He would welcome them gladly!

As he lay back, carefully holding his taped ribs, Jean's words echoed in Reed's ears. Perhaps he was a blind, stupid fool, but he could not overcome his revulsion at the thought of Kathleen carrying Jean's child within her. With an exhausted sigh, Reed closed his eyes.

* * *

Kathleen sat staring into the flames of the dying fire. It was late, and everyone else had long since gone to bed in preparation for Christmas Day. In deference to her advanced pregnancy, the Baker and Taylor clans had all come to Emerald Hill for the holidays.

Her gaze wandered to the pile of gifts beneath the tree. Come morning, Andrea and Katlin and their cousins would make a shambles of the orderly arrangement, flinging ribbon and wrapping across the room as they discovered the coveted prizes within the boxes. Squeals of delight would echo from the rafters, and when it was done, only Reed's gifts would rest beneath the branches.

Kathleen had sewn a chocolate brown smoking jacket for him and had bought house slippers to go with it. Aside from that, she had found a beautifully carved humidor and filled it with his favorite cheroots. From Katlin, he would receive a mustache cup, and Andrea had chosen a blue ascot as her gift to her papa. All would await Reed's arrival—whenever that might be.

There were two gifts there from Reed to Kathleen. Mary had brought them earlier in the week. Evidently, he had gotten them before he left for New Orleans. But the gifts did not make up for Reed's absence. Kathleen would have given much to have him near now, even if he were to behave hatefully. A rousing fight might be just what she needed to jerk her out of her lethargy.

The baby kicked, drawing Kathleen's attention to her swollen abdomen. Placing a calming hand over the mound, she soothed it in circular motions. A few more weeks, and she would be holding the child in her arms. Kathleen was frightened, not of the birth itself, but what it might precipitate. If the babe resembled Jean, Reed would never forgive her; if it did not, Kathleen was not

445

sure she could forgive Reed for his spiteful treatment of her. At times, she hated him as fiercely as she loved him. With a sigh, Kathleen resigned herself to the final few weeks; regardless of the outcome, she would love this child and protect it with her very life.

Christmas morn dawned fine and bright. Kathleen watched the sunrise from her bedroom window, wondering if perhaps Reed was watching the same sight from New Orleans. What was it like there? Had he seen Eleonore, by chance? Or Jean; or Dominique? Had the British attacked yet? Was there much fighting? Were men bleeding and dying on a battlefield beneath this benevolent sunrise? Was Reed one of them? If only there was some way of finding out what was happening; if only news of the war did not take so long to filter back from the battlefields.

Later that morning, when Kathleen sat with Reed's gifts in her lap, she almost dreaded opening them. Reed held so much animosity toward her at times, that she was uncertain what she might find beneath the wrappings. Finally, unable to delay further, she opened her presents. The larger box contained a beautiful peach-colored morning gown and matching slippers. Kathleen recognized Mrs. Fitz's handiwork in the fine stitching, and blessed both Reed and the seamstress when she found the gown designed in a loose style that would fit her both now and after the baby was born.

The second gift was smaller, and rattled when she shook it. Upon lifting the lid, Kathleen was stunned to find a dozen jeweled pins for her hair. At the tip of six of the gold pins was a glittering emerald; the other six sported shimmering diamonds.

In the lid of the box was a note. "To my lovely wife," it

read, "Whose beauty outshines any jewel." It was signed, simply, "Reed."

The glow Kathleen felt was dimmed somewhat by the realization that though he might be proud of her beauty and choose a spectacular gift to compliment her, there was no mention in his note of love.

Far from the beautiful sunrise Kathleen had witnessed, Reed watched the New Orleans sky lighten from black to a dull grey, as rain poured down steadily throughout Christmas Day. The weather suited his mood, as he thought of everyone back home.

There was one thing Reed could be thankful for. Instead of eating with the troops, he had been invited to dinner at Eleonore's. Upon hearing that Reed was in town, she had sent a message, insisting that he share Christmas Day with her and her brother. Eleonore was eager for news of Kathleen, and Reed came away with a thick letter in his pocket to deliver to Kathleen upon his return to Savannah.

It was as he was riding through town that Reed saw the woman. At first, he thought his imagination was playing tricks on him, but then he caught a full view of her face, and was positive of her identity. It was none other than Sally Simpson! Something about her furtive attitude made Reed hesitate to reveal himself, hidden as he was beneath his cloak and the hat pulled low over his face against the rain. He watched as she glanced nervously around before hastily entering a nondescript carriage.

Curiosity over her odd behavior and unexpected appearance in New Orleans made Reed decide to follow her. The carriage took a circuitous route, down side streets and less traveled byways, winding its way toward a rundown section of town near the docks. There, Reed watched as a man slipped quickly out of a doorway and into the carriage with Sally. A couple of miles further, the carriage halted to let the man alight. He scurried quickly into the trees at the side of the road, and the carriage went on.

Reed was momentarily undecided whether to follow the carriage or the man. Since he had seen the house before which Sally had entered the carriage, he was sure he could find it if necessary. Turning his horse into the trees, Reed followed the man, keeping back a fair distance. Before long, he came out along a river track.

Staying within the treeline, Reed followed the man eastward, until the fellow was met by three others in a small boat. Reed followed along the bank to where the boat disappeared into the swamplands, but he had heard the men's voices floating back to him on the marsh mists. It was apparent that all four were British.

Reed turned his horse back toward town, his thoughts spinning. Kathleen's voice seemed to echo in his head, and again he heard her warnings about Sally, warnings he had brushed off as mere jealousy. Now he began to recall the various incidents he, too, had noticed, but failed to find significant at the time. It did seem odd, upon reflection, that Sally had chosen to visit her uncle in Washington mere days before the British attack, and again afterward, when Reed had gone up to the capital. Now it appeared she was up to something devious in New Orleans.

As he came within a block of the house from which he believed Sally had left, Reed saw Jean Lafitte coming out of Pierre's home with Dominique. Much as he detested himself for it, he felt the need to confide in his former friends and get their opinions of the strange happenings.

Acting on impulse, he called out, "Jean! Wait!"

Drawing abreast of them, he launched into his brief tale. Then he asked, "You would recognize her, Jean. Have you seen her about town?"

Jean frowned. "No, I do not recall seeing her lately. Surely I would have remembered her."

"I think she bears watching," Dominique inserted. "Since she would not recognize me, perhaps I should be the one to keep an eye on her—or perhaps Pierre."

Reed agreed. After showing the men the house Sally had exited, he asked, "Do you know who lives there?"

Jean nodded. "The house is rented by one of Claiborne's aides, a man who would know everything the governor and General Jackson discuss or plan."

Reed's face was grim. "A man who might be inclined to confide all to his attractive companion in the aftermath of passion?"

"Perhaps."

"Blast! Kathleen suggested that Sally might be a spy, and I laughed at her." Reed inwardly cursed himself for a fool.

"We will watch, and if our suspicions are confirmed, we shall inform the general," Jean assured him.

At dawn the next morning, the *Carolina* was hit by British cannon fire and blown up. At the first shots, most of the *Carolina*'s crew abandoned ship and swam to safety. The *Louisiana*, immediately behind the *Carolina*, had to be rowed out of range of danger, since there was no breeze to combat the river current. Jean's men and many of Reed's manned the *Louisiana*'s guns, giving cover fire until safe shores were reached. The following day, Jackson's troops were attacked as they lay entrenched along a river enbankment. The British force advanced in a double column along the river and bordering woods, their brilliant scarlet uniforms a blazing target. The red line soon broke up, as the Britons ran for cover. Between the barrage of gunfire on land and the accompanying cannon shots from the nearby *Louisiana,* the British retreated with heavy casualties.

It was later that evening, on another mission for the British, that Sally Simpson and her contact were arrested and charged with spying. A missive was found on her person, outlining American troop movements obtained from her gullible lover. Being a woman, she would probably escape hanging, if she were lucky, but it would be a long, long time before Miss Simpson would be free to work her wiles on another susceptible male.

Chapter 25

New Year's Day of 1815 began with a bang outside New Orleans. Under cover of a dense morning fog, the British had moved up to within a hundred yards of the U.S. troops. The battle lasted until noon, with fierce fighting, as the January sun burned away the mist. Reed fought alongside Jean throughout the battle, reluctantly acknowledging the man's expertise as a marksman as well as with sword. Jean was a man worthy of respect; a good man to have at your side in a fight, as he proved on this first day of the new year. Amid the shots, the smoke, and the confusion of battle, Jean suddenly flung himself sidelong into Reed, knocking both of them to the ground.

Reed's temper immediately ignited. "What in blazes do you think you are doing?" he demanded, sitting upright in the ditch he had landed in.

Jean grinned, his strong white teeth gleaming in his dirt-streaked face. "You should be thanking me, instead of cursing, old friend," he commented casually, reaching over to retrieve Reed's fallen hat. Jean twirled the hat about, his finger thrust through the hole caused by an enemy bullet. Reed blanched at the sight of the hat, which had been on his head just moments before. Had Jean acted a split second later, Reed would surely have been a dead man.

Reed blew out a heavy breath of thankfulness. "You saved my life," he stated quietly.

Jean shrugged, going back to his station as if nothing untoward had happened.

The battle ended shortly thereafter, the British retreating to their former entrenchments. Afterward, Reed accompanied several others to General Jackson's quarters for a briefing, but his mind was occupied with conflicting thoughts. Why would any man who coveted another man's wife bother to save that man's life? Surely Jean would have benefitted from Reed's demise, claiming Kathleen at last. Was it merely in remembrance of their friendship that Jean had acted as he had? And had Reed been in Jean's place, would he have done the same? Was Jean perhaps a nobler man than he?

Kathleen saw the New Year in quietly. Mary came to take the children to church, but Kathleen stayed home, not feeling up to the jouncing carriage ride. These days, she could balance a cup and saucer on her belly, if the child inside did not kick too hard. Waddling was a more apt description of her walk; and she required help in putting on her shoes, for her feet had disappeared from view somewhere below her bulk. Luckily, her face, hands, and feet had not swollen much, but her stomach more than made up for this, in her estimation. Constantly tired from carrying the added weight that pulled at her back and made it ache, she longed for the next weeks to hurry by, so she could transfer her burden to her arms, and a convenient cradle.

As 1815 began, Kathleen wondered what the new year held in store for her—and for Reed. Would it bring terrible sorrows or aching joy—or a share of both?

* * *

Back in New Orleans, a division of Kentucky troops arrived as reinforcements—better late than never, as General Jackson wryly put it. They were on hand, as it happened, for what was to prove the final battle of New Orleans, and, though they did not know it at the time, the last battle of the entire war.

On a foggy Sunday at dawn, exactly one week into the new year, the British attacked again. Fortunately for the Americans, and fatally for the British, a breeze picked up just seconds into the battle, quickly dispersing the fog. With awed disbelief, the Americans gaped at the solid wall of British uniforms advancing from a mere six hundred yards away, across an open field, as if in fearless defiance of their foes.

Jean shook his head in amazement. "I cannot believe the ignorance of these Englishmen! They could not present a better or brighter target!"

"They are either terrifically stupid or outrageously brave!" said Reed. "I am not sure which!"

"Either way, it will be like shooting fish in a barrel!" Dominique retorted in disgust. "I will not take much pleasure in killing a man simply because his superior officer is a bumbling jackass!"

Time and again the Americans fired into the wall of scarlet, only to have the British falter and regroup as men fell and others took their places in the charge. Only because of their vast numbers did the British manage to gain the ditch at last, clambering up the banks into the American lines. For a time, fierce hand-to-hand combat ensued. This was where the privateers shone—when their guns were empty of ammunition, knives and cutlasses gleamed red in the melee.

In the thick of the battle, Reed had finished one

opponent and was about to face another, when his gaze was caught by Jean. Busy fending off an English soldier, he was unaware of the man taking aim at him from behind. Without conscious thought, Reed reacted instinctively. The knife in his belt was sent flying through the air to sink deeply between the Briton's shoulder blades. The man was dead before he could pull the trigger. Immediately, Reed swung about to meet a challenger of his own.

By mid-morning, the battle was over, both here and on the western bank of the Mississippi, where the Americans had been forced to retreat until reinforcements arrived to turn the tide. In the end, more than twenty-five hundred British lay wounded or dead, including their commanding officer. Less than three hundred and fifty Americans had died; of these, six were Jean's men and one Reed's.

When the fighting was over, Dominique came up to Reed. Quietly, his dark eyes solemn, he said, "I saw what you did. You saved Jean's life."

Reed lit a cigar. "I suppose I did. What of it?" he challenged gruffly.

"Why did you save the life of a man you profess to hate so much?"

"Because we were once friends; because I still respect him, even while I loathe him." *A life for a life*, he was thinking. *Now I am no longer in his debt.*

The next day, a truce was called to allow the British to bury their dead. Finally, the English were seen disbanding their camps, and an exchange of prisoners was arranged. Early on the nineteenth of January, the English departed en masse. New Orleans went wild with joy. After a parade through the streets, where General Jackson and Jean Lafitte were proclaimed heroes, a celebration ball was held on the Place d' Armes. The city and its inhabitants were so exuberant that the third week of January, General Jackson was once again forced to declare martial law. Rumors flew of a peace treaty having been negotiated in late December, prior to the actual battles in New Orleans. Despite this, Jackson refused to ease restrictions, and after another week had gone by, Reed approached the general.

"Sir, I respectfully request that you allow me to leave New Orleans now," he said.

"Give me a good reason why I should make exception for you, Captain Taylor," Jackson countered.

Reed's jaw tightened in an attempt to restrain his rising temper. "You declared martial law to restore order in New Orleans. Your men are needed to maintain that order." Reed drew a deep breath, looking the general square in the eye. "My men neither have personal concerns for New Orleans, nor is their presence necessary. If anything, boredom is leading them to become disruptive."

"You are saying *my* job would be easier if I let you go, taking your men with you," Jackson concluded with a sly look.

"Since the English are no longer a threat, and a peace treaty is either being negotiated or is already in effect, yes."

Jackson squinted in concentration. Finally, he stood. "Go then!" he barked in his usual gruff manner. "Be off with you!" As Reed let himself out of the office, Jackson added, "And thank you, Captain Taylor, for your help. You are a good man to have around when the going gets rough."

It was a compliment in the extreme, coming from the tough old general, and Reed recognized it as such. "My pleasure, General." He saluted on his way out.

Anxious to be on his way before Jackson changed his

mind, Reed wasted no time readying his men and ships. On the day he was to leave, Jean and Dominique came to see him off.

Dominique handed him a letter for Isabel, asking if he would deliver it for him. "Tell her I will come for her as soon as I can," he requested.

"I will," Reed said stiffly.

Jean offered his hand. "I wish things could be different between us, Reed. We were good comrades once."

Reed took the proffered hand. "What will you do now, Jean? Rebuild Grande Terre?"

Jean grinned boyishly. "No. Claiborne is making rude noises again, and I get the feeling I will wait a long time before the American government reimburses me for my ships and arms. I am thinking of leaving New Orleans altogether."

"And go where?" Reed asked.

"There is an island perhaps better suited to my privateering ventures now. It is called Snake Island, or Galveston, and lies off the coast of Texas. I will perhaps set up my new base there." Jean smiled slightly. "I have the blood of corsairs running in my veins, I suppose. It is difficult for me to imagine not having a deck shifting beneath my feet. I have been harassing the English and Spanish for too long to give it up now."

"I wish you well in your ventures, Jean," Reed said, and was surprised to find he sincerely meant it.

"And I you," Jean returned.

"Farewell, Jean."

As Reed headed for the bridge of his ship, he knew that much had been left unsaid. They would never truly be friends again, but there were too many memories, and too much had passed between them for them to part as mortal enemies. Jean would go his way, and Reed back to Chimera to deal with Kathleen. The two men would probably never meet again, and perhaps this was for the best, but it was easier to have parted on a note of mutual respect.

When Reed arrived home, he was amazed at the size of Kathleen. In two short months, her figure had mushroomed to monumental proportions. She needed to be helped in and out of chairs and bed, and her back ached constantly. It made Reed wince to see her discomfort.

Since Kathleen still adamantly refused to return to Chimera, Reed decided to move to Emerald Hill. He wanted to be on hand when the baby was born, to assure himself that Kathleen came through the ordeal alright— as well as for his own personal reasons, among which was a strong desire to prevent further gossip.

Something had awakened him. Reed lay listening, wondering what it had been. Just as he was about to drift off once more, he heard a muffled moan again. He rolled over, his eyes searching Kathleen's face on the pillow next to him. By the faint moonlight, he saw the pearl white of her teeth as she bit her lower lip.

"Kat?" he whispered softly.

"Mmnf!"

He waited until the spasm passed. "How close are the pains?"

"How the devil should I know?" she mumbled. "I am not an owl, and the clock is across the room."

He almost laughed at her tart answer in the midst of labor. "Approximately," he prompted.

"I would guess about five minutes apart."

"Steady?"

"As far as I can tell."

"Damn it, Kat! Why didn't you wake me sooner?" Reed lit the bedside lamp and glared at her.

Kathleen glared back. "I didn't mean to wake you at all. And don't you dare send for the doctor—he stands there making clucking noises while I do all the work, then he takes half the glory! I would rather have Della with me."

Reed reached for his breeches. "I will go wake her."

"Reed, wait!" Kathleen threw off the covers. "Blast!" she cursed impatiently.

"What is it?" he asked, then said, "Kat, you shouldn't be trying to get out of bed."

"Help me!" she wailed. "I need to visit the water closet."

He eyed her dubiously. When he hesitated, she sighed in exasperation and rolled her eyes heavenward. "I promise not to have the baby in there!"

He helped her from the bed, but halfway across the room, water gushed down her legs onto the floor. "Too late!" she gasped. Then she could say no more as another pain doubled her over.

Reed supported her until the pain receded, then lowered her carefully onto a chair. "Don't move from that spot until I get back with Della!" he ordered sternly.

"But, Reed, I'm all wet! I'll stain the chair!"

"It is just a chair! Don't worry—and don't move!"

She waved him weakly on his way.

Della soon had Kathleen cleaned up and back in bed in a fresh gown, and Isabel was sent for, and Reed was shooed out of the room to smoke and pace the floor. Six long hours later, he stood at the parlor windows and watched the sun come up as his mother came hurrying into the house, having just arrived in the carriage with the servant Reed had sent to alert her.

"Any news yet?" she inquired anxiously, tugging off her gloves.

"None." With an exasperated glance toward the stairs, he asked, "What is taking so long? Katlin and Andrea were born much more quickly. You don't suppose something is wrong? I should have gone to town and brought back the doctor . . ."

"Now, don't fret!" Mary counciled. "Babies take their own sweet time, and they won't be rushed by anyone, not even anxious fathers. No two births are the same. Just because this one is taking longer does not mean anything is wrong. Kathleen has spoiled you by being so prompt and considerate the first two times around!"

Upstairs, Kathleen was in the final stage of her labor. The pain was constant now, with no time to catch her breath. Grunting and groaning, she was unaware of anything but the pain and the tremendous pressure, as she bore down with all her might.

"Ah sees da haid, Miz Kafleen! Couple of moah good pushes, an' its done," cried Della triumphantly.

Isabel wiped the perspiration from Kathleen's brow, and put the ends of a towel back into Kathleen's fist for her to pull on. The bedpost creaked as Kathleen stretched the toweling to is limits, straining to expel the child from her body. Deep groans filled the room; Isabel, concerned for her friend, would almost have preferred a good, healthy scream. With one last, loud groan, the babe's head and shoulders came free. A final pressure, and the infant had arrived safely into the world.

"It's a girl!" Della announced, as she wiped the child's face, and swatted the tiny round bottom. The baby let out a weak cry, then, gathering air into her lungs, began to wail heartily. "Sweetest sound on earth!" Della avowed.

At the sound of Kathleen's final loud groan, Reed would have bounded up the stairs, but Mary stopped him, her hand on his arm. A few seconds later, they heard the baby's cry.

"It sounds as if all is well," Mary said with a joyous smile, then added, "let them get Kathleen and the babe cleaned and settled first. Another ten minutes won't kill you. Heaven knows, after watching you and Ted when your children are being born, you have nearly convinced me that the waiting is worse than the bearing!"

When Reed was at last allowed into the room, Kathleen was lying back on her pillows, her eyes closed. The child was nestled in the curve of her arm, contentedly nursing.

He tiptoed closer, and saw the baby's eyes were open, the usual cloudy blue of a newborn, though he thought he saw an underlying tinge of green. The infant's hair, what there was of it, was a downy blonde, with perhaps just a hint of red. The rest of the child's features were red and wrinkled, resembling neither himself nor anyone else.

Kathleen's voice startled him; he had not noticed she'd opened her eyes to stare at him as hard as he was studying the child at her side. "It will be some time before you will see what you are looking for; a few months perhaps before she starts resembling any one of us to any great degree," she said, her voice weak, but hostile.

"It appears she may have red hair and green eyes," Reed replied cautiously.

"Perhaps."

Reed's tone was carefully neutral as he gave Kathleen a

level look. "We will wait, Kathleen, but sooner or later, I *will* know whose child this is!"

As he headed for the door, Kathleen called to him, "I wish to name her Erin Emerald, for her Irish heritage."

He nodded casually. "Then she'll be baptized Erin Emerald Taylor—as soon as I am convinced she is mine!"

Erin had made her debut into the world on February fourteenth, St. Valentine's Day. Neighbors and friends who came to call were delighted by this fact, calling her a love child, and telling Reed endlessly how adorable she was, and how proud he must be of his beautiful new daughter. Naturally, he accepted their congratulations and praise with good grace, and acted the proud father in their presence; but once they had departed, it was a different tale altogether. Every time he heard the phrase "love child," he felt as if he could bite nails in two. He wondered how close to the truth it was. Each time he considered the possibility that Jean was little Erin's father, he was filled with jealous rage. There was a sick feeling in the pit of his stomach, and the taste of bile in his throat. To imagine that Kathleen and Jean had truly loved one another as well only intensified his anguish.

When only the family was present, Reed avoided Erin, abandoning her to Kathleen's care, or to Isabel, who held the status of a proud "aunt" to the newborn. While he had been a doting father to his two other children, he shied away from Erin as if she carried a plague.

Kathleen spent much time feeding and caring for her infant daughter, so Reed spent little time with his wife. Whenever he came upon her nursing Erin, he flinched. To see Kathleen smile lovingly into the small face, or tenderly stroke the downy head, sent a shaft of pain through him. Was Kathleen looking for Jean each time she intently studied Erin's features? Was she remembering him as she held the child to her breast? These thoughts tormented Reed like evil demons gnawing at his soul, leaving him raw and bleeding inside, and outwardly irritable and distant.

Kathleen was distraught over Reed's behavior, having secretly hoped for a miracle once the baby arrived. Hiding her disappointment, she concentrated on giving her tiny daughter all the love and attention Reed withheld. The depression she had felt after the birth of her other two children seemed doubled this time, particularly during long nights next to Reed in bed. Not three feet separated their bodies, but an entire universe separated their souls.

Isabel was Kathleen's saving grace. Thoroughly enchanted with the tiny mite, she spent enormous amounts of time and energy delightedly spoiling Erin. She loved the child as dearly as if she was her own, and tried to make up for Reed's neglect and to cheer Kathleen. Even while she looked forward with longing to Dominique's arrival, she fought to pull Kathleen out of her deep depression, and Kathleen was grateful for Isabel's support, without which she would no doubt have crumpled in despair.

In this manner, life went on at Emerald Hill for several weeks. It became apparent to everyone with eyes in their head that Erin was the exact image of Kathleen, with the same red-gold hair, tip-tilted emerald eyes, and long dark lashes forming fanned crescents on her plump rosy cheeks. From the top of her downy head to the tips of her toes, she was a miniature of her mother. There was not one feature, not one single distinguishing mark, to reveal the identity of her father. After all this time, it seemed the answer Reed sought was to remain forever a secret.

This was a bitter blow to Reed, and Kathleen felt helpless and hopeless. How long could they go on living this way; strangers and antagonists, fighting through their private hell? Would they ever be able to revive the love and trust they had once had for one another, or were they to plod on forever in this state of unbearable purgatory?

When Kathleen had fully regained her health, she first became aware of his intention to resume their marital intimacy when one night, instead of turning from her in bed, Reed drew her into his arms. The arrogant set of his chin, and the intense glow in his smoky-blue eyes, told their own tale. She had seen that look often enough to know what it foretold.

Tugging at the folds of her nightgown, his hands were already searching out the familiar contours of her body, scorching her skin through the thin material. "I want you," he muttered thickly, his voice hoarse with desire.

"Why, Reed?" she whispered, "when you still hold me in such contempt?"

"It has been a long time, Kat, since I have experienced your special brand of lovemaking. I have held back as long as I can, and my patience is exhausted. I see no reason to deny ourselves what we both know we enjoy."

With this brusque and matter-of-fact explanation and no sweet declarations of love, he took her. She had neither the strength nor the will to fight him; her heart and body yearned as strongly as his for this union of their flesh, though their hearts were still estranged. As his hands ignited flames of desire, Kathleen clung to him, her one port in the storm of her reeling emotions. Distantly, she heard her moans of passion mingling with his in the quiet room. The remembered magic was still there in his touch, his kiss, his caress, but it hurt terribly to think that this physical attraction was all that was left of their once magnificent love. Soon even that poignant pain was washed away, as wave after wave of ecstasy thrilled her. In the midst of the glory radiating through her, she dimly realized that Reed was just as transported as she, carried away with her on whirling winds of fire that obliterated all else but this devastating rapture.

Afterwards, Kathleen wept.

Chapter 26

Though Kathleen had accepted Reed back into her bed and her life, she steadfastly refused to return to Chimera. Her stubborn pride would not allow him complete victory while the emotional barriers still stood between them. She resolved to remain firm as long as Reed continued to display resentment toward her and Erin. Until Reed could truly forgive her and accept Erin as his without a qualm, Kathleen would stay at Emerald Hill.

As the days passed, Kathleen's determination grew. Her pride had been severely bruised, her heart mortally wounded. Her once-brilliant love was lying in shards about her feet. She refused to give in to Reed completely. What little pride she retained, demanded satisfaction. As much as she longed to go home to Chimera, she felt it would be a grave mistake to do so. Somewhere within her, a tiny flicker of hope still fluttered; Kathleen wanted it all— his respect, his passion, and his love. She could not and would not settle for less, for something inside her would die forever if she did.

"You must be the world's most stubborn chit!" Reed exclaimed. "What, pray tell, is the difference between my living here with you, or you returning to Chimera with me?"

"If there is so little difference, then stop harping at me,

and move the rest of your things here,'' Kathleen countered. ''That, or go back to Chimera alone and leave me in peace.''

Reed sighed heavily. ''Is that what you truly want, Kat?''

''No!'' she cried out. ''What I truly want, you refuse to give. I want you to resolve your feelings for me, once and for all—and for Erin. I want you to accept her willingly and lovingly. I want you to love me as you once did.''

''I can't, Kat.'' Reed looked away, his jaw set. ''I've tried. God knows, I have tried, but I can't.''

Kathleen swallowed a sob. ''Then I do not see any future for us together. Go back to Chimera and leave me in peace!''

He leapt forward to pull her into his arms. Pinning her to him, his arms like iron bands about her, his eyes blazed into hers. ''I won't let you go, Kat! You are mine, and you will remain mine until time itself ends.''

Kathleen wilted against his broad chest, her head resting above his beating heart. ''Oh, Reed,'' she sighed wretchedly, ''is there no answer for us?''

Dominique finally arrived in Savannah. Upon finding Reed and Kathleen in residence at Emerald Hill, he prepared to rent a room in town. While he wished only to spirit Isabel away with him as quickly as possible, he understood her reluctance to leave Kathleen at this time.

Reed surprised them all by offering to let Dominique stay at Chimera. ''It is a long ride to and from Savannah each day, and you will need all your strength to court your lady love,'' he explained sourly. ''To be completely frank with you, Dominique, the sooner you can get Isabel off my hands, the happier I will be. The woman is a veritable

466

tigress, despite her diminutive stature. Are you sure you are not biting off more than you can chew?''

Dominique laughed heartily. ''You may be right, Reed, but what else can I do? I am fatally and entirely bewitched by her.''

''I know the feeling,'' Reed sighed.

''I do not mean to interfere, but if you and Kathleen could straighten matters out between you, Isabel would be more willing to leave with me. I am anxious to try my hand as a legitimate businessman, and the hotel I have bought in New Orleans needs a woman's touch. Isabel is sorely needed.''

Reed glowered. ''I will tend to my business; you tend to yours,'' he growled. ''You could always truss her up and carry her off in the night.''

Dominique's brows rose. ''A captive bride?'' he exclaimed.

Reed continued to glare at him. ''Yes,'' he hissed, ''and it would please me immensely if you could manage to abduct that blasted parrot at the same time!''

The tension at Emerald Hill rose to unbearable heights in the next few days. Reed constantly pressured Kathleen to return to Chimera, and her obstinate refusals angered him. In turn, Kathleen's insistence that Reed swallow his pride and accept Erin as his daughter despite the lack of proof enraged him further. His mind and emotions were in constant turmoil; and the more he fought them, the more confused he became.

Finally, in desperation, he threw a few necessities in a saddle bag, and informed Kathleen he was leaving.

She asked fearfully, ''Where are you going? How long will you be?''

''I don't know, Kat,'' he sighed wearily, deep sorrow

turning his eyes to a dark sapphire. "I only know we can not go on as we are. I need some time alone, to think things through. Whatever decision I come to will affect all our lives, the choice I make must be the right one."

The finality of his tone frightened her. She flew into his embrace, and he drew her to him and kissed her one last time before he left. They clung to one another like two frightened children lost in a forbidding forest. Their arms and lips said what neither could voice aloud—a fragile hope that somehow their world would right itself once more and let them find the happiness they had lost. Grief etched harsh lines in both their faces, as Reed released her and walked swiftly away.

He rode southwest, away from the towns and the coast, into the dense wild pine forests. Come nightfall, he made camp. As he stared into the flames of his fire, he thought of Kathleen and all she meant to him. He thought of the rosy-cheeked baby girl, who might or might not be his daughter. The infant was an innocent victim in this turmoil surrounding her conception. She would, in years to come, grow to be a beauty, just like her mother . . . .

Many conflicting thoughts raced round and round in Reed's head, jumbling his mind, with no clear-cut solution at hand as his stubborn pride battled with his love for Kathleen. With a weary sigh of exasperation, Reed lay back in defeat and tried to get what rest his tormented heart would allow.

Morning brought the dawn, but no resolutions, and after fixing himself a meager breakfast, Reed traveled on. Around noon, he unexpectedly came upon a band of gypsies camped in a secluded glade. Seated upon his stallion, Reed was unobserved as he sat watching them. His mind darted back in time to the day long ago when he and Kathleen had visited a similar camp near Chimera. Kathleen had become upset over something the old fortune teller had said, and Reed had had a few choice words for the old hag. Then the woman had read his palm, telling him what lay in the future for him and for Kathleen.

Now, as he sat astride Titan, Reed could almost see the old soothsayer before him. Word for word, he could recall the woman's warnings. Her wavering voice was clear in his mind:

"Your young wife is more complex than you can imagine. You and she will have your trials, but if you cling firmly to your love, you can win her. Even should you discover she has deceived you in some way, hold fast to her.

"You will reach a crisis in your marriage. You will know it when it comes. Beware! At this time, do not flee from her, for if you do, you may lose her forever. You must curb your anger and use understanding as your truest weapons. Your life and marriage will be resolved if you can learn to temper your anger with love and kindness."

Reed frowned. He had only recalled the old woman's words once before, when he had discovered Kathleen's dual identity as Emerald, and found it had been she who had been attacking his ships. He had flown into a rage, and had left her, only to return and find Kathleen gone. Chasing her over the ocean, he had caught up to her, and against all odds, they had saved their marriage and the precious love they shared.

Reed had thought the witch's prophesy fulfilled then. Now he wondered. That crisis seemed mild compared to the one they faced now.

You will know it when it comes—do not flee—use understanding and forgiveness—love— The words echoed in his head, refusing him peace.

Wheeling Titan about, Reed set a course for home, his thoughts flying faster than the stallion's hoofs. One fact alone stood out clearly, above all else. He loved Kathleen. His life would be worthless without her. She often infuriated him; she frustrated and irritated and harassed him time and again. But she also charmed him, beguiled him, enchanted him as no other woman on earth could do. She was as changeable as the weather; as mischievous as a leprechaun; as tempting as a sea siren—a proud, loyal, rare beauty.

Loyal—the word struck him like a blow. It was one of Kathleen's fiercest virtues, an intregal part of her. Once she gave her word, she kept it. She defended her children like a lioness. She was true to herself and those she cared about. A promise from Kathleen was worth more than gold. Now Reed asked himself, would a woman like that carelessly disregard her marriage vows? If Kathleen had held any hope of his survival, could she have yielded to Jean's charms? When she and the others had told him of her grief upon being convinced of his death, he had thought perhaps Kathleen had fooled them all with a tremendously good job of acting. He, of all people, knew what a superb actress she could be when she wanted. He desperately needed to know if she had truly grieved for him deep in her heart. With this thought in mind, Reed changed course, heading toward Savannah rather than Emerald Hill. He knew now where to find some of the answers.

It took him till almost dawn to reach the *Starbright* and the item he sought—the *Emerald Enchantress*'s logbook. Despite his weariness, he opened it to the date of his disappearance. A few pages later, he started reading

Finley's account of Kathleen's reaction to news of his death. He read of her pain, of her disbelief, of her immediate decision to search for him.

The following entries were Kathleen's, detailing the journey south and the search of the first islands and the waters near where Captain Guthrie had said the storm had hit. Beneath the nautical terms and succint wording ran an underlying current of desperation that Reed knew he was not imagining. At last, he came to the time she arrived at Grande Terre and asked the Lafitte brothers for their help. This date, and those of the immediately initiated search, told him how anxious Kathleen had been to find him. Reed could sense Kathleen's despair as each day failed to produce any sign of the *Kat-Ann*.

Kathleen's outrageous description of Gasparilla made him laugh. Then came her account of discovering the sunken remains of the *Kat-Ann*. The page was so tear-stained as to be nearly indecipherable.

Reed ran a trembling hand across the blurred page, feeling Kathleen's agony as he touched the evidence of her tears. A lump rose in his own throat at the pain she had endured.

Quickly, Reed turned the page, to find a separate sheet of paper folded and tucked into the logbook. From this, Reed learned of Kathleen's attempt to drown herself in grief. It was an unofficial entry—a personal soul-baring on Kathleen's part. Tears rolled down Reed's face as he read her pain-racked thoughts and absolute despair.

There was a gap of three months, during which Kathleen had returned to Chimera. The account began again in January 1814, when Kathleen had once again disguised herself as Emerald, on a bloody mission of revenge. The number of vessels she attacked and won amazed him,

471

and he could well imagine the haughty, bold image she had projected; but he also read between the lines and felt her deep anguish, her disregard for her own life, and her rage at fate for having stolen her beloved husband.

With a jolt, Reed realized he had reached an entry dated mid-February, and Kathleen was still writing of vengeance and describing daring exploits that made Reed catch his breath at the reckless chances she took with her own life. This passage had been written a mere three months before his miraculous reappearance, and Kathleen was still grieving for him. What a fool he had been to think she had not cared enough! From what he had just read, he now knew she had mourned him more deeply than she could ever convey, far longer than he would have wished her to bear such a burden of sorrow.

Quickly, he scanned the remaining entries, to the date of his return. Here, he sensed a healing. In a strange way, perhaps he owed Jean a debt of gratitude for helping Kathleen to recover from her loss—strange because it was still a possibility that Jean had fathered Erin.

This brought Reed full circle in his thoughts, and he closed the logbook and leaned back in his chair with a deep sigh. Since he had already admitted to himself that he loved Kathleen to distraction, and needed her with a deep desperation, there were now only Jean and Erin to consider.

Jean had gone out of their lives forever. If Kathleen had been Jean's lover, she had gone to his bed in the firm belief that she was a widow, having mourned her husband deeply before turning to the comfort of another man's arms. Though it still cut Reed deeply to think of it, he could now see that all hope of his survival had died in Kathleen's heart, as well as Jean's. They had both honestly believed him to be dead. With an overwhelming sense of relief, Reed let the jealous hatred and anger flow from him, as tears wet his cheeks and blurred his vision.

Finally, he thought of Erin, that tiny, innocent bundle. Could he live the rest of his life not knowing if he was her real father? Did it really matter who was responsible for her conception? Would he not be the one to raise her, to provide for her, to see to her upbringing? Wasn't that what being a father was truly all about? To protect her, to guide her—and yes, to love her? Erin was a tiny replica of Kathleen, his wife, whom he loved more than life itself. She would grow to be more like Kathleen with each passing year; and with the passage of time, perhaps his doubts concerning her would fade and die.

With fervent determination, Reed decided then and there to give Erin the same loving attention as he did Katlin and Andrea. He would treat her as though she were his own, for she was a sweet little thing, no way deserving of his rejection. He would enjoy watching her grow into a beautiful young lady, with Kathleen's copper tresses and brilliant green eyes . . . and perhaps her mother's unpredictable temper as well.

His decision made at long last, Reed sank wearily to the bunk. When he had rested, he would head directly back to Emerald Hill, and if need be, beg Kathleen on his knees to forgive him for his stubborn, pig-headed stupidity. He resolved to do everything in his power to make up to Kathleen for all the hurt he had caused her, and to convince her of how very much he loved and needed her.

Deep in his own thoughts, Reed had passed Chimera the following morning before he became aware of the strong smell of smoke in the air. Quickly scanning the countryside, his heart nearly stopped in his chest as he saw

473

thick black smoke rising in the air from the direction of Emerald Hill. With the acrid taste of fear in his mouth, Reed urged Titan into a gallop.

As he rounded the last bend to Emerald Hill, Reed gasped at the sight that met his eyes. The entire house was engulfed in flames. Several people stood on the front lawn, but he was still too far away to identify them.

Drawing closer, he saw Kathleen being forcibly restrained by two servants, as she struggled to break free of them. Her face was contorted in intense agony, and it was plain to see she wanted desperately to enter the burning building. With relief Reed saw Katlin and Andrea safely enfolded in the capable arms of Della. It was only then that Reed noticed the absence of Isabel—and baby Erin. With a groan of dismay, he rushed to his wife's side.

Kathleen was beside herself, shrieking and screaming and crying hysterically, "My baby! My baby! Oh, God! My baby!"

It was a wonder she was capable of recognizing him, but she did. "Reed!" she screamed. "Please!"

As Reed neared the cluster of people, he saw three men dragging Dominique from the house. Over Kathleen's terrified screams, he heard one of them shout, "He's alive! A beam knocked him out cold, is all!"

Rushing up to the men, Reed asked urgently, "What room were Isabel and the baby in?"

"Upstairs nursery!" one man choked.

Without thought for his own safety, Reed took a deep breath and plunged into the flaming house. There was only one thought in his mind—to save the child and Isabel.

To Kathleen, every moment seemed an eternity, as she prayed and wept and struggled against her captors. Near collapse from shock, she almost fainted as part of the roof collapsed with a roar. A deep groan of grief was torn from her throat as she realized it would take a miracle for anyone to survive that blazing inferno.

Then, just when everyone had given up all hope, Reed came stumbling through the billowing smoke, Isabel clutched in his arms. Kathleen's frantic gaze searched in vain for Erin's tiny form. It was not until Reed laid Isabel gently on the grass, that Kathleen saw the small body wrapped in a scorched shawl, held close to Isabel's breast. Freed at last, she flew to their side, terror clutching her heart.

Reed, scorched and blackened, his clothes still smouldering, was on his knees next to Isabel and the baby, gasping great gulps of air. Isabel choked, and went promptly into a fierce spasm of coughing. At the very moment Kathleen reached them, Reed became chillingly aware that the infant had not moved at all. Reed snatched the child from Isabel's arms.

Wild-eyed Kathleen shrieked, "Give me my baby! Reed! *Give me my baby!*"

Behind her, someone murmured, "Thet chile is daid."

"*No!*" Kathleen screamed in anguished denial. "No! I won't *let* her die!" She reached out to grab Erin from Reed, but strong arms again restrained her.

Instinct alone drove Reed to place his mouth upon Erin's tiny rosebud lips, forcing his breath into the infant's mouth and lungs. The baby's chest rose, and then dropped. Again, and still again, Reed breathed his own life into Erin's still form, as the others stared at him in dazed wonder.

"Reed! What are you doing?" Kathleen raged, unable to understand anything beyond the teror that held her mindless in its grip.

"Lord A'mighty! Dat poor man done lost his mind!" Della moaned in stunned grief. "He's tryin' to gibe life back to dat poor daid babe!"

Then, as if God had finally heard their prayers, Erin coughed. Miraculously, she coughed again and again. Reed clutched her to his chest in stupified disbelief. Tears streamed unheeded down his face as he raised his smoke-bleared eyes in grateful thanks toward heaven.

With a cry of boundless joy, Kathleen feel to her knees beside him, reaching out once more for her infant daughter, desperate to hold her and believe the miracle she had just witnessed.

Reed handed Kathleen the baby, then knelt with his arms protectively surrounding both of them. Their tears blended, as their heads bent together over the child, who was now lustily screaming. The piercing cries were music to their ears.

When he at last regained control, Reed choked out, "I was coming to tell you I love you, Kat, and Erin, too. Maybe after all that has happened, you won't believe me, but I ask you to forgive me and love me again."

Kathleen's heart swelled with love at his words, and she raised a grimy, tear-stained face to meet his gaze. "Oh, Reed! I have never stopped loving you!" He drew her close to his thundering heart, and she whispered wonderously, "You saved Erin's life—I will never forget that, even if you never accept her as your own."

"Oh, Kat! She *is* my own now," Reed murmured. "If she doesn't have one drop of my blood, she carries my life's breath within her from this day forward. After already deciding to love her because she is a part of you, now I love her doubly because she is a part of me, too!"

"It is truly a day of miracles!" Kathleen sighed happily, resting her weary head on her husband's broad shoulder.

She was right. No one had died in the terrible fire. Dominique had a large lump on his head, and Isabel was still recovering from all the smoke she had inhaled, but they would both be fine. The stables were far from the house and there had been no wind to carry embers toward it, so the horses had sustained no injury. Katlin and Andrea were soon safely tucked into their beds at Chimera, and Erin was snug in a cradle, breathing easily under Della's watchful eye. The Taylor family were all safe, alive, and thankful for the gift of life this day.

In their own big bed in the master bedroom at Chimera, Kathleen gazed lovingly at her husband. His vivid blue eyes were brimming with emotion as his lips grazed hers. "If you are not too tired, I am longing to make love to you," Reed whispered against her ripe mouth.

"I was hoping you would offer," she teased.

"Shameless hussy!" he growled.

Then all playfulness was cast aside as husband and wife came together in true love once again. His mouth worshipped hers, and her lips opened to gladly receive the thrust of his tongue. With tender caresses and whispered words of love and longing, they stoked the embers of their desire, until the flames of ecstasy blazed out of control, engulfing them both. Their rapture sealed their hearts and souls together, even as their passion-heated bodies united in tenderness; and their lives were forged together in a bond neither man nor death could ever separate.

Afterward, Kathleen lay curled tightly to his side, her head cradled on his chest over his heart. She sighed blissfully.

"I love you, kitten," Reed murmured against her hair,

"more than I can ever begin to tell you."

"I love you, too, darling," Kathleen whispered in return, "forever and always, with all my heart."

This day, from the ashes of their dying love, the fiery flames of ecstasy had risen anew, brighter, stronger, more abundant than ever—a blazing flame that would burn eternally, and warm them for the rest of their lives.

BE SWEPT AWAY
ON A TIDE OF PASSION
BY LEISURE'S THRILLING
HISTORICAL ROMANCES!

Make the Most of Your
Leisure Time
with
LEISURE BOOKS

Please send me the following titles:

Quantity	Book Number	Price
_____	_____	_____
_____	_____	_____
_____	_____	_____
_____	_____	_____
_____	_____	_____

If out of stock on any of the above titles, please send me the alternate title(s) listed below:

_____	_____	_____
_____	_____	_____
_____	_____	_____
_____	_____	_____

Postage & Handling _____

Total Enclosed $_____

☐ Please send me a free catalog.

NAME_____
(please print)

ADDRESS _____

CITY_____ STATE _____ ZIP _____

Please include $1.00 shipping and handling for the first book ordered and 25¢ for each book thereafter in the same order. All orders are shipped within approximately 4 weeks via postal service book rate. PAYMENT MUST ACCOMPANY ALL ORDERS.*

*Canadian orders must be paid in US dollars payable through a New York banking facility.

Mail coupon to: **Dorchester Publishing Co., Inc.**
6 East 39 Street, Suite 900
New York, NY 10016
Att: ORDER DEPT.